MW00989468

"India Holton infuses the story with wry wit and meta inside jokes. Every sentence is positively vibrating with the kind of charm that will have you pressing your lips together with laughter. And yet amid all the outrageous and camp fun, Holton also succeeds in building a genuine love story—between two people who have kept the world at a distance for years but somehow find a home within each other. And if that doesn't sell you, then you should at least know this book has one of the funniest twists on the 'one bed' trope I've read in a long time."
—NPR

"Holton continues to be the world's leading engineer of the *romp*. *The Ornithologist's Field Guide to Love* is positively confectionary: a sweetly earnest love story wrapped in layers of sharp wordplay, deadly magical birds, and cheeky narrative awareness."
—Alix E. Harrow,
New York Times bestselling author of *Starling House*

"Holton's prose winks and sparkles with wit and magic, flitting expertly between laugh-out-loud hijinks, swoonworthy romance, and adventure filled with fowl play. *The Ornithologist's Field Guide to Love* is pure, rollicking fun—and will set your heart aflutter."
—Allison Saft,
New York Times bestselling author of *A Fragile Enchantment*

"No one writes banter and charm like India Holton. Beth and Devon's love story isn't just entertaining and educational—it's swoonworthy. *The Ornithologist's Field Guide to Love* is an unputdownable academic adventure."
—Raquel Vasquez Gilliland,
USA Today bestselling author of *Witch of Wild Things*

"By Jove! *The Ornithologist's Field Guide to Love* is a delightfully madcap rivals-to-lovers romp featuring India Holton's trademark wit, genteel ladies who enjoy tea with their fisticuffs—and of course, oodles of magical murder birds. I was charmed from beginning to end!"

—Jenna Levine,
USA Today bestselling author of *My Roommate Is a Vampire*

"I adored India Holton's latest historical-fantasy romance! My heart must be a bird, because Professors Beth Pickering and Devon Lockley have captured it. Holton writes with wit and whimsy, building a tender and sensual romance while sending her characters on a madcap adventure dotted with exotic birds, ruthless ornithologists, and a gaggle of very concerned French fishermen. The story is charming, swoonworthy, and delightfully nerdy, and Holton's prose sparkles with both sly humor and gorgeously rendered descriptions. This is a magically romantic delight."

—Sarah Hawley,
author of *A Witch's Guide to Fake Dating a Demon*

"India Holton's writing is not only the most vibrantly unique I've ever read, but also the tears-in-your-eyes funniest. Her characters—from the rivaling heroes to their colorful supporting cast—all sparkle with pure wit, swoonworthy charisma, and magical warmth. I want to dive headfirst into *The Ornithologist's Field Guide to Love* and live forever among the feathered creatures and charming academia."
—Kate Golden, author of *A Dawn of Onyx*

"Few things are as delightful as an India Holton book, and every time I get the chance to read one, it feels like Christmas morning. Clever wordplay, gorgeous prose, adventure, and romance that made my heart happy-sigh over and over—*The Ornithologist's Field Guide to Love* has everything that I want in a novel, and the reading experience was like sitting in a magic cauldron, bubbling over with joy."
—Sarah Hogle, author of *Old Flames and New Fortunes*

The Secret Service of Tea and Treason

"*The Secret Service of Tea and Treason* was everything I wanted and everything I didn't know I needed. No one writes like India Holton—and I have never met a more immersive read! This Victorian rom-com absolutely sparkles! It was tenderly strong, hilariously romantic, and deliciously steamy. A pitch-perfect addition to this fantastical series!"   —Sarah Adams, author of *The Cheat Sheet*

"Oh my giddy heart! *The Secret Service of Tea and Treason* is brilliantly bonkers, romping fun—sleuthing shenanigans, explosive action, and most of all, radiant, romantic joy. I adored every page."
          —Chloe Liese, author of *Two Wrongs Make a Right*

"With moments of high comedy and incredible sweetness, a gazillion more uniquely Holtonesque shenanigans, and a wonderful neurodivergent heroine to boot, *The Secret Service of Tea and Treason* is joyous, marvelous fun."
          —Sangu Mandanna,
          author of *The Very Secret Society of Irregular Witches*

"Following up *The League of Gentlewomen Witches*, one of my favorite romances of all time, was no easy feat, but Holton manages to match its perfection with this exemplary undercover romance."
          —BuzzFeed

"Holton's trademark wit and prose are present throughout *The Secret Service of Tea and Treason*, and there is no shortage of sparks between Alice and Bixby. You'll find yourself laughing out loud and swooning at numerous parts of the story."   —Paste

The League of Gentlewomen Witches

"A brilliant mix of adventure, romance, and Oscar Wilde–esque absurdity—one of the wittiest, most original rom-coms I have read all year."

—Evie Dunmore,
USA Today bestselling author of *Bringing Down the Duke*

"There's no literary experience quite like reading an India Holton book. *The League of Gentlewomen Witches* is a wild, rollicking, delicious carnival ride of a story, filled with rakish pirates, chaotic witches, flying houses (and bicycles, and pumpkins), delightful banter, and some serious steam. You've never read Victorian romance like this before . . . and it'll ruin you for everything else."

—Lana Harper,
New York Times bestselling author of *Payback's a Witch*

"Sexy, funny, and utterly charming, *The League of Gentlewomen Witches* is like a deliciously over-caffeinated historical-romance novel. Not only does Holton treat us to a fiery feminist witch as our heroine and a dashing pirate as our leading man, but she also gives us lyrical prose and crackling banter to enjoy on the side. Buckle up, readers, because this is a ride you won't want to miss."

—Lynn Painter, author of *Mr. Wrong Number*

"What happens when a prim and proper witch crosses paths with a dashing pirate? Flaming chaos and delicious debauchery, of course. *The League of Gentlewomen Witches* is another wickedly funny romp through this glorious world created by India Holton."

—Harper St. George, author of *The Devil and the Heiress*

"When a prickly witch meets her match in a dangerously endearing pirate . . . the match bursts into flames! India Holton's joyous, swoony, genre-exploding novel is a marvel, bristling with wit (and weaponry!) and brimming with love. *The League of Gentlewomen Witches* will steal your heart, fly it to the moon, and return it to your chest, sparking with magic and just in time for tea."

—Joanna Lowell, author of *The Runaway Duchess*

The Wisteria Society of Lady Scoundrels

"Holton is having as much fun as the English language will permit—the prose shifts constantly from silly to sublime and back, sometimes in the course of a single sentence. And somehow in all the melodrama and jokes and hilariously mangled literary references, there are moments of emotion that cut to the quick—the way a profound traumatic experience can overcome you years later."

—*The New York Times Book Review*

"This melds the Victorian wit of Sherlock Holmes with the brash adventuring of Indiana Jones. . . . A sprightly feminist tale that offers everything from an atmospheric Gothic abbey to secret societies."

—*Entertainment Weekly*

"*The Wisteria Society of Lady Scoundrels* is easily the most delightfully bonkers historical-fantasy romance of 2021! Featuring lady pirates in flying houses and gentlemen assassins with far too many names, I enjoyed every absorbing moment."

—Jen DeLuca, author of *Well Played*

"The most charming, clever, and laugh-out-loud funny book I've read all year—it is impossible to read *The Wisteria Society of Lady Scoundrels* and not fall in love with its lady pirates, flying houses, and swoonworthy romance. India Holton's utterly delightful debut is pure joy from start to finish."

—Martha Waters, author of *To Have and to Hoax*

"With a piratical heroine who would rather be reading and a hero whose many disguises hide a (slightly tarnished) heart of gold, *The Wisteria Society of Lady Scoundrels* is the perfect diversion for a rainy afternoon with a cup of tea. What fun!"

—Manda Collins,
author of *A Lady's Guide to Mischief and Mayhem*

THE
GEOGRAPHER'S
MAP TO ROMANCE

INDIA HOLTON

BERKLEY ROMANCE

New York

BERKLEY ROMANCE
Published by Berkley
An imprint of Penguin Random House LLC
1745 Broadway, New York, NY 10019
penguinrandomhouse.com

Copyright © 2025 by India Holton
Excerpt from *The Antiquarian's Object of Desire* copyright
© 2025 by India Holton

Book design by Katy Riegel

Library of Congress Cataloging-in-Publication Data

Names: Holton, India, author.
Title: The geographer's map to romance / India Holton.
Description: First edition. | New York: Berkley Romance, 2025. |
Series: Love's academic
Identifiers: LCCN 2024047020 (print) | LCCN 2024047021 (ebook) |
ISBN 9780593641477 (trade paperback) |
ISBN 9780593641484 (ebook)
Subjects: LCGFT: Romance fiction. | Fantasy fiction. |
Historical fiction. | Novels.
Classification: LCC PR9639.4.H66 G46 2025 (print) |
LCC PR9639.4.H66 (ebook) | DDC 823/.92—dc23/eng/20241007
LC record available at https://lccn.loc.gov/2024047020
LC ebook record available at https://lccn.loc.gov/2024047021

First Edition: April 2025

Printed in the United States of America
1st Printing

The authorized representative in the EU for product safety and compliance is
Penguin Random House Ireland, Morrison Chambers, 32 Nassau Street,
Dublin D02 YH68, Ireland, https://eu-contact.penguin.ie.

For the sky-dreaming, storm-hearted ones.

Sometimes peace comes in stillness,

sometimes it comes in

a wild dance.

TABLE OF
SIGNIFICANT CHARACTERS

IN ORDER OF APPEARANCE

ELODIE HUGHES TARRANT . . . a specialist in chaos

MOTTHERS . . . the eye of a metaphorical storm

GABRIEL TARRANT . . . a professional curmudgeon

BEETLESON . . . a fall guy

AMELIA TARRANT . . . steady ground

ALGERNON JENNINGS . . . the human equivalent of a
marshland

MR. BLOYD . . . operator of a magnificent flying machine

VARIOUS TOURISTS

MR. PARRY . . . sees which way the wind blows

TEGAN PARRY . . . as yet uncharted land

BABY . . . with a name like that, is it any wonder he's angry?

ASSORTED LOCALS

PIMMERSBY & HAPSITCH . . . a poetic duo

MUMBERS . . . airhead

PROFESSOR JACKSON . . . a disaster expert

RANDOM STUDENTS

DIVERSE FACULTY MEMBERS

PROFESSOR SLUMMERY . . . the real nemesis

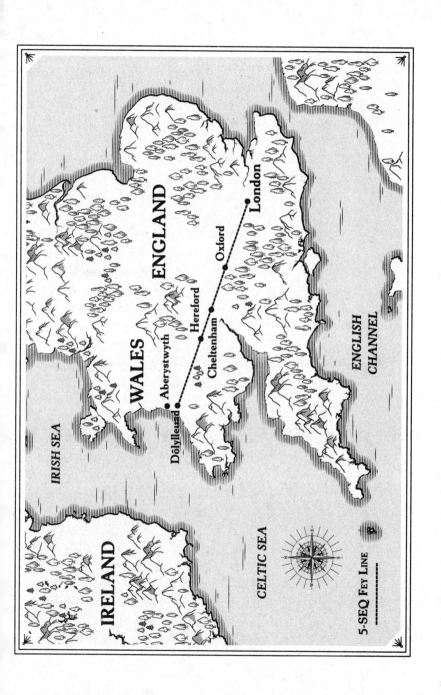

The
Geographer's Map
to Romance

Chapter One

Speak softly and carry a big telescope.
Blazing Trails, W.H. Jackson

Oxford, 1890

A GEOGRAPHER BEHAVES WITH quiet dignity at all times. Elodie Tarrant had been informed of this maxim by many professors over the years, and she took great pains to impress it upon her own students. England's surveyors and mapmakers must be known for their decorum so they are not known for their trespassing and shot at. Consequently, Elodie had chosen to cycle to the Oxford train station that morning, rather than run along the streets—walking in a dignified manner being out of the question, considering how late she was.

And this would have been entirely commendable, except for the small but not untrivial matter of her bicycle being a steam-powered velocipede.

Anyone not immediately witness to the spectacle of a helmet-clad woman perched upon a rickety wheeled contraption, with steam clouds billowing around her and a long, unbuttoned tweed coat billowing behind, was alerted to it by the loud rattling, tooting, and random belches of the machine. At least her skirt did not billow—but as this was because she had it knotted up around her knees, thus revealing her stocking-clad legs, it rather failed to argue in favor of dignity.

"Faster!" she urged the vehicle, as though doing so might make some difference to its speed. "It will be a disaster if I miss that train!"

She spoke literally. News had arrived yesterday that, following a large storm, magic was afoot in Wales, igniting trees and sending sheep airborne. The Home Office had called upon Professor Tarrant to manage the crisis. Being one of England's foremost specialists in exigent thaumaturgic geographic dynamics (otherwise known as "magical mayhem" to people who valued their vocal cords), Elodie received many such requests, and usually delegated them to graduate students. But with the Michaelmas term still a week away, Elodie rather fancied a few days in the autumnal countryside.

Besides, there existed a small chance that this job would indeed require her advanced expertise. The site—Dôlylleuad, a minor village ten miles east of the Welsh coastline—contained a deposit of subterranean thaumaturgical minerals marked as a level five trove on the Geographic Paranormal Survey map, which recorded all known sources of earth magic, along with the fey lines that connected them in a complex web around the world. Level five indicated minerals powerful enough to send dangerous sorcerous energy down the line to Oxford and its various libraries just waiting to explode, then on to London, where an incursion of wild magic would have cataclysmic results.

Immediately, Elodie had packed a suitcase, postponed her milk delivery, and organized to catch the earliest morning train to Wales. It was the perfect rapid response.

At least, up until the part where she forgot to set her alarm clock.

Arriving at Oxford Station with less than ten minutes to spare, she parked the velocipede and was untying the suitcase from its luggage tray when a young man approached, mustache trembling on his thin brown face as he hugged a clipboard of papers.

"Professor Tarrant?" he peeped.

"Ah, there you are, Motthers." Elodie turned to him with a brisk nod. He took in her entirely rational ensemble of coat, white shirtwaist, and gray skirt, and then her altogether irrational stockings exposed to general view (one black French lace, the other green, embroidered with flowers), and he winced so deeply his neck disappeared. "Is everything prepared?" she asked.

"Yes, ma'am. I have the emergency response kit, two tickets for the train, and a plentiful supply of sandwiches."

Elodie waited . . .

"Ham with cheese," he clarified.

She grinned. "Well done." Removing the helmet, she shook out her long, pale blonde hair. It tumbled down in reckless waves—magical hair, literally, having been mousy brown until, at age thirteen, she swam in a moonlit lake she had *absolutely no idea* was enchanted. "Sorry I'm late," she said, sweeping wayward strands from her face. "I overslept, then I started wondering during breakfast about how Persephone went for nine days in the underworld before eating the pomegranate seeds, and I quite lost track of time. Do you know?"

"Know what, Professor?" Motthers asked warily.

"How she survived all that time without even drinking water, of course."

"Um."

"Never mind. I'll ask someone from the classics department when I get back." She hung the helmet on the velocipede's handlebars and began to gather up her hair, looking around as if clips might appear midair for her convenience. Then she noticed Motthers's dazed stare. "What?"

"T-ticket, ma'am," he said, holding it out in a trembling hand. Elodie took it from him, her hair tumbling down again.

"Much obliged."

But Motthers was not done with trembling. "There's, um, a small problem."

"Oh?" Elodie asked, not really listening as she inspected the ticket. It provisioned her with a second class seat from Oxford to Aberystwyth, after which she and Motthers would take a hired carriage to Dôlylleuad. This was altogether a journey of several long, dull hours, but Elodie didn't mind, feeling that tedium was best described as an opportunity for imagination.

"Just a very small problem," Motthers persisted. "Which is to say, quite large actually, and—and—*problematic*."

"Uh-huh." Elodie experienced so many problems in her profession that they had to be literal disasters before she started worrying. Motthers, however, was only a master's degree student, and had not yet been caught in a raging flood, let alone outrun fiery boulders that chased him uphill. He needed several more catastrophes under his belt before he developed perspective. As a result, his voice tried to hide behind his tonsils when next he spoke.

"You recall how the telegram yesterday requested aid from Professor Tarrant?"

"Sure," Elodie said, barely listening. Suitcase in hand, she began striding through the station building toward the platform, the heels of her sturdy half boots knocking against the ground as if to announce to other travelers that a professional heroine had arrived—although apparently this was not clear enough for Professor Palgrave, who was forced to leap aside, muttering about "sinful blindness."

"Um," Motthers said, scurrying to keep pace despite his legs being several inches longer than Elodie's (which prompted him to wonder if he should mention the knotted-up skirt, but his courage failed). "It's just, well, it seems a copy was made of the telegram, and someone who shall go unnamed [Ralph Salterling] delivered it to a second office."

"Oh?" Elodie stopped near the edge of the platform and shielded her eyes with her free hand from the limpid morning sun as she peered along the tracks for a glimpse of a train. Incredibly, she had managed to arrive early.

"To be fair," Motthers continued, "we're not *exactly* sure who the message was meant for in the first place, you or . . . the other Professor Tarrant."

Elodie continued gazing out beneath her hand at the horizon, mainly because she had frozen. Then, very slowly, she turned to look at the small crowd on the platform.

And there he was.

"*You*," she muttered with such ferocity, it must be cause for amazement that the gentleman did not spontaneously combust. He did not even so much as flinch, however. Indeed, he might have been a statue erected in honor of Elodie's worst memory. All the familiar details were present: tidy black hair, almost-black eyes, olive skin, suit so immaculate he could have worn it to meet the pope, were he not an agnostic. Absent was any human warmth. Behind him, a graduate student fussed with their emergency response kit, but he ignored them, ignored the entire world, staring instead at a small, oblong wooden block in his hand with an expression so stern it made a rock seem like quivering jelly.

Yet Elodie knew that he'd seen her, without a doubt. He saw everything.

Gabriel.

Professor Tyrant to his students (and several members of the faculty when they thought no one could hear them).

Her husband.

Elodie's face blazed. She thrust the suitcase at Motthers without looking, turned on a heel, and began striding back toward the velocipede.

"P-Professor!" Motthers cried out, but Elodie ignored him. She had to get away . . . even while her mind ran headlong into the pit of memory.

SHE'D MARRIED GABRIEL on a Monday afternoon in September, almost exactly one year ago. It had been an accident.

If only she'd not gone to the Minervaeum, London's private club for academics, after attending the annual Thaumaturgic Cartography Symposium. If only she'd not felt so queasy from the odors of pipe smoke, steamed pudding, and nitroglycerine swirling through the club's Paracelsus Lounge that she'd decided to open a window. And if only doing so had not brought her close enough to where Gabriel sat with Professor Dubrovic that she'd overheard their conversation.

"Oh dear," Professor Dubrovic was saying. "*Four* Balliol students living upstairs from your flat?" He shook his head sympathetically.

"They are constantly quoting poetry," Gabriel answered,

managing to grouch in such refined tones that one naturally assumed he was in the right because he sounded like he must be. "And they debate Shakespeare's authorship at the top of their lungs. Or perhaps it's just that they want breakfast at all hours—in any case, if I hear another cry for Bacon, I will go quite mad. I need to find new accommodation before I'm driven to *educate* them."

"The place across from me on Holywell Street is vacant," Dubrovic said.

"I know, and it would be ideal. I inquired, but the landlady only wants a married couple."

Dubrovic shrugged. "So get married."

There followed a pause in the conversation, due to a chemistry professor across the room having detonated her pudding. While the other patrons variously cheered or complained, Dubrovic smirked over the rim of his whiskey glass at Gabriel. "No need to look so perturbed, old chap. *Amor est mortuus.* I'm talking about a marriage of convenience."

Gabriel frowned. "Oh? And where would I find a wife at such short notice?"

I'd marry you, Elodie thought with a wistful sigh. She'd adored him since the day they had met in Advanced Principles of Thaumaturgical Cartography, two eighteen-year-olds embarking upon a master's degree far sooner than their peers. He'd gotten there via a bachelor's degree (First Class Honors with Distinction), whereas her route had been through exceptional entry, having spent most of her life in the fields of Europe and Canada with her geographer parents. It was a difference in education that reflected their contrasting personalities, and yet Gabriel had from the very start represented Elodie's ideal of manhood, since even as a young man he'd possessed compelling gravitas and exceptional intelligence (along with perfectly aligned facial contours).

But he also scrupulously ignored her existence. Elodie could not blame him, however. She was neither beautiful nor thin, she lacked proper refinement, and then there was that time she accidentally dented his expensive, thaumaturgically charged copper sieve when using it to swat a fly in the classroom . . .

Suddenly, a ringing silence made her look up from the window's latch, whereupon she discovered that Gabriel had become very aware indeed of her existence and was staring at her in a way that made her feel like a map of some newly discovered shore.

For one frantic second, Elodie mentally cataloged every wrinkle and ink stain on her dress. Then she dragged together whatever dignity she could find within herself and stared right back at him. "What?" she said defensively.

"You'd marry me?" he asked, echoing the thought she'd apparently spoken aloud.

Oh, damn.

"The other professors don't respect me," she explained two days later, back in Oxford, as they walked to a church, the landlady having accepted Gabriel's application. Elodie's hair was unraveling from the intricate arrangement she'd spent hours concocting, her white dress was really far too matrimonial for the occasion, and somewhere along the way she'd lost her quiet dignity, perhaps in the same place as the handkerchief she'd bought for the traditional "something blue." Every few yards she glanced at her husband-to-be, still not quite believing the situation she found herself in. He just stared ahead, giving the impression he was walking alone. Nevertheless, Elodie couldn't stop talking.

"They think an unwed female professor is a terrible idea. That's why I'm agreeing to marry you." (Well, and the fact that she was an idiot, unable to keep her thoughts in her own head.)

"Uh-huh," Gabriel answered, glowering at a nearby oak that was casting its old russet leaves like wishes onto the footpath.

Actually, now that she mentioned it, Elodie felt quite heated on the subject. "Women have been allowed tertiary education for a hundred years now, thanks to Queen Charlotte's sponsoring it, and yet Oxford's geography staff think a woman with a doctorate is something bizarre. Never mind that there's a female ornithology professor even younger than I am; never mind that I know what I'm doing. I have more field experience than most of them put together, but do they care?"

"How strange," Gabriel said as he watched a squirrel scamper up the tree with a paperback novel in its mouth.

"Yes, exactly! Strange is just how I would describe it. Strange, and yet so very common. Misogynistic. The departmental secretary told me outright that I'd plague other professors with my 'tempting availability.'"

"Hm."

"My mother said that was probably just his way of asking me on a date."

Gabriel almost tripped on the edge of a cobblestone. "What?" he said, looking at her finally, his forehead creased with a frown.

"I know! Can you believe it?"

"Did *you* believe it?" he asked in return.

She huffed a laugh. "No. The only dates Hammerson knows about are the ones he buys at the greengrocer's in an effort to be cosmopolitan."

Gabriel glared at the church farther along the street as they continued toward it. He clearly did not want conversation, but if Elodie had ever found an off switch within herself, she'd lost it again long ago.

"When I'm married to you, they'll have to respect me." (For no other reason than the fear that, if they didn't, Professor Tyrant might come and *look* at them.)

"So," Gabriel said, "if we do this, I get decent housing, and you gain the respect of your peers? And you think that's a good deal?"

Elodie recognized that he was offering her a chance to withdraw, and she considered it—which is to say, immediately, completely refused it. Her proposal may have been accidental, but the opportunity to marry Gabriel Tarrant was, as her more modish students would say, a no-brainer.

In other words, she failed to apply her brain to it.

"Yes," she answered.

Twenty minutes later, she was standing in a quiet, sun-spangled chapel, trying hopelessly to repair her coiffure while Gabriel persuaded the vicar to marry them.

Ten minutes after that, they were pronounced man and wife. Gabriel lowered his head to kiss her.

"Er, we don't do that bit in the Church of England," the vicar interjected—but he could have broken into a flamboyant aria and Elodie wouldn't have noticed. Gabriel mustn't have noticed either, for he went ahead and pressed his lips gently against hers.

Although he touched her nowhere else, Elodie felt embraced by his entire being. Her heartbeat turned to stars, and her brain dissolved into a golden haze of pleasure from which she only grudgingly emerged some two days later, in Gabriel's flat, in Gabriel's bed, the marriage having been consummated to a degree that did not just meet but delightfully exceeded legal requirements. (They were, after all, two people who liked to be very thorough in what they did.) Any initial shy awkwardness had been vanquished by her joyous nature, his cool arrogance, and the excellent quality of the kissing.

It seemed a positive start, even if there was a small debate over the correct placement of used towels in the bathroom (which, Elodie learned, was apparently not "in a heap on the floor"). On the third day, they walked across to the rental house on Holywell Street, their companionable quiet feeling like a magic spell held in place by the gold ring on Elodie's finger, which Gabriel had unexpectedly produced. On the doorstep of ninety-nine, Gabriel introduced her to the land-lady as his wife. That Elodie managed not to giggle would have made her parents ~~astonished~~ proud.

But the landlady barred the threshold to them. "I've already rented it," she said.

They stared at her in disbelief. "We had an agreement," Gabriel said.

"Sorry. Dr. Costas made me a better offer."

"Dr. Andro Costas?" Gabriel asked.

"You know him?"

"Tall. Blond. A *bachelor*."

The woman winked at Elodie. "Yes, well, he's going to supplement the rent with free massages for my nervous condition. He has a special vibratory device." And she shut the door in their faces.

They stood in a silence so comprehensive it could have built a whole new house. Elodie's heartbeat began accelerating with an instinct for impending disaster. "Now what?" she asked.

Gabriel looked at her warily. "What do you mean?"

"Well, we only married so you could get this house."

Gabriel grew pale, but his eyes were darker than night as he stared at her. Belatedly realizing how she must have sounded, Elodie rushed to clarify. "I mean, I got what I wanted from our deal, but . . ."

No, stop! her brain shouted. But it was too late. Gabriel's expression turned thunderous. Pivoting abruptly, he marched away. Elodie stared after him for a moment, then left in the opposite direction.

And that had been that for their marriage.

"PROFESSOR!" MOTTHERS SQUEAKED, trying to juggle suitcase, clipboard, backpack, and wits as he hurried after her across the platform. "The train!"

"I won't be catching it," Elodie said, walking faster. In the past year since that wedding, general opinion as to her respectability did the opposite of improve; indeed, scurrilous gossip spread beyond the geography department to most of Oxford and even as far as her parents in Shropshire, who declared themselves bemused (but, alas, not entirely surprised) that she would marry a colleague on a sudden whim then abandon both him and her reputation to continue living alone. And Gabriel's search for accommodation had been completely derailed, since an estranged husband was considered even less reliable a tenant than a bachelor was. All in all, the marriage had turned out to be very inconvenient indeed. But having no grounds for an annulment, they were stuck with it.

Each blamed the other—or, at least, Elodie initially blamed herself, and wallowed in the depths of guilty despair, but since Gabriel made no effort to persuade her otherwise, she turned quite readily to blaming him. In short order, they moved from being *lovers* to *enemies*. No conversation passed between them other than a few curt greetings when absolutely required, and one particularly fiery verbal skirmish over whether to stock chocolate jumbles or plain digestive biscuits in the faculty tea cupboard.

Furthermore, Elodie learned to be a veritable escape artist, disappearing through doorways, behind hedges, and down stairwells whenever she saw Gabriel; once she even jumped out a first-floor window—the consequences of which to her ankle were luckily healed now, thus enabling her to move at speed across the train platform. Certainly, a master's student with a flimsy mustache could not stop her.

"But the magic!" Motthers cried.

"Professor Tarrant—the other one—will attend to that. You can join his team."

"But soil contamination from aeolian transportation of explosively thaumaturgized Neoproterozoic-Cambrian rock particles!"

Elodie's heart sank. *Damn.* Motthers was right. Dôlylleuad was sure to be in a bad way. She imagined the starved faces of children deprived of vital sustenance from . . . She paused to search her memory for the area's main produce . . . Er, pears.

"Fine," she muttered, coming to a halt.

"Pardon?" Motthers asked daringly.

Elodie turned, casting him a brief glare before taking the suitcase back. "Fine. I'll go."

Motthers grinned so widely, his mustache appeared in danger of sliding off. "Hurrah!" Then he grimaced. "Um, er, you might want to . . ."

As he flicked a finger at her lower half, Elodie glanced down and realized that her hem was still knotted. She hurriedly untied it, then began to trudge once more toward the tracks with the air of a French soldier approaching Waterloo. In the far distance, a cloud of steam signaled the train's approach. With luck, she'd have only a minute to talk with Gabriel before it arrived.

Approaching him was the hardest thing she'd done in a long while, and this was coming from a woman with a doctorate that had required extensive knowledge of trigonometry. She hated the coldhearted, unforgiving man. Absolutely, completely loved—wait, no, *loathed* him. Arriving at his side on the platform, she offered a terse yet polite greeting.

But Gabriel went on staring at the block in his hand, such a calm, somber beauty to his face that it made Elodie's throat ache. *Ache like I've just swallowed poison,* she amended furiously. Setting down her suitcase, she cleared her throat and, when that failed to elicit a response, tried to decide which exact swear word she would shout . . .

"Do you feel that sound?" Gabriel asked suddenly, not shifting his gaze.

It seemed "Good morning" or even "I say, aren't you my wife?" were surplus to his conversational requirements. Elodie found herself thrown from aggravation into utter confusion.

"Um?" she said.

Um. A master's degree, a doctorate, a professorship, and all she could say was *"um"*? Her intelligence rolled its eyes in embarrassment.

But Gabriel hadn't noticed, of course. Pulling herself together, Elodie tried again. "You mean do I *hear* a sound?"

"No."

Aggravation stomped back into her brain, shoving confusion aside. "I don't feel anything," she said frostily.

And then she did. A tiny sound scraped along her ear canals, whining like a student who has forgotten it's exam day. "What is that?" she wondered aloud, shaking her head.

Gabriel looked up at her then, angling the block in his hand so she could see that it was a portable weather station: the four brass-ringed gauges set upon it measured temperature, air pressure, humidity, and thaumaturgy levels. Elodie noted at a glance that all readings were normal except the latter. Its tiny silver needle quivered at the edge of the danger zone.

"Thaumaturgic resonance," Gabriel said. *Magic.*

They exchanged an expression that was pure geography, all steep hills, underground rivers, and a hot, dangerous flash of lightning. Elodie immediately looked away. She scanned the station for indications of danger, but other than an embarrassing number of professors waiting for a train out of the city just when students were beginning to return for term, nothing seemed amiss. No one else in the station appeared to suffer from feeling weird sounds. Behind her, Motthers stared at the slowly approaching train as if willing it to speed up. Even Gabriel's student was entirely focused on trying to stuff a dowsing rod into their emergency response kit. And yet, the sound of magic continued to whinge inside Elodie's air like an Oxford don who thought women professors would bring the university to ruin. A lifetime's experience with geographical

magic warned her that something somewhere was going cata-
wampus.

(No reason why scientific expertise couldn't come with a
sprightly lexicon, Elodie always contended.)

Increasingly troubled, she glanced again at Gabriel and
found him staring at her.

"Arousing," he murmured.

A blush swept across Elodie's face like a matador's cloak,
which was a particularly fitting description considering how
her pulse rampaged. "I beg your pardon?" she asked with geographic dignity.

"The resonance. It's arousing my nerves in the most disconcerting manner."

"Ah, I see. Yes, me too. The hairs on my arms are standing
up." She slid a hand beneath one sleeve to calm them. "And—"

BOOM!

CHAPTER TWO

If you want things to flow easily,
you have to not give a dam.
Blazing Trails, W.H. Jackson

A T FIRST, GABRIEL thought his senses were exploding as
Elodie reached under her clothing and stroked her bare
skin. So this was it, then. The hemorrhagic stroke he'd been
expecting since the moment an eighteen-year-old Miss Elodie
Hughes walked into Advanced Thaumaturgic Cartography
dressed in white lace and with violets in her unbound hair,
looking like a Pre-Raphaelite nymph who had strayed into
Oxford and decided to take up academia for a lark—and then
promptly tripped over her own feet, crashing against his desk
and sending his tidy stack of textbooks tumbling.

To say nothing of his mental discipline.

He'd never habituated to her. (Although, to be fair, that
was like trying to habituate to a tornado.) Even in that first
encounter, he'd failed to find words while she, apparently suffering the opposite problem, had restacked his books in entirely the wrong order, and joked about declensions, and left
violets scattered all over his feet. And matters hadn't improved
since. One glance from those amiable green eyes, and his

prodigious vocabulary simply ~~went poof~~ vaporized. The only wonder was that his health had held up as long as it had.

Therefore it was most perplexing, this desire to slip first one finger, then two, up her shirtwaist sleeve to soothe her aroused skin and make the words *my husband* come shuddering from her lips.

Fortunately, before he could, the shock wave from the *actual* explosion sent him stumbling.

Ensorcelled air hurtled past, shoving Elodie against him. Gabriel reacted without thought, catching her in his arms and holding her close, one hand cupped protectively against the back of her head. For a moment she stiffened, then clutched him as they were buffeted by raw thaumaturgic power.

Gabriel's bones rattled, but he remained firm. Only twice in his life had he lost composure: after his cousin Devon had been sent to America when they were children, depriving him of his sole friend; and on his wedding night with Elodie, when he found himself inexplicably breathless and trembling as he watched her sleep. If they survived this moment, he would tell her—

"Bloody hell!"

The pained exclamation ruptured his thoughts. Looking up, he saw his assistant, Henry Beetleson, sprawled on the ground, surrounded by the shattered pieces of a hazel and copper dowsing rod. Blood slipped from a gash on the young man's forehead, and blue sparks of magic flickered over it like tiny vampirical fireflies.

"Sorry, Professor," he groaned.

Gabriel realized the propulsive energy had vanished abruptly, leaving quiet like a long, heavy exhalation in its wake. Making a rapid survey of the scene, he comprehended that

Beetleson had somehow caused the dowsing rod to detonate, releasing the thaumaturgic energy stored within it from previous use. Other than the student himself, no one on the station platform seemed hurt; indeed, they were watching the scene with mild interest. This was Oxford, after all, where the university's presence meant that at any moment a deadly enchanted bird, possessed artifact, or over-caffeinated student might escape and go on a rampage. The explosion of a thaumaturgic device represented nothing special; all that remained was to see if those in its blast range would turn into flower bushes or large cuckoo clocks.

Frowning, Gabriel stepped away from Elodie—then discovered his body had ignored that command and was still holding her close, reveling in her soft, floral-scented warmth. Baffled, aggravated, he dispatched a stern disciplinary note to himself.

At the same moment, Elodie exhaled. As the gentle gust of air brushed against his throat, the disciplinary note went up in flames.

Mercifully for both his health and dignity, she tugged herself free. "Is everyone all right?" she asked, looking around in a rapid manner that prevented him from examining her expression beyond its blush. He could not miss, though, how excitement illuminated her entire being. "That was *fascinating!*"

"Hm," Gabriel said, crossing his arms tightly, determined not to evidence the fascination he also felt. A man couldn't just go around being keen. It was the kind of thing that led, on one hand, to getting academic degrees, but on the other to being told, *For God's sake, shut up for five minutes about alluvial plains.*

It also led to marrying a woman who clambered over hedges to avoid being seen when you walked past.

"I wish I had a thaumometer on me," Elodie was enthusing. Everything about her seemed in motion: hair, hands, intelligence. "Such atmospheric excitation due to the propulsive reverberation of intensate kinetic thaumaturgic energy is not usually—oh, hello! I say, do I know you?"

At this abrupt swerve in subject, Gabriel turned to see whom she addressed, and his expression became so dour, students still abed two miles away shuddered instinctively.

A woman stood before them, dark-eyed, dark-haired, and dressed in a sober traveling suit. She had a small leather suitcase in one hand, a book in the other, and such an aura of dignified unflappability that Gabriel saw Elodie grow calm within its influence, even while his own nerves began to twitch. She scanned Gabriel from head to foot, her demeanor suggesting that, if he was experiencing some problem, she would fix it (whether he wished her to or not) and then, as a helpful bonus, advise him on how exactly he went wrong. Determining that he was uninjured, she turned with a polite smile to Elodie.

"We haven't met," she said before Gabriel could think of a way to stop her. "I know I would remember that."

"Amelia," Gabriel interrupted brusquely. "What are you doing here?"

Blinking long, thick lashes, she turned the smile back toward him. "Well, this may seem incredible, considering our location, but I'm waiting for a train. I noticed the disturbance and wanted to check you were unhurt."

"I'm unhurt."

"That's a relief. So . . ."

"So goodbye," Gabriel said brusquely.

Amelia ignored this with perfect equanimity. "Are you going to introduce me to the lady?"

Gabriel's jaw clenched. But Elodie extended her hand without hesitation. "Professor Tarrant," she said.

"How interesting," Amelia remarked. "That's my name too."

From somewhere in the crowd behind them came the murmur, *"Oh God, there's three of them."* Amelia took Elodie's offered hand and shook it firmly. "I beg your pardon. I don't know what has become of my manners."

Elodie laughed. "Manners are for people who don't have anything more interesting to say."

That brightened Amelia's smile. "I'm Miss Amelia Tarrant, a history professor here at Oxford," she said. "Also, Gabriel's sister. And you must be his w—"

"No time to talk," Gabriel said, grasping Elodie's elbow and turning her away from his sister's fascinated scrutiny. "I'll see you at Aunt Mary's Sunday dinner."

"Nice to meet you!" Elodie called over her shoulder. Then she snatched her elbow from Gabriel's grip, speared him with a look that made it clear meeting *him* had been the opposite of nice, and redirected her attention to Beetleson, who was sitting up, wiping the blood from his forehead. Concern suffused her face. "Oh dear, are you all right, lad?"

The lad (actually a twenty-three-year-old man with a master's degree) gave her a wan, piteous look. Then, noticing Gabriel's frown, he went from pale to bright scarlet in what was obviously a very rapid heartbeat.

"F-fine," he stammered—inaccurately, since in addition to his head wound, he was on the verge of being suspended from Oxford, or by his ankles over a pit of snakes, whichever Gabriel decided was sufficient punishment for his endangering ~~Elodie's~~ everyone's life with his careless handling of thaumaturgic equipment. "I don't understand what happened. I only twisted the dowsing rod's branches so I could fit it into the pack better."

"Twisted them? Without first ensuring there was no residual energy contained in the rod?" Gabriel was furious. "You should know better than that, Beetleson. It's basic safety."

"Sorry, Professor," Beetleson murmured dolefully.

"Accidents happen," Elodie said, casting a chastising frown at Gabriel before she handed Beetleson a lace-trimmed handkerchief and winced with gentle sympathy as he pressed it to his forehead.

Gabriel bristled. "Accidents certainly do *not* happen. Not with my students. Beetleson is wholly responsible for both the explosion and the fact he now has magic eating at his face."

"*What?!*" Beetleson exclaimed in horror.

"Maybe he was in a hurry," Elodie suggested.

"*Eating at my face?*" Beetleson scrubbed his cheeks and then wailed, aghast, when blue sparks shot out, buzzing as they formed a swarm and rushed him again.

"Even a child knows to perform a fundamental Hesselthop maneuver to safely ground and discharge thaumaturgic residuum before reconfiguring a thaumaturgic dowsing rod," Gabriel said. "Beetleson's ineptitude cannot be excused."

"*Oh my God!*" Beetleson could be heard crying from within the swarm.

Elodie set her hands on her hips. "You're being too harsh."

Gabriel crossed his arms. "You're being too lenient. People could have died."

"But they didn't."

"But they could have."

"I'm going to die!" Beetleson howled.

"Is he?" Amelia asked worriedly, but no one noticed. Elodie and Gabriel were staring at each other for longer than they had in all nine years of their acquaintance. Elodie's cheeks glowed with hectic color, and Gabriel breathed more than was advisable for the maintenance of a sober reputation. Several people in the crowd whispered to one another that any moment now someone was going to get either slapped or kissed.

Thankfully, Motthers stepped forward in the nick of time, mustache quaking.

"Professor Tarrant," he squeaked. "And, er, Professor Tarrant. Sorry. The train is here."

ELODIE LOOKED AWAY from Gabriel, releasing a breath she'd not only been holding but had tied up and gagged too. There was no point trying to compel her nerves into tranquility; she might as well attempt meditation in a hurricane. Gabriel was so damned *vexing*, the most arrogant man she'd *ever* known!

(He'd also *embraced* her, risking himself to *protect* her! And his sister clearly knew that Elodie was his wife, which suggested that *he'd mentioned her to his family!*)

Oh yes, and there had been an explosion.

Preoccupied with these italics, Elodie only vaguely noted that the other travelers on the platform had begun bustling toward the train. Motthers was removing pages from his clipboard and handing them to her; she folded them absentmindedly and handed them back. Amelia, turning slowly on a heel to inspect the lingering blue tinge in the atmosphere, murmured something about "thaumaturgic residue," but Elodie only dimly registered the words. He'd *mentioned* her. *To his family!*

"What a mess," Gabriel grumbled.

Elodie managed to focus then, supposing he was about to continue their argument. Her stomach clenched. But in fact his gaze was on Beetleson, who remained hunched among the dowsing rod's remnants, trying frantically to brush away the glimmering cloud of magic that now engulfed his entire head.

"I want a full report of this episode on my desk, Monday morning," Gabriel told the young man, his voice like a dormant volcano: quiet, calm, but with the potential to erupt with terrifying effect at any moment. "Accompanied by an essay on Newton's first law of motion."

"Aghhhh," Beetleson replied.

"Motthers, help the poor boy get to the infirmary," Elodie said without thinking—then *did* think, and winced at the realization she'd just consigned herself to going on the assignment alone with Gabriel. But it was too late; Motthers had already dropped his clipboard and shrugged off his emergency response kit with such an eager haste Elodie would have been offended had the train's conductor calling, "All aboard!" not distracted her.

"Should I try to follow after you tomorrow?" he asked, making it sound like he was proposing a trek up Mt. Everest.

Elodie frowned as the question reverberated through her tangled nerves. "I don't know," she murmured, and turned to discuss the situation with Gabriel—only to find he'd picked up his suitcase in one hand, his ER kit in the other, and was striding for the train.

Just like that.

Elodie glared after him. Beside her, Amelia gave a heavy

sigh that sounded a lot like Elodie's heart felt. "He's so up-tight," the woman said. "I can't remember the last time he re-laxed, let alone laughed."

"I saw him smile once," Elodie said, then immediately shut down her memory of the moment before it triggered a cata-strophic tsunami of emotions. She looked around for her suit-case, which was in fact sitting by her feet, along with Motthers's ER kit. Motthers himself had already gone to help Beetleson, apparently thinking that, if he didn't get an answer from Elo-die, that was as good as a no. Her brain felt too askew to man-age the decision, so she just hauled the kit onto her back, lifted the suitcase, and tucked one side of her hair behind her ear in lieu of a proper coiffure. Then she nodded to Amelia.

"Sorry to dash, but it really was nice meeting you."

"And you," Amelia replied, then glanced at Beetleson. "Is the student going to be all right?"

"Oh, he'll be fine once the magic dissipates," Elodie said. Then she leaned closer to add furtively, "Besides, this fright will teach the lad not to be so careless about basic safety rules when it comes to thaumaturgic tools."

Amelia blinked for one startled moment, then laughed. "I'm off to Hereford," she said, "but when I get back, perhaps we might have tea? It's no concern if you'd rather not."

"I would like that indeed . . ." Elodie said, but her voice trailed off as she noticed Gabriel across the platform. He'd paused in boarding the first class carriage and was frowning at her, no doubt wondering if she intended to catch the train. For a moment, she considered again not doing so. Spending several days in the countryside with her husband might be a secret wish of her heart, but it was also one that only the most devi-ous of fairy godmothers would make come true.

And yet, although she often failed at being dignified, she was in every other respect professional. Whatever her personal issues with Gabriel, she was going to do her work, and do it well, like a grown-up. So there!

"Well, good luck," Amelia said. And watching her brother as he entered the train, she added, "I've a feeling you'll need it."

"Oh?"

"It's going to be a disaster zone."

"That's the job," Elodie said.

"The job?" Amelia smiled wryly. "Oh yes, that too."

"Final call!" the conductor announced. Elodie dashed for the train. She had just entered when Motthers began frantically hollering her name. Pausing, Elodie turned to see the student waving his clipboard at her. "Professor, wait! I forgot to tell you! It's urgent! There's another problem—!"

Toot!

The conductor shut the carriage door, and as Elodie tumbled into a seat, the train began its journey toward magic.

Chapter Three

What goes up must come down, although
that can take between seconds and millennia,
depending on whether one is a man or a mountain.
        Blazing Trails, W.H. Jackson

THE TRAIN ARRIVED in Aberystwyth just after noon. Both Professors Tarrant disembarked from their separate carriages, several yards apart. They looked around the station and the luminous azure sky beyond. They double-checked their luggage. They watched a seagull glide on ocean-scented breezes that scudded along the platform. Finally, when every single excuse had been used, they began to look at each other—

"Professor Tarrant!"

Elodie turned so fast she made herself dizzy. A sallow young man was running toward her, waving a clipboard. She watched him apprehensively through windswept hair, fearing he might be a student who'd tracked her all the way to Wales to complain about her course prerequisites . . .

Suddenly, Gabriel appeared at her side in a protective stance, arms crossed, expression indomitable. *Well, goodness,* Elodie thought. How ~~chivalrous~~ contemptuous of female capabilities! Did he think her some fainting damsel? Why, she'd been dragging herself out of bogs, dusting herself off after falling out of trees, and, um, perhaps this wasn't the most helpful line of thought after all.

The young man arrived in front of them, breathing heavily as a consequence of his short dash across the station platform. "Professor Tarrant," he said between gasps. "I'm Algernon Jennings, an accountant with the Home Office. I was appointed yesterday to manage this assignment, and I took the overnight train in the interests of our budget."

The implied criticism of their having caught a more expensive morning service did not escape Elodie. She gave Mr. Jennings a closer look. Dressed in a cheap, undersized gray suit, with an old suitcase in one hand and a tent rolled up under his arm, he was apparently planning to camp out in an office. His thin brown hair contained so much pomade a tornado wouldn't have been able to stir it, let alone the afternoon's breeze that played havoc with Elodie's. Testosterone was attempting to cultivate a mustache above his upper lip without much success.

This must be the other problem Motthers had tried to warn her about. Elodie did what she always did in the face of problems: she smiled. "Nice to meet you, Mr. Jennings."

The young man blinked as if only just noticing her presence. "Hello, are you Professor Tarrant's secretary?"

Her smile vanished faster than doughnuts in a faculty lounge. "No, I most certainly am not."

"I beg your pardon. How good of the professor to bring his wife along on the job."

Elodie blinked. Beside her, Gabriel developed a sudden cough.

"I'm not Professor Tarrant's wife," she said tersely. "I mean, I *am*, but that is beside the point." (Actually, she would rather like to take the point and stab someone with it just now. Either of the two men in her vicinity would do.) "I'm also a professor in my own right. Why have we been given a manager?"

Algernon Jennings looked at Gabriel as if seeking permission to reply. Fed up, Elodie picked up her suitcase, turned on a heel, and began striding toward the station exit. Gabriel joined her, and Algernon scampered to catch up.

"Too many field operations have come in over budget lately," he explained. "Just last month Mr. Kapoor bought new binoculars, even though one lens of his existing pair still worked perfectly well. And—"

"You won't need that tent," Elodie said, having stopped listening to his speech after the first sentence. She did not actually care why he was joining their assignment. She'd just realized that he would provide a convenient third presence between her and Gabriel, which elevated him from a "problem," into a godsend. "The weather forecast is too unstable for camping," she explained. "We'll be staying at the village inn."

Jennings's eyes widened. "The inn?! But the cost of renting rooms for an entire team . . . uh, where is the team?"

"We're it," Elodie told him. "Hurry up, please, we've no time to waste."

"But—but—" Algernon dropped his clipboard, then almost tripped as he hastened to retrieve it. Elodie and Gabriel did not pause in their stride, and he was forced again to catch up. "But there's been a disaster!"

"Well yes," Elodie replied briskly. "That's why we're here."

"No, I mean another one!"

They came to an abrupt halt. Gabriel frowned at Algernon. "Talk fast."

"The townsfolk are in a tizzy," the young man gabbled. "The Rheidol river's turned bloodred in places!"

"No doubt from erosion of the Old Red Sandstone common in this area," Gabriel said.

"And, a strange fog sent a whole crowd of peddlers running back to town! They swore fairies were calling to them."

"Cattle lowing. The sound would be distorted by the fog."

"Oh." Algernon seemed rather crestfallen, as if fairies were somehow more interesting than acoustic attenuation and dispersion in relation to water molecules.

Elodie set down her suitcase so as to brush the hair away from her face. "There's really no need for superstitious panic in town," she said. "Magic does exist, of course—"

"Sensible, scientific magic," Gabriel interjected. "Not fairies."

"—but the 5-SEQ fey line is some four miles from Aberystwyth. For any overflow to reach across such a distance, the energy intensity would have to be unprecedented. You'd see consequences, such as fires, between here and the line." She angled to point southward and blinked at the sight of a large smoke plume rising beyond the edge of town. "Er, well, *more* of such things."

"What does any of this have to do with getting us to Dôly-lleuad?" Gabriel asked, glancing pointedly at his wristwatch.

"No one will take you there," Algernon explained. "Even though the fog has cleared, they say they won't risk the . . . um, lowing cattle. Professor Jackson had to go out on a bicycle."

Elodie stiffened. "Did you say Jackson? As in *Woodrow* Jackson, formerly a professor of Oxford?"

"Yes. He teaches at Aberystwyth University now, so the Home Office sent him out as an advance scout."

Elodie and Gabriel exchanged a glance darker than the cave from which they and their fellow students had barely escaped after Professor Jackson took them to see singing stalactites that turned out to be razor-sharp *spinning* stalactites.

Clearly *this* was Motthers's "other problem." If Jackson was currently on-site, they could not get there fast enough.

The breeze whipped through her hair yet again, and she swiped irritably at the strands tangling across her face. Suddenly, Gabriel's hand appeared before her, an elastic band between its thumb and forefinger. "Good heavens," she remarked in surprise. "You just happen to have one of those on you?"

"Of course," he said, looking straight ahead, expressionless. "I'm a geographer."

"And I'm perfectly capable of—"

"Take the elastic band, Ellie."

She almost gasped. No one had called her Ellie in years. All at once she was back in Oxford's quaint little coffeehouse Jabbercoffee, laughing with other students and trying not to look at the handsome, bespectacled boy who sat, usually with his nose in a book, at the edge of the group. Their peers and teachers always treated them as a matching pair—*the prodigies*—but nothing could be less true. Gabriel was a remarkable scholar, Elodie a wild card. Gabriel had an instant answer for any mathematics question; Elodie could say "My, what a big rock" in seven languages. And whereas Gabriel wore smart tweed jackets and was never seen around town without a tie, Elodie had once got halfway to class before realizing she'd been so occupied with daydreaming about flame trees, lakes of jewel-colored water, and the ethereal landscapes of Tennyson's poetry that she'd forgotten to change out of her nightgown.

Even so, there had grown over the years a bond of memory and collegiality between them, a kind of belonging together that not even her wedding ring made her feel. Her stomach swooped.

Taking the elastic band, employing assiduous care that their gloved fingers did not graze each other, she murmured thanks. Gabriel did not reply, except to flex his hand against his thigh, which was certainly eloquent enough. Elodie considered employing the elastic band as a tiny slingshot directed at his face, but decided she really did need it.

"Listen," she told Algernon as she tied back her hair. "There is an obvious solution to this predicament."

"Walk?" Algernon guessed.

"No."

"Then . . . what . . . ?"

"OH MY GOD," Algernon wailed for the thirteenth time in an hour. "A hot air balloon!" He clasped the edge of the wicker basket as if his life depended on it rather than on the harness and two safety belts he'd insisted upon wearing.

Elodie looked at him wearily. She'd tried to point out that it was a *motorized* hot air balloon that operated on both kerosene and flaming hot gas, but for some reason this failed to ameliorate his concern. "We're almost there," she assured him, raising her voice above the whir of the motor blades.

"How do you know?" Algernon demanded.

"I'm paid to judge distances. Besides, just look down." She pointed to the small village that lay like a brooch on the green patchwork of countryside below.

"Look down?!" Apparently, this suggestion did not meet Algernon's standards of reasonable behavior. "When they told me this job was a ground-level position, I took them literally!"

Elodie glanced at Gabriel, if only to avoid rolling her eyes, and saw him rolling his own. He was leaning back against the side of the basket, arms and ankles crossed, tension limning his features as he stared into the middle distance. Elodie assumed he felt unhappy being on this assignment with his so-called spouse. Well, *so did she.*

She turned back to Algernon. "You're quite safe. In fact, you'd be in more danger on the ground, crossing fey lines."

"The lines are stable ninety-nine percent of the time!"

This was true; indeed, a person could go their entire life never experiencing a single disturbance from the rare, magic-infused minerals that lay scattered beneath the earth and that flared only when natural conditions mixed in unlikely ways. But for Elodie, whose career focused on the one percent, and who therefore lived within a frequent storm of magic and its disastrous consequences (interspersed by equally exhausting periods of teaching university students), Algernon's hysteria over a tranquil balloon ride was difficult to sympathize with.

Unfortunately, the pilot, Mr. Bloyd, did not help matters by saying just then, "I reckon that's some bad weather coming, it is." He pointed southwest, to the cumulonimbus formation Elodie herself had been watching for some time now. Its vast, billowing white heap was stained beneath with a heavy, somber darkness that promised storms. Belatedly she recognized that Gabriel watched it too and that this explained his taut expression.

"It'll be raining old women and sticks soon, mark my words," Bloyd predicted, his face etched with worry. "I should never have agreed to this trip."

"Think of the noble service you're providing to science," Elodie told him.

"Think of the small fortune we paid you," Gabriel added.

"Money won't do me much good if lightning hits this balloon," Bloyd grumbled.

"Oh my God!" Algernon wailed.

Bloyd sneered at him. "You're a right *lembo*, ain't you?"

"What does that mean?" Algernon asked weakly. "I studied math; I don't understand foreign languages."

"I say," Elodie interjected before someone threw the accountant overboard. "Do you think we'll be able to land before that weather arrives?"

"Land, maybe," Bloyd said. "I'm not sure about taking off again, though. And I ain't staying any more than a minute in that *rhyfedd* place." He spat over his left shoulder (and in a *complete coincidence*, the wind current flung the spittle into Algernon's face).

Suddenly, the basket convulsed.

"Aaagghh!"

Elodie winced at Algernon's scream. Bloyd, with muttered curses, began urgently adjusting the gas tank's valve. Gabriel raised an eyebrow.

"What's haaaappening?" Algernon shrieked.

"Turbulence," Elodie told him. "Don't worry, it's just air currents—"

Thwomp! A gust smacked into the basket, causing it to swing. The atmosphere flashed eerily with a bright, glimmering blue light that set the gas flame flickering wildly.

"Actually, that's magic," Elodie amended.

"But I thought magic was in the ground!" Algernon wailed.

"It is, but it rises up through fissures in the land, or in water vapor, or with the respiration of plants. That's how it ensorcells people and creates atmospheric conditions like—"

Thwack. Her lecture was interrupted by a practical demonstration that shook the basket. Algernon howled. Elodie sighed testily. Gabriel straightened the handkerchief in his jacket pocket.

"I'm not going to be able to hold her for long!" Bloyd shouted. "We've got to turn back!"

"No, wait!" Elodie urged. "We're almost there. I'll pay you another ten shillings." She reached into her skirt pocket, pulling out a handful of coins (and fascinating pebbles and a single earring whose partner she'd lost somewhere). Looking closer at them, she amended, "Eleven shillings."

"Oh well, if it's *eleven*," Bloyd said sardonically. Reducing the flame, he vented air, and the basket began to lower. *Whoosh* went the magically charged breeze. *"Eeeek!"* went Algernon as sparks flew.

"It's fine," Elodie told him. "They're coming from outside."

Algernon evidenced no reassurance at this, perhaps because one of the sparks had set a corner of the basket alight. Indeed, he began flailing his arms, creating more of a risk to their safety than the weather or the fire. Elodie nudged him aside, removed her coat, and beat it against the flames until they were snuffed.

"See," she said soothingly. "We're perfectly—"

Thud. As another gust rocked the basket, everyone stumbled.

"Just take us as low as you can," Elodie told Bloyd even as Gabriel opened one of the ER kits and began pulling out ropes and a harness. "We'll rappel the rest of the way."

There followed a thorough explanation from Algernon as to why he could not agree with this proposed action, mainly consisting of the words *never*, *oh God*, and *Mummy!* Elodie ignored

it. Behind her, Gabriel was strapping on a harness, looking
entirely calm, as if he were preparing to walk into a classroom.
Elodie hastily stripped off her skirt and petticoat until she was
left only in long drawers, thus enabling her to don a harness also.
Then, taking coils of rope from her kit, she crammed as much
of her personal luggage into the newly available space as she
could, hoisted the kit onto her back, and set about securing
the rope to one of the basket's uprights while Gabriel did the
same opposite her.

"Mr. Jennings, are you ready?" she asked as she tied a bow-
line knot.

"No!" he shouted, shaking his head with vigor.

"For goodness' sake," Gabriel snapped. "Go home, boy.
And once there, try to locate your backbone." He turned Elodie around and began tugging on the buckles and straps of her
harness to check their security, causing her own backbone to
feel like it was melting. Memories of him undressing her on
their wedding night skittered over her skin, making her tingle
and blush. Forcibly repressing them, she checked his harness
in turn, like the sensible professional that she was, then they
stepped apart, neither of them meeting the other's eye.

"Ready?" Gabriel asked.

"Of course," Elodie replied.

Without another word, they tossed their ropes over the
edge of the basket.

"Oh God, you're insane!" Algernon wailed. "You're going
to diiiiie!"

Clipping her harness buckle onto the rope, Elodie hauled
herself over the basket's edge with the ease of someone whose
job involved climbing rocks (and occasionally outrunning

them), then paused with her bootheels propped against the woven cane until Gabriel was in the same position on the other side. He looked across at her with solemn steadiness. She grinned in return.

"Race you."

Gabriel frowned. "Certainly not. Safety regulations state—"

With a laugh, Elodie pushed herself off into the sky. Half a second later, Gabriel followed.

Elodie's stomach swooped with exhilaration as she rappelled down. Wind-shredded light flickered across her face like the bright memory of birds. Magic kissed her skin, warm and sweet. Bloyd had managed to bring them directly above Dôlylleuad, and as Elodie descended toward it, she admired the picturesque cluster of white-washed cottages, tucked among lush meadows that lay between low, wooded hills. The Ystwyth River wound a placid course nearby like a glinting dream of the sea. Autumn brightness flared among the greenery as if ancient, mythical gods had scattered copper, gold, and rubies when they stalked the land. Elodie was just beginning on a simile involving sheep and pearls when she came to the village's cobblestone street and the end of her descent. Her feet hit the ground with a jolt; at the same moment, Gabriel landed.

"It's a tie," she told him, giddy with adrenaline.

"It wasn't a race," he replied punctiliously. "But just for the record, my left foot touched down half a second before either of yours."

Elodie scoffed. They unclipped themselves, and Gabriel waved to Bloyd, who immediately accelerated the balloon away. Closing her eyes, Elodie inhaled a scent of old leaves, chimney smoke, and shimmery magic. A bewitching thrill

tingled through her as it always did at the start of an assignment, when everything was wild, unknown, and free from
students begging wretchedly for deadline extensions.

"Hell's bells, what a bricky sensagger!"

Instantly, her tingles turned to ashes. She knew that dialect,
and it was not Welsh. Opening her eyes, she turned to discover
that she'd been so busy enjoying the landscape during her descent, she'd entirely missed the people within it. Two young
ladies in white lace dresses beneath white lace parasols, alongside a trio of young gentlemen with beige boater hats, beige
suits, and thin beige mustaches, stared at her amazedly. All
that was missing to complete the picture was a tea service,
someone holding a cricket bat, and an emphysemic bulldog.

"I say, that was bang up to the elephant, what!" one of the
gentlemen declared.

"Balmy on the crumpet," said another excitedly.

"Dimber-damber ekker, sure puts footer in the wagger pag-
ger bagger!" contributed the third.

Elodie was aghast. Only one species talked so incompre-
hensibly: the well-educated man. She leaned a little toward
Gabriel. "Did we somehow get turned around and end up back
in Oxford?"

"Hm," he replied, which Elodie understood to mean *unless
they are landforms that happen to resemble people, I'm not interested*. Setting down his ER kit, he began unbuckling his harness, ruthlessly leaving Elodie to deal with the human
geography aspect of the job. Repressing a sigh, she put on her
best professional countenance and moved forward, hand
extended . . .

Then stopped and looked over her shoulder as something
bashed against her thighs. Seeing a loose strap of her harness,

she tried to reach it, then concluded she'd be better off just removing the whole thing, whereupon . . .

"Good afternoon," Gabriel said, stepping forward in the bewildered silence to shake first one man's hand and then another while Elodie muttered under her breath, wrestling with her harness. "The name's Tarrant."

"How d'you do?" replied a fellow whose trim mustache lay so crookedly above his lip, Gabriel wanted to bring out a ruler and razor blade to fix it. "Pimmersby, at your service. Have you come for the fun?"

"Fun?" Gabriel repeated.

"The magic, of course. Such frabjous excitement! Calloo! Callay! 'Airy abeles set on a flare! Flake-doves sent floating forth—'"

Bloody hell. The fellow was either an incoherent lunatic or a humanities student. (Gabriel did not always find it easy to spot the difference.) "You mean the manifestations of dangerous, unconstrained thaumaturgic energy," he said, frowning severely.

"Yes, exactly! Hapsitch and I were en route to Oxford for Noughth Week when we heard the news and turned around at once. Mumbers here was holidaying in Aberystwyth—"

"Spot of pleurisy," the aforementioned Mumbers interposed with a cheerful smile. "My phrenologist says damp sea air's the best cure for it."

"—and the Misses Trevallion abandoned an exploration of Tintern Abbey. No longer did they 'repose here, under this dark sycamore,' but instead came, er, here . . ."

"And where were you when you heard about the hijinks?"

one of the Misses asked Gabriel in a voice that lifted its hem coyly and flashed a silk-stockinged question mark.

Gabriel's frown deepened from *severe* to the level of *Puritan at Christmas*. "I was in my office in Merton College when informed by the Home Office about Dôlylleuad's life-threatening situation."

"Ooh," chorused the ladies. The gentlemen, however, shuffled back upon this revelation that they faced their natural foe, a university don.

"Dr. Tarrant and I are with Her Majesty's geographic emergency response team," Gabriel explained. "We will be assessing the hazards triggered by this crisis and organizing whatever aid may be required."

It was in fact the smallest part of their job and provided cover for the greater: locating the source of the magical disruptions and, as much as possible, making any initial fixes until the secondary team could arrive. If a landslip had exposed a seam of thaumaturgic minerals that were flaring in response to the weather conditions, they would cover it again. If a magic-infused pool of water had flooded, they would shore up its banks. Such a task must always be highly classified, however, since geographers had long ago learned that if you announced a site of dangerous magic existed nearby and might explode at any given moment, it wouldn't so much induce panic as send people rushing to that site so they could poke their finger in it, take their photograph beside it, and establish a souvenir shop at the edge.

Indeed, this lot were a case in point. Only idiots rushed *toward* a thaumaturgic crisis on purpose. Excepting him, of course . . . and Elodie . . . their peers . . . thaumaturgy students . . . geologists . . . news reporters . . . army reserves . . .

nurses . . . *but* it was not at all appropriate for civilians. Storm chasing ought not be a species of tourism!

"Excuse me," a Miss ventured, holding up a delicate, lace-gloved hand. Gabriel looked at her expectantly. "I wonder if you'd help me with my sextant," she said, batting her eyelashes with such vigor it was a wonder she could see at all.

Abruptly, Gabriel reached the limit of his conversation tolerance. He snapped a glance at Elodie, and she dropped her harness, offering a smile so radiantly charming it no doubt would have won the group's full attention had she been wearing more than a shirtwaist and lace drawers. "We want to be sure everyone is safe," she explained, "and—"

Thump.

It took Gabriel a second to realize this was not his heart reacting to the sight of other men ogling Elodie's legs, but in fact Algernon Jennings landing bum-first on the road. The lad seemed to bounce a few times, yelping in fright, before Elodie hurried over to unclip his harness from the rappelling rope. Seconds later, his suitcase landed mere inches from where he sat.

"*Lembo!*" came a shout from above. Looking up, Gabriel saw Bloyd make an angry gesture before once again directing his flying machine back toward Aberystwyth.

"By George, they're all crackers!" Pimmersby exclaimed, whacking his boater hat against his thigh in emphasis.

"Such derring-do!" sighed a Miss Trevallion dreamily.

"Can we have your autographs?" begged the other.

Gabriel pressed a finger to his brow, trying to remind himself that patience was the better part of valor (or something like that; his only real experience of Shakespeare involved using a volume of the collected works to press flower specimens for a field study). He'd chosen to study physical geography not only because of all the fun math involved, but also because he assumed there'd be minimal association with humans, and by the time he'd been introduced to words like "diplomacy" and "negotiations" and "teaching students if you want to get any income from your work," it had been too late to become a tax auditor instead.

He stared at the group, waited quietly until he had their full attention, then spoke in a calm, polite voice.

"Talk to her."

And pointing at Elodie, he turned his focus away to the verdant landscape beyond.

The Geographic Paranormal Survey placed the major trove of thaumaturgic minerals northwest of Dôlylleuad. Gabriel looked in that direction, seeking evidence of a disturbed fey line, such as broken trees, charred land, or a rooftop made from feathers instead of thatch. He saw nothing of the kind, and yet this place definitely was, as Bloyd had put it, *rhyfedd*. Weird. The cool autumn air seemed to tremble with latent magic.

Beside him, Elodie was trying to explain to the Misses Trevallion that lace-trimmed drawers were sadly not the latest fashion in outerwear. Gabriel touched her arm, and when she turned with an inquiring look, he nodded northwest. "The trove is that way," he said.

"Yes, I know," she answered with just the merest undertone of *I am capable of reading a map*. For a moment they stood in professional silence, scanning the view. Then—

"There," Elodie said, pointing to a church graveyard at the far edge of the village. "That could prove a trouble spot."

"I agree," Gabriel said. "Decomposing matter tends to absorb and intensify thaumaturgic energy." His eyes narrowed as he laid a mental image of the Geographic Paranormal Survey map over the scene and traced the fey line's vector. Its scattering of minor deposits between this trove and the next, some fifty miles southeast, ran close to the village. Too close. And it was sparking. Even as he watched, blue light began flickering across the hedge-trimmed fields, causing dirt and grass to erupt along a course that trailed the fey line. Somewhere in the village, glass shattered.

Elodie grinned. "Things are about to get interesting."

"This situation appears on the verge of disorder," Gabriel said at the same time.

Crack!

A pebble farther along the road exploded. They pivoted to stare at it. *Crack!* Another went up in flames. The air blanched with a phantasmal, silvery-blue sheen.

"Magic," Elodie gasped.

"Eek!" Algernon cried, clutching his hands to his mouth.

Gabriel's pulse ticked up. "Everyone indoors!" he shouted. *"Now!"*

Chapter Four

Geography is a science of measurement;
for example, "How many minutes until I can
get out of this mosquito-ridden bog and go for a
beer?"

Blazing Trails, W.H. Jackson

For a brief, stark moment, the tourists stared dumbstruck. Then all at once they sprang into action; which is to say, produced binoculars and barometers, excitedly looked around for signs of magic, and demanded one another get out of the way because it was impossible to see clearly with all the parasols and mustaches.

"Ahoy!" Hapsitch shouted, pointing to a levitating stone. "Poltergeistic activation at two o'clock!"

"Polter-what?" Elodie murmured to Gabriel, who did not respond. He was pulling a thin coil of braided iron and gold from his trouser pocket and hooking it around his left ear. Prompted by the sight, Elodie removed a similar crescent wrapped about her wrist and attached it with practiced ease to her own left ear. The simple device offered protection against any thaumaturgic sound waves that might disrupt one's thoughts, although in Elodie's experience its greatest effect was merely to make one look thrillingly expert.

Gabriel attempted once again to warn the tourists of their

peril, to no avail. "This is ridiculous," he growled as he watched them try to catch blazing pebbles in upturned hats and parasols. "They're not even listening."

"So they get enchanted," Elodie said. "It's their own fault."

"It's our responsibility. We are the professionals here." He said this as if she needed reminding; as if he suspected she was half-inclined to join in the foolishness, which of course was utterly preposterous and insulting and *goodness what a fantastic catch from the lady with the white-feathered hat!*

"The point is," she replied, "these people have been informed of the risk. It's their choice if they wish to court a hideously painful death."

Hearing this, the tourists paused, glancing anxiously at one another. "Did she say hideously?" someone whispered.

"When people are being irresponsible," Gabriel countered, "it is incumbent upon the sensible among them to take charge before someone gets their hair set on fire."

"Egad!" exclaimed a Miss Trevallion.

"I say, that's not very jolly, old chap!" cried out one of the gentlemen.

"And what about free will?" Elodie argued, setting her hands on her hips.

"What about it?" Gabriel asked, as if free will was something he, as a university professor, simply could not countenance.

"Why shouldn't they let magic transform them into frogs if that's what they want?"

"*Frogs?*" squealed the other Miss Trevallion.

Gabriel shook his head. "The middle of a thaumaturgic squall is not the place to debate philosophy."

"Codswallop!" Elodie retorted.

"That's your best argument? 'Codswallop'?" Gabriel was too proper to scoff outright, but Elodie had no difficulty imagining that he was doing so on the inside.

"I can offer *'absurdité'* if you'd prefer me to move you in French," she said.

This provoked him into a patriotic scowl. Her took a step closer to her. She tossed back a loose strand of hair and stared him down (or, more accurately, up, since he was some four inches taller). The air between them crackled with a magic considerably more potent than that which was exploding pebbles on the road beyond.

"Er, excuse me." Algernon's thin, shrill voice crept into their taut silence.

They both snapped their heads around to glare at him, and he squeaked, leaping back. "Don't hurt me! I only thought you should know . . ."

"What?" Gabriel demanded.

"Er, the people have left."

Glancing around, Elodie saw the tourists disappearing into various buildings. A raindrop struck her face with a sudden, tiny burst of cold, followed immediately by another. The storm cloud was going to break open at any moment.

"I'm finding shelter," she declared haughtily. Snatching up her ER kit, she began to stride along the road. Some fifty yards away stood a large brown building, lumpy with old, weathered rock, capped neatly by a slate roof from which bulged two smoke-wreathed chimneys. A white picket fence encompassed its small, exuberant garden. A wooden sign hanging above its door depicted a sheep holding a beer mug in its mouth, which suggested the premises were an inn or perhaps a brewery. Quite frankly, Elodie felt excited about either of those possibilities. She quickened her pace. Gabriel followed, Algernon close behind.

None of them noticed a trio of elderly women half-concealed behind a hedge, watching them closely.

"So the servants of the old Queen come, tempest-tossed and bringing shadows with them," one remarked in a crackling voice.

"What?" said the other two, staring at her. "Why are you being weird, sister?"

She bristled. "I'm talking about those scientists. I didn't expect the Home Office would actually send someone to manage the disaster."

"It's damned annoying," another added. "I've been making a fortune from these tourists."

"I do like the girl's knickers though," said the third. General murmurs of agreement followed this.

"So when shall we three meet again, sisters? In thunder, lightning, or in rain?"

"Er, what's wrong with in the house, Betty?"

"Hey, is that a cow flying over by Lew Jones's cottage?"

"Well, damn. Looks like someone's getting steak for dinner tonight."

THE BUILDING PROVED to be an inn named the Queen Mab. Its lobby glowed with luxuriant, red-gold light from a peat-burning hearth fire that promised warmth, coziness, and slow death from carbon monoxide poisoning. The geographers could not enjoy it, however, for the proprietor stood in the doorway, barring their entry. "You're joking!" he said with a laugh. "You want three bedrooms?"

"Two, if that's all you have available," Elodie said, "since I'm sure the gentlemen will be happy to share a—" She stopped, noticing Gabriel's scowl. "Three bedrooms, please."

"I don't even have one that I can offer you, lady. I'm full up. So's the Taliesin's Harp, the Pendefig Dyfed, and the Gwalchmai fab Gwyar's Golden Tongue."

"A village this small has four inns?" Elodie said with surprise.

In response, the innkeeper took a brochure from a table beside the door and handed it to her. Elodie stared rather bemusedly at its image of sheep dancing on a rainbow above a plum orchard.

Dôlylleuad!!
For a Magical Vacation!
You'll See Stars!

DISCLAIMER: neither the Dôlylleuad village council nor associated service providers shall be liable for any injuries, up to and including concussion that results in seeing stars, due to being struck by thaumaturgic forces and/or airborne cattle.

"Oh dear," Elodie murmured. Obviously *this* was what Motthers had meant by "another problem."

"We've got tourists coming out of our ears, what with the Magical Extravaganza." He gestured with a flourish when he said this, like some kind of used carriage salesman. But his expression was implacable. "I can't help you at all."

"Drat." Elodie regretted now having made Algernon leave

his tent behind—although then again, camping near an unstable thaumaturgic fey line during a thunderstorm was, while not a risk to one's life, certainly a risk of continuing that life in the form of a shrub or unusually tall chicken.

"Three pound," Gabriel said. Everyone looked at him.

"What are you saying, mister?" the innkeeper asked.

"Yes, what are you saying?" Algernon echoed with alarm.

"Three pound," Gabriel repeated. "Per room."

A pivotal moment of silence followed . . .

"Per night," he added.

"Per night, hey?" The innkeeper grinned, stepping aside to allow them inside. "As I've been trying to explain, of course I can help! *Croeso, fy cyfeillion.* Never let it be said that a Welshman isn't happy to let Englishmen come in and take over his house! The lad can have my youngest boy's room, and my daughter's should suit you and your wife, good sir."

Instantly, Elodie's pulse tumbled into panic. But there was nothing to be done: they were caught between a rock and a hard place—or, more accurately, no place at all.

Besides, sharing a room was no disaster. After all, nothing existed between her and Gabriel except a marriage license (and a subscription to *The Fashionable Scholar* magazine, which kept turning up in Gabriel's mailbox despite Elodie having informed the publisher repeatedly, and increasingly desperately, of her correct address). The tremulous feeling in her heart as she glanced at her husband indicated no more than a desire for some tea after the tiring journey from Oxford.

In fact, not even that. An *inclination* for tea. A *vague wish.* There was no desire in her whatsoever.

The innkeeper led them indoors, saying that his name was

Mr. Parry and he was entirely at their service (so long as they paid cash, extra for linen, and purchased their meals on the premises). "What brings you to Dôlylleuad?" he asked as they went upstairs.

"Dr. Tarrant and I are geographers," Gabriel said. "We've been sent here by the Home Office to investigate the thaumaturgic disturbances."

"Investigate?" Parry echoed sharply. "What do you mean by that?"

"To inquire into the facts of a matter," Gabriel answered. "From the Latin *vestigium*, to trace."

"It's our job to identify problems," Elodie said before the innkeeper fell too far into confusion, "and fix any insofar as we're able."

"I don't see why you need to *investigate* or *fix* anything," Parry said sniffily. "No one's been hurt. Except old Ellis Jones, but he shouldn't've been smoking his pipe in the street. And it was completely unrelated that Lloyd Brown turned into a daisy bush. Besides, after the drought, we're grateful for magic, we are. It's done wonders for our economy. We're going to be the next boomtown, even bigger than Llandrindod Wells, I'm sure of it! They just have healing spa waters. Our waters explode!"

"I hardly think—" Gabriel began, and Elodie interrupted before he sacrificed the Second Rule of Fieldwork: *don't cause trouble with the locals* (the First Rule being *take your own toilet paper with you, just in case*).

"How long have the disturbances been occurring?" she asked.

"About a month," Parry said. "I'd just extended the inn to better cater for tourists coming out from Aberystwyth on day trips, so it was lucky timing for me."

"Speaking of Aberystwyth, is Woodrow Jackson a guest here, by any chance?"

"Indeed he is. Odd chap."

"Odd?" Elodie prompted warily. It was the kind of word people tended to use about Professor Jackson when they were too polite to say things like "addled" and "I didn't understand that 'disaster expert' meant literally being an expert at causing disasters."

Parry cleared his throat. "Well, for one thing, he told us he was a chair at Aberystwyth University. Obviously not in his right mind, thinking he's furniture. He went up to Devil's Knob yesterday, and we haven't seen him since. If he's not back by tomorrow, you can be sure that I'll—"

"Send a search party?"

"Rent out his room," Parry corrected.

Elodie chewed her lip worriedly. She retained an exhausting memory of the last time Woodrow Jackson went up somewhere alone then had to be dug out from the resulting landslide. Had he met trouble again, or was he just camping while he assessed the geographic situation?

Weighing these two possibilities, she added *rescue the professor* to her mental list of Urgent Tasks.

"Where is Devil's Knob?" she asked.

But evidently Parry thought that, if he told her, she'd *investigate* and thus single-handedly destroy the village's income, for he muttered something about "over that way," accompanied by an imprecise wave of the hand. "Here we are now, these rooms are for you."

Without a word, Algernon dashed into his and locked himself inside. Parry turned toward the other. "I apologize in advance for all the magazine pictures of Prince Albert Victor on the walls," he said. "My daughter is a romantic." And with that portentous word, he opened the door.

It was worse than Elodie had feared. She managed perhaps four steps into the room before every muscle in her body seized with anxiety. Beside her, Gabriel also stopped, his breath catching. Together, they stared at the bed set against one wall. It seemed to stare back at them coyly, all frilly pillowcases and pink embroidered roses. It did not even appear to be only one bed but a mere three-quarters of a bed, alarmingly narrow beneath a lavish heap of counterpanes that made Elodie feel overheated just looking at it. Light so pale as to be practically bridal white slanted through a window to illuminate the bed within the room's warm duskiness; and indeed, if other furniture existed therein, Elodie was blinded to it by the gleaming, enticing, quite terrifying *thing* that was rapidly transforming from a bed to a torture device in her mind.

She began to regret not developing calm sobriety as a character trait. Her pulse had begun acting out an Italian opera while her imagination was already cozy in that bed with Gabriel and really, really not helping matters by sending her various animated images. Beside her, the real Gabriel seemed petrified—i.e., turned to stone.

Parry, oblivious to their taut silence, bustled about, tidying things away. "I'll bring you up some fresh linen (five shillings). And if you come to the taproom, I'll let you sample Dôly-lleuad's finest plum brandy (fivepence per glass), or you might prefer a nice cup of tea to warm you up (threepence, milk and sugar extra, plus a teaspoon hire fee). It's not a large bed, I'm afraid, but I hope you'll be comfortable."

In fact, it was so opposite of large, it might have served as an official antonym for the word. Elodie guessed it would prove barely adequate for one person, let alone both her and her estranged husband-cum-nemesis . . .

And *that* was a very unhelpful thought to have under the circumstances.

"All right, then?" Parry asked.

"Mm," Elodie said.

"Hm," Gabriel said.

They set their ER kits down with a simultaneous *thump*.

"I'll leave you to it, then. And if you want—oh, bother. I didn't realize that had been left here." He dragged a rolled-up mattress from beside the dressing table. "I'll just take it away to give you more—"

"No!" Elodie and Gabriel both shouted.

"That's fine, don't trouble yourself," Elodie said with an urgent smile.

"It's no trouble," Parry assured her, hauling the mattress toward the door.

"Really, please, you'll hurt your back," Elodie insisted.

"I can manage, I can," Parry insisted right back.

Abruptly, Gabriel stepped into his path and grabbed hold of the mattress. Laughing awkwardly, the innkeeper clung on. Gabriel tugged; Parry tugged; both of them frowned. Finally, Gabriel gave a decided yank, and Parry stumbled backward, relinquishing his hold. Gabriel clutched the mattress as if the very fate of the world depended upon it.

"Thank you so much for everything," Elodie said at once, rushing to shake Parry's hand. "We're truly grateful," she added as she guided the man toward the door. "You've been marvelous. Thanks again."

And she shut him out of the room.

Turning back to Gabriel, she attempted a smile, but he had set the mattress aside and retreated to the edge of the room, where he bent over his ER kit, assiduously avoiding eye contact. *Good*, Elodie thought. *I don't want to look at you either.* She crossed to the window on the other side of the room. They were now as far from each other and the bed as possible, an interesting case of geographic triangulation Elodie did not wish to explore. She peered out through the window's mullioned panes, checking the atmosphere.

Thankfully the villagers had gone indoors, for the sky over the village writhed with a dark morass of storm that shed bright splinters of magic along with the rain. Trouble was not just afoot but organizing a parade.

"With this weather, we probably have four more hours of light at most," she told Gabriel.

"Three and a half," he said, checking his wristwatch, and Elodie rolled her eyes. "I'm going to inspect the immediate area for hazards."

"I'll survey the locals," Elodie answered. Taking a beige linen skirt from her kit, she donned it hastily. It was only midcalf length—a risqué style that was permitted in a disaster zone, since although Britain's population liked their women in long dresses, they liked even better being protected from river tsunamis and exploding wildflowers. "Shall we meet for dinner to compare notes?"

"Agreed," Gabriel said. He put on a long black coat, and while Elodie buttoned her skirt, he took a notebook and pencil from one pocket, his spectacles from another, and settled in with a contented frown to check items off a list. Then she noticed him glance in her direction, and the frown deepened. He added something to the list before promptly ticking it, his pencil moving with a stoicism that made Elodie suspect the completed item was *make polite conversation with wife.*

Although upon second thought, no, that couldn't possibly be it, *since he'd not done so the entire day.*

She ought to have been annoyed. Instead, mischief bubbled up within her like a witch's brew. Dignity tried to repress it— but given that an extensive education, the opinion of society, and several warning letters from her head of department had always failed to do so, her rather scrawny allotment of dignity had no hope. She smiled at Gabriel.

"And how are you?" she asked in a pleasant voice.

He looked up at her blankly over the fine silver rim of his spectacles. "What?"

"Well, I hope? Enjoying your days?"

A shadow of wariness darkened his eyes. "Why do you want to know?"

Elodie's smile lounged back, putting its feet up on a metaphorical table. "Just making friendly chitchat."

The shadow of wariness became a midnight of distrust. "Chitchat is inappropriate under the circumstances."

"I would contend that the circumstance of a husband and wife about to sleep together in the same bedroom veritably *demands* chitchat."

"Your argument contains several fallacies."

Ah, here came her annoyance now, shoving mischief aside and tilting her chin up. "Only if one is being pedantic," she replied coolly.

"One is being *accurate.* For example, I will be sleeping on the mattress on the floor, therefore the word 'together' does not apply."

Elodie huffed a laugh that was about as far from real humor

as one could travel without requiring a whole new kind of map. "You're a geographer, you ought to appreciate the concept of relative distance. Also, you can't sleep on the ground. Everyone knows that doing so gives you a headache."

He cast her a look that said *you give me a headache* so plainly, no words were required. The conversation slammed to an abrupt halt. Elodie yanked her ER kit open with enough force to tear the lining. Gabriel removed the umbrella from his own kit with such vigor, it smacked against the dressing table. Elodie dragged out a coat (not noticing it was actually a purple velvet dressing gown) and pulled it on. Gabriel tossed his notebook on the dressing table (then straightened it and set the pencil exactly parallel alongside). Finally, snatching up her own umbrella, Elodie strode for the door.

At the exact moment Gabriel also strode for the door.

They collided.

BOOM!

Thunder shook the house—or else it was Elodie's pulse rampaging through her veins. "Excuse me," she said primly as she moved aside.

"Excuse me," Gabriel said at the same time, stepping forward to open the door for her.

They collided again. The very air seemed to clench its thighs together.

"Ladies first," Gabriel said with a politeness so extreme, it could have established its own religion.

"No, no," Elodie said. "After you."

"I insist. I think we've had enough troubles at doorways to last us a lifetime."

This reminder of their wedding day, and her thoughtless comment that had so offended him, made Elodie blush scarlet.

Without further ado, she marched out to the corridor. Gabriel closed the door behind them and followed.

Arrogant sod, Elodie grumbled to herself as she stomped over the creaky, timeworn floorboards. *Obnoxious, irritating, arrogant sod.* She could feel that arrogance pushing against her back, inspiring her to walk faster. Light from a window at the end of the corridor sent the shadow of him to loom like bat wings around her, domineering and darkening her world. *Even his bloody shadow is arrogant,* she thought.

Suddenly, she could repress her feelings no longer. Stopping abruptly, she turned, and Gabriel only just managed not to collide with her a third time.

"Just to be clear," she announced, "I didn't mean what I said about our deal."

"Deal?" he repeated confusedly. He'd forgotten to remove his spectacles, and Elodie could see herself like a white star in one lens, superimposed over the night of his eye.

"On that day," she clarified.

"What day?"

Elodie shook her head, astonished by his deliberate obtuseness. How could he so easily forget The Scene in Holywell Street After Their Wedding? The look on his face when she'd told him she'd got what she wanted from their marriage deal occupied a prime position in her own memory. She could not blame him for having been so aghast at the time; after all, they had just spent two days transforming the notion of "marrying for convenience" into something a great deal more interesting, and if only Elodie had taken better care with her words, she'd not have given the brutal impression that she considered their relationship to be anything less than a beautiful, enrapturing dream.

She'd also have followed Gabriel after he walked away, instead of going in the opposite direction.

Of course, standing in a pub's corridor a year later did not exactly represent the ideal opportunity to explain herself, but she'd not had Gabriel so close to hand before—which is to say, she'd not dared to linger so long in his presence lest she trip over her own tongue again and make matters even worse. But considering the proximity they had been forced into on this assignment, clearing the air at least seemed worth an effort. And thus, with a perturbed spirit, and much fluttering of her heartbeat, she said, "I misspoke, that day. Although really, I cannot wholly blame myself. I'm sure any newlywed woman finds herself quiverish—"

"Quiverish," Gabriel repeated blankly, as if she'd just spoken in Old French.

"Yes. And who can be eloquent under those circumstances? However, I take full responsibility for my mistake. I'm good at doing that, you must agree. I've certainly had enough practice. 'Never was there a girl so proficient at making mistakes,' as my mother likes to say. Indeed, one might even—what is that?"

Gabriel blinked at her. "What is what?"

"That." She pointed over his shoulder at a framed picture of the Queen Mab that hung crookedly on the corridor wall.

Gabriel glanced back. "It's a painting," he said.

"I mean, what is the symbol drawn above the inn? The three spirals?"

Gabriel peered closer. "A triskelion. It's an ancient Celtic symbol."

Elodie raised her eyebrows. "I'm surprised you know something like that."

"Then why did you ask me?" He straightened the painting,

moving it back and forth by tiny degrees until it was exact. "As it happens, there's one etched on the door of my parents' house, since my father is originally from Snowdonia."

"Really?" Elodie could not contain her amazement at this revelation. "You're Welsh?"

"Half-Welsh." He looked at her with mild surprise. "Surely you knew? You've borne the name Tarrant for a year now."

While this wasn't quite so exciting a statement as *You bear my name, you're mine* would have been, had he only applied a little zest to his vocabulary, it nevertheless made Elodie feel like the storm had swooped in through her body, leaving her scattered and a little damp in places. "Thank you, but I need no reminder," she replied archly. "So . . . do you speak Welsh?"

He frowned. She took this to mean yes.

"In that case, shouldn't you be the one checking on the locals instead of me?"

His frown darkened. This time, she translated it as a most definite no.

"Fine." Her feelings bubbled over again, and she didn't even try to contain them. How could she simultaneously adore and dislike this man so much? (Mind you, she felt the same way about blue cheese, so clearly it was possible.) "This should be a straightforward job. Today we assess the immediate situation, tomorrow we make any necessary repairs to the fey line, and the next day we go home. Then you won't have to be bothered anymore. And I'll sleep on the mattress on the floor, so don't worry about that either."

"Bothered by what?" he asked.

Pretending she hadn't heard this question, Elodie went to leave, but Gabriel moved to block her path. Arms crossed, head tilted aslant, he regarded her in much the same way he would a new rendition of an old map. "Bothered by what?" he repeated.

But Elodie hadn't spent the past year ducking out and disappearing as often as possible from any potential confrontation to start now. "Shouldn't you take those spectacles off?" she asked. "You only need them for looking at things up close."

"My focus is exactly where I want it to be. Bothered by what, Elodie?"

"We ought to keep moving, we're wasting daylight."

He stared at her for a further taut moment, then shrugged and turned away. "I'm never bothered by anything," he muttered as he went down the stairs.

Elodie almost laughed. How could such an intelligent man be so lacking in self-insight? He was a six-foot-tall, perambulating, jaw-clenching embotheration, and Elodie was not prepared to suffer any dictionary on the matter. Gabriel Tarrant's level of tetchiness deserved a whole new word all its own.

She made a face at him (which didn't count as undignified behavior since he had his back to her, therefore could not see it). Behind the grimace, however—er, and several inches beneath it—her heart ached like a heroine standing on a cliff's edge, wistfully contemplating the horizon.

"If I was the sort of person who got bothered, I wouldn't be working as an emergency geographer," Gabriel grumbled. "And I will be the one sleeping on the floor."

"I'm not asking you to do that," Elodie said.

"I know you're not. I'm saying it. I am a gentleman."

"A gentleman wouldn't argue with a lady. I will sleep on the floor."

Reaching the lobby, he stopped, turning to her once again.

For a fleeting second, she glimpsed in his eyes something that looked a lot like her own repressed misery . . .

BOOM!

Thunder crashed, reminding them of the disaster awaiting them beyond that of their own relationship. Elodie rubbed her forehead wearily. Gabriel frowned, of course.

"We'll discuss this tonight," he said. Which meant he considered the conversation permanently closed.

Elodie's wistfulness combusted in a flame of irritation. "Don't talk down to me," she retorted, stepping on the lobby's stone floor with a clunk of her bootheels, forcing Gabriel to move back. Unfortunately, because she was shorter than him, this resulted in him literally talking down at her.

"I'm not," he said.

"Listen, I know you're miffed—"

"Miffed?"

"—but if we're to do a good job here—"

"Miffed!"

"—we need to work as—what is that?"

"What is what?" he asked with unconcealed exasperation.

Slowly, Elodie raised a hand, pointing behind him. "That."

Gabriel glanced back, and his expression unraveled.

"Good lord. What the hell is that?"

Chapter Five

Territory could fairly be spelled with "terror"
when one is discussing thaumaturgic geography.
                                    Blazing Trails, W.H. Jackson

"A*AAAGGHHH!*"

The scream shook everything out of Elodie's brain. Which might have been a good thing, since she was obviously hallucinating. After all, inn lobbies generally did not contain a white billy goat with a tufted beard, pink knitted pom-pom hat, and more to the point (literally), large sharp horns protruding from said hat.

A moment later her wits returned, however, and she found herself still looking at a sizable goat. In the intervening two seconds, the animal had turned from glaring at her and Gabriel to ducking its head and huffing as it lined up an angle of attack against Algernon, who apparently had entered the lobby, taken one look at the goat, and suffered an instantaneous internal landslide. His scream having made the situation worse, he was now trying to crawl into the five-inch-high space beneath a sideboard.

"Let's go while the creature is distracted," Gabriel murmured to Elodie.

"But poor Mr. Jennings," she argued.

"Just think of the money we'll save on feeding him. He himself would approve."

Ignoring this, Elodie stepped forward, clicking her tongue softly and holding out a hand to the goat. He really was an adorable fellow in his pom-pom hat, to say nothing of the fluffy—

"MEHH!"

The goat pivoted toward her with terrifying speed, rearing up on his hind hooves and beating at the air. Elodie's pulse stammered. But she had barely enough time to withdraw her hand before Gabriel moved, pushing her back roughly. Well, how obnox—

Thwomp.

His umbrella burst open. He held it out like a shield between Elodie and the goat, and the creature dropped to all four hooves.

"Mehhhh," he declared (the goat, that is, not Gabriel), managing to combine surrender and utter disdain in one noise. There followed a moment of dire silence as the geographers waited to see what he would do next.

"Baby!"

The call snapped out like a whip from the inn's kitchen doorway. Everyone jolted, including the goat. A young woman with a tempest of black ringlets stepped into the corridor, rolling pin in one hand and apple in the other. She tossed the latter, and the goat bounced forward to catch it expertly in his mouth. Elodie was so impressed by this feat, she felt compelled to applaud.

Algernon shot her a look of outright horror from where he huddled against the sideboard. "How can you *clap* for a *beast* that just tried to *kill* you?" he asked, his syllables leaping more than the goat itself had done.

"Because that's the kind of person she is," Gabriel said, punctuating the comment with a brusque *click* of his umbrella's latch as he closed it.

Elodie blinked rapidly. Had that been an insult or a compliment from her husband? She began to ask, and no doubt incite another argument, but at that moment the young woman called out.

"Come on, Baby, be a good boy!" She patted her thigh and the goat trotted to her, apple in mouth, tail wagging. The girl scratched his neck before stepping aside so he could pass. The sound of his hooves tip-tapping across the stone floor and away into the kitchen ought to have been relieving, but somehow conveyed that "defeat" was just another word for "eventual revenge" in goat parlance.

Algernon rose, wiping sweat from his face. "Now I see why geographers claim hazard pay," he said shakily.

"I am sorry, I am," the young woman told them, her voice lilting as it swayed between the apology and a barely repressed amusement. "Baby is usually such a shy fellow. I don't know what's got into him that he's being so friendly now."

Elodie rather thought that Baby's idea of friendliness was more murderous than was usually applied to the word, but she refrained from saying so on the grounds of the Second Rule. She smiled at the girl. "He seems like a charming pet," she lied graciously.

"I'm Tegan Parry, my father owns this inn," the girl said. "Can I get you some tea?"

"No thank you, we're just going out."

Tegan's eyes grew wide with astonishment. "But it's raining! You might catch a cold that sees you slide rapidly into pneumonia, and despite our valiant efforts, die in this lonely, distant village, far from all those you love."

"*Egad!*" Algernon cried, eyes growing wide.

"We're quite used to inclement weather," Elodie explained, "and want to make the most use of our time." Indeed, Gabriel was already halfway along the lobby and moving fast. "But I'm sure Mr. Jennings could do with a soothing cup of tea."

"*Tea?*" Algernon echoed. "Tea, when the beast might return at any moment?"

"Or you could come out into the storm with us," Elodie replied in the deceptively mild tone that her students knew meant danger. "Do you have a fireproof umbrella in case of explosive rain?"

"I'll stay here and have tea," Algernon answered at once. Gabriel shut the front door behind him with a *thunk* that managed to sound disgusted. Smiling tightly, Elodie turned back to Tegan.

"Is it your bedroom we've taken over, Miss Parry?"

The girl flushed with delight at being addressed formally. "I'm happy to give it. Scientists, here in little Dôlylleuad! So exciting! If you don't get struck by lightning or tricked into a bog by a *pwcca*, I want to ask you all about geography!"

"Of course," Elodie said, and made her escape before the girl could get started on a new doom.

Immediately upon stepping outside, Elodie discovered the afternoon had turned cyanic (a special geographical term for "weird-as-hell blue"). The inn's garden glistened with diaphanous rain that drummed lightly against her umbrella. Chimney smoke stained the cold, rustling breeze, its scent making her wish she could curl up in a plump armchair beside a fire, enjoying hot chocolate and a really good map. But she could also taste the bitterness of magic with every breath and knew there would be no comfortable scenes in her near future.

Despite the gloom, Dôlylleuad was quaintly charming, its ambling paths flanked by ramshackle stone walls overgrown with thyme and briar roses, the slate roofs of its cottages singing with rain. A wealth of trees shivered as the breeze rummaged through them. Their fallen leaves, red and gold and burnished copper, littered the ground like the memory of summer romance (and threatened to cause Elodie a dire injury as her bootheels slid on them). She felt lovely autumnal daydreams stirring in the warm, cozy corners of her imagination, and pushed them away in favor of cool, sensible observations about the lay of the land and its buildings, and how they might interact with any further thaumaturgic eruptions. After all, this was no time for reverie. The leaves gleamed blue beneath her feet, as if she stirred dreams out of the sodden earth. Walking through the nascent enchantment, feeling it waft like delicate gossamer threads against her skin, Elodie knew it could at any moment become like her marriage had been—tender loveliness that turned abruptly to disaster.

Gabriel had already vanished within the mist of rain. Not that Elodie sought him, mind you. She was professional, focused, and *oh look, what a pretty tree!* Was it a sessile or pedunculated oak? She veered toward it, then veered away again, reminding herself that there was no time to waste on random curiosity: she had important work to accomplish before nightfall. Opening the wrought iron gate of a cottage, she began up the garden's stony path, admiring its verge of potted flowers and— Was that Gabriel farther along the street, a mere shadow in the silvery haze as he strode toward the edge of the village?

If it was, she did not care a whit, she was dedicated to her own task, and—

Crash!

A stack of empty pots went clattering across the path as she collided with them. Elodie stumbled back, and a moment later the cottage door flung open.

"Who's there?" growled a man with an expression as hard as Welsh slate, despite the soft fluff of his beard.

"Terribly sorry," Elodie said, trying to hold her umbrella in one hand and tidy the pots back into place with the other.

"What kind of name is that?" the man scoffed.

One I ought to adopt, considering how often I say it, Elodie thought ruefully as her tidying efforts resulted in one pot rolling down the pathway and another spilling its contents over her boot.

"If you're a tourist," the man continued before she could answer, "we're all full up."

"Thank you, but I'm from the Home Office," she said, giving up on the pots to straighten and look at the man directly. "My colleague and I are here to investigate the magical disturbances in the village. My name's Dr. Tarrant."

She seldom used the title in regular life, but when in the field it could be a convenient way to establish an air of authority. However, the man did not reply, and she guessed he'd misunderstood her. "To be clear, I'm not your pulse-taking, medicine-dispensing species of doctor . . . although actually a pharmacist would be the one to dispense medicine, wouldn't they? I earned a doctorate in geographical science from Oxford University, which accords me the right to be known as Dr. Tarrant—although strictly speaking I am Mrs. Dr. Tarrant, I suppose. But it's just by chance (and some unfortunate eavesdropping, but that's another story) that I'm married to a doctor, which is to say another geographer with a doctorate, and I don't want you to assume that I'm not Dr. Tarrant in my own right, despite my marriage to Dr. Tarrant. Dr. Gabriel Tarrant, that is. I am Dr. Elodie Tarrant. I have been trained in first aid, however, so in fact I *can* take your pulse should you need me to."

The man stared at her blankly, but Elodie was used to that expression on people's faces, and gave him a geographer's smile, the kind that suggests private property is merely lines on paper and can she please come in? In response, the man gripped the edge of his door, preparatory to slamming it shut in her face. "What do you want?" he demanded.

Elodie lowered her hand unshaken. "I'm just here to ascertain—"

"Osian?" came a feminine voice from inside the cottage. "Who is it?"

"A doctor," Osian replied, while still eyeing Elodie as if he suspected "ascertain" involved assassinating him.

Suddenly, a great clamor filled the room behind him. He was shoved aside by a woman, a crookbacked old man, and a youth with a mustache as wispy as pampas grass.

"Lovely to meet you," the woman said with an old-fashioned curtsy. "I don't suppose you know anything about carbuncles?"

"No, sorry," Elodie answered. "I'm not that kind of doctor."

"Ach, Meggie, carbuncles probably require a specialist," the old man said with a wink to Elodie that suggested he not only had considered himself a charmer in his youth but still did. "On the other hand, I've a rash that the lady doctor might be so kind as to look at?" He did not await her reply before proceeding to unbutton his trousers.

"Ah, er, um," Elodie said, taking a hasty step back.

"I saw you arrive on that balloon, I did," the youth interjected, smoothing his mustache with a finger. "Amazing! I don't suppose your colleague is with you?" He craned to see over her shoulder hopefully.

"Er, um, ah," Elodie said.

"Why don't you come in?" the woman offered. "I'll make you a nice cup of tea and some scones with jam and cream, and maybe you can tell me what a person should do when their carbuncle is oozing."

Whoosh!

A sudden ferocious gust slammed through the cottage garden, frankly just in the nick of time, snatching away the umbrella along with Elodie's balance. She stumbled, and Osian, despite his antagonism, reached out to help her. But then they both stopped, staring across the garden to the south.

The hills had vanished behind thunderclouds. Lightning ripped through the roiling, malevolent blackness, tearing it apart ruthlessly, like a mournful heart struck by memory. The rain was darkening from a veil to a shroud.

In the doorway, Osian crossed himself. But Elodie took a step toward the storm, shielding her eyes with a hand as she assessed the lower horizon. Wind shoved at her viciously, but she ignored it. The locals were saying something about it getting a little chilly; she ignored them too. The enchanted wild filled her mind. Eerie, deadly, it felt like home. She always bumbled her way through university corridors and human conversations, but here, at the edge of disaster, where the world was delirious with weather, and where all certainties unraveled, leaving only the hope that held the heart of all existence—*here*, she was centered. Standing quiet, she waited . . .

Then it came. In a graveyard behind the old stone church at the edge of the village, several bright blue lights flickered, as if poets were out with lanterns, looking for themselves among the dead.

Very tall poets, creeping steadily closer to the heart of Dôly-lleuad.

Elodie's instincts leaped, flinging her pulse up with them. "Get inside!" she shouted at the family. "And shut every door, every window!"

There was no time for further explanation, and Elodie could only hope they obeyed. She ran down the path—skirting the fallen pots—wincing as sodden wind slapped her face— not stopping when she reached the gate. Setting one hand atop it, she vaulted over with an ease that wouldn't have matched the even greater ease of spending two extra seconds opening the gate and walking through, but that was admittedly more impressive.

Turning left, she raced along the street toward the dark maw of the wild, boots splashing through murky puddles, hair unraveling from its knot, dressing gown billowing dramati- cally as the wind shoved at her from behind. Thankfully, ev- eryone seemed to be indoors, where she hoped they would remain, safe from the magic that had begun to flare through the storm-wrecked atmosphere.

Even with iron and gold hooked around her ear as protec- tion, Elodie could feel that magic limning her nerves like a siren song. She could feel it warming deep places inside her body where the most fragile of her dreams were tucked away like pressed flowers among old receipts and scraps of child- hood drawings. Most of them involved Gabriel, and were blushed with the recollection of their nights together, gentle and quiet nights that swayed with a shy rhythm coiling slowly into wishes she'd never dared to tell another soul. And although she knew it was a deadly earthborn enchantment, still she wanted it to continue until it slipped right inside her, killing her with a blissful little death, right there on the road.

Apparently not even iron and gold were enough against some magic or memories.

But this was something geographers trained for, relentlessly and essentially, and Elodie was not afraid. Indeed, she felt invigorated by the threat. *"Gods do what they like, they call down hurricanes with a whisper, or send off a tsunami the way you would a love letter,"* she called out to the sky in ancient Greek, laughing.

Passing the old church, she followed the road as it bent around a vast oak tree—then stopped abruptly, her heartbeat tripping over itself.

Gabriel stood beside the entrance to the church's graveyard, his long black coat swirling like tamed storm shadows. He held his umbrella aloft as thaumaturgic lightning struck its metal tip in one continual, delicate beam of energy that would have killed him had it been real lightning and the umbrella been a real umbrella instead of a Weather Mitigation Device constructed with silver and enchanted oilcloth. He looked like a dark angel, leashing perilous weather for the sake of the dead.

Ooh, Elodie's very soul gasped. Never mind earth magic; the witchery of her own lust caught fire within her, so that she felt surprised the rain didn't start steaming above her head.

Gabriel glanced over his shoulder, one eyebrow raised. Damp, wind-tangled strands of hair had fallen across his face, and as he looked through them with his dark, dark eyes, Elodie's internal flames became an inferno.

But she had been suffering reactions like this from the moment she first laid sight on the man nine years ago, and it was a matter of little effort to make a show of indifference now.

"Hello," she called, walking closer, hands in her skirt pockets. "Aeolus is certainly out to play this afternoon."

Gabriel did not reply. She couldn't decide if this was because he failed to recognize the name of the Greek storm god, or because he was *an obnoxious, arrogant sod*, despite his physical charms. Then she noticed the thaumaturgic compass in his black-gloved hand.

"Lost your way?"

"No," he said, raising his voice calmly above the crackle of the lightning, and Elodie reflected that he wouldn't recognize banter even if it hit him smack in the face. She had a sinking feeling that this assignment was going to prove methodical, orderly, and effective—all of which would look great in the official report but would make living through it a tedious misery.

"You might want to stand back," Gabriel warned her. "As we anticipated, the graveyard has attracted excessive power from the fey line, and thaumaturgic sublimation is emitting magic into the atmosphere. Matters may become dire at any minute."

Stand back? As if she weren't a professional, the same as him! A calm, sensible professional with unfaltering mental discipline! Indeed, she was so professional, she could take that umbrella he was holding, lightning and all, and shove it—

"Ahem." Elodie cleared her throat before the sudden violent idea turned into words and got her into the kind of trouble that thinking aloud had done in the past—for example, married to the arrogant sod with the umbrella.

"I can see that," she said instead, maintaining her stride. Indeed, she'd have had to be a humanities scholar to not recognize the danger. Above the lush, leaf-strewn grass of the graveyard, several sparks of ignited gases formed out of leaking thaumaturgic energy were being drawn together to become a single greenish-blue globe that pulsed with magic as it grew. Dancing over headstones, illuminating them with its ephemeral, sinister light, it made the name "will-o'-the-wisp" seem far too dreamy. *This* ghost light was a nightmare.

Elodie hastily calculated the globe's probable trajectory and realized that, without a doubt, it was going to hit the village like a bomb. And although ignis fatuus phenomena, even when thaumaturgically activated, generally did not have a high charge density, still the danger of civilians being scorched or turned into a flock of chickens remained.

If only she'd not lost her own umbrella, she might have been able to attract and contain the energy bomb with its silver tip, like Gabriel was doing with his. But as it was, there seemed no way to prevent the impending disaster.

"*Think, Elodie Hughes; think,*" she muttered under her breath, an old habit that had not changed even after she'd married Gabriel and taken on the name Tarrant . . .

"Aha!" she exclaimed with such force, Gabriel raised his eyebrow at her again. An idea whipped through her imagination, and at once she began to run. Leaping over a narrow, weedy ditch that cut across the graveyard's entrance, she wove a haphazard route through the headstones, heartily grateful for the shorter length of her field skirt as she skipped over thistles and splashed through murky puddles.

"What are you doing?" Gabriel demanded.

"My job!" Elodie shouted in reply. The rain began to fall

harder, filling her eyes with stars of watery light and ending any possibility of conversation. She felt herself enter the thaumaturgic energy flow. It prickled against her skin and beneath her boots, lifting her some three inches until she was running literally on air and magic. She laughed, delighted. As the sizzling bomb of blue light rushed at her, she raised her hand like she had any hope in the world of stopping it.

And everything turned to gold.

CHAPTER SIX

A geographer must become familiar
with danger, in order to define safety.
Blazing Trails, W.H. Jackson

FOR ONE HORRIFYING moment, Gabriel's heart relocated itself to the pit of his stomach. He could see nothing but burning light and, at its core, a stark after-image of Elodie raising her hand to death. Panic utterly overwhelmed him, such as it never had in all his life. He threw his umbrella aside, not caring about what happened to the thaumaturgic energy it had been harnessing, and closed his eyes—breathing, breathing, desperately trying to control his internal environment. Some five seconds later, a fucking *eternity* later, the light faded. He began to run even before opening his eyes. After all, he never really needed to look to know exactly where that wife of his stood. He was always aware of her, the same way he was aware of present dangers in a field: from sheer self-defense.

Except she wasn't standing now. She was lying on her back in the mud and grass between a headstone and a grimy marble angel, eyes closed, a strange sound emitting from her mouth . . .

Was she *laughing*?

He skidded to a halt beside her, dropping to his knees. She

was indeed laughing, a laugh like river water tumbling over rocks on a bright summer's day. As Gabriel stared in frantic confusion, she opened her eyes and looked directly into his.

Now he was the one who died, for one stark moment so infused with emotion he could not bear to exist in it. Elodie's eyes shone as green as a man might imagine the meadows of heaven looked—

And at that, Gabriel came abruptly back to his senses with a scientific, self-disgusted thud. *Imagine? Heaven?* This was what the woman did to him. Much longer in her sphere of influence and he'd be writing poetry and adopting fluffy kittens.

"What do you think you were doing?" he demanded, only just restraining himself from grasping her shoulders and shaking her. After all, the laughter might be a hysterical reaction to some injury . . .

The thought tried to kill him all over again. "Are you hurt?" he asked, urgently scanning her body. When she did not reply, he yanked off his gloves to perform a physical examination, but hesitated, his hands hovering above her, restrained by propriety or fear or some damned feeling he couldn't even begin to understand despite all his academic qualifications.

Then *she* reached up, smiling, and set a hand against his chest as if in reassurance. Or perhaps she was too dazed to know what she was doing. Either way, Gabriel felt his breath, his pulse, all the world simply . . .

Stop.

Lingering magic cast a phantasmic glow over Elodie's wet, mud-streaked face. Her nose was turning red from the cold, and her hair spilled in tangles over the dirty grass. Altogether it created such a vision of ethereal beauty, one might indeed begin to believe in a heaven that had created her. Gabriel stared wonderingly as a raindrop fell from his eyelashes to kiss a corner of her mouth. Elodie's smile faded. Her hand stroked his chest, creating warmth that twinkled with silvery magic. It soaked through clothes, skin, bone, to infuse Gabriel's heart with something as tender and vulnerable as the secret trove of memories he kept just for her . . .

And suddenly both his pulse and his rationality jolted back into beating. The sharp-edged elements of the world became painfully clear once more. Gabriel caught Elodie's hand, pulling it away from him, and pressed two fingers against her wrist to check the pulse within. It leaped and trembled.

"I'm fine," Elodie told him, contradicting this physical evidence. "Ugh, very wet though. Can you help me up?"

"No," Gabriel said brusquely. Dropping her hand, he rose and turned away, yanking his gloves back on with such violence, he risked tearing their seams. Breath strained in his throat. The rain tried to pound him into senselessness. On the road, something burned despite the weather, and he stared at it with a frown more thunderous than the sky. He didn't really see it, however. All he saw was the memory of Elodie lying on the ground as if she was—was—

Crack! The small fire exploded, turning raindrops briefly into flames. Behind him came the even more disturbing sound of Elodie muttering as she struggled to push herself up.

Good, he thought ruthlessly. She *ought* to struggle, considering how his heart was still riotous and his mental discipline unraveled. She ought to just stay lying in the graveyard all night, thinking about what she'd done.

Then he turned back around and held out a hand, not looking at her. After the slightest pause, Elodie took it. He hauled her up. As she stood, she stumbled a little, alerting Gabriel's every nerve to the possibility of collision. But she managed to stop herself, although the distance between them remained so slight, Gabriel could hear her breathing through blue-tinged lips that were slightly parted, as if awaiting a kiss to warm them. The alert became a wailing siren.

Just be calm, he told himself. She wasn't his wife in truth, nor his lover. And certainly she wasn't his student. He had no right to chastise her. He needed simply to inquire in a reasonable, professional manner as to the rationale behind her actions . . .

"Jesus Christ, Elodie, what the bloody hell possessed you?!"

She blinked as a rapid succession of emotions shot through her expression. Gabriel recognized less than half of them before quiet dignity ended the procession, stamping itself hard and unrelenting on the normally gentle planes of her face. "My job," she said.

"Suicide isn't in the job definition."

"I knew what I was doing."

"That makes it bloody *worse*, woman!"

The moment he said the words, he wanted to haul them back into silence. And sure enough, Elodie's dignity crumpled into an outraged frown. Gabriel considered backing down, but he was too ~~distressed~~ disapproving to manage it. He clenched his jaw—her eyes darkened—and both suddenly realized they were still holding hands.

They snatched them apart so rapidly, Elodie almost lost her balance again. She pressed her feet more firmly on the sodden ground, lifted her chin, and glared at Gabriel defiantly. She looked terrifying and enthralling, with wet strands of hair streaking her face like witch light, and a fire of formidable intelligence in her eyes.

"Pish tosh!" she declared. "I stopped the magic and saved the village from disaster. Although," she added with reluctant self-honesty, "it is particularly good fortune that the diverted energy just happened to miss all the gravesites."

They both flicked a glance at the ground beside her, where a three-feet-deep gash was sparking with bright fragments of magic. Elodie seemed to appreciate all of a sudden that it represented what might very easily have become of her, and she shuffled to obscure Gabriel's view of it. Immediately, instinctively, he reached out, grabbing her wrist—

And pulled her forward just before she tumbled into the crevasse. Their bodies collided with a shock of what must have been residual magic. They scowled at each other across the hazardous distance of five inches.

"You are *incorrigible*," Gabriel said furiously.

"I certainly hope so," Elodie retorted, "or nothing would get done. *You* are a pedant."

"If it is pedantic to not want my wi—colleague dying before the assignment is complete, then I stand guilty as charged." He released her wrist and stepped back, his angry frown tilting a little with confusion. "How the hell did you stop ignis fatuus just by touching it?"

"You're Welsh," Elodie replied—taking their conversation and throwing it in a completely different direction, as usual.

He blinked at her, seriously aggravated, and only just managing to stop himself from falling to his knees again in gratitude that she was still alive to aggravate him like this. (Which, of course, he would feel about *any* colleague under the circumstances.)

"And?" he said curtly.

She held up her left hand, the back of it toward him. "This

wedding ring, it's Welsh gold, isn't it? There's a dragon stamp on the inner side of the band."

Gabriel turned to stone, as if he'd been blindsided by magic, or at least by a metaphor that made his brain hurt. If he truly were stone, he'd not feel on the verge of internal combustion. "Hm" was all he said.

"You said your father came from Snowdonia, and Dolgellau is located there—a gold-rich area that's one of the most powerful troves on the 3-SEQ fey line. I speculated that you or one of your predecessors may have got the ring from there." Watching his face for a reaction, she suddenly grinned, her frown disappearing like shadows defeated by the return of sunlight. "You gave me a magic ring."

Well, damn. She was right. The ring had belonged to his paternal grandmother, and its gold was indeed sourced from Dolgellau. But Gabriel had never intended for her to know that he'd given her a precious family heirloom (merely to save money, of course, no other reason whatsoever), and he now felt an actual blush spread across his cheeks. Aghast, he scowled so vehemently, the warmth fled faster than a student leaving for home at the end of term.

"You risked your life on the basis of a wild guess like that?" He shook his head. "I've never heard of anything more foolhardy, reckless, insane—"

"Successful," she countered. "Gold is a powerful thaumaturgic inhibitor in any case, and I felt it reasonable to suppose that gold from a level five Welsh trove would be especially effective on the magic of another Welsh fey line. I simply used the ring as a shield to stop the ignis fatuus. And it worked."

"You got lucky."

His words seemed to strike her like a whip. Her smile vanished, taking its sunshine with it. "I did not. I may have a uterus—oh for heaven's sake don't wince, you're a scientist—but I can think better than most men in this country, despite what they believe. I analyzed the evidence before me and used it to form a reasonable plan of action. Within seconds, I might add. And although I don't need to excuse myself, risk assessment was part of that plan. Even if the ring hadn't been magic, it's still gold, and there was a decent chance of that being enough to counter ignis fatuus. So do not accuse me of being *lucky*, thank you. I am far too clever for luck."

Gabriel stared at her unblinking as the rain poured down their faces like years of regret, and the air gasped with wind and unspoken emotion. He knew full well that Elodie had chosen to study geography only because she loved the idea of magic. She was a scientist because it allowed her to be a professional dreamer. And yet, it was that imagination, alongside her eternally restless curiosity and the sheer joy of her mind, that had led her to become the best exigent thaumaturgy analyst in Britain—even better than him, Gabriel could admit (privately, behind several mental barricades and a forbidding glower). Elodie was the kind of person who would dance on a rooftop if dared (or even if not), whereas he was, quite properly, a ladders and read-the-safety-manual-in-its-entirety man. Dôlylleuad would be burning right now if he'd been on-site alone, since he'd never have thought to stop ignis fatuus magic by using a gold ring, of all things. His brain simply couldn't make a sharp turn sideways like that.

He also knew that most of Oxford University's faculty considered Elodie "the pretty girl that Tarrant married." Were he ever bothered to, Gabriel could have supplied them with a plethora of more suitable adjectives to describe her. Exasperating. Maddening. *Mysti*-bloody-*fying*.

And brilliant, damn it. So brilliant that, in Gabriel's rational moments, when he wasn't breathlessly anticipating her destroying either herself or half the world, he would never accuse her of relying on mere luck.

Unfortunately, her presence all too often left him irrational.

Case in point: his right hand was inexplicably lifting toward her face, and he realized with a startled hop of pulse that it was intent on doing something as dangerous as smacking a magical bomb out of the sky: gently brushing the spatters of mud from his wife's cheek. Appalled, he shoved it into his coat pocket, clenching its fingers around the compass therein. *Get yourself and your minions under control at once,* he ordered his brain.

In response, like a snarky, supercilious villain, it showed him an image of the woman Elodie used to be, blithe, sunny, randomly offering to marry him. Scowling, he focused instead on the version before him. She'd become fierce, this past year, since their estrangement. Even soaking wet, and garbed in what appeared to be a velvet dressing gown, she looked indomitable. Gabriel was not daunted, absolutely not. But if he *were* to be, now would be the moment for it.

Not that he'd ever admit to that. He would, however, accept when he was wrong. It was the only proper thing to do.

"I misspoke," he told her. "My apologies."

ELODIE WAS ASTONISHED to discover that she had been killed by the thaumaturgic bomb after all, and was now in heaven.

This was the only conclusion she could reach, considering Gabriel had just *apologized* to her. Certainly such a thing would never happen in real life.

By the time her brain had processed the matter, Gabriel was already walking back to the road, leaving her alone in a spooky graveyard as rain dragged down the shadowed sky and oak leaves whispered of their own death. With a dry swallow, Elodie hurried after him. It wasn't that she believed in ghosts and fairies, you understand. She did, however, believe quite fervently in the power of her own imagination.

"We should discuss our plan from here," she said as she caught up to Gabriel.

"There's no need for discussion," he replied imperturbably, pushing the wet hair off his face.

"Of course there's a need!" she argued. "We are a team. You cannot just make unilateral decisions."

"The rain is killing the wind. You stopped the magic. I'm going back to the inn for dinner and a hot bath. Discuss."

"Er, well, yes, I'm going to do that too." She scowled at him, which achieved nothing except future wrinkles, because he did not even glance her way. "Although tomorrow we should talk to someone about installing drainage in the graveyard to prevent—oh dear, your umbrella."

They stopped in the road, staring at the Weather Mitigation Device, which was engulfed in flames despite the heavy rain.

"So much for waterproof," Elodie remarked wryly. "It's been completely overwhelmed."

"I know how it feels," Gabriel muttered under his breath.

Suddenly a voice emerged from the gloom, growling harshly. *"Beware!"*

Elodie and Gabriel turned to see two figures in a long dark coats appear out of the deep shadows beside a hedge. Elodie's brain leaped from vampires to Hades to highwaymen. Gabriel raised one eyebrow with mild annoyance at being approached.

"Beware!" intoned one again. "'The wind is a torrent of darkness among the gusty trees!'"

Gabriel exhaled a sharp, irritable sigh. Elodie recognized the tourists Pimmersby and Hapsitch, dressed in galoshes and hooded raincoats.

"What are you doing here?" she demanded with her sternest voice (which she'd practiced so often in a mirror she could now make even her undergraduate students shiver at the sound of it—and *not* shiver with repressed laughter, thank you very much).

"Our innkeeper told us about the Gothic Flame Display that happens out here in the graveyard," Pimmersby said. "He charged us five shillings for directions, and sixpence each to hire the raincoats, but it was worth it, by George!"

Astonishment pushed Elodie's sternness aside. "He urged you to go sightseeing at a zone of volatile thaumaturgic activity?"

"He's a chuckaboo, for sure," Pimmersby said, then gestured at the umbrella. "We even get a magical fire as a bonus! 'Burning bright, in the forests of the night'!"

Gabriel looked around with grim confusion. "I would call this a grove, at the most. And it's not even five o'clock yet."

But the gentlemen were uninterested in such fiddle-faddle as accurate timekeeping. "Mumbers is going to be so narked he missed this!" Hapsitch chuckled. "I must take a sketch of the fire!" He pulled a small book from his raincoat pocket and held

it out toward Gabriel. "And will you sketch us standing beside it?"

Gabriel just stared at him. It was a Professor-Grade Stare,
as terrifying as any weapon. The sort of stare that takes the
very measure of your soul, then hands it back to you covered in
corrections. Elodie imagined Gabriel didn't ever practice it in
a mirror; he probably looked that way at the midwife when she
delivered him.

"Er, actually, never mind," Hapsitch said, his throat bobbing. Elodie could practically see exams flash through his eyes.
"I might just toddle back to the inn . . . Got a Latin textbook
that I am *very* excited to read . . ."

He tugged on Pimmersby's arm. "But the magic!" Pimmersby whined.

With one blink, Gabriel shifted the stare to him.

Pimmersby turned more ghostly pale than the subject of an
Edgar Allan Poe poem. "Uh, actually, we should probably
hurry, before we miss the dinner service," he said, gesturing
back toward the village. "Got to keep ourselves healthy for the
term ahead, after all." He tugged in turn on Hapsitch's coat.
Indeed, so much tugging occurred, the two men almost pulled
each other off-balance. They retreated down the road with the
haste of people whose nightmares involved such things as attending a lecture naked.

"The wind is only some ten knots now," Gabriel muttered,
frowning after them. "I wouldn't call that a torrent."

"I think he was taking poetic license," Elodie explained.
Turning back to the burning umbrella, she removed from her
dressing gown's pocket several paper scraps that were scrawled
with important notes long forgotten, passed them to Gabriel,

then took off the dressing gown and beat it against the enchanted fire until all that remained was a charred, soggy mess. Gabriel, hands full of paper, watched bemusedly. Once she was certain the fire would not reignite, she dropped her ruined dressing gown on the pile of ash and began walking back to the village, not caring if Gabriel followed.

Thoroughly soaked, with her boots filled with water and her gloveless fingers so cold they burned, she felt like a perambulating block of ice. Her teeth began chattering, and she hugged herself in what she knew would be a futile attempt to ward off hypothermia.

Coming alongside, Gabriel cast a dark glance her way, then began to remove his coat. Elodie's breath tripped. The cursed man was going to give it to her! How inconsiderate! He was her estranged husband; he ought to be consistently rude and arrogant so a woman knew where she stood with him! How was she supposed to maintain a healthy antipathy when he kept doing thoughtful things?

Immediately, she walked faster, trying to ignore how her feet hurt as the wet leather of her boots chafed them. Without effort, Gabriel kept pace. From the edge of her vision, Elodie saw him withdraw one arm from within the coat's sleeve . . .

"No," she said, holding up a hand in refusal as she increased her speed yet again.

"I beg your pardon?" Gabriel asked, managing to sound simultaneously confused and repressive.

"Thank you for your consideration, but please do not be charming or gallant. Do *not* give me your coat."

"Why not?" he asked suspiciously. "Do you think I have body lice?"

"Aah!" Mortified by the very suggestion, she covered her

face with a hand. "No, of course not! I just feel we ought to remain scrupulously professional." *In other words, do not make me like you, or I will remember that I love you, and that's a worse disaster for me than any storm could create.*

"Hm," he replied. In fact, not even that. Half a hm. The least amount of sound possible while still being definable as a reply. So no real danger, then, of him being actually charming. Elodie had to wonder why she was making a mountain out of a mere chalk down elevation. Besides, her teeth were now chattering so hard she feared for their integrity more than that of her character. She stopped in a band of limpid red-gold light overflowing from a cottage window, and squinting against the rainfall, she looked obliquely at him.

"Unless you would offer it to any other colleague under similar professional circumstances, that is."

At once, he had the coat off. Elodie girded her loins against the thrill of him draping it around her shoulders . . .

But he simply handed it to her. She took it automatically, rendered wordless by surprise, and he continued walking down the road.

"So rude!" Elodie muttered under her breath as she hauled on the coat. Its sleeves hung beyond her fingertips and its hem to her ankles, making her feel rather like an awkward child. But waterproofing had kept the satin lining dry and warm, and the exterior smelled of—well, sodden wool, actually, and smoke from thaumaturgical lightning, but also a dark muskiness she could only describe as masculine. She closed her eyes, allowing herself one moment to luxuriate in being *inside Gabriel's coat*. She'd spent years dreaming of this. Granted, in those dreams he'd tucked it around her, gently gathering her hair out from under the collar and then, with a forehead kiss, drawing her close to comfort her against his strength and his steady heart—

"Are you coming or not?" he called from farther along the road.

Sighing, Elodie hurried to follow.

Chapter Seven

Longitude tells you your relative position,
much the same as longing does.
Blazing Trails, W.H. Jackson

A WARM BATH RESTORED Elodie to good humor, and after she donned an old, comfortable white dress and brown cardigan, she tied back the sides of her washed hair with the elastic band Gabriel had given her, leaving the soft, rippling length to fall down her back so it might dry before bedtime. Then she unfurled the extra mattress, setting a nightgown atop it as a claim marker.

"So there," she said, hands on hips and smug smile tilting her mouth—then blushed at having spoken to an empty room. Really, she'd not behaved in such a juvenile manner since . . . Well, perhaps better not to answer that, lest memories from last month, when she dropped a water bomb on the dean of Merton College, come to mind. Instead she quickly took herself off downstairs.

The inn's taproom looked like something from one of the adventure novels about smugglers that Elodie had read as a child at the back of slow-moving carts while her parents traveled around Europe, studying its magical geography. She paused in the doorway, clasping her hands before her heart in an old gesture of wonderment that adulthood had never been completely able to eradicate (probably because she was really still just a dreaming twelve-year-old inside).

Smoky, roseate firelight swayed over the rugged stone walls and flashed against a collection of mugs hanging from the low ceiling beams. Wood-framed paintings of old schooners on wild seas and medieval knights fighting dragons in oak forests lured her imagination into a thrilling jumble of stories she set aside for indulging later that night, before sleep. Several tourists sat at hefty tables about the room, eating food that smelled of grease and murmuring together with something like the same wonder Elodie felt. Kerosene lamps illuminated the curious glances several of them were casting at Gabriel, who sat alone at a table in a corner. He had bathed and dressed in a downstairs washroom and now veritably gleamed as he busied himself writing in a notepad, several maps spread across the table before him.

Wearing his spectacles, and clad in a crisp white shirt and dark tie beneath a knitted vest and brown tweed jacket, he presented the quintessential image of male professorship; indeed, he looked like he might at any moment stand up and announce a surprise exam. On the other hand, a damp fringe of hair lying over his brow made him appear young and really rather sweet. Elodie felt herself smile wistfully as she remembered brushing that fringe away from his eyes while they lay together, gazing quietly at each other, after consummating their marriage. It had been damp then too, since he'd put himself to quite a degree of exercise. He'd stiffened a little at the touch of her fingers, as if tenderness disconcerted him, and she'd snatched her hand back, anxious that she'd ruined the mood. He'd muttered something about sleeping and turned onto his back . . . but one second later he'd gathered her against his side, holding her warmly, protectively, and giving her hope that their marriage might prove true after all . . .

"*Ha!*"

The sudden laugh from one of the tourists drew Elodie out of her rueful memories. Gabriel looked up over the rim of his spectacles with a glare that instantly incinerated "sweet" and stamped on the ashes. His attention began to shift toward Elodie, and she realized she was gazing at him, her hands still clasped together, her expression hopelessly doting. Turning away before he caught her at it, she strode over to the bar.

Algernon stood there, chatting to Tegan Parry while the young woman poured him a mug of beer. "Oh yes, getting a university education was an absolute for me, considering my intellect," he was saying. "*Cobio, ergo sum.*"

"You're a small fish?" Elodie asked, smiling teasingly as she came up next to him. Then she turned the smile to Tegan. "May I have a cup of tea, please?"

"Of course, Mrs. Doctor, ma'am."

"Please, call me Elodie."

The girl blinked confusedly at this casual obliteration of social convention. "As you wish, Mrs. Doctor Elodie, ma'am. Um . . . would your husband like a different table, perhaps . . . ?"

Elodie looked over her shoulder at Gabriel, who had set his hands against the edge of the table and was jostling it as he frowned at first one of its legs then another, trying to locate the source of some minuscule imbalance. "He's fine," she said. "He's just having fun with geometry."

"I don't think I've ever heard those two words used in the same sentence," Tegan said wryly. "Mind you, I'm not very smart when it comes to math. If I can't count something on my fingers, I'm out of the equation."

Elodie grinned, thinking the girl was probably more clever than she gave herself credit for. "Archimedes believed that mathematics reveals its secrets only to those who approach it with pure love, for its own beauty," she said, then glanced at Gabriel again. How many women, she wondered, had approached her husband for the sake of his beauty? Had he told any of them the secrets behind his lovely dark eyes?

"Hey!" Algernon exclaimed.

The aggrieved cry jolted Elodie, and she realized that she'd taken the beer mug Tegan had just set on the bar and downed almost half of its contents in one long swallow. Going abruptly still, she looked over the rim at Jennings's indignant stare and Tegan's smirk. Her dignity turned its face to the wall and wept.

"Sorry," she murmured, sheepishly passing the mug to Algernon, then wiping foam from her mouth with the back of her hand as he continued to stare at her. "Long day, half-asleep."

"I didn't think ladies drank beer," Algernon muttered, bringing out a handkerchief from his vest pocket to wipe the mug's rim with an attitude so passively aggressive it was a wonder the glass didn't break.

"Mrs. Doctor Elodie isn't a lady, she's a scientist," Tegan argued, possibly in Elodie's defense. "I wish *I* could be a scientist." She sighed, clutching a damp dishcloth to her heart wistfully.

"Why can't you?" Elodie asked.

Tegan scoffed. "A girl like me, go to university? I don't think so!"

"If you study hard and obtain good grades, there's no reason why you can't. It's true you will need a large amount of money, and you may face some prejudice regarding your gender—and class—and Welsh nationality . . . and I was going somewhere helpful with this, I'm sure . . ."

She winced, all too aware of her own privilege as the child of rich and well-connected geographer parents. In her youth, she'd soaked up the stories and theories of Paul Vidal de La Blache when he came to dinner. Sir Richard Burton had taught her how to determine the source of a river. When she applied to university, her greatest stress had been in choosing between Oxford, with its excellent science department, or her mother's alma mater, the Sorbonne, which sent her a magnificent wine and cheese basket as an enticement. Yet even with all that privilege, she'd been forced to make her career an ongoing demonstration that possessing a uterus did not preclude one from a talent for geography. And here she was even now, being called *Mrs.* Doctor Tarrant by a girl whom she wanted to convince that science was a reasonable feminine pursuit.

Of course, the *real* truth about women in higher education went deeper than gender concerns and class privilege. "I think," she said slowly, carefully, "that when the path is difficult, one must draw upon—"

"Inner strength," Tegan intoned wearily.

"All the available scholarships," Elodie corrected her.

The girl sighed again, half agony, half hope. Elodie tried to think of how else she might encourage her, but was distracted by a sudden gust of wind slamming against the building. Windows rattled, and an eerie blue luster infused the lamplight, flashing here and there with the memory of hill magic before dissipating.

Elodie straightened, instantly alert. She looked around, but

none of the tourists seemed to have noticed anything unto-
ward: they were admiring a set of crystals "guaranteed to light
up in the presence of magic or your money back." Tegan had
turned away to prepare the tea, and Algernon squinted into his
beer as if girl germs now floated in it. Only Gabriel scanned
the room in the same way she had, his expression tense as he
watched the last glint of blue-tinged thaumaturgic energy
flicker away. The atmosphere reverted to one of warm coziness,
as if the squall had never occurred—and yet, beneath the
cheerful crackle of firelight and the plump, slumbery shadows,
Elodie sensed that the evening was poised at the edge of trouble, grinning wickedly with a promise to jump.

The best gauge of thaumaturgic danger is your own intuition,
Elodie always told her students. *Well, second best to being hit in
the head by a flying tree.* But the next thing she told them was
that it took years of education, and tramping through thaumaturgic minefields, and listening to one's lecturer—yes, even
you, Mr. Hazelcroft in the back row—before that intuition
developed into an accurate tool.

Elodie had been honing hers for her entire life.

"Come on, lad, let's go sit down," she said briskly to Algernon, then crossed the room without awaiting a reply. But the
young man hurried ahead of her, claiming a chair opposite
Gabriel and shuffling it so there wasn't enough space for Elodie to sit comfortably next to him. She hesitated—

And suddenly Gabriel was on his feet, pulling out the chair
beside his own. Taken by surprise, Elodie had no flippant re-
mark immediately to hand, and could only murmur a quiet
thanks as she lowered herself into the chair. Gabriel pushed it
in with expert timing, and thus Elodie found herself rendered
safely seated, perfectly aligned with the table, and with noth-

ing to do but calm her heartbeat as Gabriel returned to his chair mere inches from her.

Eight inches, her professional brain estimated, then ran off screaming. Although this morning she'd been in the man's *actual embrace*, somehow sitting alongside each other at a table, *like a normal married couple*, felt *even more thrilling*, and any good sense she possessed dissolved *completely* into italics. Her awareness of his presence was *so intensely physical*, the tiny hairs on her arms shivered. His scent, clean and masculine, layered through her breathing until every inhalation seemed erotic, making her wish *quite desperately* for a fan. And as he brushed an infinitesimal speck off the table, her muscles clenched, imagining *him sweeping those strong fingers across her bare skin*.

She began to harbor serious doubts that she'd be able to think straight again, let alone eat dinner.

Algernon, however, suffered no such trouble. Taking up the card that supplied the inn's menu, he exclaimed happily, "Excellent! Boiled potatoes!"

"You noticed the thaumaturgical flash?" Elodie managed to ask Gabriel, albeit without looking at him.

"Yes," he answered, not looking at her either. He began rolling up the maps, returning them to their leather cases. Elodie watched as if mesmerized. His hands were geographer's hands, calloused, marked here and there with tiny scars from scraping against rocks and being bitten by enchanted wildflowers. In contrast, the cuff of his shirt, peeking out from beneath his jacket sleeve, was so pristine it seemed to shine against his olive-toned skin. How could a glimpse of plain linen be erotic? Elodie did not know but would rather like to make a physical study of the matter—in the name of science, of course.

"Are you hungry?" someone inquired, and she had to admit herself indeed more hungry than it seemed respectable to be, metaphorically speaking. Then she realized Tegan was standing beside their table with a handful of cutlery. The girl had set down a cup of tea while Elodie was woolgathering (or wool-removing, more accurately: she'd got most of Gabriel's suit off him before her imagination had been interrupted), and she reached for it gratefully. If anything could civilize her thoughts, it was tea.

"I could really do with a banger in a bun," Algernon said, and Elodie nearly dropped the cup.

"Sorry," Tegan said, "no sausages today."

Algernon sniffed with disappointment. "What's the hearty stew?"

"Mutton."

"Ugh. What about the country pie?"

"Mutton."

"And the—"

"Mutton."

Algernon sighed peevishly. Gabriel snatched the menu from him and passed it to Elodie.

"Um, thank you," she said, setting down her cup on the table, there being no room in her brain just now for such ephemera as tea saucers. She took the menu, looked unseeing at it, said "mutton pie" at random, and handed it back to Gabriel.

He put it down without a glance. "Three servings of pie, please, and some boiled potatoes for Mr. Jennings. Thank you."

"I'll bring them now in a minute," Tegan said, and placed knives and forks before each of them before hurrying off.

"Is that the Geographic Paranormal Survey of Dôlylleuad?"

Elodie asked before her thoughts could degenerate once more. She nodded at the last remaining map on the table.

"Yes," Gabriel said, bringing out a handkerchief in order to polish his cutlery. "I've been making notes about the potential hazards in the immediate zone, should there be a farther outburst from the fey line. The angle of the riverbank protects Dôlylleuad from flooding, and the hills are far enough distant that there's no threat to the village from possible landslides should a thaumaturgic disturbance result in earthquakes. Liquefaction does remain a concern, although as to that . . ."

"The graveyard is not on the line," Elodie said.

"Exactly." He tapped a finger against a red dot on the map. "Here is the trove, located inside an ancient mine approximately one mile, five hundred and eighty yards outside the village. And *this* is what I calculated the trajectory of this afternoon's thaumaturgic energy stream to be." He traced a newly drawn pencil line from Dôlylleuad's graveyard southward, passing some six hundred yards west of the charted fey line.

"It wasn't an unsurprising divergence," Elodie said. "The adjacent fields are no doubt waterlogged due to the recent storms, creating anaerobic soil conditions, which don't easily conduct thaumaturgic energy. Subterranean movement of mineral-infused water could induce not only an overflow of the fey line, but also intermittent intensities, such as the lightning that destroyed your umbrella."

"Hm," Gabriel responded.

"Excuse me, what did you just say?" Algernon asked, agog.

Elodie gave him a gentle smile. "Sorry, I suppose that was all rather technical. Allow me to explain about anaerobic—"

"I don't care about anaerobic," he interrupted. "I care about the destroyed umbrella! Do you know how much it costs to make a Weather Mitigation Device?"

Elodie's smile wavered with bemusement. "Professor Tarrant used that umbrella to harness lightning—"

"Good God!" Algernon turned to Gabriel, who was frowning at a speck on his fork's handle. "How could you be so reckless with a valuable piece of equipment?!"

"An umbrella is not worth more than a man's life, Mr. Jennings," Elodie said.

The young accountant sniffed. "I couldn't comment on that without first reading his insurance policy."

Elodie laughed. "Geography wouldn't be an adventure if we had life insurance."

"So says the woman who decided to catch magical fire with her bare hands," Gabriel remarked, setting aside the fork as if it were contaminated.

Algernon gasped. "Are you both *completely* reckless? Training specialist geographers is an expensive endeavor!" He jabbed his butter knife toward Elodie in emphasis. "Should anything happen to either of you, the cost to the Home Office would be significant! I will be writing this up in my—"

He stopped mid-rant as Gabriel grabbed his hand. With a gasp of mingled fear and outrage, his mouth fell open.

Wordlessly, Gabriel removed the knife from his possession, placed it on the table, and then returned to polishing his own cutlery. "How much would it cost if anything happened to you?" he asked in a mild, conversational tone.

Algernon closed his mouth without an answer, having apparently, albeit belatedly, discovered the profit of silence.

"We will inspect the trove first thing tomorrow," Gabriel went on as if the interruption had not occurred. "With this much thaumaturgic activity, it has clearly been damaged. After effecting repairs, we need to trace the line to check for any exposure of lesser deposits. We also need to evaluate hazards and make an action plan for the follow-up team. It's going to be a long day. Both of you be ready to leave at dawn."

Elodie's nerves, which had been twinkling after his display of manly protectiveness, now twanged with irritation as he crossed the line into manly arrogance. "Again I remind you about not making unilateral decisions," she said.

"I assumed you would sensibly agree with me, therefore I abbreviated the conversation for everyone's convenience."

"You assumed wrong," she informed him, chin in the air and eyes overbright, a pose that had made more than one gentleman professor tremble within his dusty tweed suit.

Gabriel, however, returned her look imperturbably, not the slightest tremble in evidence. "Are you admitting to not being sensible, Professor Tarrant?"

"Are you admitting to making an unscientific assumption, Professor Tarrant?" she replied.

Oblivious to their hot-eyed staring, and to the growing tension that felt almost as dangerous as a flash of wild magic, Algernon whined, "Dawn? Can't we go at a more civilized hour?"

"Thaumaturgic energy does not flow by the clock," Gabriel told him without looking away from Elodie.

"Unless it's the Exeter Cathedral clock," Elodie added, and broke their stare at last to smile at Algernon. "When they repaired it a few years ago, they used materials from Ecton Hill, a level three trove. As a result, when the clock reached the hour, it chimed three verses of 'God Save the Queen'—at least, it did until the locals were driven so mad by this, they damaged the bell. Now it just chimes 'God,' which I suppose is appropriate for a cathedral."

A moment of silence followed this absolutely fascinating interjection, then Algernon asked, "What if it's still raining?"

Gabriel gave him a dark, uncompromising look. "Then you get wet."

Tegan arrived with their food, and thereafter dinner was undertaken in an ambience so uncomfortable as to be practically a parent-teacher conference. Algernon ate fast, then fled. Left alone, Elodie and Gabriel finished the meal without further word or even a glance at each other. The degree of atmospheric tension between them grew almost painful. Indeed, had Professor Mulgrew, Oxford's senior meteorologist, been present, he'd have made an enthusiastic study of it (not because he was a meteorologist, but because he gossiped worse than anyone else in the entire university).

As they went upstairs, assisted by lanterns Tegan had given them to illuminate the way, Elodie tried to ease the mood. "I hope Professor Jackson hasn't touched anything he shouldn't have out there," she said with a smile.

"Hm," Gabriel replied.

The smile promptly stormed off in disgust. "There's no need to be like that."

"I'm agreeing with you," he answered, so pleasantly calm that a woman had *no option* but to argue.

"Someone needs to teach you how to say yes nicely," she snapped.

"Saying yes is a dangerous thing." He looked over his shoulder at her with such intensity, Elodie almost stumbled. Clearly he was talking about his wedding vows, and all of a sudden she longed to take a divorce decree and whack him over the head several times with it. Instead, she glared, although to no avail, since he'd looked away again.

"*Sod,*" Elodie muttered under her breath. And as if to concur, an icy draft swirled through the corridor. It agitated the flames of the lanterns, and although it failed to cool the furious heat currently burning great holes in Elodie's dignity, she shivered a little nevertheless, pulling the sides of her cardigan together. A scent of wild, damp magic moldered the air. They might have been walking through a moonless autumn forest that leaned, yearning and sighing in every bough, toward an old river. They might have been lost in a dream. Elodie drew slowly to a halt, the argument with Gabriel forgotten as all her senses began prickling with curiosity.

Somehow, between one moment and the next, the night had turned gothic, as if danger (for example, a necromancer, monster, or university constable who wanted to know why you were climbing out a library window) lurked behind one of the doors in the corridor. The darkness whispered to her with eerie wistfulness.

"Elodie?"

She blinked, pulling herself out of the strange reverie, and discovered that Gabriel had turned back to her again. The way he spoke her name was not at all wistful; indeed, he'd obviously been saying it for some time. He ducked his head to look closely in her eyes, and as lantern light burnished his face, it made the mild frown lining his brow seem broodingly solemn.

"What?" she answered spikily, even as her heart melted into old romantic wishes that could never come true.

His frown tilted deeper. "Are you all right?"

"Fine. Tired."

Gabriel looked doubtful. He lifted a hand as if he would

touch her face, and Elodie suspended all operations of her respiratory system.

The darkness of his eyes grew heavier. "Violets," he murmured. The tips of his fingers almost, *almost* brushed against her hair, and Elodie realized he must be referring to the fragrance of her soap. "Hm," he said.

Then he lowered the hand, turning once more toward the bedroom, and Elodie expelled a frustrated sigh.

"Considering your diminished state," he said with his regular dispassionate timbre as he walked, "it's important you get a comfortable night's sleep. We don't want you struggling on the job tomorrow. Therefore you will take the bed and I the mattress."

"Diminished—?!" Every romantic wish promptly vanished from Elodie's heart. "Struggle?!" she sputtered, hurrying after him. "I recommend that you take the bed, so if I get up in the night, I do not *accidentally* step on your face."

Although his back was to her, she would guarantee that he'd raised an eyebrow. "Threatening violence against one's team leader is a strong indication of impaired reasoning."

"Delusions that one is the team leader also indicate impaired reasoning," she rebutted.

"You are exhausted. Take the bed."

"You are obnoxious. I'm sleeping on the floor."

They arrived at the bedroom and stopped.

"Oh," Elodie said, staring at the door, which stood ajar. "I could have sworn I closed that."

"Uh-huh," Gabriel replied in a noncommittal manner that nevertheless conveyed wholehearted commitment to the idea of Elodie wandering out the door, deep in thought about rain or dinner or something completely random, such as Australian marsupial habitats—*Ooh, I wonder what they are,* she thought. *I'll have to ask someone from the animal biology department*—and thus forgetting to secure the room behind her. Only the fact that he was probably right stopped her from chastising him.

"After you," she said with a stiff gesture.

"Certainly not," Gabriel replied. "As previously established, ladies first."

Elodie almost insisted, but the look he gave her conveyed a willingness to stand there all night, exchanging politeness like arrows until she finally surrendered. So, with one final supercilious glare, she swept past him into the room.

Gabriel followed, and as he closed the door behind them, the entire world shrank down to one small chamber and the stark fact that they'd soon be undressing and lying down to sleep in the company of their ~~wedded spouse~~ worst enemy. Holding up their lanterns, they stared with mutual silence at the mattress on the floor.

And at the goat that was industriously eating it.

CHAPTER EIGHT

Geography maps the space between mountains
and the space between people, with all its
sinkholes, storms, and dangerous magic.

Blazing Trails, W.H. Jackson

"THIS IS NOT a problem," Elodie said. "I'm sure we can get a good handle on it."

"Are you insane?" Gabriel stared at her with amazed disbelief.

"No, I'm saying you need to *get a good handle* on those horns. You're not being firm enough. Pull harder."

Gabriel frowned. The woman might appear angelic in her white dress and the pearly halo of her hair, but Gabriel would swear she was an unkempt devil sent specifically to vex him. "I am pulling with perfectly adequate force," he said. "It's not my fault the creature won't budge. You need to push harder."

"I'm trying," she averred. "Besides, a proper gentleman wouldn't ask a lady to put her hands on a goat's rear end."

"You teach male university students. I'm sure you can manage one billy goat."

"And I'm sure you know all about not budging." She exhaled an impatient sigh. "Look, we're professional scientists, we should be able to use teamwork."

A moment of silence followed as they both considered where teamwork had got them in the past: into this god-awful marriage.

"Push harder," Gabriel said.

"Pull harder," Elodie said at the same time. "Angle it more toward the door, and I'll give a really big shove."

"Hm," Gabriel murmured doubtfully, but nevertheless wrangled the creature's horns as directed. Elodie leaned more heavily at the opposite end, putting all her weight into the effort.

Just then, a whistle sounded in the corridor beyond. *"Baby!"* came Tegan Parry's bright, coaxing call.

The goat reacted instantly. With a sanctimonious *mehh* and a kick of his hooves, he skipped away, tugging Gabriel with him and causing Elodie to fall forward onto her hands and knees on the torn, goat-slobbered mattress.

"Ugh," she said with disgust.

"Ugh," Gabriel agreed as he released the beast, stumbling to stay upright himself. Baby disappeared through the doorway, and a moment later the grinning figure of Tegan Parry replaced him.

"All right there?" she asked cheerfully, as if goat wrestling were one of the fun entertainments provided free of charge by the Queen Mab.

Elodie glared up at the young woman through a tumble of hair, but Gabriel saw the exact moment she remembered the Second Rule and hastily transformed her expression into a civil smile. "Just fine," she said.

"Oh dear, Baby has made a mess of that old mattress," Tegan remarked, then actually *laughed.* The jolly sound served to remind Gabriel yet again why he disapproved of other people's sense of humor. What they found amusing was, on the whole, utterly inexplicable, whereas he lived, breathed, and got science degrees for the explicable.

"Lucky the wily old scoundrel didn't jump up onto the bed!" Tegan joked.

"Yes, very lucky," Elodie said, her smile almost viciously courteous as she got to her feet. "Thank goodness Dr. Tarrant and I still have somewhere to sleep. In the sole bed. Together."

She cast a black look at Gabriel, but he averted his gaze, instead frowning into the safety of the middle distance. This provided a clear signal that the conversation was over, so he found himself confused and annoyed when Tegan spoke again.

"Mr. Jennings mentioned that you were going out early tomorrow. I'll leave a packed breakfast in the kitchen for you. You should see if you can find traces of the *pwcca* while you're out there. That upstart town Llandrindod might have fancy water, but we here in Dôlylleuad are even better when it comes to—"

A sudden flash of lightning blazed through the room, making her flinch. Gabriel automatically shifted his gaze to the window, prepared for whatever hazards it might reveal. But all he saw was a lamplit reflection of his wife against the darkness—which, frankly, represented hazard enough.

BOOM!

As thunder roared, Gabriel looked at Elodie, and she met his gaze. *The storm's worsening,* her expression said.

Don't worry, his answered.

I'll worry if I want, her eyebrows argued.

It would be a waste of your energy, his mouth conveyed with a shrug.

Energy is only wasted when it's not used, her entire body retorted, becoming as stiff as an exclamation mark. *Much like wedding vows.*

Tegan, oblivious to this professional discourse, gave a cheerful laugh. "Autumn is such a dramatic season. Last year I wrote a poem about it, which I think I can still recall . . . 'The sky is dreary, thought the oak tree fairy' . . ."

Aghast, Gabriel widened his eyes at Elodie. At once, she turned to Tegan with a bright, charming smile.

"Thank you so much for rescuing us from Baby. And for allowing us the use of your bedroom. We'll let you go now. Have a nice night, sleep well."

"'Her spirit was weary, the wind scary' . . ."

Somehow, with gentle guidance and polite murmurs, Elodie managed to get the girl out of the room before any further desecration of the English language could be committed. Then, closing the door, she sighed.

"I have a bad feeling about this." She looked at the window (or perhaps the bed; in the shadowy ambience, it wasn't fully clear which, although Gabriel had to agree with her on either count). "There's a sense of things being . . . askew."

Gabriel pursed his lips. He placed "a sense of things" in the same category as Father Christmas: fanciful, nonsensical, and one short step away from the outright horrors of *whimsy*. But there was no point in saying this to Elodie, who had chosen her specialist courses at university by closing her eyes and setting her pointer finger at random on the options list. "We can do nothing now except ensure we're well rested for tomorrow," he said instead.

Elodie clearly disliked this logic, but there was no arguing against it. "You're right, we should go to bed," she said . . .

And then some more words Gabriel did not hear over the

sudden shouting of his pulse. It sounded a lot like *bed!—bed!—bed!* Which was not only disturbing but also inaccurate, considering there existed only one (1) bed. He frowned at the mattress on the floor. Perhaps it wasn't as bad as it looked. He could stuff the wool and straw back in . . . and cover the slobber with a blanket . . . and pretend that wasn't goat dung he smelled . . .

"Sensible adults," Elodie said.

Gabriel blinked, apprehending that he'd missed a sentence, or perhaps even—judging by the snip in her voice—an entire paragraph to which he really, *really* ought to have attended. Returning his gaze to her dutifully, he could not help but observe that she was the most beautiful woman he had ever seen, all lush and cream-and-honey soft (scientifically speaking), and since he was soon going to die of discomfort within the world's narrowest bed, at least his final experience had been of listening to her say . . . uh, something about the cerebral cortex? or counterpanes? . . . through those warm, velvety lips that were so incredibly sweet to kiss—

No. He did not want to kiss his wife. He wanted only to complete this assignment without further disaster. Thus he listened soberly as Elodie talked about respect, and staying on their own side of the bed, and bloody hell he loved her eyelashes. Loved them so much that he'd spent hours in the library researching human cilium and other ocular features (which was a scientist's equivalent of mooning over poetry).

Not that he loved *her*, please note. One might harbor an affection for certain eyelashes without extending it to the possessor of them, and Gabriel was, after all, a man who extended his emotions only under extreme duress.

Besides, Elodie hated him. And fair enough, he wasn't all

that keen on himself either. As a result, he could admire things like her eyelashes (and eyes, and lips, and the near-translucent skin of her wrists) but he would not, *must not*, do anything that would overstep the firm boundary she maintained between them.

"Therefore, you should hug me," she said—and Gabriel's own eyelashes suddenly fluttered so much, he experienced an internal hurricane that sent all his thoughts scattering into shocked silence.

ELODIE SWALLOWED DRYLY as Gabriel stared at her dumb-struck. "I merely think that physical contact prior to entering the bed might desensitize us to any inadvertent bumping—er, I mean, you know. *Touching*."

She winced as this clarification not only failed to lighten the general atmosphere but sizzled through it like a burst of fiery magical energy that heated her face even as Gabriel grew pale. "Except not to say 'touching' as a verb, no, definitely not, I'm not insinuating anything so purposeful; indeed, there's no purpose at all, I assure you. Not that you need assurance. Neither do I. Why would we? We'll be sleeping together purely on a professional level, not as a married couple, even though we are married—er, which is to say, in sum, it's of no consequence whatsoever that we must share a bed, and I for one am entirely serene, unburdened by concerns that—"

"Elodie." The interjection was like a steadying hand on her shoulder. She took a deep breath, letting the jumble of words sink into Gabriel's aura of quiet.

"Of course," she added, "there's always the option of sleeping on the floor."

"Hm." Gabriel looked at said floor with such fierceness, Elodie was certain he would at any moment lie down upon it and declare himself asleep. Then he shrugged. "We've slept together before," he said in a businesslike tone. "We can do it again."

They both fell into profound silence as they recalled the last time they shared a bed, and how little sleeping actually occurred. Then Gabriel frowned. "Perhaps desensitization is a good idea. We will . . . hug. *Scientifically*," he added, giving her a stern look. No doubt he expected this to daunt her, but instead it filled Elodie with sparkles, rendering her so unscientific she essentially became a love sonnet. Taking off his jacket, he draped it neatly over the dressing table's chair, then removed his tie and unbuttoned the top button of his shirt. At this point, Elodie must have fainted just a little, because when she returned to sense, he had detached his cufflinks and was folding up his sleeves as if preparing to delve into action. The sight of his strong, toned forearms set her heartbeat racing.

"Why are you staring like that?" Gabriel asked warily. "You've seen my arms before."

"Uhhh," she replied—for despite her embarrassment at this verbal equivalent of drooling, she could not seem to produce any dry, sensible consonants.

"You've seen my entire naked body," Gabriel then added. Which did not help.

"Unuhhh," Elodie managed.

"Hm. Take off your cardigan."

Surprise jolted Elodie from her dreaminess. "Excuse me?"

"Take off your cardigan. The wool looks like it will be itchy. I can't abide itchy things. Take it off."

"But—but—"

"It's hardly risqué, Elodie. After all, I've seen your entire naked body too, remember."

She tried to summon an outraged reply—*something something arrogant sod something*—but the cardigan was already sliding from her shoulders with wanton ease. As it dropped to the ground, Gabriel stepped forward, and Elodie supposed he was going to pick it up. But suddenly he was embracing her. Or, to be more precise, he was holding his arms around her with a rigidity that felt rather like being embraced by a tree.

"Um, are you sure you want to do this?" she said awkwardly.

"Yes."

"Because if you—"

"It's fine. Do you intend to participate also?"

"Oh. Right." She hugged him close, snuggling against the rock-hard cliff face of his pectoral region. "See, this is easy," she lied cheerfully. "We should soon become desensitized."

"Hm."

They waited in taut silence.

And waited.

"This is taking longer than I anticipated," Gabriel grumbled.

"Huuhh," Elodie agreed. Speaking was difficult, for the man smelled of crisp linen and cold nights under a thousand stars, and every time she inhaled, she tipped dangerously toward dreaming.

"I'm exhausted," he said. "Can we at least lie down?"

"Good idea."

Still embracing, they shuffled sideways until they came to the bed.

"Pull back the quilt," Gabriel suggested.

Elodie reached out one hand to perform the task. The bed
was low-set, however, and she was forced to lean, taking Gabriel with her.

"Careful," he said. "Don't unbalance us."

"Of course not." She tossed back the heavy quilt, and the
movement caused them to rock on their heels.

"We're going to fall," Gabriel warned.

"We won't," Elodie scoffed, and promptly toppled over.

They dropped together onto the bed, or more specifically
onto each other on the bed.

The world's first magnitude ten earthquake took place inside their nervous systems.

"For goodness' sake," Gabriel muttered, his breath stirring
the hair on Elodie's crown (and other things farther down).
"How have you survived this long?"

"It wasn't my fault," Elodie retorted. "You were too tall, and
that made me lose my balance."

"I was too tall," he echoed amazedly. "Well, I shall endeavor
to be shorter in the future. Move farther left, please. There's a
lump in the mattress."

"Any farther left and I'll fall off the bed."

"Nonsense. I've got you."

This announcement was followed by a brief moment of
rose-tinted breathlessness. Then Elodie reminded herself that
he in fact did not have her. He'd abandoned their marriage,
and any metaphorical roses were spiked with thorns. "You've
got most of the pillows, that's what you've got," she retorted.

"Stop wriggling."

"I need to reach my dress hem, it's shifting up."

"Jesus Christ."

"Don't swear."

"I'm not, I'm praying for patience."

"But you're not religious."

"I'm being driven to it. *Must* you wriggle so much?"

"Yes. The telescope in your trouser pocket is pressing against me."

"I don't have a telescope in my trouser pocket."

"Then wh— *Oh.*"

Silence slammed down.

After several hot, motionless seconds, Elodie ventured cautiously, "Can you reach the quilt to pull it up?"

"Not without moving my . . . telescope," Gabriel said.

"That's fine," Elodie answered at once. "I don't need the quilt. I feel quite warm enough."

"Hm," Gabriel replied, the meaning of which was anyone's guess at this point.

The silence returned with a vengeance. The night beyond, however, was a cacophony of sound. Wind howled, sending tree branches and slate tiles clattering around the village. Rain bombarded the inn. It seemed like an oasis compared to the environment in the bedroom.

Elodie closed her eyes. Unable to stop herself, she sank into a dream that Gabriel held her from a sincere wish to be close with her, not just for the scientific pursuit of relief. As the storm rioted outside, she imagined them making a sanctuary for each other, Gabriel's strength encompassing her with certainty while her soft warmth eased his aches from the day's travails. She cuddled closer without consciously realizing, and his arms tightened around her.

I really do love you, dreadful man, she thought.

But even as the impossibly beautiful dream melted a smile into her heart, it was succeeded by a pang of shame. Gabriel disliked her, despite what his physiological response to their contact might suggest, so her own pleasure in his touch felt somehow unethical.

"Sorry," she said, pulling away.

But she'd forgotten just how narrow the bed was, and she would have tumbled right off had Gabriel not caught her. He pulled her close against him once more, their bodies connecting like a hard, fierce kiss. A hundred nerves endings flashed with memory, sending thrills through them like alchemy, shaking their breath to pieces. Instantly, they scrambled to turn their backs, Gabriel cramming himself against the wall, Elodie clutching the edge of the mattress lest she fall again.

"Good night," Gabriel said brusquely.

"Happy dreams," Elodie replied.

And wind rattled against the house like laughter, mocking them.

CHAPTER NINE

Just because you can read a map
doesn't mean you know where you're going.
Blazing Trails, W.H. Jackson

ELODIE WOKE TO magic. It pressed warm against her body, softening her pulse with its starlit dreams, and she smiled, cuddling closer to it despite the inherent danger of doing so, in the same way she threw herself out of hot air balloons and ran straight toward thaumaturgic bombs, wild-hearted woman that she was.

Unfortunately, despite also being a well-educated woman, her brain took a while to catch up.

And then, abruptly, it did. Making a rapid assessment of the situation, it noted the scent of quality soap and the feel of a strong arm curved over her body, and it flung her eyes open even before she could fully process its report. She thus had half a second to realize she was snuggling with Gabriel before his eyes also flung open. The expression in them suggested he'd just received an equally alarming report from his own brain.

They stared at each other across a distance that Elodie professionally estimated to be *really bloody close*. And for the first time since she'd known him, she saw fear in Gabriel's eyes.

Or perhaps it was her own fear, reflected in that heavy darkness.

"Sorry," she said, pulling herself up out of his embrace.

"Sorry," he said in the same moment, also sitting up.

Crack. Her forehead met his chin.

"Damn it," they swore in unison.

"I'll just . . ." Elodie said, and practically threw herself off the bed. Bright, rosy light filled the room, indicating that they had outslept their intention to rise with dawn. Fairly certain that her face shone with the same hue, Elodie fled to the bathroom.

"You are your own personal disaster zone," she whispered furiously to her reflection in the old, mottled mirror. Shadow-rimmed eyes looked back at her with weary agreement.

Completing the usual ablutions, she bundled as much of her long, tameless hair as she could manage into a knot at the back of her head, secured with Gabriel's elastic band, which was by now entwined with snarls. At once, the coiffure, such as it was, drooped lopsidedly. Elodie tried without success to convince herself this was charming, then decided that the heroines of mythology never fretted about their hair, and that she too was a heroine, professionally speaking, and had better things to do with her day.

Thus consoled, and daydreaming about Atalanta, and about the princess Ariadne being met by Bacchus "in his chariot, wreathed with vines," she returned to the bedroom to find Gabriel having just arrived back from visiting the downstairs bathroom. His own hair was faultless of course, his jaw shaven, a cool, fresh scent surrounding him. Elodie promptly discarded the vision of wild Bacchus in favor of this man in all his Apollonian precision.

"Good morning," she said a little shyly.

"Morning," he replied, and if there was any shyness behind the word, his tone bashed it into two crisp, sharp-edged syllables. He took his kit and moved to one side of the room, where the dressing table stood, even as Elodie took hers and moved to the other side, near the window.

"Keep your back turned, please," he said, sounding as prim as a maiden aunt, "so I can get changed."

Elodie bristled. "I have no intention of peeking at you. Keep *your* back turned, please, while I can get changed also."

"Naturally," Gabriel replied.

"Good."

"Perfect."

Elodie clenched her teeth to prevent herself from responding. Let him have the last word. *She* would rather have her self-respect. As she began unfastening her dress, she scowled determinedly out the window.

Which reflected the room with perfect clarity.

She watched in the glass as Gabriel removed his vest and undid all the buttons of his shirt before her conscience finally stirred. *Stop peeking!* it demanded.

Absolutely, of course, Elodie agreed, looking down.

Then Gabriel took off the shirt, and her eyes suffered mild whiplash as they rose again to the view.

Morning light glossed his bare skin, turning it to gold. He angled slightly, revealing an abdomen so well-defined it was practically an entire dictionary on masculine strength. Elodie's nerves trilled with the memory of that abdomen pressed against her body, and she rubbed a hand restively across her midriff, trying to calm the sensations and bring herself more firmly back into the present, in which her husband's abdomen was off-limits and indeed not even for peeking at. All she managed, however, was to stoke a warmth that threatened to spread through her entire body.

Oblivious to her suffering, Gabriel bent to his kit, withdrawing a black henley. Elodie had previously observed this species of tightly fitting, long-sleeved vest on male students during the Oxford Cambridge Boat Race, but never paid it much attention. After all, what are men to rocks and mountains? But as Gabriel pulled on the henley, muscles rippling with the movement, Elodie had to admit, he was an Everest.

Leaning forward, she rested her forehead on the windowpane. *I hate him, hate him,* she silently chanted. A shadow moved across the glass as Gabriel's reflection shifted again, and her attention automatically followed it.

He was removing his trousers.

This is it, she thought. *This is the moment I die.* (Which was not quite as hyperbolic a statement as it seemed, considering she'd forgotten to inhale.) Swallowing heavily, she turned aside from the window and attacked the buttons of her dress, determined to make no further notice of her altogether disturbing husband.

HELL, GABRIEL CURSED silently, then added a preposition for good measure: *I am in hell.* For although he'd turned his back to Elodie like a decent gentleman, he'd not counted on the dressing table's mirror giving him a clear view of his damned disturbing wife as she slipped off her dress. The sight of her upper body covered only by the flimsiest camisole, not even a corset to protect a man's sensibilities, set his nerves aflame. Hastily he looked away.

Dressing in khaki field pants, tucking them into sturdy tramping boots, he folded up the vest's sleeves (then refolded one until it was precisely even with the other), and set his ER kit on his back. Then, donning his spectacles, he reached across the dressing table for his portable weather station.

The movement caused him to accidentally see Elodie's reflection in the mirror once again. She was now safely attired in a white, lace-collared shirtwaist, plaid skirt, and the scratchy brown cardigan. The skirt was salaciously short, just four inches below her knees, and tall boots only superficially protected her legs from the scandal of visibility.

Mind you, had someone interviewed Gabriel on the matter, he'd have said she ought to wear trousers, for safety's sake. Any man ruffled by the female form lacked mental discipline.

Just then Elodie noticed a crease on the front of her shirtwaist. She brushed her hand down over her breast—

ELODIE GLANCED OVER with mild alarm as Gabriel appeared to choke on his own breath. Immediately, her own breath threatened to implode. He was wearing his spectacles.

More specifically, he was wearing a tight-fitting henley with the sleeves folded up, trousers made for action, hardy boots, and his spectacles.

Just kill me now and be done with it, she thought with a heavy sigh.

"Is something wrong?" Gabriel asked, gruff.

"Nngghghnnh," she replied. Thankfully, due to long experience of giving morning lectures while still half-asleep, this came out with serene coherence: "No, nothing wrong. Nothing at all. Absolutely fine. And you?"

"Fine," he said, and scowled so fiercely at the weather station in his hand that it was a wonder the glass covers of its brass-ringed gauges did not shatter.

"Bad readings?" she asked as she turned to her ER kit and began removing nonessential items.

"No, they're all normal. The storm has passed. We should be able to make good headway today. If we . . ."

As his voice faded, Elodie glanced over and found him staring at the pile of clothes and toiletries strewn about at her feet.

"Don't worry, I'll clean it up later," she assured him. Closing her lightened kit, she set it on her back. "Are you ready to go?"

"Yes." Gabriel hauled his attention away from the floor with obvious difficulty. *Really, it's not that much mess,* Elodie grumped, glancing at it herself—

And saw the silk and lace drawers draped lasciviously over a telescope.

Her heart gave a little wail and hid itself under a blanket of embarrassment. Her brain reminded her that she'd spent much of yesterday walking around in almost identical drawers for all the world to see, but this oddly did not help. Somehow, the garments seemed more salacious off her body. The pink bows at either side of the lace trim appeared to wink at her.

Oh God, I need coffee, she thought. Black, black coffee. Coffee so black it would make midnight seem like noon. Coffee that was actually vodka. She strode for the door at the same time Gabriel did. They very, very carefully did not collide. Gabriel gestured for her to precede him, and Elodie clicked her tongue.

"Really, 'ladies first' isn't always the kindness you think it is," she told him as she exited. "A burglar could have been lurking out here and I'd have walked directly into his clutches."

"Hm," he said in a manner that fired her up more than several cups of coffee would have done.

"However, it seems a burglar has already been, and has stolen your vocabulary," she commented snarkily.

"I'm flattered you think what I say is valuable."

"I don't think about you at all."

"Whereas I think about you constantly."

Elodie's heart stammered at this pronouncement, but before it could get too excited, he continued: "Such hypervigilance is not good for one's mental well-being but has proven necessary. I can only be thankful I have a doctorate in disaster studies."

"I wish my own doctorate was in medicine," Elodie muttered, "considering you give me a headache."

"How fortunate then that you never think of me."

Elodie glanced back at Algernon's bedroom door, which they had passed while preoccupied with each other. "I suppose we should wake the redoubtable Mr. Jennings."

"Redoubtable?" Gabriel said disbelievingly.

"As in, I have doubts about him repeatedly."

Gabriel's expression suspended between disapproval for this shocking mutilation of language and amusement over its cleverness. Elodie smirked at him, and the expression immediately crashed into a frown. "We should wake him," he agreed. "After all, we might need something to throw into the mine shaft to test the magic."

Algernon was not in his bedroom, however. They found him instead in the inn's lobby, pacing back and forth. Huddled in a Mackintosh coat and woolen cap despite the fine weather, he held a cloth-covered basket in one hand, his suitcase in the other. Seeing them, he jumped with fright.

"Is everything all right?" Elodie asked.

"Oh, no, no, no, no, no, of course it is," he said, and gave a tremulous laugh.

"That's an awful lot of 'no's for a 'yes' answer," Elodie commented wryly.

"Ha ha. I'm just waiting for you so we can go out to the trove site, that's all."

Elodie frowned with mild confusion. "You're taking your suitcase with you?"

"Oh, no, I just brought it downstairs because . . . if . . . This is our breakfast." He held out the basket. "Shall we go? Hurry, now."

He turned to the door, and behind his back Elodie and Gabriel exchanged a glance of approval (Elodie) and mild disapprobation (guess who). Perhaps Algernon Jennings wasn't such a cowardly wretch after all. He pulled open the door—

"*Eee!*" he squeaked, dropping his suitcase.

Tegan Parry was standing on the doorstep, surrounded by a nimbus of fresh morning sunlight. "Ah, there you are, Mr. Jennings," she said, smiling. "I've spoken to Mrs. Jones. She's about to leave for Aberystwyth and is happy to take you in her carriage."

Algernon shook his head with such vehemence there appeared some danger of his mustache falling off. "No, no, I, you, oh dear, such a, um, misunderstanding, ha ha."

"*Fortes fortuna juvat*, Mr. Jennings," Gabriel said sternly. And when he received a blank look in response: "Fortune favors the brave. At the very least, dare a proper sentence."

"If you want to go home, you should," Elodie said with gentle sympathy. "We won't mind."

Algernon turned to her, his expression lifting into delight. "What, really?" Then he glanced at Gabriel, and it plummeted again. "I mean, no! In the middle of a disaster? Good God, woman, are you insane?"

Abruptly, Gabriel took a step forward. "Don't speak to my wife like that."

Algernon flushed, but it was a mere watercolor wash compared to the crimson brightness that lit Elodie's face. Indeed, she could have been propped against a headland to warn ships about sunken reefs.

"S-sorry," Algernon stammered, throat bobbing.

It's fine, Elodie wanted to assure him, but all her words had dissolved into stars.

Gabriel flicked a finger at the doorway. "Time to go."

"Go?" Algernon repeated, the word freighted with hope, fear, uncertainty.

"To move from one place to another," Gabriel said. "In this instance, from the inn to the trove on the fey line. We may need your assistance, Mr. Jennings, therefore you are staying. Or rather, you are going. With us. *Now*."

"Can I come too?"

They all turned to find one of the tourists, Mr. Mumbers, standing behind them. "Do say yes!" he begged enthusiastically. "My phrenologist has advised me to get more excitement in life, for the sake of my health, and you people are the most exciting thing I've encountered in a long while. I 'could not but be gay, in such a jocund company.'" He directed a beguiling grin at Elodie, and she laughed.

"You need to broaden your horizons," she advised the young

man dryly. Beside her, Gabriel muttered something under his breath about him also needing to learn the definition of "jocund," but Mr. Mumbers ignored this.

"Then I can come?" the young man asked, bouncing a little on his heels. "I'm all prepared!" He patted the small, gold-plated pair of binoculars that hung about his neck, and that were so elegantly dainty, they probably wouldn't see a tree five feet in front of them.

Gabriel's irritation, however, was impossible to miss. "N—"

"Sure," Elodie said, shrugging. "The more the merrier."

"May I remind Dr. Tarrant that we will be entering a classified location?" Gabriel intoned.

"You may," Elodie answered, then gestured for Mumbers to precede her. She would have handed over the key to Queen Victoria's bedroom if it meant yet another person between her and Gabriel. (*He said "my wife,"* her heart whispered, its hands clasped together and its eyes raised dreamily. Her brain, however, was busy erecting a barricade. It wasn't that she expected Gabriel to hurt her; rather, she hurt herself with her hopelessly unrequited feelings toward him. Really, feeling attracted to one's husband was not safe. Best that, as much as possible, they not be alone.)

"Hurrah!" Mumbers enthused. "What fun!"

"This is geography," Gabriel grumbled as he pushed past everyone and out onto the street. "*Fun* has nothing to do with it."

ALAS, NO ONE heeded this statement of fact. The thaumaturgic trove was a mere twenty minutes' distance from Dôlylleuad— but when at the three-quarter mark Gabriel looked at his wristwatch yet again, he noted they had been walking for thirty-two minutes. Thirty. Two. He could not repress a loud *tsk*.

"Must you inspect those flowers?" he demanded as Elodie bent rapturously over a tangle of briar roses at the roadside. This was after she had stopped to chat with locals, stopped to greet no fewer than three dogs, stopped to admire what could only be described by reasonable people as a plain blue sky, and actually wandered off the road completely at one point to gather harebells—"magical fairy bells," she'd called them as she tucked a few into the ramshackle bundle of her hair. As a result, she looked more like a dryad than a scientist, and Gabriel managed to keep his irritation going only with a reminder that the woman presented a hazard to anyone with hay fever. She certainly made it hard for him to breathe.

"Time doesn't only go forward, it goes deep too," she answered him now. "I don't want to just walk down a road, I want to *experience* it. That's geography for you, Dr. Tarrant."

Then she tossed him a blithe, sun-spangled grin that had him forgiving her in an instant—at least, until the very next instant, when she stopped to watch a skylark dancing above the long grasses.

Not helping matters was Algernon's trudging attitude and continual complaints about the road's sodden condition. While Elodie was gazing birdward, and Mumbers was declaiming, "'Ethereal minstrel! Pilgrim of the sky! Dost thou despise the earth where cares abound?'" the accountant cursed autumn and rubbed his muddy boots against a tuft of weeds. While Elodie veered off for roses and Mumbers followed close behind her, soliloquizing about the sweet prick of thorns, Algernon halted in the middle of the road to pluck raisins out of the last remaining scone from their breakfast. And just when Gabriel felt himself at the verge of madness, they *all* turned to look back at Dôlylleuad.

"Such a bucolic vista," Elodie said, sighing dreamily as she slid a rose behind one ear.

"It is beautiful indeed," Mumbers agreed.

"I wish I was back in bed," Algernon grumbled, flicking a raisin into a mud puddle.

Gabriel never wasted mental energy on regrets, but now found himself wishing quite fervently that he'd snuck out at dawn before anyone else was awake, as he'd originally planned.

And yet . . . had he done that, he'd have missed the rare experience of waking to comfort. At first, he'd supposed it to be a dream, such as he'd had often enough over the past year; the kind of poignant but beloved dream of cuddling with Elodie in all her violet-scented warmth, making him linger, eyes closed and heart sighing contentedly, before he surrendered at last to the cold morning emptiness of his bed. He'd imagined kissing her sweet face, and perhaps even doing more (e.g., jointly composing a scientific paper that described spatiotemporal pattern analysis of thaumaturgic mineral degradation's effects on ombrotrophic vegetation in Scottish peat bogs) . . .

And then he'd woken fully, abruptly, to realize it was no dream at all.

Except that she *was* a living kind of dream, this wife of his. Glancing at her now, almost forgetting to frown as he took in the generous curve of her smile, and her heavenly eyes glittering with joy, and even the tangled, dirt-speckled flowers in her alabaster hair, he could only think that she looked too ethereally beautiful for corporeal reality.

Which was a problem, since he was a geographer. His entire existence focused on interpreting the world in ordinary, systematic, prosaic terms. The last thing he needed was someone in his life turning what ought to be a straightforward journey into a wonder-filled ramble.

Gabriel concluded that there was only one thing he could do under the circumstances: he marched on, leaving the incorrigible woman behind. (Algernon did not rate an inclusion in this decision, and Gabriel had already forgotten the tourist's name.) He worried *not even slightly* that Elodie might be upset by this. His elevated pulse rate was due to the physical exercise alone.

Within five brisk, efficient minutes he had reached the abandoned mine site beneath which lay the thaumaturgic reservoir. When Elodie and the others wandered in three minutes later, they discovered him standing among the remnants of broken buildings and rusted equipment in the shadow of a small wooded hill, scowling at the gauges and levels on his handheld thaumometer.

"What is it?" Elodie asked, instantly professional despite the petals drifting from her hair.

"Nothing," he said.

"It looks like something, judging by your expression," she insisted.

"It is. *Nothing.* No thaumaturgical energy signal whatsoever."

She frowned. "That's impossible." Bringing out her own thaumometer from a skirt pocket, she consulted its readings, and her eyebrows rose at least as much as the gauges' needles ought to have been doing. "Huh. Nothing. Quantity—pressure—velocity—all flat. The well appears to have gone dry."

"Aren't we at a mine shaft, not a well?" the tourist asked as he tried to peer over Elodie's shoulder at the thaumometer. He was so close, his breath stirred the fine threads of hair that had slipped down about her face.

Mumbers, Gabriel remembered. The man with pleurisy. Gabriel knew a cure for that: *I'll rip out your lungs if you don't fucking step away from my wife.*

"The shaft contains a subterranean pool of magic-charged water," Elodie said, slipping adroitly from Mumbers's shadow. The sunlight embraced her at once like a lover, gilding her body. (Gabriel had never before been jealous of the sun, and he wasn't now either, of course; he merely noted the phenomenon.) "Most such places lie dormant," she continued to explain, "unless weather or human activity impinge upon them, or the land collapses, or there's been activity farther along the fey line, causing a cascade—"

"Fey line?" Mumbers asked, the words rolling on his tongue and igniting wonder in his gaze, as if he was internally composing a poem on the subject. Gabriel found his own eyes narrowing as he watched.

"An imaginary line that runs between deposits of magic beneath the land," Elodie explained. She sounded enthused, and Gabriel couldn't really fault her for that. A young person's interest in learning was like manna for teachers.

"For example," she continued, "the 5-SEQ—England's fifth southeast quadrant line, which is the line this reservoir sits on—travels southeast across England from the Welsh coast and through London before it peters out. It's quite weighted, by which I mean there are many deposits of significant size along it. That's rare, and makes it a powerful line. But this particular deposit was only discovered by miners eighty years ago, after they were transformed briefly into mice, and it hasn't been especially active until now."

"So, if this is a pool, then magic is in water?" Mumbers ventured. "Or is it an elfin grot, wherein dwells a fair lady with wild wild eyes?"

Elodie laughed, delighted at this odd notion, her own eyes shining bright. Sudden pain snapped through Gabriel, startling him. He realized he was smacking his weather station against his thigh. "May I speak to you for a moment, Dr. Tarrant?" he said in a clipped voice.

"Mm hm," Elodie answered, but then went right on talking, like a pebble caught in a flow of—of—(Gabriel's brain twisted, attempting a melodic metaphor)—grotty elfin water. "No, magic exists within certain minerals, under certain conditions," she told Mumbers patiently. "You'll have to ask a geologist for a detailed explanation, but I can tell you that some of these minerals are dissolved in water or soil, others embedded in rocks. Early scientists recognized dispersal patterns and connections between deposits, and maps of those were created, hence the fey lines. Because they generally form radiant seams through the earth's crust, we call them lines, although a few are more like wiggles—"

"Wiggles," Gabriel muttered disbelievingly.

Elodie glanced at him, all flashing fairy eyes and tilted-up chin; all flowery and kissable, and damn he wished something in the vicinity would explode before he injured his brain permanently, trying to come up with poetic descriptions for the woman. Poetic! As if he'd been educated at a community college!

"A simple vocabulary helps people feel less daunted," Elodie said in an arch tone.

Gabriel was willing to accept that pedagogical theory, although he didn't subscribe to it himself. But he knew it wasn't the true reason why she spoke so casually. He knew *her*. She simply, unselfconsciously brought the same ebullience to her lectures that she did to everything else in life. And she was clearly more at ease talking with the rhapsodical Mr. Mumbers than with him.

She was never at ease with him.

The thought was like a punch beneath his heart. Mortified, he turned on a heel and strode purposefully across the mine site. Not running away. Just departing with precipitous intent to be gone.

ELODIE STARED AT Gabriel's retreating back, frustrated and hurt. Did he have to make his dislike of her quite so evident? And did she have to care about it so much?

Please, she begged her heart. *Stop feeling.*

To which her heart responded by sending up a mist of tears, turning the world silvery and vague, as if it were drowning in unhappiness. But Elodie never cried in front of people (apart from that one time when she was lecturing about Mount Vesuvius's eruption) (and also when Mr. Durbent explained he was late handing in his essay because his beloved grandmother had died) (and when her students gave her a cake for her birthday) (and at the end of each term). So she blinked furiously, pulled the flowers from her hair, and marched after Gabriel. After all, she truly *was* a professional, whatever he might think, she had a job to do, and she couldn't accidentally whack him in the face with her weather station from a distance.

He was standing before the padlocked double doors of a hut that sheltered the mine shaft, and as Elodie came alongside him, he kicked one of them. This had no effect besides rattling the padlock and making Elodie's nerves leap.

"Damn it," he muttered.

"There's no damage," Elodie said.

"Except to my toes," Gabriel answered sardonically. He shoved a hand through his hair, looking like a man on the verge of doing something wild and furious, such as dog-earing the page of an atlas.

"I meant the site," Elodie said, cool and businesslike. "There's no storm damage. The initial report said bad weather triggered the magical events plaguing Dôlylleuad, but where is the evidence? None here—and none along the road to here," she added with a pointed look. Gabriel returned it silently, his own expression barricaded. "No magical char either, no lique-faction, no buildings turned into trees," she plowed on. "Considering the degree of thaumaturgic activity reported, I'd expect to see consequences in the primary zone. But there's *nothing* here, as you said."

"Good heavens, you agree with something I said?" Gabriel remarked dryly. "Yet I know that music has a far more pleasing—uh—noise."

Elodie blinked at him. "What?"

The barricade seemed to develop spikes. And cauldrons of burning tar in his eyes. "What?" he echoed defensively.

She blinked again, astonished. "Did you just try to quote Shakespeare?"

"Don't be ridiculous," Gabriel snapped, flushing.

Her heart, which had been lifting at the thought of her professional curmudgeon of a husband attempting poetry, now came down with a resounding thud. She half turned away from him, glaring at the dusty weeds and empty buildings. "Not the smallest spark of magic," she declared.

Gabriel tipped his gaze skyward, squinting fiercely. "Nothing stirring at all."

Then they looked at each other again, like compasses turning inevitably to magnetic north. Elodie felt misery shadow her eyes. Gabriel blinked as if the light hurt him.

"I know the magic exists, though," she said, her voice growing as quiet and dry as the landscape around them.

"It does," he agreed.

They went on looking, not talking, until at last Elodie tugged her gaze away once more. Gabriel frowned at his thaumometer.

"There's nothing underground either," he said, "according to this reading."

"Perhaps the energy disseminated at a velocity that minimized damage here," Elodie suggested. "It also might have exhausted the lode, which would explain our zero readings. But there is a real sense of this place being . . ."

"Derelict," Gabriel said.

"Dead as a dodo," she said at the same time.

And somehow they were looking at each other again. Elodie expected another comment about her idiomatic language, but instead she saw amusement twitch at the corner of Gabriel's mouth. Her heart did a double take. Gabriel quickly turned away, his profile severe against the blank sky, leaving her to conclude that she'd witnessed no more than a trick of the light. She did not sigh then, but she did exhale rather heavily.

"I'm going to investigate further," she said, and left before he could reply.

But an hour's walking around poking at weeds, taking measurements, ignoring Algernon's complaints about boredom and Mumbers getting in the way as he composed sonnets about the various broken pieces of mine equipment ultimately brought them back to where they had started: standing side by side, trying hard not to look at each other.

"This site is exhausted," Gabriel said.

Elodie nodded, which accidentally brought her gaze in line with Gabriel's sun-gilded profile. "All the evidence does suggest as much."

"Hm." Gabriel ran a hand through his hair, which resulted purely by chance in him facing her. "The recent crisis must have been caused by an—"

"*Undiscovered thaumaturgic deposit,*" they chorused. A thrill twinkled between them. Elodie was unable to repress a grin, although she dug her heels into the ground to keep herself from leaping forward and hugging Gabriel in excitement. He seemed equally excited, his mouth straight and brow unfurrowed.

"My calculations placed the trajectory of yesterday's energy burst six hundred yards west of here," he said, squinting in that direction. The land bulged gently, covered with an oak wood whose lush autumnal canopy appeared to smolder in the sunlight. Regarding it intently, Gabriel frowned, and Elodie knew he was seeing not trees but angles and inches. "I propose we move west and see if we can pick up thaumaturgic resonance in that direction."

"Good plan," Elodie agreed. She paused, tucking a strand of hair behind her ear shyly. "I hope your foot isn't still hurting."

Gabriel stiffened, as if she'd insulted him somehow. "It's fine," he murmured, and walked off without further conversation. This time, Elodie did sigh. Then she hurried after him, because what else could she do?

After a minute she recollected the other two men's existence, primarily because Algernon pleaded for both her and Gabriel to slow down. But Gabriel was intent on his thaumometer, and Elodie felt so energized by the prospect of a new, unmapped trove of thaumaturgic materials that she did not glance even once at the incandescent glory of leaves rustling quietly overhead, nor imagine what fairy revelries the shadows below might be hiding.

Upon emerging from the woods at the crest of the hill, they met an expansive view of countryside billowing west to the sea and east toward England, villages and farmhouses tucked among its honey-colored copses and along the river, smoke rising from their chimneys like unfurled dreams. But Elodie and Gabriel saw none of this. They stopped, a shock of silence passing between them.

Some thirty yards ahead was a monolith. Six feet tall, extensively etched with symbols, it evoked a sense of antiquity, sacredness, and danger, the latter mostly due to the angle at which it leaned—and the human figure leaning in opposition, trying to keep it from toppling altogether.

Elodie and Gabriel exhaled with identical tones of weary frustration.

"Oh look," Algernon said as he came up behind them. "We found Dr. Jackson."

"How is he holding up that rock?" Mumbers asked in amazement. "It's almost like—"

"Magic," everyone said.

At that moment, the old professor noticed their arrival. Squinting through large round spectacles at them, he grimaced, his face purple with the effort of propping up the monolith.

"Hello there!" Mumbers called out, waving.

Dr. Jackson waved back . . .

"Aaahhh!" he screamed.

THUD.

"Damn!" Gabriel and Elodie swore in unison, and even as blue smoke arose from the fallen stone, they began to run.

Chapter Ten

A thaumaturgically dynamic landscape is a nonlinear system.
In other words, it's prone to going *boom* in all directions.

Blazing Trails, W.H. Jackson

O H HELLO THERE, you're the Tappets, aren't you?" Professor Jackson peered at them with curiosity as they helped him up out of the sodden grass where he'd thrown himself as the rock fell. "The ones with the weird marriage?"

"That sounds about right," Elodie muttered under her breath. The fact gossip about her relationship with Gabriel had reached the literal edge of Britain did not surprise her, considering the nature of academia. But she kept her response brisk, professional. "Tarrant, sir. Emergency response team. Are you all right?"

"I think I've squashed the sandwich in my pocket," the old professor said, patting his tweed jacket (and thus squashing the sandwich in its aforementioned pocket, which had in fact survived the fall). "Bother, it was chicken too."

Dismayed, he shook his head, sending his white cloud of hair fluttering and making him stumble. "I *am* a tad woozy. But I've not had a cup of tea in two days, so that's only to be expected." He rubbed one eye as if this might improve his sense of balance—applying his finger to the task directly through the frame of his spectacles, which proved to be without lenses. Then, with sudden, belated awareness of the diaphanous cyanic smoke drifting around them, he grimaced. "Oh dear, that can't be good."

"What happened?" Gabriel demanded, arms crossed as he frowned severely at the man.

"It wasn't my fault," Jackson replied with all the speed and fervency of a naughty boy caught in some trouble that was plainly and incontrovertibly his fault. "I just looked at the rock."

"Just looked," Gabriel repeated, dubious.

The professor shrugged. "Maybe a modicum of poking was involved. But the etchings on its surface are so fascinating. And how was I to know it was a thaumaturgic object? It doesn't smell like it." He pulled the flattened sandwich from his pocket, grimaced at the lint speckled on it, then took a large bite.

Elodie set down her ER kit and crouched to inspect the tor more closely. "These etchings really are fascinating," she said, tilting her head as she visually traced them.

"Runes?" Gabriel asked without ceasing to stare at Jackson.

"No, circles and spirals, remarkably alike those on the Newgrange tomb."

Gabriel looked over then, interest lighting his expression. Newgrange was the site of the greatest thaumaturgic mineral deposit in all Ireland, and considering how magical in general the island was, that really was saying something. Elodie grinned up at him. *A new trove*, their mutual gaze said. (Also,

God, I want to kiss you, but each translated this in the other as
eye strain.)

A gasp sounded as Mumbers and Algernon arrived on the
scene. Elodie could not discern which of them had gasped—
Algernon with horror at the faint thaumaturgic smoke, or
Mumbers in excitement.

"Ancient pagan designs!" the latter exclaimed. "I simply
must get a picture!" He pulled a sketchbook from his jacket
pocket and passed it to Algernon. "Will you draw me beside
the rock? And Miss Tarrant, stand with me!"

"*Mrs.* Tarrant," Gabriel growled, taking off his kit and
pushing his sleeves up farther as if he were planning to chal-
lenge Mumbers to a boxing match.

"Actually, I don't think these designs are ancient after all,"
Elodie said, her excited grin fading as she ran a finger over the
stone's surface. "The indentations are sharp-edged, not weathered, which suggests they're only recently made. Also, there's
no lichen on the rock."

"Knob," Professor Jackson said through a mouthful of bread
and chicken. Everyone looked at him confusedly. "Devil's
Knob," he clarified, waving his sandwich at the monolith. "It
marks a doorway that Arawn takes out of Annwn on Nos Ca-
lan Gaeaf, according to the locals."

"The Welsh king of the underworld!" Mumbers exclaimed,
his eyes growing wide as if expecting Arawn to appear at any
moment and claim his soul (which would be a jolly sensagger
indeed!).

"Folklore often conveys local knowledge about thaumaturgic activity, and serves as a warning that people should stay
away," Gabriel grumbled, clearly wishing the three men would
take that warning to heart.

"I doubt it's a warning," Professor Jackson argued, "considering Mr. Parry, the innkeeper, offered to bring me up here on a sightseeing tour, complete with a chance to see and pat one of Arawn's supernatural hounds, all for the cost of one shilling."

"There's no sign of thaumaturgic material in the ground itself," Elodie said as she bent over the hole from whence the monolith had toppled. "And this worm population appears healthy and normal. I'm guessing what happened is that the thaumaturgic energy we're seeing here is an overspill from another source, and the rock has absorbed it. In fact, I think—oops!" She straightened hastily, batting at a strand of magic that sizzled in her hair.

"The thaumaturgic pressure is building," Gabriel said, sounding like he was talking about the weather—although maybe not that, considering their profession, but some other, boring subject. He frowned at his thaumometer. "Overspill or not, this is powerful energy, and I don't know that the granite will contain it for long. Judging from these readings, there could be a perforative eructation at any minute."

"A perfor-what?" Mumbers asked warily.

"It's about to go boom," Elodie explained, fisting her hands then opening them to illustrate.

"We're all going to die!" Algernon wailed.

"Nonsense," Professor Jackson scoffed. "You're perfectly safe, trust me."

Crack!

A split opened in the monolith, blue sparks shooting from it. Everyone ducked.

"Aaahhhh!" Professor Jackson cried out, flinging up his sandwich as it spontaneously metamorphosed into a large white hen. The bird flapped frantically, squawking and pecking at his face, then it fell to the ground and scurried off while the professor was swaying in shock at having had his carnivorism literally come back to bite him.

"Aaahhhh!" Algernon screamed, because he was Algernon.

"I say, jolly good fun!" Mumbers exclaimed, blood dripping from a cut on his forehead.

The air around the monolith began to glow with a pulsing silver radiance. Elodie and Gabriel stepped closer to it.

"The tip is blue," Gabriel noted. "It's going to discharge from there."

Elodie grinned. "Would it be unladylike of me to point out the phallic imagery?"

"Yes."

"Where's it pointing?"

They squinted at the horizon. "Aberystwyth," Gabriel said.

"Egad!" Professor Jackson exclaimed. "There are medieval books in the university library that will cause mayhem if magic hits them!"

Pivoting on a heel, Elodie gestured urgently at the others. "We have to turn it! Hurry, before it erupts!"

"It's a whopping great rock," Mumbers said with a laugh. "We'll never be able to lift it."

"The magic has eroded its relative density," Professor Jackson said. "It's as light as a feather."

They arranged themselves alongside the monolith and, wrapping their arms around it, hauled it up to waist height.

"Bloody hell," Algernon groaned. "I thought you said 'light as a feather.'"

"I meant a mammoth eagle feather," Professor Jackson said.

"The lady shouldn't be part of this work," Mumbers spoke up nobly. "She might get hurt."

"For God's sake," Elodie muttered. She looked to Gabriel. "Which direction?"

"West," he suggested. "Send it out to sea."

Shuffling awkwardly, they angled the monolith as directed, but an invisible force dragged against their efforts.

"It's trying to align to the fey line," Elodie realized.

"Ow, that was my foot you just stepped on!" Mumbers cried out.

"Was it? My apologies," Gabriel said, his voice as stiff as the rock itself.

"Never mind feet!" Professor Jackson shouted. "No one will care about their feet if the university's original volume of the *Malleus Mephitidae* explodes!"

"*The Hammer of the Stink Badgers?*" Elodie translated bemusedly.

"Exactly!"

"I can't hold on much longer," Algernon panted.

"Think of me, I've only just recovered from pleurisy!" Mumbers told him. "'Mortality weighs heavily on me like unwilling sleep.'"

"Keep turning west," Gabriel grumbled.

"So do the badgers have the hammer, or . . . ?"

"West!"

"Ow! You stepped on my foot again!"

"The rock's getting heavier!"

"Don't drop it!"

"Surely they don't expect people to hit badgers with a hammer? That's not—"

CRACK!

Suddenly, the very air seemed to shatter. Elodie found herself flying backward. She smacked against the ground, pain shocking through her. One second later, Gabriel was atop her body, sheltering her as shards of sword-colored magic rained down. Wind screamed in pain. The ground buckled. All of existence strained to hold itself together.

And then, suddenly—quiet.

Elodie stared up at Gabriel. His eyes behind a fall of hair were so dark, magic would have lost itself for a thousand years in their depths. His breath was barely there. Elodie felt the same exhilaration she had when, years ago, he'd unexpectedly walked between lectures with her, discussing cartography agendas. And she felt comforted too, like the time she'd sat opposite him in the Bodleian, silently studying the teachings of Eratosthenes until the librarians evicted them at the end of the day. And it was lovely, lovely, like the slow drift of light and shadow through a small, quiet church as she watched him slide a gold ring onto her finger.

"Amazing," Gabriel said huskily.

"Incredible," she agreed, the word not much more than a sigh.

"The subjective alchemic transformation was remarkably specific."

"And the voltage!" she added. "Such force from a relatively small lode!"

They scrambled up, looking around with an academic enthusiasm that was so pronounced, neither noticed their arms were touching, their hands not so much brushing against each other as mingling in a way that would have been almost unbearably thrilling under other circumstances.

The world gleamed like a tear-filled eye. The monolith was on fire, blue flames dancing along its length. A ray of energy emerged from its tip, silver-bright, angling down from the hill's summit like a great translucent path until it struck a field almost a mile away.

"Intense," Elodie breathed.

"It must be at least seven thousand conjures," Gabriel said. He looked around. "Where's my thaumometer?"

"There." Elodie pointed to pool of copper and glass bubbling in the grass a few yards away. Then her stomach lurched as she belatedly recalled the human element of geography. "Is everyone all right?"

"Nggh," Professor Jackson replied from where he lay on his back nearby, glasses askew.

"I want to go home!" Algernon howled as he clutched the ground. Mumbers stared dazedly at a patch of wheat that had previously been his hat.

"It didn't reach as far as I expected," Gabriel murmured, frowning at the thaumaturgic energy beam. Beneath it, hedges were shattering and wildflowers turning to bright dust. Birds flew up like feathered screams, trailing magic that set the air briefly alight. And where the beam met earth, fragments of rainbows swirled, as if a pot of thaumaturgic gold lay there.

"All this energy must be originating from *somewhere*," Elodie said. "Maybe the source is in that field."

"What on earth are we going to do?" Professor Jackson asked as he pushed himself up from the ground, glasses swinging from one ear. "If you'll excuse the little pun, ha ha."

Elodie grinned at him. "I'm going down to take a look," she said. Turning to her kit, she took out a utility belt containing various emergency gadgets, such as a compass and measuring tape, and began to wrap it around her waist.

"Can I come too?" Mumbers asked eagerly.

"No," Gabriel said. He pulled a short telescope from his own kit and weighed it in his hand. Blanching, Mumbers stepped back.

"Would you help Mr. Jennings down to the village?" Elodie asked the man, smiling distractedly at him. "Professor Jackson will escort you, for your safety."

At the sound of his name, the professor looked up from smacking his jacket pockets in search of another sandwich. "What? What?"

"Take these men back to Dôlylleuad," Elodie ordered him while checking the gauges on her portable weather station before slipping the device into her skirt pocket.

"Telegraph the Home Office to advise them of the situation here," Gabriel added as he strapped the telescope around the calf of one leg. "We're going to need help."

"Also please take our kits with you," Elodie said. "I don't want to carry any extra load."

"And you should probably warn Aberystwyth," Gabriel said, "in case of spillage along the line."

"And make sure the people of Dôlylleuad are safe."

"And most of all, *don't poke at any more things.*"

"Right." The old professor nodded in a way that made it clear he'd not processed even half of what they'd told him. "Do you want to use my bicycle?"

Elodie straightened from tucking a dowsing rod into her left boot. "Thank you, but I know a shortcut." She grinned sidelong at Gabriel. He'd donned his long dark coat and was placing a map in an inside pocket, but he seemed to sense her attention; he looked up with cool, dispassionate professionalism. And yet, his eye held something that Elodie would describe as an anti-glint: excitement so sober, so dignified, it was the blackest black, more intense than any sparkle. She quirked her grin.

"Ready?"

"Ready," he said.

They turned to face northwest. The cobalt flames of the burning monolith illuminated them with a witchical glow. The breeze stirred their hair. In unison, each hooked iron and gold around their left ear. Altogether they presented a heroic picture, lacking only the dramatic billowing of capes for a full effect.

"Botheration," Elodie whispered, tipping her head a little toward Gabriel so he might hear her. "If we don't survive, someone's going to find my pile of underwear at the inn."

He laughed.

Laughed.

Or perhaps it was just the wind, for in the next half a second his face was stony once more. The opposite might be said for Elodie's heart, however, which began to flutter more wildly than a summer storm.

"Be careful!" Algernon called out weakly from where he was propping himself up, white-faced, on the ground.

Elodie gave him a radiant smile. Disaster burned behind her, disaster raged ahead, but all she knew was delight. Gabriel had laughed (possibly) (probably not) (but she was going to pretend it really had happened). "Don't worry about us," she told Algernon gaily. "This is our job. We'll be perfectly safe."

"You'd better be!" the young accountant answered. "It will cost a bloody fortune to transport your bodies back to Oxford!"

"Let's go," Gabriel said. Then, without further word, he broke into a run.

"See you later!" Elodie said, waving to the others. And while they stared open-mouthed, she sprinted away from them, following Gabriel right off the edge of the hill into a silver-veined sky.

CHAPTER ELEVEN

A thaumaturgic geographer needs to be skilled
in mathematics, analytics, and running like hell.
Blazing Trails, W.H. Jackson

WHEN ELODIE WAS a child, she considered geography the most boring subject ever known to humankind. Traipsing endlessly around the countryside with her parents, dependent on the kindness of their various assistants to compensate for a lack of other children's company, she'd sought entertainment in the splendors of nature, spending hours lying in the long grass dreaming as tiny winged insects flittered like sparks of wonder above her . . . rummaging through forest shadows . . . gathering wildflowers that she wove into crowns and necklaces more beautiful than jewels. But whenever the adults in her life looked up from their work and belatedly remembered her, they turned the grass-scented dreams into lessons on soil characteristics, tore the flowers apart to explain their components, and reduced nature's magic to a series of numbers, charts, and long, somber conversations at dinner parties while she struggled to stay awake. For the first ten years of her life, geography equaled tedium.

And then they taught her how to fly.

———

THE GLEAMING RAY of thaumaturgic power streaming out from the monolith on the hilltop to the field below sang beneath Elodie's feet as she raced along it, high above the meadows, angling steadily toward the ground. It was the sound of energy and wind and joy. It was exultant magic chiming with her every step. She had learned as a girl how to assess the intensity of these kinds of thaumaturgic beams, to calculate their density, and to make a sensible judgment as to whether they were safe enough, despite their bright translucence, to support her weight. The math went on inside her brain, effortlessly rapid, even as she ran right off the edge of the hill. But her spirit, empty of all good sense, just soared.

Air whooshed against her and she flung out her arms, palms facing forward to scoop the cool sweep of it, hair flying behind her, skirt billowing. The land blurred like a dream of green and gold. She closed her eyes, and life hollowed out to pure freedom, flashing with light through her inner darkness. Her heart seemed to expand as if it would become a new sun for the ensorcelled sky. Any moment, she might misstep and tumble to her death, but Elodie couldn't find it in herself to fear. More than magic, she felt like she was running on sheer passion.

Only some four or five seconds later—barely any time at all, if you think about it, and therefore not *completely* reckless—she opened her eyes once more and saw Gabriel standing already on the ground, facing her with his arms crossed and exasperated frown in its usual place. Elodie could just imagine the safety regulations that were ticking over in his brain. She grinned, waving to him. And although he was too far away to hear, she just knew he responded with a tetchy "hm."

The beam began to angle more steeply, wavering as its energy diminished. The field beneath looked old, rusty with fallen leaves, and extremely solid. Gravity cleared its throat officiously, and Elodie's brain began calling out urgent instructions to be careful, sensible, and to slow her descent.

Woo-hoo! her spirit replied, urging her to go even faster. To outrun gravity. To defy the laws of physics with absolute impudence and hope they didn't notice. After all, she was still alive after years of such behavior, and you couldn't get a more logical argument that that.

(Elodie had read a little philosophy, here and there, but the laws of thought were to her what New Year's resolutions were to other people: *affirmed in all their wisdom and value!* then instantly forgotten.)

Gabriel stood awaiting her with an expression so intense, Elodie suspected her every step was being assessed toward a final grade. *Not* literally *final, I hope,* her brain muttered. She laughed.

And the path dissolved.

As AN EXPERT scientist, Gabriel held one thing as certain: there was always something new to learn. New techniques, new theories . . . and new levels of utter, breathtaking terror. As he watched Elodie run along the disintegrating ray of magic *with her eyes closed*, Gabriel experienced an entire bachelor's degree course in fear.

By which he meant "fear about the time-consuming

accident report he'd have to make should she fall," that is, nothing more.

His body burned with an overwhelming instinct to run back up along the magic and catch her, hold her safe in his embrace (and lecture her stridently on the importance of prudence), but that was impossible. He could not reach her. He could only watch, arms crossed tightly against the pain of his thundering heartbeat, brain roaring its helplessness.

At last, ~~seconds~~ eons later, she opened her eyes, thank God. Then the confounded woman grinned, and actually waved, as if she hadn't just done something so reckless, so heedless, so *bloody stupid* that every cell in Gabriel's body, and every atom in the world around him, felt like it was going to shatter from the sheer force of the danger. And if it did, that would be fine. He couldn't exist if she fell from that magic and died. He couldn't bear to even begin imagining a world without her.

The breath staggered loudly in his throat—it sounded like *hm*, brusque and sharp, even while the hysterical shouting in his brain began to calm. Elodie was drawing closer to the ground now, closer to safety.

Then, all at once, between one step and another, the thaumaturgic beam disintegrated beneath her, three feet off the ground. Gabriel's heart stopped. But Elodie went on moving with her own irrepressible womanly magic, tipping over in an effortless cartwheel. Flowers shed from her moon-colored hair. Lace flashed like a provocative wink from beneath her skirt. She landed upright, her boots making a thud on the earth that was echoed by his heart jolting back into rhythm.

"Well, that was fun," she said, smiling with such joyful exhilaration Gabriel knew she was still running on sunlight inside her mind. It almost unbalanced him, sending him to his knees before her, but he held himself rigid with a frown. His pulse, however, was a fluttering wreck.

"You are—"

"Incorrigible," she interrupted blithely. "Irresponsible."

"Unrivaled," he corrected her, then looked away. He thought he heard a tiny storm, as if Elodie had gasped, but nothing could have induced him to look at her, lest he see what his word had done to the expression on her face. And, quite frankly, he rather feared that he might cry, or shout, or offer an extensive explanation as to why running on magic in the sky *with your bloody eyes closed* imperiled the health of people who loved you.

Not loved. Admired. Respected as a colleague.

He scowled at the field in which they found themselves.

The ground was damp, bruised from the week's storms. Fragments of the thaumaturgic beam littered the air like broken rainbows but were fading fast, leaving only a ruin of torn hedges and ripped-up grass in the wake of magic. A lone farmhouse stood some quarter of a mile away, white smoke arising placidly from its chimney. Everything appeared calm, as if the shock of magic had been no worse than a brief, bright gust of wind. The late morning sun burnished tawny leaves and gently spun Elodie's hair to gold, and Gabriel realized he was looking at her yet again.

"Any sign of a thaumaturgic trove?" she asked.

"Not immediately."

"It must be here somewhere." She gazed out at the surrounding countryside, no doubt accumulating romantic adjectives about its trees and mud puddles—and although she didn't bite her lip as was her habit, she did tuck a stray curl behind her ear, which was almost as ~~alluring~~ uninteresting. Gabriel's heart fluttered again, watching her. He began to worry about his blood pressure, and made a private note to decrease his morning intake of coffee—except no, he'd not drunk coffee this morning, had he? *Because he'd been in bed with his blasted wife.*

"Annoying," he grumbled to himself, even as other things within him began fluttering. Elodie heard, and cast him an offended glance, and for a startling moment Gabriel feared he might blush. "I am not referring to you," he said hastily, his brain racing through the tidy stack of its thoughts, tossing them hither and yon, in search of a reasonable explanation. "It's annoying that we're dealing with such a conundrum."

Which was a ridiculous thing to say about two people who loved nothing better than a good conundrum to exercise their mental faculties. Disgusted with himself, Gabriel turned away, shoving a hand through his hair. The field really was very quiet. Eerily quiet. No birds sang, no breeze stirred. It was as if the world held its breath behind a smirk, poised to spring a practical joke upon him.

Then Elodie sighed. It was a sound so ecstatic, Gabriel couldn't prevent himself from looking back at her. She stood with her hands clasped, face tipped up with a rapturous expression, soaking in the eeriness as if it fueled her very soul. Baffled, Gabriel regarded her, his head tilted to one side as if doing so might give him a better perspective on this wayward woman.

Her linked fingers were half-hidden in the sleeves of the scratchy-looking brown cardigan. One fine, rippling strand of hair snagged in her eyelashes. She seemed young, and yet Gabriel couldn't even begin to fathom the strength within her— this woman who threw herself out of hot air balloons and into marriage without a second thought, and held her ground among the fusty old men of the geography school who, despite having accepted her as a student because she was undeniably clever (and because the university's chancellor forced them to), were appalled by the very thought of her as a professor. Had she been a man, they'd have proved welcoming, with much back-slapping and advice about the best pipe tobacco. But for *a woman* to become their equal was deemed insufferable.

In fact, as a member of that same faculty, Gabriel believed Elodie superior to them all. Certainly she possessed far more strength than he did.

Oh, he could lift her off her feet and over his shoulder (*note to self,* his brain interjected: *try to make that happen*), but he could never match the power of her spirit. How did she feel so much emotion all the time and not collapse with exhaustion from it? He himself was still recovering from the brief interlude following their wedding, during which he'd spun from passion to astonishment to delight (upon Elodie making him a truly excellent omelet for breakfast) then shock and pain as it all came to a crashing halt. And that recovery would now take significantly longer, considering in the past two days he'd watched Elodie run pell-mell directly into a magic bomb and race blindly down a magic beam . . . to say nothing of the hug last night, which perhaps had been the most discombobulating of all.

He wanted to hug her now. But that was insane. For one thing, she was wearing the blasted scratchy cardigan again. For another, a man didn't just hug his wife indiscriminately. Especially when she'd made it very clear she was his wife in name only.

But damn it, he wanted to hug her more than he wanted to

breathe. No, that wasn't true. He wanted to *kiss* her. And to undress her, slowly, gently, until he'd absolutely confirmed that no inch of her being was at risk of further peril.

Which was more than insane. It was heartbreaking.

Clearing his throat gruffly, he directed himself back to the safe territory of science. "Atmospheric conditions suggest no ongoing thaumaturgic forces in the immediate zone," he said, squinting at the sky, where no trace of magic lingered against the bland expanse.

"That's true," Elodie answered. "And yet, things feel iffy."

"Iffy," Gabriel repeated with a frown. "Elucidate, please."

She shrugged. "I have a tingle down my spine." Then she grinned at him sidelong. "I know, that's not scientific."

"Hm," he said. "No, it's not. But under the circumstances, one shouldn't discount the subconscious awareness of an expert."

"Good heavens, are you saying I should trust my instincts?" Elodie laughed and nudged him with her elbow. *Nudged him*. With her *elbow*. Everything in him clenched against a sudden bizarre impulse to laugh with . . . what was this feeling? Appreciation? Dyspepsia? Joy?

"My instincts tell me that we have a long day ahead of us," she said. "The source of the magic emissions must be somewhere, although I don't see any significant disturbance of the earth, or blue lights, or an enormous hound of darkness and thaumaturgic fire that chars the ground beneath its claws . . ."

"Such a specific example," Gabriel said dryly. He was trying to repress the disconcerting amusement that had started to grow like colorful weeds in his heretofore neatly trimmed psyche, but Elodie made it difficult when she ~~existed~~ said things like that.

"Um," she replied. She was staring to the northwest, eyes wide, and Gabriel turned to see what had so captivated her.

"Well, that's aggravating," he said.

Across the field crept an immense, hunched figure of mist and fury, a hellhound shaped from hill shadows and old, buried magic. Vicious blue light spiked its back and spat broken fragments like pain-colored stars that blistered the land when they fell. A memory of volcanic fire served as eyes, flashing and roiling with malevolent hunger. There was nothing substantial about it, only feral enchantment and an echo of mythology, but Gabriel knew that, if it caught them, they would be swallowed, bones and soul.

"Run!" he commanded.

And snatching Elodie's hand, he pulled her with him into the haunted wild.

As ELODIE SPRINTED through woodrush and old quaking grass, she felt magic sparking around her ankles, fierce and spiky even through the leather of her tall boots. But it was nothing compared to the magic in her heart. *Gabriel was holding her hand.*

She'd spent most of her life escaping things—parental rules, a provocative husband, enchanted trees. But she'd never before escaped with someone else. Oh, there had been students to guide across treacherous fields while pursued by a boulder, and colleagues whose kisses beside campfires helped her elude melancholic thoughts brought on by too much wine. But no one had taken her hand and run with her, literally or otherwise.

Within seconds, she learned that it was the most incredibly, extraordinarily unhelpful experience.

Gabriel's pace was much longer than hers, and she stumbled repeatedly as she strove to match it. Mud splashed up under her skirt, charring the lace of her drawers with hot, fetid thaumaturgy. At one point she almost fell, and was saved only by Gabriel yanking on her arm, an intervention that rescued her knees from bruises but just about dislocated her shoulder.

"Faster!" he shouted, as if she could somehow extend her legs at will. Elodie tried to point out the unreasonableness of his demand, but her every breath was otherwise engaged.

Jagged rocks thrust violently through the subsoil, sending dirt and shards of sandstone flying. A clump of thistles exploded in green fire, forcing them to swerve or else be impaled by burning prickles.

Then they swerved again, avoiding a sudden mud geyser.

And again, batting at swarms of dead leaves that flickered about their faces like ragged brown butterflies.

"The farmhouse!" Gabriel called out, and they angled toward it. Groundwater began to rise all around them, a muddy, backward kind of rain that rapidly twisted into high, thin columns spun by furious magic. Elodie counted three—*five* waterspouts that screeched with witchlike fury as they began plowing through the field, churning up grass, dirt, and flaming stones. Water blasted the air. The hellhound was instantly shredded, black, jagged remnants of its magic slicing through the air like knives.

Elodie could barely see anything, her eyes full of grime and strands of hair. She could hear only the screaming of agonized wind. Gabriel's hand was her center of gravity, and she clung to it desperately as they ducked and dodged a way through the maelstrom. Survival seemed an impossible hope, violently ripped apart and slapped in their faces.

Then the farmhouse appeared out of the turmoiled shadows before them, solid as—well, not as a rock, considering Elodie's experiences of more than one rock turning into a bonfire or a gaggle of fanged geese that chased her, but since she did not presently have the luxury to contrive a better simile, it would have to do. They stumbled up to its door, and Gabriel raised his free hand to knock.

Elodie flung him an incredulous look, then grasped the doorhandle, shoved open the door, and pushed him over the threshold, following immediately behind. A dim impression of a cozy, firelit room barely registered with her senses. She and Gabriel moved against each other while he shut the door again and she bolted it, as if they were one person with double the usual limbs. They pulled across a large wooden box filled with boots and old shoes to serve as a barricade, although that would hardly keep out any force determined to get in. Then, stepping back, they stood side by side, panting with near exhaustion, to stare at the door.

Magic slammed against it, causing the heavy oak to rattle on its hinges. Wind speared through gaps between the wood and its frame, howling, shattering into tiny silver stars. But the door held, and after a minute Elodie and Gabriel exhaled in unison.

"Well, that was—" Elodie began, but she tumbled into an astonished silence as Gabriel turned to grasp her head between his hands. Her pulse, which had just begun to slow, leaped up once more, racing around wildly with no idea of what on earth was happening.

"Are you all right?" he demanded. His voice was rough, as if he'd dragged it behind him through the squall. His eyes were fierce, urgently assessing her mud-streaked face. He appeared enraged by the possibility that she might be injured.

"I'm fine," Elodie lied. In fact, she felt completely wrung out by a force more intense than that which raged beyond the door: her hopeless, unrequited love for this man. The thought that he'd been in peril, that he might have died, made her distraught. She ran her hands across his chest, his arms, checking him for injury, even while he did the same to her. His fingers stroking her face slid through mud and filthy water and, ugh, something slimy that she suspected was part of a worm. But Gabriel, the world's most fastidious man, did not even flinch. As he grew sure she was unharmed, his breathing slowed, but still something shook through it, something that almost seemed to Elodie like fear.

"I'm fine," she reiterated. "Just a little damp. Are you—"

"Fine," he said brusquely.

Their gazes locked. The building might have smashed apart with magical tornadic winds in that moment and neither of them would have noticed. Their entire world had compressed into the small, desperate space between them, its atmosphere a storm of adrenaline and longing and years of unspoken love.

"You—" Elodie began.

"You—" Gabriel said, his voice layering over hers.

And then, suddenly, they were kissing.

Chapter Twelve

Sometimes place is a feeling.
Blazing Trails, W.H. Jackson

I F THERE EVER was a kiss that stopped time, this was it. They stood in a cottage deep inside the storm-wrecked Welsh countryside, lips meeting with desperate passion . . . they stood inside a small Oxford chapel, sealing their marital vows with unrequired tenderness . . . and the year between those moments seemed like a shadow adding depth to their ardor.

Gabriel's hand slid down to cup the back of Elodie's neck as he intensified the kiss, and she twined her arms around his neck, drawing him closer. He tasted of water and dirt and perfection. He warmed her so thoroughly, the icy bitterness of magic shed from her skin. She felt transported by desire—and yet she also felt like she'd always been here with him, kissing him. Gabriel was as much part of her existence as were skies and trees and apology letters to her head of department. She knew him the way she knew the shapes of the continents. His kiss was home.

All her longing dissolved into a bright haze of love. She lifted herself on tiptoes, and he wrapped an arm around her waist, everything hardening and softening, aching and easing with relief. For less than half a second, Gabriel pulled away an inch to change his angle, and Elodie thought her heart might break. Then they met again with even greater fervor, lips heating, tongues . . .

"*Oy!*"

They jumped apart. Belatedly, and now rather urgently, Elodie took in the room. It was charming in a rustic kind of way, with a spinning wheel in one corner, a table laden with food at its center, and most noteworthy of all, a man walking through the doorway at the far side of the room with a bowl of peas in his hands and stunned amazement gripping his face. Behind him came a woman carrying a toddler propped on her hip, and behind her a little boy who was craning to see.

Elodie blushed as red as a poinsettia flower at Christmas, although with significantly less festive cheer. "Uh, hello there," she said, waving awkwardly.

The family made no reply, but she could see trespass notices and rifle barrels in the man's eyes. Clearly, immediate reassurance was needed.

"We're from the British government," she told them with a smile.

Crash. The bowl of peas shattered as it fell to the floor.

Gabriel winced. "Perhaps not the best thing to say after barging into a Welshman's home," he murmured.

Indeed, said Welshman clenched his hands as if more than a bowl was about to be shattered.

"What should we do now?" Elodie asked Gabriel out of the corner of her smile. But before he might respond, the man took an abrupt step forward, clay shards crunching beneath his boots.

"What are you doing here? Apart from canoodling, that is."

Canoodling! Elodie's sensibilities bristled at having her romantic moment with Gabriel described thus.

Gabriel, however, was untroubled. "Good afternoon, sir," he said with such dignity that everyone in the room stood a little straighter. "I'm Dr. Tarrant, a geographer from Oxford University. And this is Dr. Tarrant. Er, also."

"We're married," Elodie contributed, holding up her hand to display its wedding ring.

"Mama," said the little boy in the kind of sweetly innocent voice that sends a shiver of fear up the spines of adults everywhere, "why were the funny people hugging with their faces?"

Elodie's blush grew so hot she was in some danger of setting the house alight. "Well, you see," she said, "when two consenting adults—"

"We apologize for intruding so precipitously," Gabriel interrupted. "The squall forced us to seek urgent shelter."

"*Pfft.*" The man sneered. "You're scared of a little rain? *Saeson!*"

Sensing that the time for dignity had not only come and gone but was now catching a ship for foreign parts with no intention of ever returning, Elodie stepped forward, broadening her smile and replicating the doe-eyed look that had got her out of trouble as a ~~grown-up university professor just last week~~ child.

"We are *so terribly* sorry for not knocking," she said. "We will of course pay to have the bowl replaced. In fact, we'll buy you a bigger bowl. A much prettier one. And please, allow me to clean up those peas for you before they stain your rug even worse . . ."

———

PLODDING ACROSS THE field some ten minutes later, Elodie tried to puzzle out how things had gone so wrong. At least the thaumaturgic emanations had subsided, which meant that eviction from the farmhouse at the tip of a red-hot poker didn't result in being killed by ferocious magical tornadoes. And hiking through waterlogged fields back to Dôlylleuad was going to provide healthful excellent exercise. Furthermore, the breeze now sweeping across the land wasn't *entirely* freezing, offering some hope that she wouldn't perish from hypothermia in her sodden clothes. Really, when one considered the whole picture, it could not be called such a bad morning at all. Elodie did like to think positively.

Beside her, Gabriel kept his gaze fixed ahead as he squelched through the muddy grass. Everything about him communicated *bad, bad, bloody terrible morning*. His expression was like a rock that had been encased in ice then set in a wintry tundra at midnight (and even that description veered a little warmer than was accurate). His silence roared in saturnine tones. Elodie felt fairly certain "positive thoughts" had dipped one toe into his brain and been instantly destroyed by frostbite.

Biting her lip, she glanced at him through a wet tangle of hair. Although his gaze did not shift, he clearly sensed her attention, for the temperature surrounding them dropped another degree. Elodie noted rather resentfully that, although he was as soaked through as she, it only served to make his hair smoother and his skin gleaming.

"I'm sorry," she ventured.

Gabriel did not respond. The man was a sod. Fabulous kisser, but still an utter, arrogant sod.

"However," she added heatedly (although alas, not literally) "it's not my fault they were so inhospitable."

After all, she could not be blamed for offending the farmers with her comment about the bowl. And the rug. And the quaintness of their decor, which had been *meant* as a compliment. Exhaustion had knocked her senses askew, therefore absolving her of responsibility.

And she couldn't be blamed for slipping on the spilled peas. That was an accident, as was her consequent stumbling against the food-laden table.

Therefore, according to logic, she *also* wasn't responsible for a jug of milk tipping over when the table jolted.

Although maybe, just maybe, it was her fault that, upon removing her cardigan with all the haste of mortification and using it to blot up the milk, she dripped muddy water on the food.

"I'm sorry," she said again, rather more contritely this time. A blush tried to stir, but without success, for she'd been forced to leave her cardigan in the middle of the table due to their hasty departure, and her cotton shirtwaist felt like an icy shroud clinging to her skin.

Gabriel's eyelashes flickered.

"I'm entirely to blame," she added.

His jaw twitched.

"Really, I should beg forgiveness, on my knees no less, and offer a penance of—"

"It's not your fault," he interjected gruffly. "I also am partly responsible. But we needn't dwell on the matter; it was, after all, merely a physical response to the danger we'd just been through. Nervous overexcitement, nothing more."

Elodie blinked in confusion. Then her stomach flipped as she comprehended what he was talking about.

The kiss.

The kiss.

It absolutely deserved sparkling italics. Such a kiss! Not even the memory of those they had shared on their wedding night could compare. The sweet, tentative explorations that had sparked two days of delight, then burnished her dreams for a year afterward, now seemed tepid in comparison. Certainly her earlier experiences with other people were instantaneously nullified.

As for the future, all her ambitions had shifted. Being published in *The Journal of Thaumaturgic Sciences* now became "being published in *The Journal of Thaumaturgic Sciences* and kissing Gabriel again." Exploring the Pennine Alps was now "exploring the Pennine Alps while kissing Gabriel" (although perhaps a warm beach somewhere would be a better goal, since it would necessitate fewer clothes on his body). She'd even go so far as wanting to marry him, had she not already done so.

"Nervous overexcitement," she echoed musingly. Then, shrugging her mouth, she nodded. "Sounds rational." *And also entirely wrong.* But Elodie understood that, in this matter, patience must be her compass. Granted, she may ultimately take that patience to her deathbed, considering the man hated her, but she was willing to do that. For there had been no one else in her heart even before Gabriel married her, and she now knew for certain that there never would be.

Not that she could tell him this, good God no. Throwing herself out of hot air balloons was one thing; confessing her love to her husband another entirely.

"In fact, I was apologizing for my behavior *after* the—uh, the physical response to danger," she said. "The farmers were right to evict me. I made a mess of things, as usual."

She laughed, because she'd meant the words to be light, and hugged herself, because of the cold of course, and stared at the wan sky until her eyes hurt because what she'd said had touched more on the secret hollows of her psyche than she'd intended. *Pull yourself together, Elodie Hughes,* she grumbled, or her mother did (sometimes it was hard to tell the difference between those two inner voices). She had never liked journeying into the depths of herself even on a good day—a day when, for example, her hair was tidy and she hadn't almost been killed by enchanted twisters—and had no desire for it now. She felt Gabriel's gaze upon her, silently contemplative, and she lifted her chin with a pride that shuddered somewhat as her teeth chattered together.

"Come here," he said suddenly. Elodie did not even have time to comprehend the instruction before he stepped into her path, requiring her to make an abrupt halt. And then—*and then!*—he gently gathered her into his arms.

Even while Elodie was blinking with confused astonishment, he wrapped his coat around her—most pertinently, with him still inside it. True, he held her with patent awkwardness, and yet it must be stressed, *he held her.* Indeed, one might even classify it as an embrace.

That was the last rational thought Elodie managed before her mind was buried beneath an avalanche of emotions. She could do no more than stand there, embraced, her arms hanging, her eyes wide as they stared over Gabriel's shoulder at the gossamer haze of light.

"I am employing emergency first aid," he explained, his voice thrumming through her bones. "You're freezing, and I do not wish to endure a lecture from Mr. Jennings about the cost of your funeral should you die of hypothermia."

"Okay." Hypothermia was no longer a risk; indeed, she had grown so hot in the span of mere seconds that she was surprised steam did not arise from her body.

"This is not a hug."

"Understood."

"It is first aid."

"Yes, so you said. I really am sorry about what happened. If it helps, I am trying to change."

"Change what?" Gabriel asked in a confused tone.

Elodie's stomach tried to curl up into itself bashfully. "Myself, of course."

Gabriel clutched her shoulders and pushed her back a little so he could frown at her. "Don't you dare."

Elodie blinked, astonished at such a fierce response. "No, no, I do appreciate that I'm absent-minded and lacking just a little in dignity—"

"So?"

"Um . . ." She hadn't expected such a question from Gabriel, of all people, and found herself falling into honesty. "It's stopping me from getting what I want." After all, a man as distinguished as Gabriel could never love such an oddball—which of course was just as well, since she hated him (. . . didn't she? It was getting harder to remember that). And she actually rather liked herself, when she wasn't dripping dirty water on food and accidentally proposing to people, a fact that did tend to make self-improvement a long and slow process.

"If you have to change yourself to get something, then it's not the right thing for you," Gabriel said tetchily, and pulled her back into his embrace. "Never apologize for who you are." His tone became businesslike, even as he snuggled her closer. "Diversity is as important in humankind as it is in nature. We each have something unique to offer our community. In your case—"

"Chaos," she supplied, and smiled even though he could not see it.

"Vivacity," he countered sternly.

Oh. Elodie's heart gasped. *Vivacity.* That was a word a woman could enjoy for quite some time before overthinking it to the degree of deciding it was an insult.

"As for you offending those people with your apologies and generous attempt to help," Gabriel continued, "that wasn't why they denied us shelter. It was because you mentioned that we're from the British government. I suspect they're smugglers."

"Really?"

"Yes. They had a bowl of strawberries on the table, despite it being autumn."

"Strawberry smugglers," Elodie said, managing not to laugh.

"Yes."

It was the most ridiculous thing she'd heard, and the fact Professor Tyrant, advocate for absolute truth, was clearly just saying it to protect her from self-castigation, made everything inside her grow so warm she felt like she was melting. She could not prevent herself from tipping her head to rest its cheek against his shoulder.

"Do you think it's going to be a disaster?" she asked quietly.

A few uncertain seconds passed before he replied. "Not necessarily. We just have to be mindful of the situation's complexities."

"Thoughtful."

"Yes."

She lifted her arms and set them hesitantly around him. He

cupped one of his own hands against her head, employing the other to stroke her back. Thus the wrecked, boggy field was transformed into paradise.

They stood together for what felt to be hours (and yet not nearly long enough) while the sweet, timid quiet slowly deepened to something richer, more robust, like coffee that had been allowed to steep. Elodie was inclined never to let go. Now that the initial shock of his embrace had eased, Gabriel began to feel like solid ground, untroubled by weeds and impervious to enchantment. Standing within his embrace wasn't quite a feeling of safety, for she was too shy and too aware of his potent masculinity; half her senses clamored for more kisses, whereas the other half wanted to do what she always did and run away. So not a comfort—but certainly a delicious unease.

"We should get moving," she said finally, with a reluctance she could not quite hide. "We need to find the source of the disturbances before someone is hurt or worse."

"Agreed," Gabriel answered.

No moving occurred, however, other than him tilting his head to rest it against hers, and her pressing her lips to the strong plane of his shoulder (not kissing; merely a placement of the mouth), and much leaping and trembling of pulses.

"Oh my stars and garters!"

Elodie jolted, supposing that she'd shouted her feelings aloud. But in fact it was a woman emerging from behind a high hedgerow nearby, leading a group of some half a dozen people. They presented what Elodie could only describe as a catastrophe of colors. Orange, purple, green, and red jumbled together—and that was just on the first woman's dress. The entire group was similarly attired.

"Look, Bobby!" the woman shouted. "It's fixin' to be a real firecracker show!"

Elodie and Gabriel hurtled apart. The woman, however, was pointing beyond them. Glancing around, they discovered that, while they'd been hugging and dreaming like a pair of undergraduate coeds, magic had been creeping up on them. Several small ignes fatui hovered over the boggy ground some fifteen feet away, looking remarkably malevolent for mere balls of light.

"Ain't no need to yell like a cat making kittens, Roberta!" a man shouted back. "I'm standin' right here!"

Elodie and Gabriel shared a grim look. *"Americans,"* they muttered.

"Stand back, please!" Elodie called out, gesturing for the group to retreat from the ignes fatui. They did not move, except to lift binoculars that they trained on the magic—at least the men did. Elodie noted most of the women seemed to have focused on Gabriel's forearms. Frowning, she strode toward them with sudden, authoritarian vigor. This was a trick she'd seen other professors use to disperse students who wanted to ask questions at the end of a lecture, and it worked: the tourists hastened backward until Elodie had them shepherded out of the ignes fatui's direct path and, as a bonus, no longer ogling her husband quite so overtly.

"Hello!" came a familiar voice. From the midst of the group emerged Tegan Parry, carrying a large picnic basket. "What a surprise, seeing you here!" she exclaimed. "I thought you were going to the old mine this morning. I guess geographers really know how to cover ground."

She turned to the group of tourists. "Everyone, everyone, we have an extra-special treat for you today! These people are famous scientists who have traveled all the way from Oxford University to study the enchantments of our picturesque village. Exclusive to guests of the Queen Mab, and for only a penny each, they'll be happy to answer your questions about magic."

"We will?" Elodie said dazedly.

"We're not famous," Gabriel grumbled.

"Well . . ." Elodie shrugged. "I'm a little famous."

He raised an eyebrow. "You are?"

"Yes. In Kent."

His other eyebrow joined the first. "You're famous. In Kent. For what professional achievement?"

"Oh well, not anything *professional*, exactly. I'm famous for . . ." She murmured something, and Gabriel leaned toward her.

"I beg your pardon?"

"For walking along the roof ridge of Canterbury Cathedral."

Gabriel stared as if he didn't know whether to laugh or shake her. She stared back defiantly. His face was gold and blue-spangled in the magical sunlight, and his lips looked like they had been kissed and needed to be again. Elodie felt her own lips parting . . .

"Ahem."

They turned their heads to see Tegan and the tourists watching them in fascination.

"I have a question!" A young woman thrust her arm into the air, and from her expression it was clear the inquiry would involve not geographical but biological science.

"Just hold your potato, Sue-Ann," a man shouted, despite there being no evidence of Sue-Ann possessing any root vegetable whatsoever. "I have a more important one. Should that blue light be spinning quite so fast?"

BOOM!

A hot wind blasted through the group. Elodie and Gabriel ducked immediately, throwing their arms around their heads. The atmosphere flashed silver, then faded to a quiet, shaken pallor. Straightening, Elodie and Gabriel turned to each other. She touched his face, he touched hers, ostensibly assessing for injury, although rather more stroking and yearnful gazing went on than was medically necessary—then they snatched their hands back as if burned by the realization of what they were doing.

"Are you hurt?" they asked, words tangling.

"I'm fine," they answered.

"Mmuuhhhhh."

The low, mournful sound had them looking around belatedly at the group. "Oh dear," Elodie said.

Tegan was standing open-mouthed with stunned horror among a half dozen orange and yellow cows that had, a few seconds before, been American tourists.

"This is terrible!" the girl wailed.

"Don't worry," Elodie assured her. "Ignis fatuus energy tends to be short-lived. In about an hour or so they'll transform back into people, with no lingering harm other than an inclination toward vegetarianism."

"They're Texans!"

"Oh dear," Elodie repeated, wincing.

"Allow me to offer you a solution," Gabriel interjected.

Tegan nodded eagerly.

He gestured to her picnic hamper. "If you give us some of the food, it won't go to waste."

Tegan gaped at him incredulously, but Gabriel, unrepentant, just displayed the unblinking calm of a man who has seen countless magical transformations during his career and no longer considers it a reason to go without lunch.

"Try to herd them back to the village," Elodie advised while Tegan handed over sandwiches and tea cakes. "Or at least get them onto more solid ground. Magic is leaking up through the groundwater here to enchant the atmosphere."

"It's only been pretty lights so far," Tegan said with a touch of accusation in her voice, as if the geographers themselves had caused an escalation of the danger.

"Pretty lights are hazardous in themselves," Gabriel told her severely. "You people have been playing with fire. Literally."

"Oh." Tegan's voice was small but her eyes grew huge as she looked around her, as if taking even one step might transform her into some variety of farm animal.

"Don't worry," Elodie told her, smiling with warm reassurance. "Just go carefully, stay alert, and you'll be fine. Probably. Almost certainly."

The girl did not seem too encouraged by this. "Can't you help me herd the tourists back home?" she asked.

"No, we have important work to do," Gabriel said. "This chaos is being triggered by something. We need to find the source before it sends the whole fey line into cascade."

"'Cascade' sounds pleasant?" Tegan ventured.

Gabriel frowned. "A line cascade means thousands of people being transformed into cows or worse. Not. Pleasant."

"Come on, Professor Tarrant," Elodie said, tugging on his arm before he terrified the girl even further. "Let's go find our magic."

Chapter Thirteen

A map is a translation of what we see,
evidence of what we consider valuable,
and a handy place mat if we need one.
Blazing Trails, W.H. Jackson

Y OU'RE LOOKING IN the wrong place."

Gabriel forced himself not to sigh. Again. "On the contrary, I am following the fey line exactly." He held up his thaumaturgic compass as proof.

Elodie dismissed this with a wave of her dowsing rod. "'Exactly' doesn't count in geography."

"What? Of course it does!"

"You have to feel the ambience."

Gabriel regarded her with stiff irritation. They'd been out here for five hours now, feeling the ambience, measuring the ambience, and traipsing through so many mud puddles in the goddamned ambience that his boots were completely ruined. He'd have called it a wild-goose chase (to be more precise, he'd have called it *a profitless errand*, except Elodie's devil-may-care attitude toward language seemed to be invading his brain), but damned if he knew what else to do at this point other than wander around frowning at things.

It didn't help that, despite him being as fit as any field

geographer needed to be, the day's escapades had left him bone-tired. Only thanks to the energy provided by Tegan Parry's sandwiches (and a good ration of stubbornness) had he not given up an hour ago, retiring to the inn and its bathing facilities.

Elodie, on the other hand, was possessed of an enthusiasm that seemed indefatigable. She'd thrown herself into the work, quite literally in the case of a weed-filled ditch she'd sworn had been twinkling suspiciously. Her skirt hem was filthy, torn flower petals littered her hair, and there existed beneath her fingernails enough dirt to harbor a dozen germ colonies. She was, in short, a perambulating biological weapon—and simultaneously the most beautiful creature Gabriel had ever seen. The lowering sun infused her hair with glory and flashed against the silver of her dowsing rod, making it seem like she'd stepped out of a fairy tale. Gabriel's irritation grew so stiff he had to think with some urgency of cold tea to bring himself under control once again.

"Are you paying attention?" Elodie demanded, tapping the dowsing rod against her thigh impatiently. Her lovely, curvaceous thigh that felt like silk beneath a man's palm. Not even the passage of a year could erase his memory of caressing it, and of gently hooking it over his own thigh . . .

"Uh-huh," he managed to answer.

"Then what did I just say?"

Something about kissing? his brain suggested. Something about laying her down in the soft white clover and using his lips to map every delectable contour of her body? That seemed unlikely. She had displayed no inclination to further their earlier intimacy. Indeed, her lower lip was ragged from where she'd been biting it, her gaze kept flicking to him then away, and she carried with her an uncharacteristic quiet tension—all of which informed Gabriel plainly about her dislike of him. At one point their hands accidentally brushed together as they navigated a narrow space between two trees, and Elodie's breath had shuddered audibly, her face shining red. Dislike. There could be no stronger proof of it.

Thankfully, he disliked her too. He only thought about kissing her because even such an excellent mind as his fell prey now and again to the baser qualities of manhood. As soon as they returned to Oxford, he could once more take up the austere mental discipline that was his comfort and stay.

"I was too occupied with examining the ambience to hear every word you said," he answered with a fine show of disdain.

Elodie flung out her arms, and he stepped back with mild alarm. But her face was doing that lighting-up thing it did whenever she was about to say something whimsical or heartfelt (or probably both), and Gabriel prepared himself for an onslaught of colloquialism.

"The magic is everywhere," she said, turning from side to side to indicate the fields and copses surrounding them.

Whimsical, indeed. "More poetry," Gabriel muttered.

"*Tsk.*" Elodie shook her head, as if he were a first-year student who'd failed to comprehend the simple fact that heterogeneous colluvium incorporating disaggregated thaumaturgized paleosols is a telestic hazard resulting from downslope creep. "I'm talking science. So far today we've encountered thaumaturgic manifestations, waterspouts, ignes fatui, and there was that exploding puddle a mile back. But it doesn't all align to the fey line, and the dispersion patterns don't immediately suggest a point of origin. This is all just ricocheting spillage."

She gestured indiscriminately, but there was no real need

for greater precision. She was right; everywhere Gabriel looked, he saw magic. The horizon, a darkening blue behind the swollen shadows of hills, was strung with fey lights. Rainbows floated between trees. His wife brushed a luminous strand of hair away from her cheek. Three quarters of a mile west, where Dôlylleuad nestled beside the slow curve of the river, plumes of chimney smoke became dandelion fluff that drifted like a thousand wishes.

Without the gauges of his weather station, it was impossible for Gabriel to judge the environment in any quantifiable way unless he resorted to adjectives that he was unprepared to entertain. But he did suppose it might be called "magical" without risking accusations of lyricism. Before he could say so, however, Elodie jabbed her dowsing rod at him, as if she were in a lecture theater and he her student.

"The fact we've failed to locate the originating source is very worrisome, considering how much magic is afoot. I really expected to arrive at Dôlylleuad and be met by a single trove venting thaumaturgic energy, rather than all this mess. The only thing I can conclude is that pressure is building in the unmapped deposit, wherever it is. The leakage through geographical vulnerabilities, such as the village graveyard and these sodden fields, is strong enough to cause all this intense spillage. I worry it could explode at any moment."

"I agree," Gabriel said. "The source lode must be immense." He paused, his thoughts sparking with theories and concerns. "It might even contain platinum."

"Or it may have absorbed the energy of the original trove beneath the mine site," Elodie said, "which would explain why that was completely drained."

Considering this, Gabriel shrugged his mouth then nodded. "That's a reasonable hypothesis."

"Vampire minerals!" She grinned, and Gabriel had all he could do not to grin in response. It sent alarm bells through him, for he was not a grinning man. He was a man who considered amusement a precursor to anarchy, and the fact that he'd been close to it all day suggested an imminent and catastrophic failure of dignity. Why, the last time he'd smiled had been—

Abruptly the thought was slammed into silence by a vanguard of self-restraint. His countenance hardened, and his heart followed suit. Safe again, Gabriel exhaled quietly in relief.

Alas, however, his breath trembled just a little, sigh-like, and emotions took this encouragement to rush in again . . .

Elodie, unaware of his internal struggle, continued to smile and shine and generally light up the world with her presence. "Mark my words," she said, "we're dealing with something even stronger than level five. When it does erupt, it could trigger the fey line into cascade."

"Hm," he said.

She huffed a little. "Might you perhaps expatiate further than one syllable?"

"I'm thinking." And it was true. He thought about her luxuriant beauty. He thought about the softness of her lips, and about how glorious it had been to taste the magic on them. He thought as well about what a bloody fool he'd been to do so. A disaster zone was not an appropriate place to reacquaint oneself with the charms of one's wife. He should be focusing instead on the far more deadly charms of ensorcelled meadows and potentially explosive rocks.

It was just that every time he tried to do so, all he saw was Elodie standing in the sunlight, with her wild fair hair and stormy eyes flashing with magic.

Gabriel was at a loss to understand what was happening to him. Many, many times he'd escaped life-threatening thaumaturgic squalls in the company of associates and felt no subsequent desire to kiss them (perhaps because the majority possessed greasy mustaches and an odor of pipe smoke). But he'd been physically unable to stop himself from kissing Elodie, despite how wet and filthy they'd both been. Had he studied biology, he'd have been able to reason through this situation in cool, scientific terms. As it was, the only explanation he could generate was *idiocy*.

"We should return to Dôlylleuad to consult a topographical map," Elodie said, clearly having given up on waiting for his reply. It was sensible advice, and in fact what he himself would have suggested were he in better control of his brain right now. Back at the Queen Mab, they could not only chart the morning's experiences and run theoreticals, but also change out of their filthy clothes. Gabriel envisioned it: a crisp map, a shining protractor, and Elodie undressing, cotton and candlelight drifting over her bare skin, revealing curves that both softened and hardened a man, making him want to . . . *To listen to the woman now as she spoke*, he interrupted himself sternly. She was talking about potentially evacuating Dôlylleuad. Her voice was like velvet soaked in honey. He might lick it from her tongue . . .

Ahem, he interrupted himself again, and adjusted the iron and gold hook around his ear, since obviously magic was messing with his mind.

"And I want to telegraph the Home Office," Elodie continued. "I doubt Professor Jackson remembered to do so, and we really are going to need a bigger team here."

She sighed at the thought. Gabriel couldn't discern why, and he wondered whether he'd done something to cause it.

"I agree," he ventured, since that seemed the safest response.

Elodie nodded. Then she wrapped her arms around herself, gazing over his shoulder at the magical light show (*the profusion of aeriform thaumaturgic materialization,* thank you very much, his intelligence corrected him indignantly). It washed her over with rainbows and gleaming blue-green shadows, and Gabriel would have sworn she was more lovely than any enchanted sky could ever be. If only he might kiss her even one more time in his life . . .

Then again, he was no doubt confusing a desire for dinner with desire for his wife, and a good serving of steak and potatoes would soon cure him of this undignified romantic nonsense.

"Let's get going," he said gruffly, rubbing a thumb knuckle against his forehead. He needed to get back on track, walk a straight line, and perform other cartographical metaphors that would stabilize his thinking.

They began trekking toward the distant village. "Do you think the tourists will have transformed back by now?" Elodie asked.

"Impossible to say," Gabriel answered disinterestedly.

"Perhaps they'll take it as a lesson. Too many people treat the environment as property . . . a resource . . . entertainment, rather than a community to which we all belong. I don't wish to criticize the villagers—"

"I'm entirely comfortable criticizing them," Gabriel interposed. "They're money hungry."

"Or just hungry," she suggested.

"The mice in this field were hungry too, no doubt, until the moment thaumaturgic energy smashed through them."

Elodie winced. "True. And without those mice to scatter seeds, make tunnels that aerate the soil, and so on, the environment that people want to give them crops and orchards wouldn't be so healthy. It's all a magic web with colors gay."

"Poetry," Gabriel muttered, managing to fit an entire critique of the genre into three syllables.

"It's that too," she answered, then grinned at him. Why did she insist on doing that so often? Was she deliberately trying to set him off-balance? If he kissed her, would she stop? He should try!

No, he bloody well should not. He should frown at her so she understood he was a tyrant and not to be smiled at like a man adored.

She looked at the frown and her grin widened. *Widened.* "I'm surprised you recognized a Tennyson reference," she said.

"Yes, well, I've heard excerpts from 'The Lady of Shalott' recited in moony tones by a certain geographer for years now, during faculty meanings and in library corners where people are *supposed* to be silent. It's inevitable I would recognize its mumbo jumbo."

"Mumbo jumbo!" she sputtered. The grin vanished, thank goodness. If he kissed her, would she bring it back? If he told her that he'd bought a volume of Tennyson's collected works just so he could read that poem late at night and let it bore him to sleep, would she stop hating him? "You can't call great poetry *mumbo jumbo*," she said.

"You call undulating fey lines *wiggles*," he retorted.

"That is a perfectly reasonable synonym."

"And 'The Lady of Shalott' is a perfectly ridiculous rhyme."

"Rhyme!" Now she closed her mouth so firmly, a muscle in her jaw leaped.

They trudged on, side by side, shadows weaving together, furious silence between them. A few minutes later, however, Elodie asked with a timbre that managed to be both huffy and conciliatory, "Did you know that field mice sing to each other?"

"Yes," Gabriel said.

They glanced at each other. Elodie smiled tentatively. Gabriel gave her a clipped nod in lieu of the highfalutin poetry his wrecked and aching brain was urging him to express instead. And for one beautiful moment, magic flittered between them.

Literally . . .

"Ooh, look!" Elodie said, reaching for the star-colored thread of thaumaturgy.

Boom!

THE HORIZON REALLY was beautiful, Elodie thought as she gazed at it. Blush-colored and soft and far, far away. If only she were in it. Or back at the Queen Mab. Or even better, in her own Oxford home, hiding under the bed. Anywhere, dear God, except sitting here in the damp grass, watching Gabriel examine her bare foot. All that kept her from dying on the spot from mortification was that she'd got a professional pedicure before coming on this assignment. (It hadn't take much intuition to prepare just in case she got tossed hither and yon by magical explosions and thus injured her ankle, considering how often that befell her.)

Gabriel looked like a knight errant on one knee before her,

sober-faced, illuminated with late golden light; but the impression was spoiled by the way he *tsk-tsk*ed. Elodie was sure Lancelot had never clicked his tongue at Guinevere. Then again, Guinevere no doubt never had to surreptitiously pull a leaf from her hair while a handsome man tended to her injury.

"You need someone going around behind you at all times with a safety manual and first aid kit," Gabriel grumbled as he carefully moved the foot to ensure she'd not broken her ankle.

"It wasn't my fault," Elodie retorted at once, even though it absolutely had been.

"So it was a pure accident that you tried to catch magic with your bare hand—*again, may I add*—causing it to explode and knocking us both to the ground?" He gave her a severe look, but something glinted in it that made Elodie's stomach glint in response.

"Er, parts of that may have been my fault, and other parts accidental." She smiled, and he shook his head a little, and some ten seconds later they both blinked hard and looked away.

"Does it hurt?" he asked.

"Yes," she said, her voice a plaintive breath. It hurt to look at him and to not. It hurt to breathe the air he'd walked through, but hurt worse when he was absent. It hurt so beautifully, she could not bear it, and if only . . .

Wait. He was probably talking about her ankle.

"It aches a little," she confessed. "But I'm sure I can walk on it."

"Hm." Clearly, Gabriel doubted her, but nevertheless took her stocking and slipped it back onto her foot.

"I can do that myself" is what Elodie *should* have said, and indeed would have said, had it been any other man. Instead, she sat in a sweet-glazed silence, watching him unfurl the stocking up her leg. Thank goodness it was sturdy green wool rather than black lace, or she'd have died from internal combustion right then, and Professor Coffingham would get her office, which he'd always coveted.

Once the stocking was in place, Gabriel moved on to replacing the boot. This was safer; no one could take anything erotic from a man placing a dirty old boot on a woman's green-stockinged foot. He pushed it over her heel and proceeded to button it.

His fingers were strong yet nimble as they grasped a small, round button and slipped it through the corresponding hole. A little sensation of completion followed, and Elodie found her muscles tightening as he worked. She realized belatedly that her skirt was rucked up, exposing the lace hem of her drawers, but she could not seem to make herself move to remedy the situation. Then Gabriel began to slide his thumb across each button after fastening it, and all hope of doing anything beyond staring at his hands was lost. She watched, mesmerized, her nerves quivering delightfully.

"I can do it," she managed to say, although she made no real attempt to intervene.

"Hush," Gabriel replied.

By the fifth button, she'd become so taut, and yet so trembly, she felt like she might implode. By the seventh, when Gabriel inserted two fingers between boot and her bare leg to hold the boot's flap steady, she had forsaken breathing altogether. After he had all nine buttons secured at last, he withdrew those fingers, stroking them against her calf as he did so. The tension in Elodie abruptly snapped, setting her nervous system into cascade like a fey line. She closed her eyes, the breath shaking out of her.

"All right?" Gabriel asked.

"All right," Elodie managed to reply. Decidedly quivering, and knowing her face was flushed, she dared to look at him. His face was lowered, hands blotching red as they gripped his knee.

"We should get on," she said. "It will be evening soon."

Gabriel cleared his throat. "I just—in just a moment," he answered, his voice rough.

Elodie regarded him as she would any thorny problem: enchanted rosebush, explosive cactus, arrogant sod of a husband. But his eyes were hidden beneath his lashes, and his shoulders hunched as if he strove to control something wild inside himself. Elodie, being the intelligent and insightful scientist that she was, concluded he was upset by the dirt he'd got on his fingers from her muddy boot. Taking a handkerchief from her skirt pocket, she lifted one of the hands off his knee and began to clean it.

Gabriel jolted as if she'd attacked him with pumice instead of delicate lace and lawn. "You needn't do that," he said, although he did not pull away from her grip.

"Pish tosh," she replied amiably. "Sit still."

The injunction was unnecessary: he was so stiff, even his breath did not seem to stir. Elodie, conversely, now felt like she was turning to hot pudding. Perhaps this had been the "other problem" Motthers had tried to warn her about: the risk that she'd end up sitting alone with her husband in the middle of the enchanted Welsh countryside, caressing his hand minutes after having come apart merely from him putting her boot on her foot. Had she known it would happen, she'd almost certainly have . . . well, undertaken the assignment just the same, but at least first polished her fingernails.

She'd always considered her hands ugly although capable, the fingers too blunt, the nails too often broken during field-work to justify pampering them. Whereas her feet needed care after continually wading through bogs and rivers, her hands were hardy.

But now, as she touched Gabriel's own strong, olive-skinned hands, her fingers seemed delicate, feminine, in a way they never had before. And Elodie was surprised to discover that tending to him made her feel as quivery as when he'd but-toned up her boot, but with an *even deeper* level of satisfaction. Not only her body was aroused, but her heart.

Suddenly Gabriel made a strange, broken sound and yanked his hand from her, simultaneously rising and whirling away. Elodie stared up at him gobsmacked.

"Where the bloody hell is the village?" he demanded, shov-ing a hand through his hair.

Elodie dared not reply at once, or else she risked suggesting a location that was neither physically possible nor dignified. Blast the man and the way he made her spin between love and anger so exhaustingly. Dragging calm from the corners of her brain, she took a deep breath, then pushed herself clumsily to her feet.

"It's there," she said in a clipped tone, pointing east-southeast despite the fact that Gabriel had his back to her and couldn't see the gesture. Dôlylleuad crouched in tree shadows by the riverbank, almost a mile away. It had the quality of a fairy-tale illustration: pretty, quaint, a little blurred through a diaphanous haze of fading sunlight. The sky beyond it was purpling with a promise of night.

"I need wine," Gabriel muttered as he turned, still facing away from her, and began to stomp toward the village. Then he stopped abruptly and glanced over his shoulder. "The ankle."

By which, Elodie supposed, he meant, *How is it?*

"Fine," she said acidly, and took a step.

Pain shot through her foot.

Which is to say, her *other* foot. Looking down, she discovered she'd trodden on a jagged stone. With a hissed curse she looked up again—

And Gabriel was gone.

Chapter Fourteen

Weeds are plants that belong where they grow,
it's just that we don't want them there.
Blazing Trails, W.H. Jackson

WELL THIS IS a fine muddle!" Elodie declared as she turned in a slow circle to confirm that Gabriel had indeed vanished completely from sight.

It is worth noting that her tone was not annoyed but excited, for a muddle was a rare thaumaturgic event—*vanishingly rare, as it were*, she couldn't help but think with a chuckle—and this an exceedingly fine example of one indeed.

Setting her hands on her lips, Elodie blew a wayward strand of hair away from her face as she tried to discern whether it was she or Gabriel who had inadvertently walked into a puddle of magic. Either way, there could be no denying this was her fault. As soon as she'd noted the haze of sunlight, she ought to have appreciated that such a thing was unlikely on a cold autumn afternoon and that instead it was a muddle's perimeter. And she'd almost certainly have done so if only Gabriel hadn't infuriated her so much.

Which, come to think of it, made this situation *his* fault.

"Gabriel!" she called out, an experiment she suspected would fail. Sure enough, only silence replied.

She considered her surroundings calmly. A muddle occurred when an excess of caustic thaumaturgic material in the environment poisoned a small body of water, sending up a bubble of sorcerous energy. On one hand, this provided exciting evidence that the suspected new trove contained a sulfur element, which Elodie had already half suspected due to the intense but off-and-on nature of the magical storm these past two days. Enchanted sulfur tended to be unstable in that way, for reasons Elodie could have explained had she attended more chemistry lectures as a student.

On the other hand, *oops!* To not notice the muddle's membrane was a basic error. If anyone at Oxford saw her now, they'd wonder how she'd ever managed to get her doctorate. The only positive to this situation was that Motthers hadn't joined the assignment. Her various misadventures would not exactly have offered a good teaching opportunity, unless to demonstrate that he ought to take up a safer course of education, such as ornithology.

Maybe I *was his "other problem,"* Elodie thought sourly. Maybe he'd intended to shout out, "Professor, remember that you are an idiot!" And he wouldn't have been wrong. As her mother liked to point out at regular intervals, Elodie possessed the kind of intelligence that overshot normal thinking and landed frequently in the zone of ridiculousness.

"Gabriel!" she called again, a touch more emphatically this time. The result was the same.

"Drat," she muttered. Most likely she was the one trapped, because that was par for the course. And also likely was that her sod of a husband, having realized she was in a muddle, had

headed back to the inn to wait in comfort while she got herself
out of it. After all, the majority of people did manage an escape. They turned up back in their villages with wild tales of
pwcca or some other fairy that had led them astray, such was
their state of dehydration, hypothermia, or exhaustion. But a
few others disappeared forever, swallowed by muddles that
were so strong, not even a specialist in thaumaturgic geography noticed them.

"Damn it, Gabriel!" she shouted, angry, worried. There
came no reply.

"I suppose he's going to grumble at me when next we meet,"
she said as she began scanning the grass for the stone she'd
accidentally stepped on. "It really was the worst day of his life
when he married me. Best day of mine, but there's certainly no
need for me to tell—aha!" Finding the stone, she snatched it
up. Weighing it thoughtfully, she shifted it to a comfortable
angle in her palm. Then, swiveling on her heel, she threw it.

Thwack.

With a hollow sound of impact, the stone vanished abruptly
from sight. "Ooh," Elodie said, enlivened, for the air had rippled as the stone passed through it, allowing her to briefly
glimpse the muddle's perimeter. It had been convex shaped,
which meant she was standing on the *outside*. She was not the
one trapped, after all.

She smirked. Professor Perfect Tarrant had got himself into
a muddle. Ha!

"Ahem." She cleared her throat solemnly, reminding herself
that she was an adult, and it did not do to laugh about a colleague being in trouble, let alone one's own husband. Besides,
it really was quite serious trouble. The fey line's instability
might lead to all kinds of atypical consequences, such as the

muddle collapsing in upon itself while Gabriel was still trapped inside.

At that thought, Elodie's pulse shook. Without further ado (or, alas, further reflection) she leaped forward. Magic flowed around her like sheets of cold, opulent satin. The world shone with a pearlescent gloss for one strange and beautiful second.

And there he was. Standing with his feet apart, arms crossed, eyebrows raised as he looked straight at her.

Whew, she thought with relief . . . even while her heart sighed a wild prayer of thanks . . . and she stumbled a little as she forced herself to stop, rather than to keep running forward and fling her arms around him.

"No," he said conversationally, "my wedding wasn't the worst day of my life. That would be this one."

Oops. (Again.) He'd heard her. Elodie winced, biting her lip.

"Have you come to rescue me?" he asked in the same politely inquiring tone that inspired his students to greatness (or sent them fleeing Oxford in tears).

Elodie shook back her hair, chin angled high in the manner of a plucky heroine who had absolutely given serious thought to entering a muddle and had in no manner whatsoever panicked. "I have."

"Thank you," Gabriel said in that same even tone, which was beginning to make her nerves rattle. "One further question, if I may?"

"Hm?"

"How are you going to do that from *inside* the trap?"

Elodie blinked at him. Forget *oops.* This was an *oh, darn.* There remained to her only one recourse.

Shrugging, she smiled.

———

GABRIEL REGARDED ELODIE steadily in austere silence. He'd spent his whole life studying magic—deconstructing it beneath a microscope—writing papers bristling with footnotes about it—watching its filaments sift through his fingers on a riverbank. In all that time, he'd never seen anything more spellbinding than the sight of his wife leaping through the muddle's perimeter to rescue him.

"You were foolhardy," he told her sternly. (She was sublime. She was a dream come true.)

"Of course I was," she replied, scoffing. "You surely must expect that from me by now."

Gabriel huffed. But it was perilously close to a laugh, so he hastily frowned as well, just to press home the point that he was ~~so in love with her~~ disapproving of what she'd done—not only her heedless jumping into a muddle, but having driven him into it in the first place. For if he'd not been so hot and bothered by her gorgeousness, and by the feel of her bare skin beneath his fingers, he'd have paid better attention to where he was going. Consequently, this was all her fault.

And if only he weren't a pedant about truthfulness, he could have quite happily believed that, instead of knowing all too well that he'd behaved like a libidinous idiot.

"Do you have a plan to effect an escape for us both?" he asked.

"Yes," she replied at once in a tone that said, *Obviously,* but with a shadow in her eyes that said, *Um* . . . She turned, looking around thoughtfully. Then all of a sudden, "Aha!" she declared, her attention fixed on the tiny pond of water that Gabriel had already determined was the source of the muddle (a conclusion reached by the scientific method of accidentally stepping in it).

"No," he said automatically.

Elodie stared at him in indignant surprise. "I haven't suggested anything."

"But you will." He shook his head in anticipatory disapproval. "You'll come up with some mad idea that will almost kill us but ultimately prove a brilliant success."

She grinned so brightly the entire muddle seemed to light up—or perhaps it was just his brain, which organ Gabriel was beginning to accept as a lost cause. "You called me brilliant," she said.

"No," he disagreed, his crossed arms tightening. "Yes. But I also called you mad."

It was hopeless. She looked like she might at any moment take flight. Gabriel considered kissing her, to make her forget what he'd said, but concluded regretfully that this would only make matters worse.

"I do have a brilliant idea, as it happens," she told him as she began to unfasten her skirt.

"What are you doing?" Gabriel demanded warily.

"I'm going to use my skirt to soak up the puddle."

"Bloody hell." He pinched the bridge of his nose. "That's incredibly risky. Besides, you can't walk around in your drawers again. It's too cold."

She hesitated, considering this. "Fair point," she said, and Gabriel breathed with relief as she refastened the skirt. Never mind the temperature—he feared for his dignity if she exposed her underwear like that again. After all, just touching her bare foot had resulted in him bumbling headlong into a thaumaturgic muddle.

Then the blasted woman reached up under the skirt and pulled down her drawers, and only three decades' habit of imperturbability saved Gabriel from hysterics. He did, however, somehow manage to raise his eyebrows and frown at the same time.

"What are you doing? We should just wait; the muddle will eventually dissipate."

"No, I'm sick of waiting," she said, and flicked her gaze away from him, eyes darkening. "I can't bear it."

"You've only been in this muddle for two minutes."

She muttered something under her breath and began to roll up the drawers in a wild, rather violent movement that caused Gabriel's eyes to widen in alarm. "I believe we're dealing with thaumaturgically charged sulfur," she said, her voice all sharp edges and snapping consonants. "That means instability. The magic could collapse in on us."

"All the more reason to act with care and precision," Gabriel argued. "There will be a seam in the perimeter, we just have to find it."

"That'll take too long," she countered, and strode toward the little flooded hollow.

"Don't—"

She shoved her drawers into the water.

Boom! (Again.)

ELODIE WATCHED WITH smug satisfaction as the muddle shuddered violently and began dissolving around them. Its lustrous shell became a gentle rain of argent magic that looked like a thousand tiny, sugary kisses she wanted to lift her face to. Before she could (not that she would have, she wasn't entirely stupid . . . although maybe she could just catch a speck on her fingertip, the tiniest of morsels to taste . . .), Gabriel grabbed her wrist and pulled her to safety. They ran, hunched against the perilous shower, their hair sparking, their boots stamping on flashes of blue fire among the grass.

"So bloody foolhardy," Gabriel was complaining as they came to a stop beyond the danger zone. He took her by the shoulders, turning her to face him, his eyes a furious dark storm.

"Actually, I believe your earlier word, 'brilliant,' is most appropriate here," Elodie argued, but he ignored this. Grumbling curses, he began to brush thaumaturgic flakes from her hair and arms. A sweet prickling danced over her skin, either from his touch or the deadly magic that was beginning to burn through her shirtwaist. She swept Gabriel's hair in turn, then pulled his coat off him and ran her fingers down the tight sleeves of his henley and over his chest. Granted, these areas were unaffected by magic, thanks to the shelter of the coat, but as a professional she felt it important to be meticulous.

"I was right about the sulfur," she said as they worked.

"You were," Gabriel agreed, his fingers sweeping the column of her throat, startling the breath within. "Which is one of a dozen reasons why you shouldn't have *exploded* the muddle."

Elodie bristled, and not because he was now brushing specks of magic from her bosom. "It got us out, didn't it?"

"Hm."

"Just say I was brilliant, you know you're thinking it."

"I don't know what the hell I'm thinking anymore."

The urgent brushing slowed, his hands stroking the tumbled length of her hair, her fingertips gently grazing his cheekbone. No trace of the magic remained, yet they continued to touch each other, in the name of being . . . um . . . *thorough*, of course . . . and *cautious*, yes! . . . and goodness the stubble developing along his jaw made her fingers twinkle.

"You shouldn't have risked yourself for me like that," Gabriel said. It would have been a whisper had it not sounded rough, like pebbles shaken by a cold wind.

"Of course I should have," Elodie replied. "Close your eyes."

He gave her a fiercely suspicious look, she returned it with an exasperated one of her own, and he finally obeyed. With great gentleness, she brushed her thumb over the abundant, thick lashes of first one and then the other eye. It would have been a tragedy if magic burned that lavish darkness; she absolutely *had* to ensure it was safe.

"There," she breathed, withdrawing her touch reluctantly. Gabriel opened his eyes again, the lashes swooping like a nightbird dreaming of the sun. He gazed at her for so long, she felt the muddle of her heart dissolve. They drifted close, lips parting, breath stilled in delicious anticipation . . .

And Gabriel jerked away. Elodie stared blankly as he stepped back, his usual frown gathering once more as he gazed out at the fields.

"Where are we?"

I wish I knew, she thought in wild, aching frustration. Then she turned to consider a more literal answer.

To her surprise, they stood on calm green land that swelled gently into low hills around them, dipped into shadows lined with beech and fir trees, and rang out in its secret places with the melodic commotion of roosting birds. Evening had begun to settle, soothing the air with tranquil duskiness. Plump clouds were thickening, darkening. To the northwest, an aura of brightness blanched part of the vast crimson sunset, and from this Elodie oriented herself, assuming it to be the city lights of Aberystwyth. Otherwise there were no signs of nearby civilization, and certainly none of Dôlylleuad.

"The energy from the muddle's bursting must have propelled it across considerable distance while we were still inside," she said. "I didn't know that was possible."

"You needn't sound so excited," Gabriel grouched as he shook his coat to remove flakes of magic.

"But it's a fascinating scientific discovery!"

"Which you only made because we were not killed by it."

"Yes, yes." She waved this point away.

"We're going to have a long walk back to Dôlylleuad. In the dark. With magic erupting everywhere."

Elodie grimaced at the thought. Then shook her head and smiled. "No, it's worth it. I'll get an article in *The Journal of Thaumaturgic Sciences* with this."

"Hm." Gabriel put on his coat, then took a map from an inner pocket. He frowned at it while Elodie gazed at the deepening southeastern horizon, seeing all the way to Oxford and some six months into the future, when the head of the geography department shook her hand and called her "as good as a man" for her work on thaumaturgic simulacrum theory.

It was an unlikely dream, and she gave a little melancholy sigh, although she could not quite bury it in a graveyard of hopes—for it was dreaming that had got her through the loneliness of childhood, when so often she felt like just another piece of luggage her parents had to take on the road . . . and through the loneliness of university, surrounded by men who wanted to see her fail . . . and she would not even think about the loneliness of her marriage. Holding on to hope, she smiled at Gabriel. He looked beautiful, all shadowy and blushed in the last breath of day, and made luminous by her secret wishes.

Sensing her attention, he looked up from his map, and his eyes darkened. The blush flared.

"Ahem." Clearing his throat, he turned toward the southeast as she had done, but with a far more somber expression, as if all his own dreams were nightmares. "From what I can tell," he said, "we're almost two miles northwest of Dôlylleuad. I'd rather not risk traveling in the dark. Besides, those clouds look like they're going to rain. Therefore, I suggest that, unless we come across a farmhouse or mining operation within the next few minutes, we find somewhere to make camp until the morning."

Elodie agreed, and they set off walking. "Ankle?" Gabriel asked brusquely.

"Still fine," Elodie assured him. "It's not sprained."

"Hm."

Silence descended. Gabriel read his map, and Elodie tried not to squirm as the rough fabric of her skirt rubbed against her bare skin. Then, with an abrupt swing of mood, she sighed aloud.

"What?" Gabriel asked disinterestedly, not looking up from his map.

"I'm sorry," she said.

"Oh?"

"It *might* have been a mad idea to collapse the muddle in the way I did, causing it to displace us such a distance."

He glanced at her then, a tint of amusement in his eyes. "Are you tired of walking already?"

"No. But we're without food and water, and goodness only knows what trouble Professor Jackson will be getting into back at the village."

Gabriel did not reply as he rolled up his map, securing it with an elastic band. Elodie assumed he'd abandoned the conversation. But then he said, "To be fair, considering the intense energy output upon its dissolution, I suspect *any* escape attempt would have met the same result."

Elodie blinked, astonished. Then her eyes narrowed with suspicion. "Stop being reasonable."

He slipped the map back into its special long pocket inside his coat. "Stop criticizing yourself."

"You said my actions were foolhardy and could have got us killed."

"Well, upon reconsidering the evidence, and with a new set of calculations that suggested—"

"Get to the point, please."

He frowned at her. "I was wrong."

Elodie's jaw dropped, which inspired Gabriel to frown even more severely. "Being wrong is necessary for me sometimes," he said, "in order to illuminate my general record of being right."

She closed her mouth with a clash of teeth and strode forth away from him, trying to ignore that he kept pace easily. But she managed only half a minute in angry silence before she burst out, "You are so—the most—cottage."

Gabriel gave her a strange look. "I'm a cottage?"

"No, there!" She pointed to a small building visible among a small cluster of trees in the near distance. No light shone at its window nor smoke arose from its squat chimney, which quite frankly Elodie found encouraging, considering her earlier experience with locals. "Come on!" she said, and began to run.

She *felt* Gabriel shake his head disapprovingly at her. But when she glanced back, she saw him following her, his pace calm and steady. He made a grim, brooding figure in the deepening shadows, like some manifestation of old Welsh myths, and Elodie's imagination immediately transformed her into a springtime maiden, bedecked with wildflowers, stalked by the terrifying but darkly romantic winter king . . .

"Be careful," Gabriel said blandly.

Be careful? That was the best he could do as a creature of haunted midnight? Elodie scoffed.

And ran straight into a bush.

FOR AS LONG as she could remember, Elodie had been excessively fond of a cottage. Perhaps this was due to a childhood spent living in tents and caravans, or perhaps it was from too much time spent in those tents reading romances. She liked to daydream about finding Mr. Darcy not at his grand manor but in a cozy, single-bedroom house at which she was forced to seek shelter due to stormy weather. He would be stony and brooding, but she rather liked that, and she would be dignified, witty, calm like Elizabeth Bennet, instead of the Marianne Dashwood she knew herself truly to be.

Alas, if only she'd read Jane Austen's works as scrupulously as she did maps, she'd have been forewarned about the dubious wisdom of loving a cottage.

The little house beside the trees was comfortable in the way a heap of used rags would be comfortable. That it proved unoccupied was no surprise, for the grime and the dank smell would certainly have driven away any reasonable tenant. Enough daylight remained for Elodie and Gabriel to see very quickly that dust covered the few shabby pieces of furniture in its living room, old ashes filled the hearth, and an entire civilization of spiders had built cobweb empires at each ceiling corner. Elodie, chewing her lip, tried to summon some positive comment; Gabriel, however, did not spend even three seconds inside before making for the exit.

He was met there by a sudden torrential downpour. Consequently, there was only one thing to do: cheerfully make the best of it! (Elodie) / suffer (Gabriel).

Inspecting the house more thoroughly, they found some canned food in the kitchen, firewood stacked beside the hearth, and a bedroom containing only one bed.

Now this is more like it, Elodie thought. Granted, the notion of sleeping alongside Gabriel after an afternoon of kissing, embracing, and shoe-putting-on was a little nerve-racking, but she was prepared to be brave. The bed had an old iron frame, a blanket hopefully made from brown wool and not some other color that had become brown with grime, and just enough width for two occupants, provided they snuggle.

"You may take the bed," Gabriel said. "I'll sleep in the chair by the hearth."

Elodie's racked nerves twanged with irritation. "How gracious of you," she said in a wry tone, for it was obvious he wasn't being magnanimous but feared the state of the mattress. *She*, however, was not a pedant. *She* did not wobble at the mere sight of dust. "I'm looking forward to a comfortable sleep," she remarked gaily.

"I suppose that's the benefit of having an imagination," Gabriel replied, albeit as if it was a bad thing.

They also found a few tallow candles, and Gabriel supplied matches from a pocket of his coat, thus providing them with light. Whether this was fortunate or not can be debated, for it allowed them to see more clearly what they were doing, but also to see more clearly the place they were doing it in. They got the fireplace cleaned out and lit—then very shortly thereafter discovered a possum had colonized the chimney. Only after dousing the flames and ensuring the possum was not going to come out to wreak revenge did they know peace.

By this point, Gabriel's jaw was clenching so hard a dentist would have wept to see it. But Elodie kept her spirits up by dint of sheer obstinance. After all, she wouldn't be Elodie Tarrant if she admitted how ghastly the situation was. The deeper Gabriel scowled, the brighter she smiled. The less he said, the more she filled his silence with cheerful observations that involved words like "quaint," "pastoral," and (when even her imagination began running out of positives) "quirky." This resolution did waver slightly upon her visiting the outhouse, but a nearby tree served her needs just as well, and it was *refreshing* to get wet and cold in the rain.

"And will it be *a jolly jape* if you come down with pneumonia?" Gabriel countered.

Dinner managed to be almost charming, partly due to the candlelight, but mostly because they were both too tired to argue and too hungry to care that they were eating corned beef and peaches from tins. Elodie attempted some fun conversation.

"If the new thaumaturgic trove does contain magically charged sulfur, it may have originated from pyrite. We should get a map of the regional mining operations."

"I have one, back at the inn," Gabriel said.

"Of course you do," Elodie murmured, then felt a clenching of her stomach that wasn't entirely due to the corned beef. "I meant that as a compliment," she added hastily. "You're always so prepared, I'm quite envious of it. I really ought to work harder to follow your excellent example, because the most—"

"It's fine," Gabriel interrupted. "I know what you meant; I wasn't offended."

"Oh." She stared at her tinned beef ruefully. "Good."

A peaceful quiet followed, with the rain outside making soft—

"Are you sure you're not offended?" Elodie blurted out. "Because it came out all wrong, I really did mean it in a positive way."

Gabriel gave her a calm, steady look. "I know."

"I'm always putting my foot in my mouth. Which, by the by, is what this corned beef tastes like."

"Hm," Gabriel agreed. In fact he did not seem to mind the beef so much, but was clearly struggling with everything else, from the table's weathered surface to the crookedness of his chair to the very air he breathed, which was rather pungent with tallow smoke.

"We should have just camped in the woods," he grumbled.

"Nonsense!" Elodie said with a touch too much good cheer, even for her. She winced privately, then resolved to keep her chin up. After all, the world was what one made of it. "Yes, the house is a little rustic, to be sure, but it's not so bad as you're making it out to be. Really, you ought to try relaxing your scruples."

"If I did, the spiders would come down and eat them," Gabriel muttered.

Elodie stared at him. "Was that a joke?"

Glowering, he stabbed the corned beef with his fork. "What do you think? Have you ever known me to joke?"

This casual acknowledgment that she knew him well made Elodie's blood tingle. As they returned to silently eating, she began to weave a romantic tale in her imagination of her and Gabriel as a genuinely married couple sitting together at their dining table, a little weary after working all day, a little grouchy, and wholly comfortable being so with each other. She sighed.

"What?" Gabriel asked.

"Nothing."

"Do you have enough food? I can open another can of corned beef for you."

"No, thanks." She smiled at him; he frowned in return, of course. She didn't mind that, not truly; it was just who he was. Self-defended, suspecting trouble from the world all the time. And what it most made her feel, beneath her protestations of annoyance, was hope that one day she might win a path through those defenses, to his heart.

Suddenly he reached across the table and turned her peach can to a new angle that presumably satisfied him better. Elodie gave him a surprised look; he gazed back unblinking. Something capricious in her heart flared in response to such inexplicable fastidiousness. She took hold of the peach can to move it in one haphazard direction or another—and stopped, seeing the ragged metal at the edge that he'd turned to be farthest from her.

She flushed. "Thank you."

"Hm," Gabriel said, and stabbed the corned beef again.

The silence returned, newly awkward as Elodie was forced to acknowledge to herself that some of Gabriel's defenses probably existed because of her. He'd done her a kindness, ensuring she wasn't hurt by ragged metal, and she'd automatically assumed he was just being finickity. Really, no wonder the man hated her. She wasn't so fond of herself in this moment.

"I'm sorry," she said—then lost courage for explaining why, since no doubt her words would come out all wrong, and she'd make things even more difficult than they already were. "I know this shelter is not ideal," she said instead. "But we're really quite lucky to have found it. We must try to cheer up. A bit of dust won't hurt us. We can—*aaaggghhhh*!"

Her scream pierced the candlelight.

♡

Chapter Fifteen

You are not in the world,
you are in the universe.

Blazing Trails, W.H. Jackson

GABRIEL LEAPED UP, his chair crashing to the floor, as Elodie screamed. A second later she was grabbing hold of him, attempting to climb his body.

This was not as romantic as one may suppose.

"What's wrong?" he demanded, pulse thundering in response to her panic and, moreover, her proximity to parts of him that had only just recovered from their excitement earlier in the day.

"Mouse!" she wailed.

"Mouse," Gabriel echoed in bemusement. From her reaction, he'd been expecting something truly dire, along the lines of *fire!* or *there's mold on these peaches!* He put his arms around her, embracing her firmly in the hope this would stop her writhing. "A mouse won't hurt you, Elodie."

To which she replied with singular eloquence: "Aaaaghhhh!"

"You're a geographer," he pointed out, albeit with some difficulty as her hair was covering his face. "You must have seen hundreds of mice over your lifetime."

"Field mice!" she retorted as if this made all clear. Tightening her arms around his neck and her legs around his waist, she clung to him desperately. "Outside! Hurry! Now!"

"It's still raining. Let me just set you down on this—"

"Aaaaagghhhh!"

Thus persuaded, Gabriel walked them to the front door and, with some angling, some painful twisting of his arm, managed to open it. The rain had eased, but still they were going to get wet. Torn between delight at her seeking his protection and an equal dismay at the miserable discomfort of the night outside, he hesitated. "Are you sure you—"

"Oh God, it's looking at me!" Elodie wailed. "Hurry! Go!"

So Gabriel took his coat from the hook beside the door, glanced at the fireplace to ensure it was completely cold, and stepped into the night. At this point he expected Elodie to get down, but she continued clinging with a tenacity that really was quite endearing. It made him feel strong, heroic, and just a little strained, but he wasn't about to admit that. Indeed, he found himself having to wrestle a rather foolish smile into his more habitual frown. Draping the coat over her, he headed for a nearby oak tree as quickly as possible under the circumstances.

But as soon as they reached its shelter, Elodie declared it was too close to the mouse. And so Gabriel continued on through the sodden darkness, risking possible tripping hazards, pneumonia, and worst of all, a hopeless lovesickness creating havoc in his stomach, as if he'd swallowed a swarm of magical vampire butterflies. At last an elm tree was pronounced safe, and with a rather tired exhalation he stopped.

Elodie loosened her grip on him and slid down until she

was standing. This had the unfortunate consequence of shifting Gabriel's internal havoc several inches below his stomach, and he'd have immediately stepped back were not Elodie still holding him captive. Oh, she'd removed her arms from around him—but her *eyes*, they were merciless. In the dark Gabriel could not see the sea green shade of their beauty, but he didn't need to. It had long ago colored his soul.

"Sorry," she said, the word a tremble that might have been laughter or the precursor to tears. "I know, 'girl who catches lightning is scared of mice'—it's ridiculous."

"It's a relief," Gabriel answered. "At least now I know you have some sense of caution within you, which hopefully can one day be applied to such things as, well, catching lightning."

Elodie was quiet as she tried to work through whether he'd just insulted her, and Gabriel took the opportunity to brush a strand of hair away from her face, his fingers warming with exultation as they glided across her skin.

The air seemed to gasp excitedly and clamp a hand over its mouth. Elodie went very still. He brushed a raindrop from her cheek next, then another from her temple. He could not seem to stop touching her, taking care of her in this small way. He would do more—he would do anything she asked of him. He was at her service forever. And he wished with all his heart that she'd cling to him once more, for he knew now he was physically incomplete without her.

But he also knew that if they stood there staring at each other, they'd catch a chill and end up in separate graves. So he stepped back, although it hurt all through his body to do so.

"Sit down," he said gruffly. And once she had done so, making herself comfortable in the soft, red-gold leaves fallen from the tree, he added, "Have this," handing her his coat. She took it automatically. With a brisk nod, Gabriel turned to leave.

"Wait!" Elodie said with some alarm. "Where are you going?"

He looked down at her dispassionately, never mind the butterflies now fluttering around his heart. "To sleep under another tree, so you'll have privacy."

"Oh." She sounded forlorn, and Gabriel hesitated, not sure what she wanted. "You'll freeze without your coat," she said. "Stay here, we can share it."

"Under only one tree?" He looked around as if faculty secretaries were lurking in the darkness, hoping to witness something they could gossip about.

"It's a logical solution," Elodie said.

She had him there. With an inarticulate grumble as his nerves trembled, he sat beside her, keeping a polite and safe fifteen inches' gap between them.

(Thirteen inches, after he shifted to avoid a stone, then shifted again to avoid an itchy leaf.)

(Ten inches, after Elodie moved to cross her legs.)

(Five inches, after Gabriel spread the coat over them both like a blanket, requiring them to shuffle closer so it fit across their laps.)

(Half an inch, when they both placed their hands down in the intervening gap beneath the coat, where it was warm and insular like a cave. Their smallest fingers drifted across the last tiny distance, meeting in the secret dark.) They sat like that, quiet, goosebumps rising along their arms as they stared out into the slow-dripping night.

"I'm sorry," Elodie said after a while.

"It's fine, I didn't want to stay in that place anyway."

"I know. That's why I'm sorry." She looked at him, her eyes big and soft and full of feeling. "I should have listened to you instead of insisting that you ought to feel comfortable."

Blindsided by this statement, Gabriel could do no more than shrug. He'd never received such an apology in all his life and didn't know how one properly responded. *Thank you* seemed paltry; taking off her clothes and kissing her from brow to toes seemed possibly excessive (although enjoyable).

"The second I was upset, you helped me," she went on. "Thank you. I wish I had been kind like that to you."

Gabriel stared at her. *Say something,* he urged his brain. But the traitorous organ had transformed itself into a loveheart and was no longer aware of anything but the beautiful woman at his side.

"It's too easy for me to get caught up in the moment," she said, "and not think more carefully. I'm so truly sorry if I hurt you."

"You didn't hurt me," Gabriel answered gruffly. Of course she hadn't. He didn't get hurt by things like that. He was a persnickety curmudgeon; a need for comfort was the last thing people would associate with him, therefore they never considered it. And his extended family, half of whom were academics, the other half civil servants, could have taken "Keep a Stiff Upper Lip" as their official motto. For them, comfort was something that happened only in the nursery, and generally consisted of firm pats on the back by a starchy woman in an even starchier uniform. When a child dared to become more emotional than a stern look could quell, they were packed off—to America, in the case of his cousin Devon, who'd failed to recover swiftly enough from his mother's death—or to boarding school, as happened with Amelia, after which she returned only during the summer holidays, a guest in the family house, no longer quite belonging.

Gabriel had learned better, quicker, than Devon and Amelia, perhaps because quiet had always been his natural instinct. He protected himself from the risk of needing comfort by expressing no more than a grumpy frown, even though in truth *everything* hurt, the whole noisy, itchy, crooked world, all the fucking time.

But Elodie continued gazing at him as if she saw right through that defense to where an aching boy huddled inside, just wishing for . . . not a hug, exactly, but perhaps a look that was like a hug . . . the type of look that Elodie was giving him now, in fact.

Damn, she was going to make him cry.

"The hovel supplied us with a meal," he said, "and so it all worked out for the best."

"I don't know that I'd ever equate tinned corned beef with 'the best,'" Elodie remarked, sardonic but smiling gently.

Damn again, now she was going to make him laugh. Determined to control himself, Gabriel nodded tersely. And Elodie, wise woman, understanding that the topic was closed, nodded also. They looked away from each other, into the hollow night.

Silence fell again.

Altogether it was as awkward as an eighteen-year-old boy trying not to blush when a gorgeous, pale-haired girl smiled at him. Then the moon emerged from behind a cloud, gossamer-thin and wry, its light transforming the elm's canopy into a roof of lambent gold that sparkled with raindrops like diamonds. Elodie gave one of her dreamy sighs.

"This reminds me of when George Lowbridge and I were studying the effects of thaumaturgic silver deposits on apple growth in North Yorkshire. It rained the entire time, despite being summer."

George Lowbridge? The perpetually sniffing junior professor from Cambridge?

"Oh?" Gabriel inquired with all the cool disinterest of someone who was in fact interested to the point of near combustion but determined not to show it.

"We sheltered under a tree very similar to this."

"Indeed?"

She laughed at some memory that made her eyes shine, and Gabriel felt several large, sharp boulders locate themselves to inside his respiratory system, in defiance of all geographic science. He knew perfectly well that Elodie had the right to sit under any tree she pleased with another man, but he also had the right to *absolutely hate the very thought of it.* She was *his.* Granted, only in legal terms, and he would *never dare* to state the claim aloud to her face. She was her own woman, and he believed that *implicitly.* He just also believed, deep down, where decency turned into a wild jungle, that she *belonged* to *him.* Indeed, he felt this *so vehemently,* he could not save himself from the alarming bout of italics.

Nevertheless, he remained outwardly dispassionate as he said, "So . . . where might I find Professor Lowbridge these days? I'd quite like to have a little chat with him."

"Oh, George went to Australia," Elodie said, oblivious to his spiking emotions.

Hopefully George would get eaten along the way by crocodiles.

"That's fine," Gabriel said. "I can go to Australia." On the other hand, he wouldn't shift his gaze just slightly to the left and see the warm, teasing smile he could *feel* her directing at him. "Why is he there, of all places?"

"My uncle is doing in-depth research on the songlines—Australian natives' method of navigation," Elodie said, drawing up her knees, wrapping her arms around her legs as she gazed out into the whispering night. "George went to study with him."

Her voice was . . . melancholy? Wishful? Showing signs of a chill? "That makes you sad," Gabriel hazarded. If he was right, then forget crocodiles. *Poisonous spiders.* Large, black poisonous spiders with incurable venom. Even better, he'd toss George into a pit of crocodiles for making Elodie sad, and then toss poisonous spiders in after him for daring to even think of Elodie at all.

"I'm only sad insofar as I wish I could study in Australia myself, and South America, and really the whole world," she replied. "But I'll never leave Oxford. I love . . . teaching." She shook her head. "It was better that George took the position Uncle Jasper had to offer, rather than me. And Clifford was happy about it too."

"Clifford?" Gabriel had been with her for half that speech, but all the human names at the end bamboozled him.

"George's particular friend."

Oh. He knew what that meant. Well then, perhaps this George wasn't so bad after all. In fact, one might even call him an excellent fellow for ensuring Elodie had shelter from the rain. Gabriel would buy him and Clifford coffee, should they ever meet.

"Goodness, aren't the stars so beautiful," Elodie murmured

complacently, even while Gabriel strove to regain the inner balance that jealousy had so profoundly rocked. He considered the inky vista with mild skepticism. The rain had stopped while they'd been talking, and the sky stretched clear into forever, blue-black, littered with stars.

"I suppose if I point out a constellation, you'll insist on telling me the whole mythology behind it," he grumbled.

Elodie tipped her head against her knees so that she was smiling at him. "You know me well."

Bloody hell, could a man cope with any more temptation? *Kiss her,* his body exhorted. His mind, however, began supplying reasons why such an action was inadvisable, from (1) she might reject him to (12) he hadn't been able to clean his teeth after eating the corned beef.

Kiss her anyway, fool! his body insisted.

His mind muttered and writhed and finally decided *fine*, he could attempt one small kiss . . .

And she looked away.

Everything inside Gabriel slumped. Scowling at himself, he pointed skyward. "Pleiades," he said.

"The seven sisters," Elodie responded as he expected. She began to unfurl one, then another tale, her voice warming Gabriel until he forgot he was sitting damp-haired and cold beneath a tree, lulling him until he felt half-inside a dream. Gradually her voice slowed and she began to sway with tiredness. So Gabriel grunted at her that he'd had enough, and she came back to reality with a quiet sigh.

"Do you think the village is safe tonight?" she asked.

"I see no fires," Gabriel replied.

"We need to establish a baseline for—"

"Tomorrow," he interrupted. Even if Elodie weren't half-asleep, he himself felt utterly exhausted by all the feelings he'd suffered this evening.

Elodie murmured something grim beneath her breath. Hearing his own name, Gabriel turned his head to ask her what she was saying. At the same moment, she turned hers, no doubt to tell him.

And somehow, completely by accident, or perhaps some conspiracy between fate and physics, their lips met.

Could he call it a kiss? It was barely more than the soft touching of mouths. Even so, a powerful sensation rushed from his lips to the pit of his stomach, where it set off a number of small explosions. He watched Elodie's eyes widen. He felt his heart do the same. With tender gentleness, the kiss began to warm . . .

And they pulled away, both of them blinking wildly in panic.

"Sorry," Elodie said, peering up at the leaves.

"Sorry," Gabriel said, glaring at the horizon. He heard Elodie's breath hitch. His pulse raced. From the corner of his eye he noticed her glance toward him. He lifted a hand . . .

And the panic slammed through them again. Nine years of shyness, and of watching the woman run away from him again and again, pushed Gabriel's hand down so hard, it smacked against the ground. He wanted her so much, his heart cringed and his eyes grew heavy, forcing him to employ an emergency scowl. Elodie, for her part, was looking so far in the opposite direction from him that her neck must be hurting with the effort.

"It's been a frazzly day," she suggested.

"Our nerves are overexcited," Gabriel contributed.

"We should sleep."

"Yes."

They lay down, back-to-back, in the leaves.

"This is really quite snug," Elodie said with a cheerfulness that sounded like it might at any moment snap from over-straining.

Gabriel dared not reply. He was being scratched against every inch of his body that touched the ground, even through his clothes. The coat lay crooked over his legs, and the corned beef churned in his stomach. But it was fine, all fine, so long as there was no more conversation . . .

"Are you terribly uncomfortable?" Elodie asked.

"No, I'm snug too," he replied gallantly. A stick jabbed him in the ribs, and he swallowed down a curse.

"You're lying."

"I am not."

"I can tell when you lie, Gabriel."

"I don't lie, Elodie."

"You've never used the word 'snug' in all the time I've known you."

"That's because you've never seen me sleep in a pile of leaves."

"All right. Good night, then."

"Hm."

Thank God, Elodie didn't reply. Sleeping in company was difficult under any circumstances; Gabriel hated being vulner-able like that. But sleeping with his wife (who smelled like violets despite her muddy clothes, and who had no drawers on beneath her skirt, and who was moreover the most beautiful woman in all existence) felt almost impossible. She was wrig-gling in the leaf pile, making herself even cozier, and Gabriel had to silently chant mathematical formulae just to stop himself from envisioning her wriggling naked beneath him.

But his lips burned from their sweet, accidental kiss, and his stomach continued to clench, making him feel literally lovesick. At least they weren't touching, their backs to each other and five inches of safety between them. Gabriel closed his eyes . . .

"Happy dreams," Elodie said, like a lovely line of music.

And Gabriel opened his eyes again, staring out into the dark, utterly lost inside his own heart.

"*WHAT THE BLIMMIN' heck?!*"

Elodie woke in a tumble of confusion and alarm as the exclamation broke through her dreams. One minute she was strolling Lyonnesse, mapping its shores, the next a man was shouting at her. Opening her eyes, she found herself cuddled up with Gabriel beneath the elm tree. He blinked at her dazedly, as half-awake as she. Together they came into focused awareness, their eyes growing increasingly large as they realized that his arms were holding her close while one of her bare legs hooked over his thigh. At least, this was the case for approximately 1.3 seconds before the information filtered through their brains and they flung themselves up in a tangle of limbs and apologies.

"*Vagrants!*"

At this point, they realized a man stood in front of them. Or, to be more precise, they noticed a broom being shaken at them, behind which was the man, snarling as he wielded it furiously. Gabriel leaped to his feet, pulling Elodie up and behind him in a display of chivalry that would have made her swoon were they not under immediate threat of being bashed by dirty, cobwebby rushes.

"Are you the blighters who messed up my house?" the man demanded.

They stared at him in amazement. "You—you actually live in that cottage?" Elodie asked.

"Of course!" the man sputtered. "I go away one night and come back to find I've been looted!"

"We shall of course pay for the food we consumed," Gabriel said.

"Too right you will! And what about the table?"

"Uh . . ." Elodie and Gabriel said in bemused unison.

"You did something to it!" The broom was rattled violently at them.

"We . . . cleaned it?" Elodie suggested.

"Blighters!" the man roared.

"Now, now, my good fellow." Gabriel's voice took on the polite, mollifying tone of a geographer who, having inadvertently trespassed on both property and sensitivities, has only the dignity of Her Majesty's service to help him escape the predicament. This was, of course, the exact way one should manage such a situation. Elodie had been taught the same by her parents, mentors, and professors, and knew how well it worked. So she took half a step forward, smiling nicely.

Then—"Oh my gosh, look!" she gasped, pointing to behind the man. "What on earth is that?!"

The man turned to see what she meant, his broom lowering as he did so. At once, Elodie grabbed it with both hands and twisted.

The man stumbled to his knees, and Elodie caught Gabriel by the shirtsleeve. "Run!" she urged, tugging him.

Gabriel stared at her with an incredulousness that wavered between disapproval and admiration. Elodie tugged him again. "Come on," she hissed.

"Hooligans!" the man shouted, clambering to his feet.

They ran.

AFTER A QUARTER of a mile's dash down a muddy slope, they finally stopped. Not only had the furious man been left far behind, scrambling in the grass for the coins Gabriel had thrown him, but they'd come to accept that there could be no outrunning the awkwardness of having woken in each other's arms again. Breathing hard, they looked across the quiet, misty land to where Dôlylleuad stood, softly wreathed in chimney smoke, beside the river.

"It's not too far," Elodie said. "We should be back there in time for breakfast."

"The mist has a blue tinge," Gabriel noted, staring at it fixedly so he would not be tempted to watch the way Elodie's breasts heaved with her breath.

"I think it's just a trick of the light," she said. "Everything seems calm."

They surveyed the view awhile longer until their gazes happened to meet. Memories filled the silence between them: waking to find themselves cuddling, the kisses yesterday, the morning after their wedding night, when they sat cross-legged in Gabriel's tumbled bed, eating toast and eggs, talking about their favorite maps . . .

Elodie's eyes darkened with blatant longing. *She must be starving for breakfast,* Gabriel thought, and looked away.

"We'll be there soon," he said.

"I don't think we ever will," she answered wearily. They began walking toward Dôlylleuad.

Blessed silence reigned for all of three minutes before Elodie broke it with the air of a woman unable to restrain herself a moment longer. "What a pretty bird!" she exclaimed.

She pointed toward a feathered creature in a nearby tree, but Gabriel's instincts warned him that this was merely a prelude to deeper conversation.

"No," he said.

Elodie halted, turning to him with stormy eyes. "What do you mean, no?"

"I mean no," he answered tersely. "Ornithology is an exceedingly dull subject, trust me. We will not be discussing it."

She gave an astonished laugh, and the storm in her eyes flashed with her lightning-fast temper. "You can't tell me what to discuss."

"Of course I can."

Her jaw dropped. Gabriel just stared at her in the way he'd perfected over years of teaching: implacable, inscrutable, unwilling to be convinced that an essay deadline should be extended or a conversation about birds be undertaken. But the heat in Elodie's gaze burned a hole in his heart. He wished he could just tell her how he really felt. Her every rambling conversation, her every stormy look, made him love her more than he thought possible. And yet, considering she once jumped out of a laboratory window upon seeing him enter, confessing his secret adoration would almost certainly inspire her to run off into the wild, where she'd meet a carnivorous tree or river tsunami, knowing her luck. So he found himself frowning, because he did not know what else to do.

Abruptly, her jaw snapped shut. "Well—I—arrogant—

humph." Thus communicating God only knew what, she stomped off ahead of him, grumbling about mice and men and how she was looking forward to a hot bath, in which she would like to drown a certain spouse.

Grateful that conversation had been avoided, Gabriel followed. It was a placid morning, at least, and they would soon be back in Dôlylleuad, with other people to come between them. Thank goodness for small mercies! Thus thinking, he quickened his pace, all the while gazing hopelessly at the sunlit magic that was his wife.

Chapter Sixteen

What we see of a tree is its own underneath.
Dirt is its sky, and light its dreaming.
                                    Blazing Trails, W.H. Jackson

TWO MILES AND twelve hours later, they finally arrived back at Dôlylleuad.

Exhausted and aching, they trudged into the Queen Mab's lobby, where they found Algernon and Professor Jackson wrestling for possession of Algernon's suitcase while Tegan looked on in amusement. As Gabriel shut the door with an eloquent thud, both men froze, astonished, the suitcase dropping to the ground between them.

"Leaving again, Algie?" Elodie asked, her voice dry with weariness.

"We thought you were dead!" Professor Jackson exclaimed.

"Algie?!" Algernon blustered at the same time.

"To be fair," Elodie said, "I feel a little dead."

"You do seem like you've been through the mill," Tegan remarked, managing to balance neatly on the fine line between politeness and *oh my God is that cow dung in your hair?*

"Not so much the mill as the tornadic storm," Elodie told her grimly.

"The exploding tree," Gabriel added.

"The mud bombs and a magic-crazed bull."

"And don't forget the volcano."

"Good God!" Professor Jackson exclaimed, whipping off his lensless spectacles to stare at them with amazed horror. "A volcano outside Dôlylleuad?"

"A foot-high volcano," Elodie clarified. "But considering we didn't notice and almost stepped on it . . ."

"How could you not notice a volcano?" Tegan asked bewilderedly.

"Our attention was otherwise occupied."

Indeed, after hours of navigating what had turned abruptly from a placid morning to a maelstrom of fiery, deadly magic, they had been so busy arguing over whether the fey line was already in cascade or merely being zany . . . and if Gabriel would allow this as a topic for discussion . . . and furthermore whether Elodie was able to point to "zany" in a science dictionary . . . that they'd barely noticed anything else around them. Elodie would have received a highly educative practicum on the effects of magma had not Gabriel, annoyed by the sudden odor of hydrogen sulfide, seen the volcano in the nick of time.

He'd grabbed her by the waist, lifted her over his shoulder for some reason Elodie could not fathom, and after she finally convinced him to put her down two minutes later (not that she'd insisted with especial force), they discovered that the volcano had burned itself out and so had their ability to form any conversation whatsoever, whether an argument or otherwise. The remainder of their walk had been undertaken in profound silence.

Frankly, Elodie no longer cared about the state of the fey

line or any danger it presented to Dôlylleuad. Besides, despite the surrounding countryside having been bedeviled by ricocheting magic, the village itself proved peaceful, and now her sole preoccupation was to have a bath. A nice long, quiet bath in cold water. Icy water. Water so arctic she would emerge entirely dispassionate about over-shoulder carries, and embraces, and kisses that Gabriel had been quite right to call "nervous overexcitement" after all, considering their ongoing effect on her. Even a day's hard slog through magical chaos had not dislodged them from her consciousness.

"The degree of spillage suggests increasing thaumaturgic pressure, but all our readings have been too cluttered to pinpoint a source," Gabriel told Professor Jackson, who murmured worriedly. "It's *somewhere* nearby; that much is obvious from the intense activity. But damned if we can find it. Has there been any magical activity here? Any injuries?"

"None," Professor Jackson assured him. "Obviously the trove isn't inside Dôlylleuad itself."

"Did you telegraph the Home Office?"

"I was on my way to do so when I caught Jennings here about to escape."

Gabriel did not bother pointing out that he'd tasked Jackson with sending that telegraph a day and a half ago. "We need to call for reinforcements," he said. "It's imperative we locate the source of this disruption before things worsen. We also need to alert nearby villages and towns to the risk."

"And I want to hold a public meeting here in Dôlylleuad," Elodie added, "to discourage tourist activity before someone gets turned into—oh, wait, that already happened, didn't it?" She turned to Tegan with belated concern. "Are the Americans back to form?"

A brassy peal of laughter from the taproom answered her even as Tegan said, "Yes." Gabriel winced at the noise, pressing fingertips against his forehead as if pained. Elodie nodded, but did not have enough energy for a smile.

"I'm going to have a bath," she declared, "and eat dinner in my bedroom."

"As am I," Gabriel said. Then his eyelashes flickered and Elodie's pulse did the same, recollecting the fact of their shared room and its sole bed. "Mr. Jennings," he said briskly, "since you are leaving, I'll take your bedroom."

"He can't leave," Professor Jackson argued. "We need every scientist we can get."

"But I'm not a scientist!" Algernon wailed. "I'm an accountant."

"You're also a man without a bedroom now," Gabriel told him, and marched off upstairs, leaving the others to stare at each other in stunned silence.

"Look on the bright side," Elodie said. "You two gentlemen can share a room. You're bound to become great chums."

"I've never had a chum," both men said, the professor wistfully, Algernon with a grumble that suggested friendship was too costly to allow.

"Well, there you go, then," Elodie said. "It's perfect." And she fled before the conversation entered dangerous territory— that is, the swampland of why her husband didn't want to spend the night with her.

A long, perfumed bath eased her bodily aches, dinner cured at least some of her empty feeling, and an evening of poring over topographical maps of Dôlylleuad's surrounds while sitting on the bedroom floor kept her from knocking on Gabriel's door and demanding what he'd meant when he'd said she had "vivacity." Finally, she forced herself to retire so she would be well rested for the next day.

But the bed that had previously been too small now seemed lamentably overlarge, and the room's quiet served only to make her thoughts as loud and disturbing as thunder. Assisted by two glasses of wine, Elodie managed to enjoy "sleep that knits up the ravell'd sleeve of care," but woke feeling suffocated, as if not only the sleeve but the entire cardigan of care were currently wrapped around her like a straightjacket.

She writhed irritably, then sat up all at once, blowing crumpled strands of hair away from her face.

"Confound it," she said to the wan light that softened the room. What exactly she confounded was unclear, even to her; essentially, a general atmosphere of confoundment surrounded her heart, the professional situation, and pretty much every choice she'd made for nine years that had ultimately led her to this room, at this time, with her husband sleeping on the other side of the wall.

Flinging back the quilt, she rose and paced to the window, automatically drawn to check on the village's status. Dawn was unfurling across its slate rooftops and red-gold trees, giving them a cold, delicate luminescence that capped the lingering shade of night. The eastern horizon blushed like a woman who had just woken to the kisses of an adoring spouse, and the steam fog drifting over the river might have suggested bridal veils or tumbled white sheets had Elodie not found herself become half-sick of metaphors.

Most importantly, she saw no disasters farther than her own reflection in the shadowy windowpane. With her white cotton nightgown and loose, unbrushed hair, she looked spectral, lost, and unmourned.

Or, more prosaically, a little hungover from last night's wine.

Deciding that "prosaic" should be the order of the day, since "romantic" had got her nowhere thus far, she left the peaceful view of the slumbering village and visited the bathroom. Upon returning, she was about to dress when a soft flicker caught her eye through the window. She paused, watching cautiously.

Windblown leaves floated past outside, and the world gave a sigh that seemed to echo what she felt in her own heart. Reaching automatically for her weather station, Elodie felt a slight flicker of concern. The general readings were normal, but the thaumometer's needle trembled in a strange way. It was surely nothing . . . and yet, before she knew what she was doing, she found herself walking downstairs, barefoot and still in her nightgown, hair streaming down. By the time she reached the front door, that flicker of concern had become a hard knocking in her heart. It was probably too much imagination. Or perhaps it was some tiny clue—an unexpected breeze, a trembling needle—that alerted her expertise. Whatever the case, something definitely felt odd . . . shivery . . . *rhyfedd*.

Opening the door, she looked out at the dusky morning. The unlit houses of the village seemed to be part of the land, little stone hillocks with their right angles blurred by shadows. The faint breeze was a poem Keats might have written. And the inn's narrow, bright garden smelled like a geographer's heaven, loam-rich and with a slight fetid odor of rot. Elodie found herself being lured outside. Through the white picket gate, onto the street, she wandered toward the dawn.

Mist swirled around her, strangely warm, like steam from

a bath. *Mist and yet a breeze,* she thought worriedly. The street's cobblestones felt warm too beneath her feet. The oddness of it slowed her, making her strides heavy. She stopped in a wide patch of oak shadow, and pressing her hands to her heart, she closed her eyes as she drank in the quietness.

There's nothing wrong, she told herself. The possibility of a line cascade had her nerves humming, that was all. She ought to go back to the inn and ~~ask Gabriel to kiss her again~~ look at her maps again, instead of wandering around out here getting cold.

Only it wasn't cold, was it?

"Cold enough to want a good, strong coffee," Elodie grumbled aloud. She turned back.

And could not move.

Startled, she looked down and realized that what she stood in was not oak shadow. It was quirksand.

Like quicksand but much, *much* worse.

Its thick, implacable magic clung to her legs, making every step an agony. She had probably less than five minutes to get free or else be clamped to the ground forever.

"Oh, drat," she muttered.

GABRIEL HAD BARELY slept through the night, acutely conscious of his wife lying on the other side of the bedroom wall while every muscle within him ached to hold her close again. At dawn he gave up and rose, aggravated, restless, and desirous of a good, brisk walk to enliven himself.

Which was the truth, as far as it went. There did exist an even truer truth, however: that he desired a far more interesting manner of exercise, if only it weren't made impossible by the bedroom wall (and more to the point, his wife's dislike of him).

But this was swiftly and decisively repressed by his brain, which avowed that, henceforth, good sense would rule. Two days in Elodie's company had rendered him an emotional mess, and Gabriel could not abide mess. It made his blood itchy. Consequently, the time had come to reinstitute self-discipline, self-respect (and a rather desperate self-entertainment, which had probably contributed to his lack of sleep).

He dressed in a shirt, field trousers, and a brown jumper made of the softest wool, and was in the process of buckling his boots when a sudden argent brilliance swamped the window, scattering dapples of light through the dim room. Gabriel reacted instantly, not even pausing to make the bed before he rushed out. Finding Elodie's room empty, he ran downstairs and out into the dawn.

Almost at once he saw strands of moon-bright magic forming overhead, binding the village within their compass. Only *almost* at once, however, because *the very first and most imperative* thing he noticed was Elodie standing farther along the road, hair and nightgown billowing around her as she gazed up at the sky. She was a wild goddess. She was an angel come to rescue him from a slow, cold fate of loneliness.

She was a bloody nuisance who was going to get herself killed! Furious, Gabriel took off at a run toward her.

Thaumaturgic energy wove above him like the Lady of Shalott's web. Little breezes dusked and shivered. *I'm being enchanted*, Gabriel thought, reaching for the iron hook around his ear only to remember that, in his haste, he'd left it on the bedside table. He began seeing images of Elodie lying in a boat that drifted downriver while he lay beside her, kissing her closed eyes and soft mouth and the gentle swell of her—

"The square of the hypotenuse is equal to the sum of the squares of the other two sides of a right-angled triangle," he chanted, trying to barricade his mind. Simultaneously assessing the situation, he found nothing to measure, only endless twining magical threads making a ring that surrounded Dôlylleuad. A closed system, pointing nowhere.

It's here, he realized suddenly, his blood chilling. *The thaumaturgic deposit we're looking for is right here in the village.*

Just then, Elodie glanced at him, her eyes alight. Gabriel could tell she'd reached the same conclusion he had, and excitement shot between them. He wanted to lift her up and spin her around with that excitement—which must be the most ridiculous, most undignified idea he'd had in years. It certainly showed the degree of disaster that had befallen him. Never mind explosive earth magic; he was completely ensorcelled by his half-wild and exasperatingly beautiful wife.

But as he jogged close to her, Elodie held out her hand with the palm raised in a warding gesture. "Stop!" she shouted.

Her attitude was grave, professional, and Gabriel immediately tried to obey. But momentum kept him going, even as his legs grew oddly heavy, causing him to stumble . . .

Then he did stop—so fast, and with such a wrench, that he tipped into her arms. Elodie lurched from the force of his weight. Catching her, Gabriel pulled them both into balance, then released her with a murmur of apology. He tried to step back but could not move his legs.

"It's quirksand," Elodie told him, well and truly after the nick of time.

"Damn," he said.

"Bit of a sticky wicket," Elodie agreed. (Gabriel wondered if she'd been thinking up that joke the whole time he ran toward her.) "I'm awfully sorry for the bother."

And then the blasted woman went and smiled at him again.

REALLY, THE SITUATION was not funny. It was extremely serious. But Elodie felt herself on the verge of helpless, anxious laughter as Gabriel bristled automatically. "I am not bothered," he declared.

"No, no, of course not," she said, nodding fervently. Gabriel scowled, not at all taken in by her supposed agreement, then turned his irritation on the magic underfoot.

"Well?" Elodie prompted.

He looked back at her, his face tighter than the grip of the magic around their legs. "Don't panic," he said, much in the same way he might tell a student not to panic about losing all their lecture notes: as if the path forward had not just turned significantly arduous.

"Don't panic?" Only the constrictive magic prevented Elodie from ~~stropping off~~ making a dignified exit. Did he think her one of his juniors?! Or was he quite simply the most arrogant sod to ever have arroganted?! "Do you see me panicking?" she demanded, setting her hands on her hips.

Gabriel did not reply, only shifted his attention to her left eye, beside which a muscle was twitching.

"Fine, so my spirit is slightly ruffled," she conceded. "But you feel the same way, I know it." She pointed a finger at him; he raised one eyebrow. "You're just as ruffled! After all, there's only one way to escape quirksand."

"Hm," he said.

"Waltzing."

"Hm," he said again.

"Walt. Zing." *The dance of romance.* The dance they'd have performed at their wedding, had it been genuine. "I did warn you to stop."

"I would have entered anyway," he said. "You rescued me from the muddle, now I have the honor of rescuing you."

As far as charming statements went, this would have been really quite nice indeed, had he not made it in such an offhand tone. Perhaps he did not realize the extent of the situation. "Waltzing," she reiterated. *"Together."*

Gabriel did not reply, exuding such dispassionate calm he might well have been standing in front of a blackboard, about to teach seventy hungover undergraduates how to map the relative gradients of thaumaturgic intensity within the vector of a fey line by employing isothaums. And yet, when Elodie advanced her left hand, he appeared to forget the mechanics of breathing.

"You do know how to waltz?" she asked.

"Every emergency geographer learns how," he answered stiffly.

"Because I can lead if—"

He silenced her with an affronted look. Taking her hand in his, he gripped it firmly while placing his other against her upper back. A delightful frisson went through Elodie, no doubt due to the surrounding magic. Trying to ignore it, she placed her right hand on Gabriel's shoulder.

"We can do this," she said through gritted teeth. "Slow, steady movements."

Crrrack! The ground nearby split open under the magic's

pressure. Vicious spikes of thaumaturgic energy shot out, searing through the shadows, leaving hot black scars.

Crrrack! Again, closer.

"Actually," Elodie amended, "perhaps quite fast movements, what do you think?"

Gabriel did not reply. He moved his left foot forward, and Elodie moved hers back, wincing against the burning pain of the effort. It was like trying to get through setting concrete or a boring lecture on a hot afternoon. They dragged themselves out of one step and to the side, then turned to repeat the procedure. One, two three . . . one, two three . . .

Elodie exhaled a tremulous breath. She was dancing with her husband, and her heart showed no signs of breaking. (Her ankles, however, were a different matter.) Indeed, the beat of her pulse was so strong, sending such a swirl of emotion through her—happiness, and giddiness, and embarrassment over being dressed in her nightie—that she began to see stars.

Silver and blue stars, glinting in the pink glaze of early sunlight.

Blinking, she became aware that their dance was loosening the thaumaturgic bonds of the quirksand and scattering fragments of them into the air—a hundred bright, tiny stars of magic.

"Beautiful," she said sighingly.

"Yes," Gabriel said. His voice was so gruff, Elodie almost chided him for having no sense of wonder in his soul. Then she realized that he was not looking at the enchantment of the stars. He was looking at her.

She blushed the color of the sky.

Crrrack! A fissure opened mere inches from their feet.

Scorching thaumaturgic electricity hissed from within the broken ground, transforming tiny insects into jewels.

Gabriel said nothing more, just continued to lead them in aching, gliding steps toward safety. Each turn of the waltz was easier than the last until it felt to Elodie like they moved in a seamless dream. And perhaps the magic had shifted, for they could not seem to look away from each other. Gabriel's eyes were as dark as the ink they'd used to sign their marriage certificate. Each time he blinked, Elodie's pulse stuttered. She forgot the quirksand, forgot Dôlylleuad. Nothing existed for her at all but the breathless quiet between her and her husband as they moved through the chaos of the world.

"Miss Hughes is better at forecasting probabilities," he'd said once, when they were students and their professor had been allotting responsibilities for a group task. His voice had been impassive, and he'd glanced so briefly across the classroom at her that he might actually have just been blinking, but nevertheless Elodie had treasured the compliment.

"Leave that last tea bag for Miss Hughes to use, Fotheringay," he'd commanded a fellow lecturer in the faculty lounge, thrilling Elodie so greatly, she'd been quite unable to drink the tea she made from that bag (possibly also because she'd had four cups already that morning).

"I will," he'd said at the altar, marrying her.

Elodie carried the memories of a dozen such perfect moments with her always, private little joys that sheltered her on maudlin days. None though came anywhere near the perfection of this moment, waltzing with Gabriel in silence.

A warm gust of magic curled around her ankle, inciting her to glance down . . .

"Oh," she said softly.

The quirksand had completely shattered. The fractured street lay quiet beneath their feet, magic swirling in slow, opalescent waves among the remnants of stars.

"Don't panic," Gabriel said.

"I'm not," Elodie assured him.

"I was talking to myself."

Elodie was bemused. "The spell is broken. We're safe. Why would you panic now?"

"Because I'm going to kiss you."

"Oh." Panic immediately swept through her too.

"It is no doubt a consequence of the magic, sensitizing my nerves," he said. "Or possibly the radiant effervescence of your spirit, which has fascinated me for so long now that my resistance to it has weakened." He frowned with intense botheration, as if she were a table that wobbled on side and he a chair that wobbled on the other, and he'd run out of little bits of folded paper to make them properly straight. "I'm compelled, Elodie. I'm driven. My every thought circles back to you. My every breath wants to kiss you. I know you despise me, and I will never speak these words again, so don't be afraid. But I l-l—" He winced. "Like your hair. And the way you draw topographical maps. And, well, *you*."

"Oh." Elodie would have thought herself dreaming were it not for a fresh breeze gusting up beneath her nightgown, acquainting her intimately with reality's existence. "Truly?"

"Truly."

"Oh," she said again. "But why would you think I despise you?"

He frowned in confusion. "You run away or hide every time you see me."

She wriggled a little in his hold, embarrassed. "That's because I l-like you but I know you hate me."

His eyes widened. "You *like* me?"

She shrugged, and nodded, and stared at an exceedingly fascinating piece of air over his shoulder. But Gabriel took her jaw between his fingers and gently guided it so that she was facing him again.

"I have never hated you, Ellie."

To which massively life-changing information there was only one response: "Gosh."

"Indeed," he answered wryly. "Hence the panic."

"But goodness, there's no need for it," Elodie told him. "We kissed rather comprehensively yesterday in the farmhouse."

"Nervous overexcitement."

"And under the tree," she added.

"An accident."

"And on our wedding day," she said with just a little exasperation. "Indeed, we did a great deal more than kissing for those two days . . ."

"This is different."

"I understand." In fact, she understood nothing, but now was not the time for contemplation. "Would it help if I kissed you first?"

"Probably not. I just have to get it over with."

She strove not to roll her eyes. "Heavens, what a romantic line. I shall have to record it in my diary."

Gabriel frowned, seeming more confused than cross. "We're dancing among magical stars as the sun rises over a quaint country village. Isn't that romantic enough for you?"

"Considering that I'm starting to get goosebumps in unmentionable places," Elodie answered dryly, "I'm going to

require a very thorough kiss to make things 'romantic enough.'"
Which wasn't true; she thought her heart would never recover
from the gorgeous romanticism of this morning (the risk of
dying in quirksand notwithstanding).

Gabriel gave her one of his thrillingly intense looks. "I'm
good at thorough," he said—and proved it.

Chapter Seventeen

The sensible geographer always knows the safest path, even if they don't take it.

Blazing Trails, W.H. Jackson

ELODIE CLOSED HER eyes as Gabriel gently pressed his lips against hers. Even so, light filled her, warm and rich and gleaming with pleasure. Their first kiss yesterday had been a storm of passion, their second a sweet accident. This, though, was more like the fulfillment of what the early days of their marriage had promised, tender and deep, with a divine slowness that suggested Gabriel intended to kiss her at his leisure for the rest of their lives.

Gravity settled beneath her heart. She leaned into Gabriel's strength, and he held her there with an embrace that was so calm, so certain, they might have been standing safe inside a stone-walled room, not on a cracked road while lingering, glimmering magic encircled them and gold-soaked shadows swayed around their feet. The moment was transcendent. The kiss was like dark coffee, smooth and rich, with a sugary tingle as their tongues met. Elodie could have wept from the beauty of it.

Finally, they eased apart. A little dazedly, Elodie looked

around, half expecting the morning to be burst open and brightly lit by love's enchantment. But the sun had still barely risen above the trees. The village remained quiet. They might have been the only people in the world—which, Elodie reflected, was rather fortunate, since public smooching probably did not count as decent professional behavior.

"Are you all right?" Gabriel asked, looking at their feet to ensure they were indeed free from the quirksand and unharmed.

"I'm fine," Elodie responded in correct English style. The French half of her, however, reached for him again, and he reached for her, and their lips met with such yearning it was as if it had been years since they last kissed.

"Mehheehhhh!"

Startled, they jerked around. The Queen Mab's goat, Baby, had appeared in front of them as if from nowhere. He was glaring with the kind of malevolent complacency only a creature with dangerous horns and a fluffy pom-pom hat can manage, all the while chewing noisily on a mess of leaves and flowers.

"For fuck's sake," Gabriel muttered, his face blanching in reaction to the slurping noises. In turn, Baby ducked his head and glared as if to say, *Mind your language, young man!*

Elodie laughed. After all, she'd just been extensively kissed by her husband, and as a bonus had not been permanently clamped to the ground by magical quirksand. All was good with the world, at least for now—and to a disaster specialist, "for now" was the only moment that could be relied upon. Besides, it would take a truly stony heart to disagree that Baby really was very cute, in a rustic kind of way.

"Diabolical creature," Gabriel muttered, crossing his arms with stern disapproval.

Elodie clicked her tongue chidingly at him. Then she leaned down, hand extended to Baby. "What are you doing out here, you silly thing?" she asked in a coaxing voice.

Baby whipped his glare around to her, and Elodie retreated with a gasp. Gabriel instantly put an arm around her back to steady her, but she didn't even notice, such was her alarm, for the animal's eyes burned with a fierce, witchy blue, and the sharp flick of his tail suggested she and Gabriel now faced the double hazard of a goat that was enchanted and at the same time a regular goat—both conditions fraught with danger.

"That's interesting," Gabriel said mildly.

"Meehh," replied the goat. The slobbery tangle in his mouth fell to the ground, where it burst into green flames.

"That definitely is interesting," Elodie agreed. "Perhaps we might discuss it further . . ." She pointed both hands to the left. "Over there, yes?"

"Hm," Gabriel agreed. They began to sidestep.

"*Meehh!*" Baby protested, rearing up. Fire belched from its mouth in a foul-smelling burst, which was a little more interesting than Elodie would have preferred.

"Hurry!" she urged Gabriel, tugging on his sleeve.

They skirted with breathless care around the goat while it stood on two hooves, screaming at them, then immediately began racing down the road toward the Queen Mab. Seconds later, Baby took up the chase.

Glancing back through the swirl of her hair, Elodie glimpsed the cobalt sparks flashing off the goat's hooves as they struck the ground, and she felt a rush of sympathy for the

poor creature. He must surely be hurting from the thaumaturgic power that coursed through his body. This, however, did
not prevent her from urgently considering ways in which they
might detain or destroy him—provided of course they managed to survive his murderous intent. For Baby proved terrify-
ingly fast, and soon was snapping at the air so close behind
them that Elodie could hear the clash of his teeth and feel the
nasty heat of magic.

Calling on a strength developed over years of outrunning
dangers in the field and determined bursars wanting to chastise her for blowing up expensive laboratory equipment *yet
again*, Elodie sprinted hard alongside Gabriel as they gained
distance on the creature. Pain shot through her bare feet, making her wince, but she dared not slow.

Coming to the Queen Mab, Gabriel grappled with the
latch of its garden gate as Elodie patted his back and urged,
"Hurry, hurry," in a manner that was no doubt tremendously
inspiring. Baby was drawing close once more, flames snorting
from his nostrils, pom-poms wobbling violently.

"Let me try opening it," Elodie said tetchily, and in the next
moment found herself being picked up and lifted over the gate
in one swift, powerful movement. She did not even have time
to decide whether this action was romantic or outrageously
offensive before it was done, and she was dropping to the
ground on the other side. She hastened back to give Gabriel
room for a more dignified vault himself, which he achieved
only half a second before Baby rammed the gate at full speed.

Crack! A wooden picket split upon impact with the goat's
horns.

"Meeehh!" Baby bleated, a clear declaration of war.

"Poor wee thing," Elodie crooned. Gabriel threw her a disbelieving look. "What?" she said defensively. "It's not his fault he was struck by magic."

Crack! Baby rammed the gate again, sending splinters flying. Elodie and Gabriel edged toward the inn's door.

"Was he?" Gabriel said. "Hm." Hands on his hips, head tilted to one side, he regarded the goat thoughtfully. Elodie had seen him make the same pose in front of a particularly gnarly map, and a little tremor of love went from her heart down into her stomach. He was so . . . so *Gabriel.*

"Surely a magic strike of such potent effect would have outright killed what is a relatively small animal?" he said.

"Well, he was obviously enchanted somehow," Elodie argued, "considering his peevish behavior."

"Elodie, Professor Lipovsky is peevish. Always complaining about chalk dust and how ten o'clock is too early to face students. *This* is belligerence."

Proving his point, Baby backed up and, with head lowered and nostrils steaming, began stomping on the ground in preparation for a new assault. Elodie glanced at the front door, estimating how fast she and Gabriel could get to it if the gate were breached. Faster than the goat, she guessed, and looked back just in time to see Baby begin his charge.

Crack! He slammed into the gate.

Thud. He collapsed in a tangle of scrawny limbs and pompoms.

"Meh," he bleated pathetically, then went silent.

Elodie gasped, pressing her fisted hands against her mouth. "Is he dead?"

"I don't think so." Gabriel leaned over the gate to make a closer inspection. "Unconscious, still breathing. We need to get some rope to secure him before he awakens."

"Right." Elodie pivoted toward the door, but Gabriel caught her arm before she could leave.

"Wait."

He sounded shakier than the Pacific Rim fault line, and as Elodie turned back to him, he lowered his gaze, pushing a hand through his hair, for which there was only one possible interpretation: *I'm about to ask you for a divorce.* In preparation, Elodie both bit her lip and smiled, which made her appear more coyly excited than she felt. "Trepidation" would have been a better description. "Terror" would have been best.

Gabriel peered up through his lashes at her. Noting the smile, he shifted his own mouth slightly—just a little curve at one edge, the shyest ghost of emotion.

Elodie swallowed heavily. She had seen that same look on his face once before: the only time he'd smiled during the near decade she'd known him. As he'd stood at the altar, watching while she made a solo procession down the church aisle (since a girl needed at least that much on her wedding day), his expression had been entirely neutral until the moment she'd stepped into a slanting, glittering beam of sunlight.

And then he'd crooked his mouth ever so gently. Anyone who'd not spent years adoring him would have missed it. To Elodie, it blazed. And yet, it hadn't been a smile of pleasure, or even surprised admiration. It had simply said, *Of course.*

As if he expected always to see her in sunlight.

Among all Elodie's memories, that was the loveliest. At the time, she'd felt her heart swoon so completely, it had been a miracle she'd been able to take another step. Even a year later, the recollection still did things to her, delightful, tickly things that had no place in a polite paragraph.

And now here he was, smiling at her again.

"Yes?" she breathed.

He shoved back his hair a second time. (Elodie managed a moment's envy, despite everything, to note that it resettled impeccably.) "I know we're in the middle of a disaster," he said, "and that the ground may explode beneath our feet at any moment, killing us and scores of other people. But I must ask . . ."

He paused, clearing his throat while Elodie's nerves flailed around screaming. The smile had gone; he appeared now to be on the verge of implosion.

"Yes?" she repeated cautiously.

Gabriel shook his head. "Never mind." Turning on a heel, he scowled around the garden. "Where the hell is some rope?"

Elodie sighed with exasperation. "Really," she said rather stroppily, "people who kiss other people ought to just ask them questions if they want."

"People who have questions might not know how to ask them," Gabriel replied, his tone coolly conversational. "People might be unused to personal conversations. Why is there no bloody rope in this garden?"

"I'm going to get dressed," Elodie grumbled, and made again for the door.

"Wait."

She stopped. "What, Gabriel?"

He squinted at the sky. "Theoretically, do you think being married to a person precludes one from courting them?"

Elodie's pulse did such a double take, she was momentarily too dizzy to respond. "Um," she said eventually, which was not quite the answer she'd rehearsed for years, should such a situation arise. "No, I think it would be acceptable. Theoretically."

"Acceptable," he repeated gravely.

"Encouraged."

"Hm." He was squinting with such ferocity at a passing cloud that Elodie feared he might do himself an ocular injury. She took pity on him.

"I like flowers."

That brought him back from the sky, although he still would not quite meet her gaze. "Yes, I read your paper on how the presence of *Zantedeschia aethiopica* in bog environments serves to inhibit acute thaumaturgic emissions. Most insightful."

"Thanks. I also like coffee, and poetry, and I especially like moonlit strolls along the Thames."

"To study the bioluminescent phenomenon of the thaumaturgic carp in the river?"

Elodie grinned. "Yes, absolutely, Gabriel. To study the fish."

He looked at her without speaking, his expression having grown thoughtful (probably because her nightgown was becoming transparent in the strengthening daylight). "I really should get dressed," she said. "Will you deal with the goat? That would be most chivalric of you."

And there it was, pinching his countenance and straightening his spine even further—the tetchiness she knew so well, and that she'd even come to love, recognizing it to be not a meanness in his character but a vulnerability showing where he was rubbed sore by a world too loud, bright, and rough-edged for him. She'd teased him just a little too far.

"Sorry," she said hastily, and fled before she made a mess of things.

IN THE SHADOWY quiet of the bedroom, Elodie dressed, paying little attention to what she pulled from the kit (which explains how she came to wear a long plaid skirt; a lacy, blue-dotted shirtwaist; and a green silk opera coat embroidered with pea-cocks). She secured her hair in a lopsided braid. Then, grabbing maps, a weather station, and a field notebook, she left the room.

And a few seconds later returned to don stockings and shoes.

"It's not my fault I'm being absent-minded," she told the empty room defensively. After all, no woman cared about triv-ialities like clothing when the man of her dreams had . . . er . . . talked about glow-in-the-dark fish.

"Oh dear," she murmured. "Perhaps he doesn't want to ro-mance me after all. Perhaps he really was just talking theoret-ically. I may *possibly* have let my imagination run away with me."

As usual, replied the room, with a smug silence.

"No, he kissed me," she argued. She certainly hadn't imag-ined that.

Feeling much tousled in spirit, and needing to regain some composure before going downstairs, she crossed to the window and peered out. In the Queen Mab's little garden below, Ga-briel was carrying Baby across the grass while Tegan Parry hovered anxiously, rope in hand. His face twisted in disgust at the general goatishness to which he was being exposed, and yet he held Baby with gentle care. Elodie's heart melted, and she leaned against the window frame, sighing with such sentimen-tality that she felt embarrassed for herself. Forget being a ge-ographer; this was undignified behavior for a *woman*, or at least one with self-respect. Straightening, she assessed the view for geographical hazards, and even succeeded in convinc-ing herself that this had been her original aim.

The thaumaturgical flare had dissipated, in the random

flash-then-fade way that characterized this situation, and the most interesting thing she saw was ~~Gabriel's trousers straining against his derriere as he crouched to set Baby down~~ a mangled bush of the same flowers the goat had been chewing when they encountered him.

"Well, thankfully the world isn't on the immediate verge of self-destruction," she mumbled, "even if I am."

She went down to the taproom. A few tourists were already seated therein, perusing breakfast menus. At the bar, two local gentlemen in work clothes conversed with Mr. Parry, and they fell silent while watching her cross the room, their attitude so suspicious that Elodie rather wished something would explode to divert attention from her.

Taking a table within earshot of the locals, she half listened to them muttering, *"Twll dyn pob Sais,"* while she drew a map of Dôlylleuad. Their tone suggested they weren't commenting on her exceptional fashion sense. Indeed, by the time Gabriel arrived, wearing a new jumper and with hands scrubbed so clean they glowed, she was beginning to feel decidedly uncomfortable.

"I think we are outstaying our welcome," she whispered as he sat beside her. "Mr. Parry and his friends keep giving me grim looks."

"It's early morning," Gabriel said, shifting his chair by increments beneath him until it was aligned perfectly with the table. "Everyone is grim at this hour. What are you drawing?"

"I'm layering different themes into a map of the village, trying to pinpoint the most likely location for a trove of thaumaturgic materials. We're running out of time to find what is causing this chaos." She tapped her pencil against her weather station, all the gauges of which were now promising imminent doom.

Donning his spectacles, Gabriel contemplated the weather station somberly. "We should just go ahead and evacuate the village."

"I tend to agree. But in which direction?"

They frowned at her map. "Hmm," they murmured in unison.

Just then, Mr. Parry appeared beside the table. "Did I hear you say 'evacuate'?" he asked in a low, troubled voice. "What do you mean by that?"

Gabriel looked up over the rim of his spectacles. "To withdraw from an area for the purposes of safety. Also to empty the bowels, but that isn't relevant in this situation."

Elodie hastily turned a laugh into a cough. Then she smiled at the innkeeper. "Nothing's been decided yet. Can we please order two cooked breakfasts and coffees?"

"Sure," Mr. Parry said, but he was frowning as he left.

They worked together on the map, absently eating breakfast as they did so. They shared ideas, debated the scale of various features, and generally behaved in a manner befitting colleagues who may have recently undergone two interesting episodes of nervous overexcitement but who were otherwise not engaged in romance, let alone genuinely married.

It is true, however, that as their hands lay side by side on the tabletop, Gabriel's smallest finger brushed against Elodie's with a slowness that cast some suspicion on the idea of it being accidental. But since neither of them reacted in any way beyond a tremor of their breath, this can be dismissed.

And when Elodie bumped her knee against Gabriel's, one can accept it as a simple consequence of their nearness, understanding that she was too tired after the morning's exertions to move it away.

Furthermore, when Gabriel took his hand off the table and

laid it on that knee . . . well, actually, there is no banal interpretation of this, but since it happened out of sight, beneath
the table, it need not be counted.

Professor Jackson arrived, resplendent in a quilted dressing
gown, with the cloud of his hair bundled atop his head and
pierced through with a dowsing rod. A bleary-eyed Algernon
shuffled behind him. They sat opposite Elodie and Gabriel,
and Algernon immediately took first her mug and then Gabriel's, peering inside for any coffee. Finding some dregs in
Gabriel's, he drank them with an unhygienic desperation that
left Gabriel staring, appalled.

"I'll buy you your own," Elodie said, raising her hand for
service. "I'm sure the Home Office can stand the expense."

Algernon did not argue. "Professor Jackson lectured me all
night about the art of cartography," he said grittily, rubbing his
face.

"Why didn't you tell him to stop?" Elodie asked.

"He was asleep."

The professor shrugged and grinned unrepentantly. "A
mind as great as mine takes no rest," he explained, even as
Algernon, groaning, bent until his face was on the table.

"Next time they offer me a field assignment," he muttered
into the wood, "I will shoot them. With a crossbow. Using a
flaming bolt. The consequences will be more pleasant than this
week has been."

"Have you found the trove yet?" Professor Jackson asked,
tapping Elodie's map. As he did so, a faint blue stain washed
through the air, and all three geographers went still. But in the
next second it was gone again.

"Not yet," Elodie answered. "But I think it's down by the

river. Magic may be rising in water vapor and being trans-ported by the prevailing southerly wind through the village, causing the atmospheric disturbances."

"Oh look!" came a sudden cry of delight from the far side of the room. Everyone glanced over to see a glimmering blue globe spiraling gently up toward the ceiling beams. The Misses Trevallion giggled, reaching in an effort to catch it. One al-most succeeded, only to have it pop like a bubble. Shards of light fluttered away, winged dreams of the sky.

Elodie turned back to the map. "Or it may be in the fields outside the village, where a lack of proper drainage has led to—" She paused as the floor trembled, rattling the table and making Algernon sit up with a yelp. "Magic leaking from groundwater and decaying plant matter," she concluded once things had settled again. "But we searched there and found nothing. It's so strange. I suggest we split up and go over both locations as soon as possible."

Gabriel looked inclined to argue, but before he could, Tegan appeared, her face alight with happiness. "Baby's awake," she said, "and shows no signs of being enchanted. But he is a bit unsteady on his hooves."

"Poor little darling," Elodie answered obligingly. Gabriel muttered under his breath about the beast having slobbered green muck on his best jumper, and Elodie was about to call *him* a poor little darling, but she stopped herself just in time— then stopped altogether, staring wide-eyed into the mid-distance between Professor Jackson and Algernon.

"What?" Algernon asked nervously, checking over his shoulder.

"Stupid!" she said. Algernon's face fell, and she winced.

"Oh, I didn't mean you, Algie! I'm the one who's stupid." She turned to Gabriel. "The flowers and leaves Baby was chewing were what enchanted him."

Gabriel considered this, then nodded. "Makes sense. He was breathing fire, which suggests ingestion of magic."

"They were from the Queen Mab's garden."

His eyes widened. "Are you sure?"

"I noticed the bush he'd torn them from. That means . . ." The words felt too heavy to speak. She swallowed them back, shaking her head. "Professor Jackson," she said instead, "may I use your dowsing rod?"

The professor pulled the rod from his hair, resulting in a mild explosion of white curls. Taking it, Elodie stood, and all three men watched with close interest (Gabriel), wariness (Algernon), and admiration for her opera coat (Professor Jackson) as she pointed the dowsing rod at the taproom's floor.

It began to shudder in her grip.

Chapter Eighteen

There are worlds within worlds, and
entire universes in the heart of a woman.
Blazing Trails, W.H. Jackson

Whirling back to the table, Elodie grinned. "I've found it! It's here!" she said in an excited whisper. Then the meaning of the words struck her belatedly, and the grin vanished.

"It's *here*," she repeated in a tone of horror. "The unstable trove. It's beneath the inn."

"What?" Professor Jackson and Algernon exclaimed in a tumble of excitement and horror.

"Mr. Parry said he's recently extended the building," Elodie recollected, her pulse quickening as the answer finally came together. "He must have damaged a deposit of magic beneath the land—one dormant for so long, it's never been discovered. But once activated, it sucked in the energy from the trove beneath the mine shaft, and . . ." She opened her hands, fingers spreading, in an evocative gesture.

Gabriel stood, not even noticing how his chair scraped across the ground. "Evacuation time," he said emphatically. "I want the entire village emptied."

"Yes," Elodie said. "South?"

"That's probably best. The most important thing is to keep people calm, or—"

"Aaagghh, we're all going to diiie!"

Algernon leaped up, his chair crashing to the ground. Everyone in the taproom stared in shocked bewilderment as, wailing, he fled.

"Baby!" Tegan shouted (almost certainly in reference to the goat, not the man), and ran after him.

"I'll do the bell!" Professor Jackson announced indecipherably and also dashed out, dressing gown flapping.

Elodie and Gabriel exchanged a weary look. "Evacuation Plan A?" Elodie suggested.

"With a level four withdrawal," Gabriel said.

Nodding in agreement, they turned to depart, but stopped abruptly at the sight of three large, scowling men in front of them. Mr. Parry and his friends had come for a word. Specifically: *"Evacuation?!"*

"Do you in any way appreciate the financial damage such an overreaction will cause?" Mr. Parry hissed angrily, then glanced sidelong at his customers to be sure none had heard him.

"It's not an overreaction," Gabriel said, crossing his arms and frowning over the rim of his spectacles in a manner that would have had the men blubbering were they university undergraduates. But alas, they were hard-bitten denizens of the real world, and they didn't understand that they were supposed to be daunted. "I must urge you to listen," Gabriel continued nevertheless. "We are professional scientists who have compiled extensive instrumental and experiential data and concluded that there exists unequivocal danger of an imminent, significant thaumaturgic eructation."

The scowls wavered into confusion.

"We're brainy," Elodie translated, "and we're warning you, things are about to go boom. You need to get everyone out of here."

"Oh well, if you put it like that," Mr. Parry said. He turned to his friends. "Come on, men, let's get moving!"

"This really is a disaster!" Elodie exclaimed as she surveyed their situation.

"It isn't ideal," Gabriel concurred.

She threw him a vexed look. "We're locked inside a cellar directly above an immensely potent source of thaumaturgic energy that might erupt at any moment."

"I am aware." He rubbed a scratch on his hand, obtained during their several attempts to bash down the cellar door or find another exit among the shelves and boxes in the underground chamber. But after Mr. Parry and his friends had hauled them to the cellar, forced them down the stairs, and told them to bloody well stay there until they came to their senses and stopped messing with people's income, the men had bolted the door to ensure that they did so. There was no way out. Well, except for the ultimate exit when the magic beneath them inevitably erupted, that is.

Elodie did not want to think about that. Unfortunately, her body would not let her forget. Its pulse shouted *You're going to die!* at her unceasingly, and her nerves were even more strained than that time she'd taken a train all the way to Edinburgh before remembering she'd not turned off the gas lamps at home.

"I can't believe they imprisoned us!" she said, wildly gesticulating.

In fact, Mr. Parry had insisted they were doing no such thing. "We're providing you a special opportunity to meditate— free of charge!" he'd explained with a benevolent chuckle before he slammed the door shut. But Elodie did not feel especially meditative.

"The floor is beginning to warm," she said, stamping her foot against the flagstones. "And it's grumbly."

"Yes," Gabriel agreed, so tense he did not even argue about semantics.

"We're going to die here."

"Yes."

Elodie went very still. Gabriel saying it made everything feel a thousand times more real, and all at once she could scarcely bear to breathe, let alone speak.

They stared at each other through the dim lantern light and musty shadows. Fear and regret, grief and intense yearning crammed into the space between them, draining Elodie's warmth, turning Gabriel's eyes darker than the core of a storm. The cellar walls trembled, shedding dust, but neither of them noticed. Elodie thought of the sunlit fields they might have walked together, the joint lectures they might have given, the children that might have been born to them if only she'd had enough time to weave wishes into hope, and then into a beautiful truth. Her heart broke, and broke, and broke.

Gabriel's hands clenched as if he were trying to stop time. Elodie felt love swoop from her throat to the pit of her stomach, like a bird falling from the sky. All around her, the room began to tremble as if it too were frightened. A jar of preserves tumbled from a shelf and rolled noisily over the stone into a corner, where it caught alight with sullen, silvery magic. Fine cracks spread across the floor like the veins of a leaf. The bitter scent of fatal magic filled the air.

Abruptly, Elodie took three paces toward Gabriel, even as he moved toward her. They met in a swirl of dim light and glinting blue dust—reaching, grasping, so that nothing remained between them.

They were kissing before she realized it.

Neither spoke, but their bodies were eloquent: arms encompassing, lips conspiring, blood shouting ardently. They staggered, although whether from an excess of passion or the quaking of the floor cannot be determined. Had Elodie but taken a moment to sit quietly with a biology textbook, she would have understood the effect peril was having on her hormones, and as a result she would no doubt have thrown the textbook aside, then gone back to kissing Gabriel. As it was, she thought of nothing but him. His strength enclosing her, his hands gripping her hair. His jumper getting in the way of what she wanted. She tugged on it, and he released her so as to assist in the process. Then together they stripped her of her opera coat, letting it fall to the dust. Elodie slid Gabriel's suspenders off his shoulders; he unfastened her long skirt; she wrangled with his trouser buttons; he pulled down her skirt and drawers in one efficient move. She held on to him for dear life as he lifted her, pressing her back against the stone wall. Her ankles locked at his back. He did not hesitate. And then suddenly, *finally*, they were together.

They stopped, staring at each other in amazement.

Elodie's breath shook, wordless. Gabriel's eyes grew heavy.

Slowly he kissed her, a deeper, more intense kiss than ever before, as if he needed her in order to sustain himself. He began moving inside her, and it was just like Elodie had remembered, strong and steady, proving that he'd always belonged there. A tidal wave of sensation overwhelmed her. She moaned against his mouth, and he chased the sound with his tongue, and everything grew hotter, faster, desperate, as a long, miserable year of pining compressed into passion then barreled toward what the trembling, steaming floor promised would be an abrupt end.

Still holding her, Gabriel turned, pushing a wicker basket of plums off a sideboard before setting her down in its place. As her bare skin met the wooden surface, Elodie felt like she was being electrified. She tipped her head back so she could gasp a breath, and at once Gabriel seized the opportunity to kiss her throat. But just as her pulse rushed to meet him there, he stopped, and he withdrew altogether from her, leaving her feeling more bereft than she'd ever been in her life. She murmured a protest. Not answering, he lay her back gently on the sideboard.

It was not the most comfortable of beds, and Elodie considered making a polite complaint—but then Gabriel began kissing the soft curve of her naked belly, making a scintillating course southward. Elodie promptly decided that backache (and what felt awfully like a splinter in her hip) was a small price to pay for such delight.

He was so tender, and yet it seemed like he was igniting wildfires in her blood. Elodie didn't know whether to laugh with joy or cry with overwhelming wonder that she lay naked beneath Gabriel's mouth. As he arrived at the secret place she'd never allowed any other man but him to reach, his kisses grew more elaborate, and Elodie pressed one hand over her eyes, the other against his head to ensure he did not stop what he was doing. All the while, the sideboard quivered beneath her and dust showered from the ceiling, but Elodie didn't care. Let the world explode! Life couldn't get better than this moment anyway.

Then Gabriel lifted his head again, leaving her on the brink of something that felt like everything, and she swore at him. He calmly raised her up and guided her to the edge of the sideboard, where they reunited in one swift and thrilling movement that took Elodie's breath away. This time, Gabriel escalated matters by also using his fingers in the same way his mouth had so profitably been employed, and Elodie's breath returned like a tempest. She was ablaze; she was going to perish before any thaumaturgic explosion had a chance to kill her. It would be an undignified way to go, but God, so worth it.

"Wait for me," Gabriel whispered, half command, half plea.

A wry laugh shook from Elodie's throat, that he should say such a thing after all these years, here at the end when they'd no time left to them. "Hurry," she urged.

"No."

Stubborn, arrogant sod. She caught his face between her hands, and their lips met with painful urgency. It felt like both a reunion and farewell, and the poignancy of it fanned Elodie's internal flames to such an intensity that she was forced at last to break the kiss with a sob. Still Gabriel would not hurry.

"You're mine," he growled. "I won't let time take you from me."

"Such a tyrant," she complained, and kissed his jaw, his temple, and all the places on his beautiful face that she'd spent so long dreaming over. Fear and grief faded away. The disaster surrounding them became a mist, a rattling song. They cared for nothing but each other. Gabriel's movements quickened at last, and he gazed with such reverence into Elodie's eyes, it was as if he saw her soul. She felt it shine for him.

I love you, she thought, and came apart in a billowing of bright, singing stars.

At the same moment Gabriel went still, gasping. Elodie could have sworn magic poured through her, every nerve lighting up in response.

A soft, tremulous quiet followed (which is to say, clattering and rumbling followed, and the smash of glass as jars fell from shelves, but that was in the universe beyond their hearts). Gabriel drew her against him, enfolding her in a strong embrace. They held each other tight, eyes closed, pulses throbbing heavily, fingers digging in as they awaited the end.

BANG!

They hugged even tighter, every muscle tensed.

But it had only been the door slamming open. "Are you still in there?" came Mr. Parry's shouted voice from above.

It was as though a map had been flipped over, showing a whole new world on the other side. Instantly, Elodie pushed Gabriel back as she scrambled down from the cabinet, her boots sending up clouds of sparking blue dust as they hit the floor. Gabriel, blinking rather dazedly, positioned himself in front of her as a shield against Mr. Parry's view—never mind that his own nakedness made it clear what they had been doing. But Mr. Parry, on the landing, only called out once more, "Hello, are you there?" and Elodie realized the shadows and the rising thaumaturgic mist concealed them from sight.

"Where the hell else would we be?" Gabriel shouted up to the innkeeper. "You locked us in!"

"Yes, sorry about that," Mr. Parry answered contritely. "You were right after all. There will be a discount on your bill, as an apology. But now we're getting out. Hurry!"

Elodie's nervous system imploded with hysterics. She did not know whether to laugh or scream. She'd just had desperate, urgent sex with her husband by way of farewell, and now *the bloody door was open*!

Which was, of course, a good thing.

Maybe a good thing, part of her responded darkly as Gabriel half turned away from her to restore his clothing. Death by thaumaturgic explosion would have been more comfortable than the certain demise from panic that she was about to experience. What had it all meant? What—what—what what?! Had it merely been incited by the danger and the banging and the impending death? The absolute in nervous overexcitement? Or had it been as heartfelt for Gabriel as it had been for her?

Actually, thank goodness the door *was* open, because she intended to run away as soon as she got her knickers on.

They dressed hurriedly while the room filled with a heat that was not due entirely to their mutual agitation, considering the smell. "Sulfur," Elodie said, wrinkling her nose. "I knew it."

Suddenly, a high set of shelves toppled, its load of jars smashing to the floor in a violent explosion of glass. Gabriel yanked Elodie protectively against him, their heartbeats crashing together. Flames were igniting from the broken glass, and cracks widening in the floorboards, and hot steam began to belch from within the tormented earth.

"Go!" Gabriel shouted, pushing Elodie toward the stairs. They raced up, even as the steps behind them caught fire and spilled fruit transformed into twisted black trees. Reaching the corridor above, they stumbled on trembling floorboards.

"I'll clear the building," Gabriel said, steadying himself with a hand against one wall. "You begin evacuating the village."

Elodie nodded. "Be safe."

"You too."

She did not linger for a poignant goodbye. (After all, that had been thoroughly accomplished in the cellar.) Her professional instincts engaged, some ten minutes later than propriety would have liked. She turned and ran, skipping over fissures that were ripping open in the floor as she went.

GABRIEL COMPLETED AN evacuation of the Queen Mab in minutes, assisted by its shuddering walls and floorboards. Frightened guests in various states of dress pushed him aside as he came to rescue them and fled on their own initiative. Once certain that every room was empty, he ran to his own to retrieve his coat and ER kit, for the sake of the vital things they contained, then raced into the street.

The church bell was ringing, its doleful clang echoing through the village. Locals and tourists streamed out of buildings. They formed an exodus south into the fields with the efficiency of people who had been living with thaumaturgic activity for some time. Gabriel jogged through them, looking for Elodie.

There, his heart said, and a second later he saw her emerging from a cottage. At once, he released muscles he hadn't been aware he was clenching. She led the cottage's occupants onto the street, then pointed south. They joined the fleeing crowd, and Elodie turned toward the neighboring house. Gabriel pulled his attention away from her and ran to assist an elderly man who had fallen.

A foul odor of rotten eggs saturated the air. Cracks tore through cobblestones and trees slanted precariously as shock waves rippled out from the Queen Mab. When at last the village stood empty, the bell tolling into an otherwise portentous hush, Gabriel walked to the center of the street and looked back at the inn. Steam was billowing from its windows and chimneys.

"Well, at least we finally located the source," said a light voice, and Gabriel glanced aside to find Elodie arriving next to him. His stomach squeezed as if he were seeing her for the first time, an unkempt dryad tripping into his life to mess up its nicely regulated schema. He frowned in automatic defense. But she wasn't quite looking at him, her cheeks flushed with uncharacteristic shyness. Gabriel couldn't blame her. His entire body felt like it was flushing for the same reason.

Well, maybe not his entire body. Certain parts of it ached to reach out and be with her again, kiss her again, and to make the bed in the morning after spending a long, sultry night with her. But there was the small matter of the disaster that was their relationship . . . er, which is to say, *the disaster engulfing Dôlylleuad*.

"All clear?" he asked, his voice gritty.

She nodded. "Professor Jackson is ringing the church bell. Everyone else has—"

BOOM!

They ducked. The Queen Mab's roof burst apart, stone and dust flying. Roaring up from beneath it came an enormous jet of boiling water.

"Huh," Gabriel said.

"Gosh!" Elodie breathed.

"Now that's what I call magic!"

At this shout, they straightened, turning to see Professor Jackson jogging toward them, his dressing gown flapping open to reveal a disconcerting lack of sleepwear. Algernon followed, cowering as he ran. Gabriel could hear the accountant's whimpers even from the distance.

"Stay back!" he shouted to the men as the geyser shot almost two hundred feet high, enshrouding the inn and its neighbors in clouds of steam. The rush of heat, and more emphatically the speeding fragments of shattered stone, inspired Gabriel and Elodie to retreat up the road, meeting Professor Jackson and Algernon beneath the dubious shelter of an oak tree.

"Is the world ending?" Algernon wailed from where he huddled behind the trunk.

"Maybe," Professor Jackson told him cheerfully.

"Of course it's not," Elodie said. And her confident attitude might have gone some way to reassuring the young accountant had not jagged rocks begun to burst through the cobblestones of the street while she was speaking. Dirt and burning pebbles went flying. The sky glowed blue like the color of a scream. In that moment, Algernon found religion (and Professor Jackson found half a muffin in his dressing gown's pocket, but that was less impressive).

Elodie turned to Gabriel. "An eruption of this size is sure to trigger the fey line into cascade," she whispered so that Algernon would not hear her beneath his frantic praying.

Gabriel looked over her shoulder to where venting magic was rising like blue smoke in the east, transforming into birds that swooped and spiraled through the morning light before disintegrating again as ash. "I believe it already has," he said grimly.

Taking a map from his ER kit, he held it open so Elodie could read it along with him. They mentally traced the 5-SEQ line through a range of colors and contour lines.

"The Bronze Age cairns and stone circles of Elan Valley might stop it," Elodie said, tapping that area on the map.

"Maybe," Gabriel said, meaning *no.* Thaumaturgic energy was going to sweep right over those old stones, smash through Hereford and Cheltenham, and then slam into Oxford, where libraries and museums crammed with magical artifacts, and aviaries with magical birds, created a vast thaumaturgic reservoir that would be ignited with cataclysmic effect.

And then that energy would continue on, burning, snarling, ripping magic out of the earth all the way to . . .

"London," Elodie breathed.

They stared at the gray sprawl of the city on the map, then lifted their eyes again to the east. Lightning tore through the magic-stained sky.

"Amelia's in Hereford, studying an ancient copy of the Magna Carta," Gabriel said.

Elodie patted his arm reassuringly, sending ~~delightful tingles~~ electrical impulses through his nervous system. "She'll be fine, I'm sure."

"I'm not worried about her," he said. "If anyone knows how to handle magic, it's my sister. I'm thinking that the charter's parchment is the skin of a sheep who drank from Ullswater."

Elodie gasped. "That's one of the lakes claiming to be where Nimue handed Excalibur to King Arthur! It's a level six node."

"Exactly. According to Amelia, the parchment has an

extremely high thaumaturgic charge. This new trove is not so distant from those currently mapped along the 5-SEQ that it couldn't represent a . . ." He winced very slightly. "A wiggle in the fey line. If we place the Magna Carta at a point along the line, ahead of the cascading energy, it could act like a reflective shield and make that energy rebound."

"Aah," Elodie said in approval. "Reverse the cascade and squelch the magic." Gabriel looked at her, all bright and lovely and slightly rumpled from the things he'd done to her some fifteen minutes ago, her eyes reflecting magic from the sunlit geyser, and he nodded. The surrender to colloquialism was worth it just to see her smile in response.

"You'd be risking a massive explosion in the village," Professor Jackson remarked through a mouthful of buttered muffin.

"As a matter of fact, my team and I did something similar a few years ago in Sheffield," Gabriel said, "although on a smaller scale, and the result was a squelching rather than an explosion."

"It's a good plan," Elodie said. "So we need to reach Hereford at all speed."

"I still have my bicycle here somewhere," Professor Jackson said. He looked around as if he expected the bicycle to be propped against the tree.

"That's not necessary," Gabriel told him. "We are dignified professionals. Bicycles have no place in this assignment. We will hire horses to get to Aberystwyth and catch a train from there."

"And hopefully outrace the cascade," Elodie said.

"I'll come too," Professor Jackson offered, licking butter from his fingers.

"No, we need you to stay here in case of further trouble," Gabriel told him. "Mr. Jennings, you also stay."

Algernon squeaked from behind the tree. "What? Here? Are you mad?! I'm going home to Leicester, where it's safe."

"Perfect." Gabriel rolled up his map, then looked directly at Elodie. As she looked back at him, the silence between them seemed to pulse with the memory of that mad, beautiful experience in the cellar.

I love you, disaster girl, he thought.

Then he turned from her, his expression hardening as he stared into the horizon.

"Let's go."

♡

CHAPTER NINETEEN

Philomel's razor notes that, if a rational cause
for natural phenomena cannot be found, it must be
magical.
That or you've drunk too much beer.
Blazing Trails, W.H. Jackson

LESS THAN TWO hours later they were in Aberystwyth Station, impatiently awaiting the next train. Elodie shivered within the cold sea wind as she glanced surreptitiously at Gabriel standing nearby. He might have glanced at her too at some point, but if so, she didn't catch him doing it. Mostly, he frowned at his wristwatch. He'd sent a telegram to his sister in Hereford, advising her of the situation, but one historian would be no match for a cascade of magic, and Gabriel looked like he might at any moment just start running along the train tracks to reach her.

Beyond him, Algernon was pacing nervously and startling at every little noise. And beyond the young accountant, Pimmersby, Hapsitch, and Mumbers posed in various states of manly swagger alongside the Misses Trevallion. The tourists had been so determined to "follow the fun" that not even Gabriel scowling at them had provided deterrent enough. Pimmersby, who'd spent much of the mad gallop to Aberystwyth shouting at intervals, "'Half a league, half a league, half a league onward!'" was now declaiming, "'O the wild charge they made!'" and gesturing grandly, while Misses Trevallion sighed adoringly in a manner Elodie would *never* do.

At the edge of the group stood Tegan Parry. Her ostensible role was to organize the return of the horses, but she'd insisted on waiting to see them off properly—not so much from any fond feeling, Elodie suspected, but more to soak up every moment of dramatic pathos. Her father had given them only a brief farewell back in the village, having been preoccupied with intense emotion over the destruction of his inn. (The emotion of delight, that is, since not only would his insurance pay for an even better premises, but he now had a source of magical sulfur waters on his property that was even more significant than those in Llandrindod Wells, and visions of the spa he would create dominated his attention.)

"I'm sorry for doubting you about how dangerous the magic would become," he'd said, however, smiling sheepishly as they saddled their horses.

In response, Gabriel had *looked* at him.

"Er, and I'm sorry for almost getting you killed," Parry added.

The look intensified.

"Er, and compliments to your lovely wife, sir." He'd bowed to Elodie, and Gabriel had at last allowed him to retreat in continued possession of his limbs.

Thankfully, the geyser and its earthquakes subsided enough before they left that Elodie was free to stop worrying about the death and destruction they might cause in Dôlylleuad and focus instead on the death and destruction that might strike along the fey line—not to mention the death she herself was about to experience due to freezing.

Gabriel glanced over just then, and she read coat-giving in his eyes. Her stomach dissolved into sparkles. She could still feel his hands clamping her hips while he did things to her that made the violently erupting magical super-geyser seem dull in comparison. But the fact that they'd not since spoken a word unrelated to work confused her. Notwithstanding such interesting claims as *"you're mine,"* she wondered if Gabriel had merely been suffering from nervous overexcitement (yet again) or if he only had enough room in his consciousness for one thing at a time, and that the potential end of the world had seized it. To be fair, she could have done with such focus herself. As it was, her thoughts skipped between disaster and kisses and the possibility of being pregnant—which sent her back to disasters again—until she began developing a headache. Perhaps it was she who was the confusing one, not Gabriel, she mused with a weary sigh.

"Such a mournful sound, Miss Tarrant," came a polished voice behind her. Elodie turned to see Mr. Mumbers looking romantically windswept and smiling, like a poet in search of a rhyme. "I fear you must be chilled by this breeze," he said, and began to remove his coat.

"Excuse me," came a voice that was the opposite of suave. It was grim and severe, a granite mountain against a stark winter sky.

Elodie turned back to see Gabriel arrive, just an inch closer than "associates" would politely allow. He began removing *his* coat. Elodie bit her lip, feeling rather like a damsel caught between two knights except that, instead of weapons, they wielded cashmere garments.

"Thank you for considering *Mrs.* Tarrant's welfare," Gabriel told Mr. Mumbers with stolid civility. The other gentleman blanched, understanding all too well that what Gabriel actually meant was *get away from my wife or I'll suffocate you with that cheap coat hanging crookedly from your flimsy shoulders.*

Elodie considered scoffing and then marching away, but instead, inexplicably, she blushed scarlet. This was far from the behavior of a plucky, intelligent heroine, and the only possible conclusion she could make was that sex had deranged her nervous system.

Oddly, kisses and various minor fumblings with other men in her youth had never induced this problem. Mind you, she'd not spent almost a decade dreaming about those men. And Gabriel certainly had not fumbled; he'd got straight to the point. When he'd lifted her off her feet, it had felt like her only connection to the world had been his strong and vigorous . . .

She blinked suddenly, noticing that Mr. Mumbers had gone and Gabriel was standing in patient silence, holding out his coat. *Focus, Elodie,* she grumbled to herself as she took the coat.

"Thank you," she said, smiling.

"Hm," Gabriel replied, and went to ask the ticket clerk how much longer the train would be.

Finally it arrived, and the group made haste to board while Tegan waved goodbye, a rather forlorn look in her eyes. Elodie wanted to run over to hug the girl and put in a final encouraging word about tertiary education, but there was no time. She found herself jostled as she tried to board. Just as she was contemplating a bit of unladylike elbow-jabbing and hip-shoving of her own, Gabriel stepped up behind her, acting as an effective bodyguard. Entering the train compartment, she turned to thank him.

"I'll see you in Hereford," he said before she could speak. He stepped back—

"Wait!" Elodie stared at him in astonishment. "Are you not coming?"

"Of course I am," he replied.

"But—why—?"

"I bought myself a first class ticket. I could not tolerate hours in company with those tourists and Jennings."

(*"Hey!"* Algernon cried out indignantly from behind him.)

Elodie watched, utterly gobsmacked, as her husband departed for the front of the train without another word.

Of all the confounding behavior! Of all the arrogant soddishness! Elodie flung herself into the corner of one bench seat in a haze of fury, ignoring the others settling in around her. She glared with such intensity into the middle distance that, as the train began to move, Algernon could be heard pompously advising Mr. Mumbers that "Dr. Tarrant is a brilliant scientist, and it's best not to interrupt her when she's cogitating about disasters."

"Cogitating about disasters" summed up pretty well what was indeed occurring in Elodie's imagination. She had Gabriel divorced before the train even cleared Aberystwyth Station, rendered homeless as they passed Bow Street, and trapped in a Scottish bog during a thaumaturgic thunderstorm that rained down worms upon him while Mr. Mumbers led everyone else in a game of charades.

But there is only so long a woman can torture her husband *in phantasia* before she grows bored. Charades offered no distraction (indeed, she would rather have jumped into quirksand than taken part), and the view out the window was blocked by a Miss Trevallion's hat. Thus bereft of entertainment, she rummaged in Gabriel's coat pockets, discovering therein something small, flattish, and wrapped in a white linen handkerchief.

Instantly enlivened, she stared at the little parcel. The handkerchief was so well ironed it might have been fresh from a boutique store's cabinet, but it carried the clean, cool aroma of soap that always accompanied Gabriel. The folds were so carefully made, he had clearly lingered over them. Elodie sensed this was a treasure of some kind—perhaps a small collection of leaves, from the feel of it—and she told herself to put it straight back in the pocket.

Unfortunately, her fingers did not hear this and had the handkerchief opened before she could stop them.

Inside were several raggedy bits of paper, stacked with care. Curiosity rather than nosiness (*Yes, there is a difference,* she told her horrified manners) saw Elodie lift the first piece and unfold it.

Her pulse swooned. She refolded the piece, set it aside, and turned over another. Now her breath threatened to swoon also.

These were *hers.* There were notes about a river's flow through a farm outside Chipping Norton . . . an old shopping list . . . a limerick about cheese that she'd composed during her Thaumaturgy Theory lecture while her students were copying down equations from the blackboard . . . sketches of wildflowers growing around Oxford. She'd taken them from her own pocket outside the graveyard in Dôlylleuad and handed them to Gabriel while she extinguished the fire that had engulfed his umbrella. She'd forgotten to take them back. Evidently he'd kept them.

No, he'd done more than keep them. He'd smoothed out their wrinkles, folded them gently, and wrapped them in linen and . . . *oh my goodness* . . . pressed a wild violet between two.

Stunned, Elodie felt her fingers tingle as if the tiny flower were imbued with magic, rather than a sign she was hyperventilating. Trying to reconcile the romanticism of Gabriel treating her pocket detritus as treasure and his standoffish behavior at the Aberystwyth train station, she found herself caught, as it were, between the devil and a beautiful, sparkling, deep blue sea, with no compass to guide her.

Folding the handkerchief around the notes as accurately as she could, she tucked the tiny parcel back into Gabriel's coat pocket and reengaged her imagination.

By the time the train reached Shrewsbury, she had Gabriel and herself installed in a handsome town house on the outskirts of Oxford, with a green velvet sofa, a magnificent library, several detailed maps on the walls, and a large, comfortable bed, which she put to such good use that Mumbers, seeing the brightness of her eyes as she stared into the middle distance once again, declared that "Dr. Tarrant looks like she's cogitating up a veritable storm!" Which actually wasn't that far from the truth.

A changeover of trains at Shrewsbury required fifteen minutes' waiting in the tranquil aftermath of a rain shower. The sun was the color of light reflecting off a wedding ring. White wishdoves fluttered about the station with trailing ribbons of magic that rippled through the air like hope made visible. Elodie found the quiet serenity rather eerie, considering they had left one disaster and were racing toward another. Tapping her foot restively, she gazed south as if she might see evidence of trouble. Nearby, Gabriel was doing the same. But the sky was an innocent azure blue, with nothing more deadly in it than chimneys.

While the others sought tea within the station, Elodie approached Gabriel, intent on demanding why he had abandoned her to the second class carriage. It would be most annoying to die in the coming magical cataclysm without having been at least that brave. But his expression was so guarded, as if she were equivalent to a marauding band of Vikings come to loot him, that she quite lost the heart for confrontation. Instead, she took off his coat, with its hidden treasure of notes, and returned it to him.

"Are you no longer cold?" he asked.

"I'm quite warm, thank you." The lie fell clumsily from her lips, and to compensate she attempted a smile. It seemed to stretch her mouth like a grimace, however, so she tried sobriety instead. But then she felt like she was dour, so she just looked away into the distance—which did not help, for the view really was lovely, peaceful, bejeweled with silver drops of light after the recent rain; and moreover, she was alive in it, when not too long ago she'd been anticipating death's imminence. Her eyes filled with tears.

Gabriel took an alarmed step back. "Are you unwell?"

"Lovesick for the beautiful world," she told him.

This apparently was poor reassurance. "All I can see are a lot of buildings," he muttered. "And Mr. Mumbers staring out moonily through the station's window. I suppose the two of you have had much intercourse on the journey so far."

Elodie nearly choked on her breath. "No, we haven't talked at all," she said. "The group played charades most of the time."

"Oh my God." He stared at her, aghast.

"Yes, it made my headache considerably worse."

His frown deepened. "I would have bought you a first class ticket also, but I assumed you'd want to be sociable."

Elodie blinked at him. Or, at least, at his right ear. Looking into those heavy dark eyes felt far too intimate now. "Why would you assume that?"

"You like people."

"I like *my* people. I'm not so keen on quantities of random strangers." *I like* you, *daft man,* she would have said had she been able to locate courage anywhere within her.

Gabriel tilted his head as he regarded her, seemingly at a loss. "But you smile at them all the time."

"And you frown," she answered.

"Ah." Comprehension lit his face. "Wait here," he said, and without further discussion he departed for the station's interior. When he returned, it was with a first class ticket. "My apologies for misunderstanding," he said, handing it to her.

"Oh, gosh." Elodie came perilously close to fluttering her eyelashes. "I'll repay you once we get back to Oxford."

"There's no need," he answered gruffly.

"Oh," she said again, which was all she could manage since her intelligence was busy wrestling with her emotions to prevent her from hugging the ticket. "Thank you."

"Don't thank me. The Home Office is paying."

Upon that romantic note, he turned away, for the southbound train was arriving. They crossed to it, and Gabriel opened a compartment's door for Elodie. She stepped inside.

And watched bemusedly as he turned to the neighboring compartment. "See you in Hereford," he said. "Try to get some rest, it's going to be a long afternoon." He entered the compartment and shut its door, and Elodie found herself blinking at the space from which he'd disappeared.

"Phooey," she grumbled to the elegant velvet emptiness of her compartment. Now that she was alone, courage sprang to the fore again, armed with all manner of clever retorts and bold statements she should have made while talking to Gabriel on the platform. Agitated, she tried to pace, but there was inadequate room. She tried to sit nicely, but her legs jiggled and her thoughts dissolved into a melee of irritated opinions. She even considered returning to second class, where at least she'd have people to scowl at, but the train began to move.

For several more long minutes (two), Elodie continued to brood, then jumped to her feet, flung open the compartment's inner door, and stormed down the corridor to knock on Gabriel's door. He looked up in surprise from the map he was reading, and she nearly squeaked and ran away to hide. But she forced herself to stay, for while her time in Wales had not necessarily made her into a stronger woman, it had at least shown her that Gabriel was a gentler man than everyone assumed. Arrogant, yes. Obnoxious, aloof, enigmatic, and annoying . . . uh, but definitely gentle too. When he was not scowling and grumbling and making demands, that is . . .

Quickly abandoning this increasingly unhelpful line of thought, Elodie ~~flounced~~ moved with energetic purpose into the compartment and sat down opposite Gabriel.

"Er?" he said.

"Are you angry with me?" she demanded, crossing her arms and glaring at him.

"Um?"

"'Um' is not an answer," she informed him tersely. "Why are you angry with me?"

He removed his reading spectacles so as to better stare at her in utter, complete confusion. "I'm not."

"Then why are you avoiding me?"

"Avoiding you?"

She rolled her eyes. The man had all kinds of university degrees; surely he could conduct a conversation more efficiently! "Is it because of what happened in the cellar?"

He went red. "No."

"Are we even going to discuss that?"

"No."

Whew, thought her heart, which was only just holding on to its rhythm as it was. "Fine. But at least explain the separate compartments."

Gabriel went stiff, his expression opaque. "You said you have a headache. I purchased you a private compartment for the sake of your comfort. The attendants will be bringing you cream of chicken soup from the dining cart, along with a rug and pillow."

"Oh." Elodie gulped. "Cream of chicken, you say?"

"Uh-huh."

"That's my favorite."

"I know."

"And a pillow?"

"Hm."

She rose awkwardly, pointing with both hands to the door. "I'll just be—I'll—uh, see you in Hereford, shall I? Much obliged for the soup. Cheerio."

"Elodie."

"Yes?" She paused in the doorway but was too mortified to look at him.

"You can stay here if you would prefer."

The offer was made in rigid tones, and yet Elodie did not think he spoke reluctantly. In fact, she wondered if his stiffness was perhaps akin to her own jitteriness, and if he felt as shy and awkward as she did after their cellar adventure.

"I'd appreciate your opinion on this map of Hereford, and where we might make a defense against the cascade, if your head isn't too painful," Gabriel added, gruff, cold . . . and yes, *bashful*, Elodie was sure of it. The realization was profound, making her question everything she'd supposed about his behavior these past years. Could there be a soft heart beneath that grouchy exterior?

"*Tsk*," he said just then. "You'd think the railway company could spare a little effort to make these seats less torturously uncomfortable."

Elodie pressed her lips shut and laid her forehead against the glass panel of the compartment's door, trying to ward off laughter. Clearly, the grouchy exterior went all the way through. Thank goodness. What would she do with a soft-hearted man? He wouldn't be her beloved Gabriel.

Smiling, she turned back in to the compartment. Gabriel shifted so she could sit beside him (nearest the window, he insisted, for the sake of her headache), and they discussed the geographical surrounds of Hereford (quietly, ditto). When luncheon was served, they set aside the map to eat, and the conversation turned instead to where one found the best soup in Oxford's winter . . . how snow made the city appear "wondrous" (Elodie) and "white" (Gabriel) . . . and what lectures they most enjoyed giving in the Hilary term. Upon both of them answering "magical cartography," Gabriel shared with her the gist of his latest studies on the topic.

But he stopped suddenly, in the middle of describing recent developments in thaumaturgic theodolites, and his expression hunched in on itself with troubled thought. Then he began again, more slowly. "Indeed, the lens is an enchanted mirror of silver grace, unveiling a world of magic."

Elodie gave a confused laugh. "What?"

Gabriel shrugged uncomfortably. "I am not so hidebound that I can't take a lesson from a young man, such as that

Mumbers fellow. I know you appreciate language that is more . . . lyrical."

Elodie stared at him, incredulous. "No. I don't want poetry from you, Gabriel."

His eyes shuttered with darkness. "You don't?"

She smacked his arm lightly, causing his lashes to flutter and his breath to catch. "You invigorate my mind with your intelligence and your scrupulous vocabulary. Don't try to be something else, I beg you."

"I invigorate your mind?" he repeated in wary astonishment.

"Of course," she said cheerily, and stole a leftover piece of bread from his plate.

The train staff came to clear the dishes away, after which Gabriel laid the rug over her lap. But Elodie needed no pillow: lulled by the rhythmic motion of the train and Gabriel's low voice talking about angles and measurements, she fell asleep where she was sitting, her head leaning against his shoulder.

GABRIEL WAS NOT a religious man, but in that moment he knew heaven.

CHAPTER TWENTY

The apple doesn't fall far from the tree . . .
Unless it's picked up by a thaumaturgic breeze,
carried half a mile, and then transformed into a
banana.

Blazing Trails, W.H. Jackson

THEY ARRIVED IN Hereford too late.

Even the tourists evidenced horror as they looked upon the chaos that had ripped through the city. Roads were torn up, trees tossed about, roofs stripped from buildings. Cold blue flames sprang up from the river, sending coils of magic into the shock-white sky like malevolent clouds that rained deadly glittering hail. A tumult of sirens and shouted voices told a story far more grim and somber than that of Dôlylleuad.

"This is most unpleasant," a Miss Trevallion declared, delicately waving a gloved hand before her face in an effort to ward off a few dainty tears.

"The cost of these damages is going to be major," Algernon said.

"'Oh, this rueful sky, this pageantry of fear!'" Mumbers quoted, sweeping his hat in an effusive gesture that might have been more compelling had not some drifting magic struck said hat from his hand, transforming it into a small black rabbit. The Misses Trevallion squealed with delight.

"Use the station's telegram to contact the Home Office," Gabriel ordered Algernon as he shouldered his ER kit. "Tell them to dispatch an emergency response team at once."

"But my train for Leicester leaves in fifteen minutes," Algernon whined.

"Then type fast." Not waiting for a response, Gabriel strode away.

"Bye, Algie dear!" Elodie said, clasping one of the accountant's hands between both of hers and thus managing to horrify him even more than Hereford's ruined buildings had done.

"Mrs. Tarrant," he replied in starchy farewell, giving her a look down his nose that made it plain he still considered her to be no more than Gabriel's wife. "I shall send you and Dr. Tarrant a copy of my report."

"Marvelous!" Elodie said with an easy cheerfulness that came from having no intention of reading it. She kissed the lad's cheek just to bedevil him, then, to the sounds of his outraged sputters, she hurried after Gabriel.

As they sped toward Hereford Cathedral, her heart strained at the sight of despairing locals gathered outside damaged buildings while crews worked to clear immediate hazards. She wished she could stop and offer help, but that would make her only another pair of hands, instead of an expert who could ensure worse catastrophe did not hit farther down the line. So she looked ahead to the cathedral and ran, following Gabriel past rubble and around hot spots of magic, along the efficient route he'd mapped out during the train journey.

Incredibly, the great stone church remained untouched, not even one window broken. This was entirely thanks to Professor Tarrant (i.e., the Amelia one), according to the wardens whom Gabriel and Elodie questioned.

"She was remarkably efficient in the way she directed us all in creating a defense for the building," said one gentleman in breathless tones.

"She was impressive," said the other, eyes huge.

"She was bloody terrifying," added the first, and they both nodded vigorously.

"Where is she now?" Gabriel asked with unrestrained impatience.

"In the south transept," came the reply, "helping prepare for any wounded that are brought here from the city. But are you *sure* you want to see her? I wasn't exaggerating when I said 'bloody terrifying.'"

"I believe you," Gabriel answered grimly. "She's my sister."

After a few murmurs of sympathy, they were directed to said transept, where they found Amelia directing a group of nuns to lay choir bench cushions on the floor as beds and tear up priests' robes for bandages. Light streaming in through the great stained glass window illuminated her dark hair with a glinting blue aura, making her seem enchanted. Noticing Gabriel and Elodie arrive, she gave a last crisp order to a pair of tremulous novices, who clearly believed they were going to hell for destroying the dean's gold-embroidered chasuble but dared not refuse her, and then she walked over, heels tapping against the stone floor like a teacher's pointer tapping against a blackboard.

"You're here," she said, stiff and dispassionate as she scrutinized them both. "Unharmed?"

"Unharmed," Gabriel said in the same cool tone.

Immediately the tension in her body eased, allowing a sigh of relief to escape her. She gave them a bright and really quite beautiful smile, and Elodie wondered how anyone could consider this woman terrifying.

"And you're unhurt also?" Gabriel asked. The question wavered ever so slightly; glancing at him, Elodie saw warmth and worry in his eyes as he regarded his sister. Almost at once he composed himself and frowned with aggravation, but the damage was done. His familial love was exposed.

"I'm fine," Amelia said. "Kinetic thaumaturgic energy coming down the fey line struck Hereford approximately thirty-seven minutes ago." She paused, consulting a delicate silver watch on her wrist. "Thirty-eight minutes. Thanks to your telegram, we were as prepared as we could be. Much of the population was evacuated northward, and the cathedral protected by certain iron and gold items at key points around its perimeter, as you recommended. Staff were reluctant at first to obey my directions, but that was soon remedied."

She spoke with such incisiveness, Elodie got a sense now of why the wardens had been so jittery. Amelia was not stern and pedantic like her brother; rather, she appeared to be efficiency personified, a trait all too often equated with "terrorizing" in women. Elodie rather wished she had a little of it herself.

"Unfortunately, our defenses were breached in one place," Amelia continued, "as a result of which the ghost of King Ethelbert is at present wandering around the Bishop's Cloister, complaining that he can't find his bones." She rolled her eyes as if the spectral king were just a silly lad behaving in naughty fashion. "Otherwise, none of the artifacts in the cathedral were triggered. I've obtained the Magna Carta for you. It's in that leather case."

She pointed to a large satchel propped up on a nearby chair. "Hm," Gabriel said with a nod.

"Thank you for your help," Elodie added more effusively. "I'm sorry for interfering with your study of the charter."

"Not at all," Amelia reassured her. "To be honest, the study was just a cover story to get me into the cathedral. I'm looking for a long-lost . . . well, never mind. In the case you'll find the 1217 issue of the Magna Carta, along with an accompanying King's Writ and a fourteenth-century book of prayers illuminated with thaumaturgic gold. Together they contain a formidable amount of magical power, but I do fear not even they could stop a cascade."

"Frankly, we don't have any other options to try," Gabriel said. "We're out of time. In fact, we'll be lucky to get in front of the cascade at all. I didn't think it would have reached Hereford by now."

"Well, there's an ancient yew tree on a site of pagan worship not far from here, which may slow its progress," Amelia said, providing them with hope but simultaneously taking it away with her doubtful tone. "I suppose though you'll just have to put your faith in the British rail system."

A taut and painfully eloquent moment of silence followed this, then Amelia's expression shifted, becoming one Elodie had seen all too often on Gabriel: officious, determined. "I shall come with you," she announced peremptorily.

"No," Gabriel said at once. "It's obvious they need you here. And we need you here too, in case the energy rebound causes further problems for the city."

"Hm. Very well." Amelia was clearly not pleased, but nevertheless recognized his logic. Elodie began to feel pity for these Tarrant children, raised to be so very sensible. If she'd been in Amelia's place, no amount of good sense would have restrained her from doing what she wanted. Er . . . which probably wasn't such a great recommendation of her own character, come to think of it . . .

"Just take care of yourselves," Amelia admonished them. "And mind you don't damage those documents. They're great treasures, and the cathedral's archivist is upset enough with me as it is."

"Why is he upset with you, Amelia?" Gabriel asked, suspicion freighting his voice.

"Because I tied him up and put him in a cupboard so I could steal those treasures for you," she answered, much in the same way another person would have said, *Because I accidentally stepped on his foot.*

Elodie and Gabriel exchanged a glance, then shrugged. The archivist could complain to the Home Office *after* they'd saved the world.

"We'll do our best to keep them safe," Elodie promised, trying not to think about the gallons of water that had exploded in her vicinity over the past couple of days.

"And don't get killed," Amelia added, giving Gabriel the stern look that Elodie was beginning to understand represented love, Tarrant-style. "Aunt Mary is preparing a rather nice dinner for this Sunday, and she'll complain horribly if the family has to attend your funeral instead."

"I'll save the world for the sake of Aunt Mary's roast lamb," Gabriel told her. Brother and sister frowned at each other for an intense, poignant moment that almost brought tears to Elodie's eyes. Then, taking up the leather case from the chair, Gabriel walked away, no doubt expecting Elodie to follow. But even as she took one step, Amelia hissed to her.

"Professor, wait."

When Elodie turned back, the woman made a *come closer* gesture, and Elodie obeyed rather nervously.

Amelia glanced over Elodie's shoulder at Gabriel's departing form, then regarded Elodie amazedly. "He's looking almost *cheerful*. What have you done to him?"

"Er . . ." Elodie said, blushing.

"I see." Amelia's nose wrinkled with sisterly distaste. "I'm sorry I asked. But I must say, I do admire you, Professor. When Gabriel told me you were a remarkable woman, I assumed he was talking about your career success. Now I understand what he actually meant. Anyone who can make our Grouchyboo smile like that is remarkable indeed."

Elodie felt rather overcome by this speech. *Remarkable woman! Grouchyboo!* But most of all: "He was smiling?" Had she blinked and missed it?

"On the inside," Amelia explained. "A sister can discern these things. Please, take care of him."

"I will," Elodie assured her, and they both pretended not to know that the advancing tidal wave of magic might just overwhelm her every effort to do so.

"Now excuse me," Amelia said. "I see one of the nuns trying to hide the dean's silk stole . . ."

Leaving her to it, Elodie hurried after Gabriel, her thoughts swirling with ~~the disaster threatening Oxford and London~~ what Amelia had said. She felt so charmed by the information, she could have been identified as a level nine thaumaturgic node.

"To Cheltenham next?" she asked Gabriel as they strode through the nave.

"The cascade reached here in only four hours," Gabriel replied. "At that speed, it will be through Cheltenham before we can get there. We have to make straight for Oxford and hope we arrive in time. The next train leaves in . . ." He consulted his wristwatch, and his frown leaped. "Twenty-three minutes."

Elodie's swirling thoughts tripped to a standstill. "You have the Hereford rail schedule memorized?"

"Of course," he said as if it were obvious. "Needing to make a quick turnaround was always a possibility. One must be prepared."

"Somebody should give you a badge for Best Geographer."

"You mean my 1887 Mercator Award for Excellence in Exigent Geographical Science?"

She laughed. "That would do, yes."

She wanted to ask him how he'd felt, accepting the award, and whether he'd hung it on his office wall, and what his favorite color was, but she had no chance. Exiting the church, they raced back through Hereford to the train station.

Thankfully, although there existed no official award for running fast, it was a skill emergency geographers tended to excel at, as is usually the case when one regularly finds a flood or furious rosebush hot on one's heels. Consequently, they reached the station just in time to board the Oxford-bound train before it departed.

The following three hours were spent in the train's first class dining car, where they laid maps and notes across a table, drank copious amounts of tea, and planned to yet again save the world methodically (Elodie rolled her eyes at Gabriel) and safely (Gabriel frowned at Elodie). He was polite, listening to all she suggested. She was also polite, pouring his tea and not calling him Mr. Grouchyboo.

Indeed, their conduct was so exceedingly polite that Elodie felt like the morning's tryst had never occurred and the words *"my every thought circles back to you, my every breath wants to kiss you"* never spoken. (Gabriel might be able to memorize train schedules, but Elodie remembered the *important* things.) The closer to Oxford they traveled, the more their conversation faltered, until Gabriel resumed using "hm" instead of actual, polysyllabic words, and Elodie chewed her bottom lip so much it bled. Evidently having passionate sex, followed thereafter by narrowly avoiding death, did not automatically resolve relationship issues. Elodie was at a loss as to what to do next.

Gradually, they dwindled into an uncertain silence. Gabriel stared out the window. Elodie stared at the silver teapot. In fact, both were watching the other's reflection in said window and pot.

Patience shall be my compass, Elodie decided at last, reminding herself of the determination she'd made in the fields of Dôlylleuad. If she proceeded with care and gentleness, she might unearth the secret troves in Gabriel's heart. Impressed by this rather nifty pun, she turned back to him with studied casualness. "I hope Professor Jackson hasn't caused any further explosions in Dôlylleuad," she said.

As conversation starters went, it had promise, but Gabriel only responded with "hm" again. The silence clamped back down.

"I wonder if Baby recovered fully from the magic he ingested," she tried while the train was paused in Evesham.

"Probably," came the reply.

The silence dug a hole in the space between them and began laying concrete foundations.

"This is a very long journey," she commented with perhaps a tad less patience than one might wish for as they traversed Moreton-in-Marsh. Gabriel inhaled, surely for the purpose of answering . . . Elodie held her own breath . . .

Then he nodded and went on staring out the window. At which point, Elodie reached for the sugar canister, but withdrew her hand again, since throwing it at her husband's soddish head really *would* be undignified behavior.

But no one had ever called Elodie Hughes Tarrant a quitter (perhaps because they were too occupied with calling her scandalous). "Your sister is interesting," she remarked in a carefully offhand way as the outskirts of Oxford appeared in view.

At this, Gabriel did look up, teacup suspended en route to his lips. *Such kissable lips,* Elodie thought with a quiet sigh, and her own cup shook so much in her hand that tea splashed into the saucer. Gabriel watched expressionlessly as she hastily set it down.

"She's always been the most interesting one in our family," he said. "When she chose to study history instead of science, it caused a general uproar, but she insisted. The fact she was able to exorcize two ghosts from our aunt's house did rather help her cause."

Elodie was hard-pressed to restrain her excitement at this voluble response. Gabriel had never spoken much about his family, and she'd never dared to pry. But now, encouraged by his revelation, she propped her elbows on the table, rested her chin upon them, and looked at him with big eyes. "So, do you have any other siblings?"

"No." He began folding his napkin to within an inch of its life, and Elodie thought that was that. Frustrated at his refusal to share anything of himself, she reached for her teacup again. But then he said, "I do have a cousin who is like a brother to me, however."

Once again, tea splashed, and the teaspoon tumbled right off the saucer, clattering against the table and eliciting disapproving murmurs from nearby diners.

"Indeed?" Elodie asked, the nonchalance in her voice betrayed by the mayhem she was causing with her dishes.

"Devon. He's currently on honeymoon in New Zealand."

"Ooh, wonderful landscapes there."

"Hm."

She thought the conversation had ended yet again. Gabriel laid down his napkin and took great pains to smooth it to perfection. But then he took a deep breath and said, "Do you have siblings?"

Although he appeared to be addressing the linen, Elodie felt the question barrel right through to her heart, which shook in panic. The conversation was actually going forward! She'd played with fire and now had to face the consequences! How should she answer? Lightly? Wryly? Oh God, what if she messed it up? Five seconds had passed since Gabriel had asked his question, and she really, really needed to make a response . . .

"It's just me," she said with a smile.

Gabriel looked up at her again. His face was shadow, then gold, then shadow again as light flashed and faded through the carriage window, but his expression remained dark and still, much like an inn's cellar. Elodie swallowed heavily, unable to look away.

"It's never *just* you," he said.

Elodie immediately and spontaneously combusted, albeit only in metaphor. In reality, she dared not move as warmth pooled at her core. In front of her, the teaspoon, set trembling by the train's motion, was inching its way toward the edge of the table. Behind her, a half dozen passengers engaged in quiet conversation. And somewhere out there between Hereford and Oxford, a fey line was in terrifying cascade. But Elodie noticed none of it. In her imagination (a *much* more pleasant place to be), Gabriel was pulling her into one of the sleeper compartments and having his delightfully arrogant way with her.

And judging from the unrelenting depth of his gaze, he shared the same idea.

Just then the train began to slow, indicating that it would soon be arriving at Oxford Station. Elodie sagged internally at the thought of the return to normal life (providing, that is, magic didn't explode the university into pieces). Gabriel went on gazing at her, however. He was unblinking, uncompromising, not setting her free. All the air in the carriage seemed to vanish. Elodie began to feel dizzy, her pulse thundering in her ears. She tried to look down, for relief, but Gabriel's attention had always been her own personal gravity. She could not deny it. She could not even breathe. Would he lean across the table and kiss her? His eyes suggested it. They spoke of lips brushing, tongues stroking, and a foot sliding up beneath her skirt.

Alas, none of this occurred. But Gabriel's gaze did intensify, and Elodie realized all of a sudden that his eyes truly were suggesting things. He was communicating with her, albeit wordlessly. His heart was in that fierce gaze—exposed, honest, and offered freely to her. *I want you,* it plainly said. *I cannot stop thinking about you. I've had a little too much tea and am suffering the effects of this but nevertheless desire to kiss your throat and all the way down to your gorgeous bosom.*

Well, perhaps that last part was hers, since she doubted Gabriel had ever used the word "bosom" in all his life; but even so, she was entranced. And abashed too, understanding now that lovingly accepting her husband's taciturn nature wasn't enough. There would be much thoughtful work ahead to learn the wealth of language in his silence. With her usual positivity,

Elodie trusted that she would have a lifetime to devote herself to the task—especially considering the way Gabriel's gaze was currently stroking the front of her shirtwaist, then pausing as if it could see right through the cambric. Such eloquence set her own language into twinkling disarray and she almost moaned, but was saved from this indignity by her teaspoon finally making a dive for the floor.

The clatter of its landing, and the gasp of a scandalized waiter, broke Elodie from Gabriel's thrall. She bent with such speed to retrieve the spoon that all the blood rushed to her head—which at least provided an excellent excuse for why she was red-faced and dizzy. Straightening, she found Gabriel busy rolling up maps as if nothing interesting had occurred.

"Ready?" he asked, brisk and professional. But he glanced through his lashes at her, and she saw the warmth in his eyes. Not heat now, nor fierceness, but a soft and amiable warmth that wrapped around her, making her feel for the first time like she truly *did* belong to him, or more specifically *with* him—the two of them in a partnership that extended beyond their marriage to the many years they'd grown into adulthood together, even through the months they'd tried to stay apart.

"Ready," she said, grinning, and tossed the teaspoon on the table with a zestful *clink*.

Chapter Twenty-One

What goes up must come down,
just not necessarily in the same form.
Blazing Trails, W.H. Jackson

IMMEDIATELY UPON DEBOARDING the train in Oxford, Gabriel and Elodie turned to the northwest horizon. Travelers bustled around them as they stood together in tense silence, watching for magic.

The sky was blanched and cold, strewn with diaphanous cirrus clouds that drifted across a pale, swollen sun. White-gold light girdled the world, dissolving it gently into a dream.

My God, Gabriel thought in horror. *This is it. I've started thinking in poetry. I should never have kissed her. Those dear lips have corrupted me so sweetly . . .*

"Oh for goodness sake," he grumbled. Perhaps he should just surrender his doctorate and write romances instead.

"What is it?" Elodie asked with some alarm. "I can't see anything troubling."

"There isn't anything." Pivoting on a heel, Gabriel scrutinized the various rooftops of the city. They, at least, were uninspiring. No one would want to write poetry about Oxford, especially not in October. "All seems normal. We've managed to outrace the cascade."

"Maybe it petered out," Elodie suggested, although she sounded dubious.

"I'm not willing to take that chance." Consulting his wristwatch, he did some hasty mental calculations. "We have an hour at most. Are you confident in our plan?"

The question was a good excuse to look at her, but the moment he did, his mind proceeded to effuse about her starlight hair and the soft curve of her jaw. He flung his attention at a nearby tree instead. It trembled, despite the lack of breeze, as if his dark-eyed glare frightened it.

"I wouldn't call myself confident," Elodie said, "but I hope we . . . What are you looking at?" She glanced over her shoulder nervously.

"It's coming," Gabriel said in a low, grim voice. "The trees know."

Elodie's eyes widened as she considered the several trees within view. All had begun shivering, their dry red and gold leaves scratching against the crisp air.

Gabriel caught sight of a young man bearing the hallmarks of an undergraduate student: shabby suit, the pallor of a hangover, hair so glossy with pomade the sunlight was reflecting off it. "You!" he shouted, pointing at the youth.

"What? Me?" The youth clutched himself, eyes bulging with the instinctive terror of a student who might be studying medicine but had nevertheless heard all about Professor Tyrant.

"Do you know the police station on High Street?"

The youth flushed scarlet. "What do you mean? Why

should I know it? I didn't break the office window of Balliol's dean."

Gabriel exhaled impatiently. "I don't care if you did or not. I need you to run to the police station and tell them Professor Tarrant invokes Protocol D."

"But—but I have a train to catch!"

"Come on, lad," Elodie said encouragingly. "Think of what Jeremy Bentham would say about your duty of beneficence!"

"Bentham?" Confusion glazed the young man's terror. "Is he captain of the rowing squad?"

Gabriel glared at him.

"*Eep!* Yes, sir. I'll go right away, sir. Protocol D. Thank you, sir." And he dashed away as if his life and, more importantly, his enrollment depended on it.

Gabriel turned back to Elodie. "Are you sure we shouldn't be going to the Geography School to find the professors?"

"On an afternoon during Noughth Week?" Elodie huffed a laugh. "Absolutely not. Far too much risk of having students turn up. They'll be at the pub, mark my words."

"Hm." Gabriel had heard whispers among the faculty about outings to drinking establishments, and he understood that they were whispering so he didn't hear them and ask to come along. For which he was *grateful*. And not the kind of grateful that covers up feelings of hurt and unhappiness. Pubs were noisy. Smelly. Fraught with an unrelenting joviality that made reading impossible. Gabriel far preferred a snifter of brandy in one of the quiet lounges of the Minervaeum Club, primarily because no one there was stupid enough to approach him.

On the other hand, did the professors invite Elodie to these pub gatherings? Did they laugh with her, exchange anecdotes with her? If so, there was only one logical conclusion.

He needed to get such gatherings banned.

Or, a wild thought—perhaps he could join in one day. After all, he'd go to the ends of the earth for Elodie; he could spend ~~an hour~~ half an hour in a pub.

Providing, of course, Oxford did not burn to the ground this afternoon.

"Let's go." Grasping Elodie's hand, he began to run.

"Wait," she said, tugging on him to stop. "I have a better idea."

As he gave her an inquiring look, she grinned in such a way his blood shook with alarm. When Elodie grinned like that, shenanigans were almost certainly to ensue . . .

TOOT!

Elodie pumped the velocipede's horn, causing students to scatter off the road. Steam clouds billowed up from the shuddering engine, and behind her, arms clinging around her waist, Gabriel groaned as his dignity imploded. Elodie laughed.

"It was the sensible option!" she told him—but considering she had to shout over the clanking and rattling of the contraption, inspiring any passersby who weren't already staring at them to do so, it must be conceded that "sensible" really had no place in a description of the scene. "It's faster than running!" she tried instead.

"Only if we survive!" Gabriel shouted in reply.

"Don't worry, it's perfectly saf—"

Alas, Elodie could not finish this assurance due to Gabriel clutching her tightly, impeding her breath, as she swerved precipitously to avoid a classics professor who'd been attempting a pedestrian crossing. With roars of *"Cruentum stulti!"* following

them, they sped on through the city, leaving their good reputa-
tions far behind.

Minutes later, they arrived at Beaumont Street, wherein
was located the Bacon Butty, a public bar favored by Oxford's
science professors (mostly because Oxford's science students
hated it). Upon entering rather unsteadily, Gabriel trying
without success to tidy his hair, and Elodie filled with stars at
having had her husband's arms around her for the journey,
they found a half-dozen tweedy geographers clustered around
a table laden with plates of fish and chips. The men were enjoying a loud (Gabriel winced) and jovial (Gabriel frowned) debate about whether Descartes was influenced by Eratosthenes,
while a large portrait of Roger Bacon on the wall behind their
table looked on in boredom. All were equipped with beer tankards of a size known as *the lager majus*, and had evidently
emptied them enough that they slurred the phrase "Cartesian
equations" into something that sounded quite ribald indeed.

Seeing them, Elodie drew a taut breath like she always did
when faced with these men, anticipating insults or lecherous
stares. As if he sensed this, Gabriel reached to grasp her hand,
squeezing it encouragingly; surprised, she flung him a grateful
smile. He smiled back fleetingly, and her internal stars flashed
and spun.

"Everyone!" she called out as they approached the table. But
it was to no avail: she may as well have been methane in a
wetlands.

"Ahem." Gabriel cleared his throat discreetly. At once the
professors fell silent, tankards halted mid-gesture, egos on de-
fensive alert.

"The 5-SEQ is in cascade!" Elodie said, the words tumbling
with her haste to speak.

Half a dozen pairs of bushy eyebrows elevated.

"It's heading right this way!" she elaborated, pointing to the window, which actually faced northeast, but that was not important. Besides, no one even glanced at it. Instead, they exchanged amused looks.

"The situation is dire," Gabriel added.

"Oh?" Professor Diggley, a specialist in oceanography despite not having left Oxford for the past fifteen years, smirked—or at least his shaggy white mustache tilted in a manner that suggested he was smirking beneath it. "I should say, young man, that there's a more interesting situation right before us."

Both Elodie and Gabriel stared at him with impatient confusion. He waggled a finger in their direction. "This, here."

Elodie noticed that every professor's attention was now angling toward her lower body. She glanced down and realized she and Gabriel were still holding hands.

Aghast, she went to pull away. But Gabriel gripped her hand more firmly.

"Gentlemen," he said in such a domineering manner, several of the professors had to remind themselves they'd graduated decades ago. "Professor Tarrant and I are going to establish a defense out past Wytham Village. Should it fail, a secondary defense will be needed."

"Aren't *you* Professor Tarrant?" Professor Coffingham asked Gabriel with a drunken chuckle.

Alas, poor fellow, it took him three weeks to recover from the mental injury caused by Gabriel's glare.

Elodie, torn between wanting to bristle at Coffingham's insult and swoon at Gabriel's response, settled on just wishing she had a tankard of beer too. With luck, the cascade would hit Oxford before this conversation became any more stressful.

"What kind of defense do you recommend?" asked Professor Abness, an elderly gentleman of the Scottish persuasion who tended to get so directly to the point that his lectures lasted only twenty minutes. Elodie smiled at him with gratitude.

"Iron and gold barricades have proven to work against this particular energy signature," she said.

The professors turned their heads as one to Gabriel. He scowled. "Why are you looking at me? She just gave you the answer."

"It doesn't matter," Elodie murmured.

His scowl darkened. "Yes, it does."

"No, it really doesn't." She'd spent years worrying about what these men thought of her, studying all through the night so they had no cause to fail her, marrying Gabriel in the hope it would stop them from looking down their noses at her (or, more specifically, at her bosom). She'd succeeded in her career despite them—and because of herself. Because she was tenacious, and clever, and had great sources of funding. And now here she stood, an expert in disaster management, with the fate of Oxford in her hands, and they were no more than a group of old fools who discounted vital information simply because it came from a woman. She didn't intend to waste another moment on their stupidity.

"The prime location for a defense is by the observatory," she told them in a cool, professional tone, bringing from her skirt pocket a sketched map with calculations she and Gabriel had made during the train journey.

Abness hesitated the merest second, then took the map and perused it carefully before nodding. "That does make sense," he admitted (mainly because he recognized Gabriel's handwriting on the map, although he had at least enough intelligence not to confess it). "We shall get to work at once."

This pronouncement seemed to invigorate the other professors. They set down their tankards, smoothed their mustaches, and began to rise. Chairs scraped against the floor, and Elodie squeezed Gabriel's hand in sympathy as she watched him try not to wince at the noise.

"How long do we have?" Professor Dunning asked.

"Less than an hour," Gabriel told him.

"Right!" Rubbing his hands together briskly, Abness looked around at his colleagues. "Summon the graduate students! Bring out the spades! And somebody get a box for this food. If we're saving the world, we'll be wanting snacks!"

This apparently was enough for Gabriel; he pulled Elodie from the pub without another word, as if rescuing her from certain death via the mingled odors of fried fish and mustache wax. Bright daylight swamped her vision, and when she closed her eyes against it, she saw an afterimage of herself standing in front of her peers, holding Gabriel's hand.

Oh my God. They couldn't have been more obvious if they'd outright shouted, *We had sex in a cellar!* The academia rumor network was going to go wilder than a triggered fey line. Elodie released a shaky breath, and beside her, Gabriel did the same. Their hands tightened in each other's grip.

Then they turned to assess the northwest sky, because they might be muddled-up nitwits who couldn't manage a sensible adult relationship, but they were also still professionals.

"Nothing yet," Elodie said.

"Nevertheless, we need to hurry. It's at least half an hour's walk to Wytham."

"Not on the velocipede," Elodie observed, and Gabriel muttered something about preferring to literally die in a magical cataclysm than mortify himself riding that infernal machine again. Elodie would have laughed were they not on the verge of said cataclysm. But when she tugged on him, he went with her, and awkwardly mounted the velocipede behind her with the attitude of a knight preparing to sacrifice himself in battle.

Leaving the city, they followed a narrow path winding through fields toward Wytham Village, the velocipede juddering boisterously over packed dirt and pebbles. Cool breezes swept across the fields, scented with a tang of river water and the fresh sweetness of grass. The sunlight shone warm and soft on Elodie's face. It would have been a lovely afternoon but for the sense of approaching doom that seemed to grip everything in the environment. Elodie heard no birdsong, no farm noises, no laughter of students returning from drunken gambols through the meadows. As they rode through Wytham, she noticed windows being shuttered as if the habitants sensed stormy weather. Even the sky looked like it was trying to escape, clouds swept thin by fast winds at its heights.

Past the village, farmland stretched to the northern edge of the woods some half a mile away. It was an area much studied in various university courses, so here and there among the rye-grass could be seen ranging poles, rain gauges, roped-off quadrats, and a yellow raincoat someone had left behind. Elodie and Gabriel clambered off the velocipede, and as Gabriel adjusted his trousers' seat he gave Elodie a frown that warned against her making some provoking comment. Elodie considered teasing him nevertheless, but she could see that he was actually quite painfully frazzled by the loss of his dignity, and she did not want to cause him any more hurt. So she turned away again, all professional briskness and wifely care, to assess the horizon instead.

"Smoke," she reported. "Somewhere near Witney, I'd say. Might be unrelated."

"Definitely related, considering it's blue," Gabriel pointed out as he removed the ER kit from his back. "And the breeze is starting to pick up." He tossed her a dowsing rod from the kit, then took out a thaumometer for himself. Shouldering the kit once more, he pushed windswept hair back from his forehead as he regarded the view. "Thankfully no one's here."

They began to cross the field. Both had spent many hours guiding students to investigate its natural and thaumaturgic features; as a consequence, they strode forth with calm certainty. Beneath Elodie's confidence, however, anxiety fluttered. Would this mad plan succeed? Or was that death burning its way closer? Her usual steady optimism began to falter in the cold, fraught wind. To distract herself, she said lightly, "Someone might well be here. It's possible to go unseen if you lie down in the long grass."

Gabriel glanced at her askance.

"I've been stepped on more than once," she explained.

"Why were you lying in the grass in the first place?" he asked in bewilderment.

She shrugged. "Just feeling the world."

"Feeling the world," Gabriel echoed, clearly unable to grasp the concept. "How do you quantify the results of that?"

"I don't. I just . . . *feel* them."

His face wrestled with confusion. "That sounds like the geographical equivalent of reading free verse."

Elodie laughed. A friendly quiet came to rest between them, quivering ever so slightly with the possibility of more questions and sweeter discussions (should they not be killed in the next hour by an overwhelming force of magic, that is). Then Gabriel halted abruptly.

"Fey line," he said, tapping his foot against the ground.

They looked at the unremarkable stretch of grass beneath them. Elodie pointed her dowsing rod at it, and the silver branches quivered.

"Well done," she remarked. "I suppose you counted your steps."

"Of course not," Gabriel said, affronted. "I triangulated the lay of the wood's shadow at this point in the afternoon with the position of the church tower and the willow that marks the 5-SEQ-107 deposit back there close to the stream. How do you find it?"

"Oh, the same way, for sure," Elodie said, nodding emphatically.

Gabriel checked the thaumometer. "Two thousand and fifty conjures. Fifty-one . . . fifty-two . . ."

"It's coming," Elodie said. Goosebumps arose along her arms.

Setting down his kit, Gabriel withdrew from it the leather satchel containing Hereford's artifacts. Elodie removed her opera coat, dropping it to the ground, and began rolling up her sleeves.

"Here." Gabriel passed her a trowel. She handed him back the dowsing rod in turn, then knelt to thrust the trowel as deeply as she could into the ground.

"I feel like Merlin," she said. "Except, you know, with a little spade instead of a sword. And dirt instead of a stone. On second thought, ignore me."

"Right," Gabriel said absentmindedly. He was holding the thaumometer over the leather satchel. One eyebrow arched.

"Good reading?" Elodie asked.

"Off the scale."

Thus encouraged, she began digging with heightened vigor, creating a trench that dissected the surface of the fey line. Once she had it deep enough, she used her hands to brush away dirt and roots. Gabriel crouched to prop the charter, writ, and prayer book upright in the space she had created, establishing an unassuming and unlikely barricade.

"Paper to stop a torrent of supercharged earth magic," he said with disbelief.

"Enchanted paper," Elodie reminded him cheerfully.

"This will either work or make the situation immeasurably worse."

"Well, we having nothing to lose at this point."

Gabriel frowned, biting his lip. "We should have brought gold artifacts from the Ashmolean."

"We didn't have time," Elodie said. "And I'm sure the other professors will be adding some to the secondary defense."

In fact, she harbored doubts about whether that defense would prove effective, given that none of the professors were emergency specialists; indeed, their experience of disaster generally involved eight a.m. lectures and the faculty lounge running out of tea.

"Besides," she said, more in an effort to encourage herself than anything, "using items from Oxford itself might draw the magic into the city, rather than repel it. These papers belong to Hereford, so if Lazaar's theory about sympathetic attraction is right, they will send the magic back that way, and then momentum should keep it going on to Dôlylleuad."

"Hm," Gabriel responded, in lieu of pointing out that Elodie gave a lecture last year rebutting Lazaar's ideas.

She shrugged, for she'd happily be proven wrong under the circumstances, and moreover journey out to Morocco to shake Professor Lazaar's hand in a formal apology. After all, if the Hereford artifacts failed, their power would be added to the cascade before it sped into Oxford, absorbing the university's hoards of thaumaturgic items and racing on down the line to London. People now strolling blithely through that grand city . . . playing with their children . . . holding hands with their beloved . . . were going to be obliterated before they even understood themselves to be in peril.

Her stomach lurched, and she looked instinctively to Gabriel. In that same moment, his gaze rose from the Magna Carta to meet hers. They stared at each other, worry and hope and exhaustion mingling in the narrow space between them. Gabriel's eyes were all the synonyms for darkness Elodie had come up with these past couple of days. She could feel her own shine bright in turn. Smiling, she bounced her eyebrows.

"We're all set."

"Hm," Gabriel answered, his eyebrows hunching.

They stood, moving several yards aside from the barricade. Each hooked gold-charmed iron around their left ear before turning as one to look along the line.

The smoke over Witney had dispersed into a cerulean haze that stained the sky with fear. Wind rattled the world.

"I owe you an apology," Elodie said suddenly—out of the blue, as it were.

"Oh?" Gabriel responded, not shifting his gaze from the horizon.

"I didn't mean what I said on our wedding day."

He was silent for a few nerve-racking seconds, then he asked with apparent nonchalance, "Your vows?"

Oh God, this was why she shouldn't be left unsupervised with a conversation! At once, Elodie shook her head. "No! No, not at all. When I said I'd got what I wanted from our deal. I only meant to sympathize with you about losing the house."

"Oh." Gabriel blinked, his shoulders relaxing. "I did wonder."

"You did?" Elodie tried not to frown as she turned to look at him, apocalypse momentarily forgotten. "So why didn't you just ask, instead of walking away?"

"I was afraid," he admitted with a slight half shrug. "I didn't want things between us to end, and I'm—I'm not good at personal discussions. I thought I might ruin everything." He huffed dryly at how that had turned out.

"Well, I thought I *had* ruined everything," Elodie said, tapping her chest with a little too much fervor and causing a tiny sharp pain to her heart. "And I was too scared to talk to you about it in case I made matters even worse."

Gabriel looked at her finally, a dark, wry regret in his eyes. "It seems we both could have used some courage," he said.

Elodie's pulse leaped, tossing a sardonic laugh from her throat. "Courage or a basic ability to communicate. We could have solved everything with *one conversation*."

"Apparently."

"Well, damn. What is it that people call us, again?"

"You mean 'geniuses'?" Gabriel suggested.

"Hm," she said darkly.

"Hm," he agreed.

In stunned silence, they turned back to stare along the fey line. The sky beyond Wytham Woods was turning cyanic, the lambent blue speckled with dazzling silver and gold as if laughing at them. Elodie felt much the same way within herself.

"Twinkles," she said.

"Eruptive thaumaturgic scintillations," Gabriel corrected her automatically.

"Pretty," she countered.

He looked at her. "Yes," he said. And then he smiled.

Elodie stared back at him, enraptured. The smile was real, fond, unafraid. It softened his face and lit his eyes with a warm reflection of his heart, and it sent delight melting like honey and slow kisses all through Elodie. She wanted to reach up and touch it, but her fingers were dirty from having dug the trench, and she knew Gabriel wouldn't appreciate them on his mouth. She knew *him*. Every line of his face was familiar to her, every smooth plane that she'd watched strengthen over the years.

You're mine, she thought. From the corner of her eye she could see leaves explode from the woods' canopy. Beneath her feet she felt the ground tremble. And part of her mind noted with sensible anxiety that she had seconds until the line cascade slammed into their paper barricade.

But the rest of her was absorbed in the truth that had been her magnetic north for the whole of her adult life. And if this moment were to be the last she ever had, she wanted it filled with that truth.

"I love you," she said.

Gabriel closed his eyes, opened them again like night giving way to dawn. His smile wavered a little with emotion, then deepened.

And the magic arrived.

Chapter Twenty-Two

You're already where you want to go.
Getting there is part of being there.
Blazing Trails, W.H. Jackson

THE LAND ABOVE the fey line buckled and groaned as if an enormous subterranean snake were moving through the field. Grass and dirt exploded, sparking with thaumaturgic energy. The wind began to scream.

Elodie and Gabriel tensed, not even daring to breathe, while their clothes and hair swirled in the leaf-strewn wind and the ground shook beneath their feet. Two and a half miles behind them, Oxford stood in a calm that made Elodie's heart ache. The power racing toward the little paper barricade was enormous. It would bring the beautiful old city absolutely to ruins.

The plan's going the fail, Elodie thought with a sudden rush of horror. She needed to think of a better solution in the next three seconds.

But there wasn't even that much time. The cascade slammed into the barricade.

With a hollow roar, the air shuddered. Translucent flames

THE GEOGRAPHER'S MAP TO ROMANCE

of raw magical energy whipped at the documents; earth cracked, fissures ripping through the grass.

Elodie tried to inhale a calm, professional breath, but it shook wild and hot down her throat. "The barricade's not going to hold!" she warned Gabriel, shouting through wind-blown strands of her hair.

"It will!" he shouted in reply, even as the thaumometer in his hand began to smoke. Cursing, he tossed it away, and they both flinched as it burst apart midair, scraps of metal becoming black dragonflies with wings of flame. The cascade howled in response. Enormous weeds began shooting up from the cracked earth, their jagged leaves snapping at the dragonflies and long stems slashing the air.

"It's not going to hold!" Gabriel conceded.

Elodie looked around desperately as if something nearby might help. But grass and wooden marker poles offered no hope, and while the yellow raincoat might have some application, Elodie could not immediately think of what. The prayer book was rising out of the trench, its pages flapping. The King's Writ was aflame.

Elodie wedged a knuckle between her teeth and began to gnaw at it. But magical luminescence flared against her wedding ring and she winced, snatching the hand away . . . then lifted it again to stare at it wide-eyed. Or, more specifically, at the ring of thaumaturgic gold.

"No," Gabriel said instantly, guessing her thoughts.

"Yes," Elodie argued, tugging at the ring. "Or, at least, maybe. It's worth a try! After all, it stopped the thaumaturgic bomb outside Dôlylleuad."

"Ignis fatuus is nothing compared to this!" he shouted.

Black hair streaked his brow like anger; the wind tore his voice apart. "It's too much risk, Elodie!"

"I don't need to get close. I can just toss it into the trench." She waved her hand in demonstration.

And the magic caught it. Elodie was yanked off her feet so fast, the world seemed to blur around her. She cried out with shock, arms flailing as if she might be able to grab handfuls of air and stop herself. But the thaumaturgic force was inescapable. Mercilessly it dragged her toward the cascade.

"Ellie!"

She barely heard Gabriel's alarmed shout as blood and enchanted wind thundered in her ears. He grabbed her legs, wrapping his arms around them and digging his heels into the ground so as to anchor her. But magic buffeted them both, howling, wrenching, and even Gabriel's arrogant, determined strength failed. He stumbled, cursing vehemently. And then he too was being pulled into the danger zone.

"Let go!" Elodie yelled.

"No!" With the power of desperation, he managed a step backward, and then another, hauling them into retreat. *You're mine,* he'd said, and Elodie was beginning to believe that he actually meant it. And she thought that maybe, incredibly, he would be able to defy the force of an entire fey line in cascade.

But the ground ripped open beneath his feet, emitting gusts of pure, feral magic that shoved him off-balance, and immediately he was sucked into the air. Using what Elodie could only suppose was the might of stubbornness, he managed to keep hold of her, and together they were dragged toward the raging magic that crashed and crashed against the shuddering barricade.

Now Elodie was angry. No stupid, zappy rock was going to

take her Gabriel! Grasping the wedding ring, she tried to pull it free. But since the moment Gabriel had placed the band on her finger, she'd never removed it, and now it would not budge past her knuckle. She tugged and twisted it desperately, thinking that her finger might break in the effort. That was the least of her problems, of course; indeed, if she could deliberately break the finger, and so get the ring off, she would do so without hesitation. But with no way of achieving that, she resorted to placing it in her mouth and sucking. After all, as she'd said to Gabriel, dignity was not a priority in a disaster.

The tactic worked: with its path thus lubricated, the ring at last came free. Elodie held it out like an offering, and the magic grabbed it away.

As if a thread snapped, she and Gabriel dropped to the ground only one yard's distance from where the cascade rioted against the barricade.

BOOM.

A shock wave smashed into them. Elodie clung to the shuddering earth and Gabriel clung to her, and if she feared that he was going to restrict the blood flow to her feet, this seemed an inopportune moment to complain. The world screamed in agony. Then abruptly—

Silence.

Elodie held still for a moment, just in case the magic turned around and said, *Fooled you!* before exploding over her. But the stark, blank silence eased into a gentle quiet, and finally she knew she was safe. Her breath staggered out of her lungs and collapsed dramatically with exhaustion and relief.

Gabriel dragged himself up next to her. "Are you all right?" he asked, brushing the hair away from her face. Elodie turned on her side, smiling weakly at him.

"I'm fine," she said. "But only in the British sense. Every fiber of me hurts."

"Poor girl," he murmured, still stroking her hair.

"And you?"

"Fine," he said. And when she looked dubious—"I'm not caught in the center of a cascading fey line; anything else is absolutely fine."

"Good point. Is it done?"

They both tilted their heads to see . . . nothing. A field of grass bathed in late afternoon sunlight. A somnolent woodland thick with shadows against the tranquil western horizon. From somewhere nearby, small birds of the meadow recommencing a cheerful melody.

"I knew it would work!" Elodie said triumphantly. Gabriel scoffed, and she smacked his arm without looking. "Gentlemen don't point out ladies' little exaggerations."

"Ladies don't call bald-faced lies 'exaggerations,'" he answered, but humor tinged his voice, making Elodie think for a brief, mad moment that she had been more affected by the magic than she appreciated and was now experiencing auditory hallucinations.

They waited for half a minute to be sure no further eruptions were likely to occur, then went back to more important matters: each propping their head up on a hand, they gazed at the other, watching mesmerized as emotions burgeoned in their eyes.

"Say it again," Gabriel commanded, his words a dark, hoarse whisper.

"I knew it would work," Elodie repeated.

"No, the other thing."

He stroked gentle fingers across her cheek, which was very

nice but also distracted her from clear thinking. "What other thing?"

"You know."

Oh. *That* thing. She grinned. "I love you."

He lowered his eyelashes, blushing sweetly, but she hadn't finished. "I've loved you from the very start, Gabriel Tarrant. The first time I saw you, I wanted you so much I tripped over my own feet and made a mess of everything."

He contemplated her for a long, thoughtful moment, then suddenly rose to his feet. Elodie did not have enough time to feel bereft before he was reaching down and taking hold of her hands, pulling her up in one strong, easy motion. She swayed, hair tumbling around her, heart not sure which way was up. Still holding her hands, Gabriel stepped closer, as if he thought she might suddenly make a run for it. And, Elodie had to admit, as her pulse thundered and her eyes grew wide, he wasn't entirely wrong. So much of her life had been about escaping, in dreams and books and out of windows, that she didn't quite know how to stay.

But Gabriel just stood there as if he'd found his place, marked a claim, and never intended to leave. "You didn't make a mess," he told her, stern and austere, the way he always was in his first lecture of the year, so his students knew they could trust what he taught them. "Well, you did, but it was like a fresh breeze. You brought me wild joy in a life that had always been about safety, and excellent school marks, and mapping my every step exactly. Ellie, my sunshine, I loved you that first day when you tripped right into my heart, and I've loved you every moment since."

"Oh," she said.

"It's always been you for me. No one else, ever. You're in

every dawn I watch rising over cities and fields. You're in everything I do and dream. You are the heart of the world for me."

Delight cascaded through Elodie, spilling over as a jittery laugh from her throat. "Oh my, Professor Tarrant. You can indeed talk in poetry."

"I must have hit my head when we fell," he grumbled.

She grinned. "You're *mine*, Gabriel. I love you with all my soul."

Which wasn't a declaration anywhere near as gorgeous as his had been, but she could not seem to summon better words. They had all turned to *love, love, love.*

So instead she just stared at her husband with the fierce adoration she felt for him, utterly, indescribably beloved man that he was. And as if she'd willed it into being, a smile blossomed, gentle and ravishing, from his solemn expression. He lowered his head, and she raised hers, and they kissed, there in the ruins of the magical explosion.

"Elodie Tarrant, you are so beautiful," Gabriel whispered against her lips. It sounded like he was commenting on a map that bore a clear visual hierarchy: passionate, intense, leaving her breathless. "That fact is far more real than some poem."

"Gosh," she sighed as dreamily as any Miss Trevallion. Hearing herself, she rolled her eyes with exasperation, then glanced around at the grass surrounding them. "I could have sworn I left my intelligence around here somewhere."

But her levity faded as she saw the long black scars in the land. "Bloody hell, we're lucky to be alive."

"Hm," Gabriel agreed.

They shifted apart, although only by inches, and turned to assess the fey line. It lay quiet, with only a length of charred

and broken earth to show that it had been violently active minutes before. The woods were unstirred. And northwest, where
low sunlight blanched the horizon, there existed no sign of
smoke or magic.

And yet, Elodie thought of the energy that was now re-
bounding up the line. Would it squelch vulnerabilities as it
went, or cause even more turbulence?

"We need to get to a telegraph station," Gabriel said a second before she was about to suggest the same thing. "If things
don't go as we expect, Dôlylleuad's going to require more help
than Professor Jackson can give it."

"And if they do go as expected, the village will require help
being rid of him before he causes new mayhem," Elodie added,
making Gabriel snort with amusement. "We should also check
our own lot haven't burned down the observatory in their effort to build a defense."

She turned toward where the velocipede stood at the edge
of the field, but Gabriel caught her wrist. When she gave him
an inquiring look, he frowned.

"There's something I need to do before anything else," he
said.

"Oh yes, I forgot about the Hereford artifacts." Elodie bit
her lip guiltily as she looked at the paper strewn about the grass.

"More important than that."

"Confirm the stability of the terminal point?"

"No."

"Clean up the litter that your broken thaumometer—"

"Ellie." He pinched the bridge of his nose, then apparently
managed to restore his briefly lost patience, for he smiled at
her. "Just stay there, all right?"

Elodie nodded, thinking that she could certainly get used

to those sweet, shy, heart-melting smiles of his. She watched him cross to the barricade and crouch down to inspect its tumult of dirt and charred grass. The ravaged prayer book lay open some distance away, the King's Writ in its charred leather sleeve nearby. The scroll of the Magna Carta was half-buried inside the shattered trench. Gabriel pulled it free, checked that the casing was still intact, then tossed it aside with all the heedlessness of a geographic scientist for whom history meant tree rings and river sediments. Then he stood, brushing dirt from something small in his cupped hand.

Her wedding ring. A breath of riotous emotion spilled from Elodie, and Gabriel looked over, his expression daring her to flee.

Instantly Elodie responded by lifting her chin and staring at him with magnificent hauteur. His mouth twitched, and she could have sworn she saw a hint of swagger as he walked back to her. It made her grin. By gods, she loved him, egotism and all.

An arm's length away, he stopped as if meeting some hard boundary, and he held out the ring before him. It was completely unharmed by having blocked an ultrapowerful cascade of devastatingly lethal magic; indeed, its thaumaturgic gold seemed to dazzle even more gloriously. Elodie had never before seen a piece of jewelry look quite so smug.

"To think," she mused, "one ring saved the world."

"Well, Oxford," Gabriel amended.

"And London," she added.

He shrugged as if the fate of the great city was neither here nor there in his conscience. "So . . ." he said.

"So," Elodie agreed.

"You're going to want me to kneel." He made it sound like

she required him to dance naked through the university grounds, singing of his love for her.

"I made no such suggestion," she said.

"It's proper."

Now Elodie was the one to shrug. "Just be yourself, Gabriel."

"Hm." He seemed dubious as to the wisdom of this. "You'll be able to fix me over time, I'm sure."

She shook her head earnestly. "You don't need fixing."

"I agree."

Elodie had to quickly bite her tongue to keep from calling him an arrogant sod considering he was, after all, in the middle of attempting a romantic scene. That would be undignified of her at the least, and at the most it would make a terrible mess of . . .

"Arrogant sod," she said, nudging his foot with hers.

He just looked at her complacently. Then he took a deep breath, and Elodie held her own. This was it. The impossible dream, actually coming true.

But he paused, and Elodie watched as his jaw clenched. She sensed that he was waging a silent, internal battle against the spikiness that protected him from what everyone assumed was general botheration but she had come to understand was a painful sensitivity. He really needed to exist in a microhabitat, this darling grouchy man of hers, and the fact that he went about in the greater world teaching people, addressing conferences, and riding velocipedes when needed, despite the constant assaults on his tender spirit, made him heroic in her eyes.

"Don't kneel," she urged with a burst of feeling. "I don't want a grand gesture. I want *you*."

He looked through his eyelashes at her in that devastating

way he had, all midnight and secrets. "Here," he said abruptly, holding the ring out. "Will you be my wife?"

There was no need to ponder it. "Yes," she answered with a radiant smile. Gabriel took her hand with exquisite gentleness and slid the ring back on where it belonged. Then, while Elodie's heart pulled her intellect into an exuberant waltz, he lifted the hand and kissed it.

Oh my, she thought, going warm and sparkling. Who needed grand gestures when a man did things like that?

"I hope you don't have many possessions," he grumbled, fastidiously turning the ring as if there were some exact place on the plain gold band that should face outward. "My lodgings are not expansive."

"We should live at my place," she answered, practically singing the words, so joyful did she feel. "It's quite sizable, and I have only one neighbor, a venerable old lady who is so silent you'd never know she—"

Suddenly Gabriel pulled her into his arms and kissed her with all the fervor of a man who had waited years for this moment: love, *and* quiet accommodation! A soft breeze swirled around them as if in benediction. Sheets of ancient illuminated paper drifted on it, and as one brushed Elodie's leg, she broke away from the kiss to watch anxiously as it tumbled away across the grass. "Oh dear, Amelia is going to be so cross."

"Please don't talk about my sister while I'm kissing you," Gabriel said, and possessed her mouth again with determination. *Such a tyrant,* Elodie thought, and let herself sink into the delight of it.

"Oh my God, I'm going to be sick!"

The sudden exclamation made them look around irritably. Some twenty feet away a young man was sitting up the long grass, wine bottle in one hand and hair fallen over half his face. Elodie recognized him as a student from her Dynamic Geography course (subtitled When Things Go Boom). He swayed, his throat lurching with nausea, then jolted as he realized two university professors were standing nearby, watching him. His face went white as he sobered instantaneously.

"Dr. Tarrant!" he said, voice shaking like a triggered fey line. "What are you doing here?"

"Canoodling with my husband," Elodie answered at the same moment Gabriel growled, "Saving Oxford, young man." Each shot a look of exasperation at the other, but their eyes gleamed.

"See, I told you so," Elodie said, grinning. "If you lie in the long grass, no one notices you."

"*Feeling the world,*" Gabriel muttered with disapproval.

She shrugged. "Hiding from students."

At that, unexpectedly, Gabriel laughed.

And the whole world sighed dreamily at the sound of it.

CHAPTER TWENTY-THREE

They say home is where the heart is, but in truth
it's where the food is. But, by God, you can
have a lot of heart for a good potato!
                        Blazing Trails, W.H. Jackson

T HE WHOLE WORLD sighed dreamily" was in fact what Gabriel would have more sensibly described as "a rising wind." It swept over Oxford, promising rain. This was a disaster for young gentlemen who had finally got their hair looking perfect before meeting girls on a dinner date, but felt pleasantly refreshing to Elodie as she and Gabriel made their way back into the city, the undergraduate jogging alongside the velocipede with his arms full of priceless, albeit rather ragged, historic documents.

Proceeding to the police station on High Street, they called an end to Protocol D (much to the bemusement of the sergeant in charge, who'd never got the message in the first place), then requisitioned the station telegraph to send messages to towns and cities up-line. A dinner of sandwiches was brought in, the kettle boiled, and by the time news started arriving from Wales, they were half-asleep, leaning against each other on the scratchy old sofa in the sergeant's office.

"Only mild earthquakes," Elodie said with satisfaction as they considered the stack of telegrams.

"And that one rain of frogs in Much Marcle," Gabriel added.

"Yes, but that could have been just a regular, everyday rain of frogs. Most importantly, a complete squelching of the trove in Dôlylleuad." Elodie grinned as she tapped a finger against the telegram from the village. "The secondary team made excellent time in getting there. And with Dr. Ngoma in charge, I feel confident in their assurance that the line has stabilized. They've even convinced Professor Jackson to go home."

"Home," Gabriel said, frowning with what a casual observer would have called irritation but that Elodie knew was longing. Shadows lay beneath his eyes, and she'd even noticed him add sugar to his last cup of tea. The man was nearly done in. Setting aside the telegrams, she took his hand.

"Come with me, husband."

"Always, wife," he replied, awkward but clearly prepared to take a good stab at being romantic, for her sake. Elodie's heart melted. Besides, what he lacked in conversational flirtation he made up for in his silence: the look he gave her was so hot, Elodie went from melting to steaming.

They rose together from the sofa, still hand in hand, and moved toward the office door, not once taking their eyes off each other (as a consequence of which Elodie bumped into the sofa's edge and Gabriel knocked against a side table, sending a teacup clattering from its saucer). Elodie reached for the door handle . . .

"I know they're here!"

They stopped, eyes growing wide. "Oh my God," Elodie whispered. "It's Professor Slummery!"

How the head of the geography department had tracked them to the police station was anyone's guess, but Elodie personally suspected that supernatural telepathy was a skill possessed by university department heads everywhere.

"Almost running over a professor!" the man was shouting. *"Sending drunken geographers to harass the observatory staff! And I've had Hereford Cathedral's archivist on the telephone all afternoon! Tell me where they are, Constable!"*

"Quick!" Elodie whispered, tugging Gabriel across the room. "We'll go out the window!"

"Why?" Gabriel asked, perplexed. "Can't we just talk to him? He'll be glad to see us; we did after all save the city."

Elodie paused in unlatching the window to cast him a panicked look. "Well, you see—"

"And while I'm here," Slummery could be heard saying, *"I want you fellows to find out who stole my brand-new leather chair and suspended it from the cupola of the Radcliffe Camera!"*

BUT IN THE end, Elodie surprised Gabriel by bringing him peace. Clambering out a police station's window . . . running through the lamplit rain . . . hunting among an assortment of potted plants on the stoop of her town house until they found the hidden front door key, never mind that at any moment a student or fellow teacher might walk past and see them . . . careening through cluttered, unlit rooms while they kissed and kissed and pulled the clothes off each other . . . it all faded from mind once he was ensconced in the warm

tangle of her bedsheets, naked against her lovely soft nakedness.

He'd been exhausted until this moment. He'd yearned for
nothing more than sleep. And yet, as Elodie snuggled close,
murmuring *love* and *so strong* and what sounded suspiciously
like *Grouchyboo*, he felt himself become marvelously reinvigo-
rated. And his body held clear ideas about how to proceed,
namely:

(1) worship her,
(2) adore her, and
(3) give her any pleasure she desires.

Free of any deadlines, such as becoming literally dead in a
magical explosion, Gabriel was able to luxuriate, and to show
Elodie that he too had an imagination. For half an hour he
explored every pathway to the destination most beloved of his
heart: Elodie's happiness. Then it was her turn, and he lay
quiet, surrendering absolutely, while she made a wide-ranging
expedition with lips and fingers around all the sensitive places
on his body. *Beautiful*, she murmured as she went, and *delicious*, and *oh my God no wonder you're arrogant*, until he found
himself laughing with joy.

No one had ever before focused on him so exclusively (other
than the senior scientists who examined his doctoral thesis,
and about whom he did not want to think at this moment), and
Gabriel began shifting out of a waking dream of pleasure into
something more transcendent. By the time they finally got
around to the central element of the activity, no compass could
have directed him back to sensibility. All he knew of the world

was Elodie beneath him, her smile his polestar. And when they reached their mutual goal with a synchronicity that charmed the last fragment of Gabriel's brain still operating, he felt as if they were, together, the entire universe. Dark and light, stone and storm, love.

"Oh my goodness," Elodie gasped as they cuddled afterward. "To think we wasted years when we could have been doing that every day."

"Not a waste," Gabriel said, letting bits drop out of the sentence in his dazed tiredness. "You existed—that was always enough for me."

"First thing tomorrow I'm going to a bookstore," Elodie said, "and I'm going to buy half a dozen poetry books so I can study how to say such gorgeous things back to you."

"Third thing tomorrow," Gabriel corrected her. "First thing, I'm going to make love to you again."

"Acceptable. And the second thing?" she asked sleepily.

"Actually, that one's more of a forever thing. I'm going to court you, Elodie. At least insofar as a curmudgeon can. I'm going to move us and this relationship forward."

"You don't need to do that, Gabriel," she said, snuggling up to his warm, slow-beating heart. "I'm right where I where I want to be."

"Right where you belong," he grumbled with tetchy arrogance.

Elodie smiled as she drifted asleep.

"PROFESSOR TARRANT!" MOTTHERS's voice through the door was unrelenting.

"He means you," Elodie said, her voice lush with drowsiness. She nudged Gabriel.

"It's your house," Gabriel muttered into the pillow.

"Ours," Elodie grumped, but eventually she clambered out of bed and went to answer Motthers's incessant knocking.

The graduate student's eyes grew so big when Elodie opened the door that she experienced a moment of alarm for his health. But then she realized he was trying (and failing miserably) not to stare at her clothing.

"What is it?" she asked with as much politeness as she could muster, despite the hour (which was, in fact, ten o'clock in the morning).

"You're . . . you're wearing a man's shirt," Motthers squeaked, painfully squinting at said item of clothing, or perhaps the bare legs beneath it, not even a mismatched pair of stockings covering them. Elodie just looked at him steadily, since students who knock on their professor's door at an ungodly hour (again, it was halfway to noon) deserved all they got. Motthers blinked, recollecting himself—and more importantly, the fact that Elodie was his superior. "Sorry, Professor. I meant, *there's been a disaster!*"

"Another one?" Elodie asked wearily.

"I'm afraid so. In Leicester. Thaumaturgic bogs spontaneously combusting all throughout the city."

"Can't someone else go?" Elodie yawned as she pushed back the tumult of her hair. She did not want to be traipsing through Leicester today, with or without bogs. She had *plans*, and they were decidedly more horizontal than that. (Well, mostly horizontal. After all, Elodie had a very good imagination.)

"Sorry, Professor," Motthers said, holding up a telegram

like a shield for his eyes. "An accountant from the Home Office . . ." He squinted at the telegram. "Mr. Jennings . . . is trapped in one of the bogs, and he specifically demanded Professor Tarrant's help."

"Oh dear, poor Algie," Elodie said, trying not to laugh.

"Did he say which Professor Tarrant?" came a grumbled voice behind her. Elodie glanced over her shoulder to see Gabriel crossing the room in trousers, a jumper, and bare feet, his hair mussed. *Mussed!* She felt her heart swell at the sight, and she suspected this was going to be her fate from hereon: to fall in love with her husband over and over again, like a scientist always discovering something newly wondrous about the world.

"It doesn't matter which one of us, does it?" she told him. "If you go, I go with you."

"And if you go, I'll be coming too," he agreed, frowning.

"Oh my God," Motthers could be heard muttering queasily. But when Elodie turned back to him, he straightened with all the dignity of someone who hoped to achieve his master's degree that year, so long as he survived his professor. "Train tickets," he said, handing over an envelope. "And all the pertinent information."

Elodie thanked him and went to shut the door. But then she stopped, pinning Motthers with a gaze so sharp, his mustache quivered.

"Before I left for Wales, you tried to warn me of a problem. What was it?"

"Oh." The young man glanced at Gabriel, terrified, and then his expression loosened into abject surrender. "Some Merton students (not me, of course!) had a wager going about your marriage. And some of them—who are now very, very sorry—" He glanced again at Gabriel and winced. "*So very sorry*—might have unadvisedly bet their entire funding for the coming year. Because of this, I wanted to tell you, 'Whatever you do, don't fall in love with your husband.'"

He cringed as if she were about to slap him with the train tickets. Elodie closed her eyes. Behind her, Gabriel laughed.

Then they shut the student out and, together, headed off for another disaster.

♡

ACKNOWLEDGMENTS

THIS WAS ONE of those stories that appeared out of the blue, fully formed and expecting me to know how to write it. I had some trouble finding my way in, however, so the story sent Elodie chugging a path through my imagination on her ridiculous velocipede, and from there on, all that remained was for me to run after her, wondering the whole time how on earth Gabriel was going to cope with her unkempt ways. I needn't have worried. He loved her long before I even knew the color of her hair.

This being a historical fantasy novel, I've made every effort to accurately depict various aspects of life in 1890 England (the history part), but I've also taken considerable artistic license (the fantasy part). Dôlylleuad does not exist on any real map, although the riverside meadows upon which I placed it do. Furthermore, Oxford University's School of Geography was only established in 1899, nine years after this story. (I'm sure it would have been earlier if it had to deal with enchanted landscapes!) And I offer my sincere apologies to Halford John

Mackinder, who was appointed Oxford's first geography lecturer in 1887 but who makes no appearance herein.

Immeasurable thanks to Kristine, Taylor, Mary, Jasmine, Anika, Kalie, Stephanie, Stacy, Katy, and everyone behind the scenes. Thanks also to Rebecca, Jorgie, Kallie, and all at Michael Joseph Books, and my foreign publishers. Warm gratitude to the PRH audio team and Elizabeth Knowelden for their wonderfully perfect audiobook renditions of my works. And special thanks to Katie Anderson, who brought me to tears of happiness in the Dubai International Airport when I received an email with the beautiful cover she created for this book. While I traveled through Elodie and Gabriel's England, that cover came with me as the wallpaper on my phone.

Hugs and thanks also to everyone who picks up my books, and to those who send me lovely messages that brighten my days and inspire me to keep writing joy-filled stories for you all.

And as always, forever, love to my darling family.

Keep reading for an excerpt

from India Holton's next book in the

Love's Academic series . . .

THE ANTIQUARIAN'S
OBJECT OF DESIRE

In history, there is no single point of beginning.
                I, on the Past, Cornelius Ottersock

I T HAD JUST gone six o'clock in the evening and nothing had exploded yet. This was good news for the staff of the Minervaeum, London's premier club for academics, where arguments and experiments all too often detonated into chaos. They dared not relax, however, for the night was still young and the library full of historians. No one is more dangerous than people who have little interest in the future.

Some fifty gentlemen cluttered the somber, book-lined chamber, enjoying sherry, nibbles, and a haze of pipe smoke. A few dozed in leather armchairs, for they had been up since the twelfth century, academically speaking, to prepare for a symposium that commenced the next morning.

Only one woman was present, alone at a table in a corner. Several books lay open before her, and she consulted them as she wrote page after page of notes. Lamplight dappled with rain shadows from a nearby window flickered over her dark brown hair and white dress, making her seem evanescent, like a ghost trying to research a way back into life.

"Who is that charming creature?" asked Mr. Beaulieu, a junior professor who had come over from Paris for the symposium. Studying the woman's quiet poise as she sipped from a dainty porcelain cup, in particular noting the lack of a wedding ring, he felt something flutter in his heart where before there had been only midterm breaks and Brie cheese.

"That's Amelia Tarrant," Mr. Dummersby of the British Museum told him. It sounded rather the same as *that's a Viking ship coming toward us.*

Beaulieu's eyes widened. "The antiquarian professor from Oxford University?"

Dummersby nodded solemnly. "Correct."

"Mon Dieu!" Beaulieu reared back, crossing himself. "In France we call her *La Érudite Terrifiante.*"

"In England we try not to call her anything, in case she hears us."

They regarded the woman from behind the safety of their pipes. She set down her tea to stir it before laying the teaspoon on a napkin and taking another sip. Her eyes closed at the taste.

"She looks so genteel," Beaulieu remarked rather wistfully.

"Looks can be deceiving," Dummersby warned. "I once paid her a compliment, and she's refused to work with me ever since."

"No!"

"Yes. I ask you, what kind of woman doesn't like being told by a colleague that she has beautiful lips? And last week she argued with Professor Sterling over a magical candlestick, causing a fire that nearly burned down the Ashmolean Museum."

"Mon Dieu!"

Dummersby gave a shrug that said quite plainly, *it's all you can expect from antiquarians.* They were forever causing drama with magical antiques instead of just quietly reading about drama like proper historians.

"Sterling," Beaulieu mused. "Isn't he the one who found Jane Seymour's lost ghost in a jewelry box?"

"That's him. He and Tarrant are fierce enemies."

"Fascinating," Beaulieu murmured, eyeing Amelia once again. Then the library door swung open, admitting bright light from the corridor beyond and dazzling his attention. Beaulieu turned to see a man enter, reading a book as he walked.

Beaulieu gasped, for the newcomer was scandalously close to being naked. Clad in no more than trousers and an open-collared shirt, he had no pomade in his blond hair, not even the merest hint of a mustache anywhere about him, and worse, his fingernails were polished with a red tint. Beaulieu had never seen the like before, and was uncomfortably interested.

The man looked up from his book and, discovering a crowd of historians staring at him, blinked with surprise. "Good heavens," he remarked mildly. "What have you done to the kitchen?"

"*It's next floor down,*" someone called out.

"Oh." He paused, seemingly hoping that the library might transform itself into a kitchen if he but waited a moment. Then he caught sight of the buffet table and, with a shrug, headed for it. Historians scattered from his path.

"Who is he?" Beaulieu whispered rather trepidatiously.

"That," Dummersby intoned, "is Professor Caleb Sterling." *Clink.*

At the small, sharp sound, both historians jolted. Amelia

Tarrant had set her cup down in its saucer. She stared across the room at Sterling.

THUD.

Now the entire gathering jolted as Sterling slammed his book shut. He stared back at Amelia.

Beaulieu had considered himself an expert on the Black Death until this moment, seeing the expression in Sterling's eyes. Amelia, for her part, did not even blink.

"Oh dear," Dummersby murmured. "Here we go again . . ."

AMELIA WATCHED COOLLY as Caleb approached. He took his time, pausing now and again to chat with people in the crowd, but he flashed her dark glances just to prove himself an absolute villain. She frowned in reply.

She'd not seen him since the Ashmolean incident. After the flames had been extinguished and the museum's curators settled with tea and biscuits, she'd been summoned by Professor Ottersock, head of Oxford's Material History faculty, and made her attitude clear to him.

"I hate the man," she declared, albeit in the polite, gently modulated tones of a well-brought-up lady for whom hatred was something expressed only in strictest privacy. "I certainly did not intend to meet him in the museum at night. We argued, which is how the candlestick got dropped. It won't happen again, I can assure you."

In response, Ottersock just *looked* at her over the glass of laudanum he was about to drink for his sudden migraine.

"Sterling is a scoundrel," she added for good measure. And then, worried that she'd gone too far—"He's also an excellent historian and valued colleague, of course."

"Sit down, Tarrant," Ottersock said wearily, gesturing at a chair in front of his desk. "Talk to me about what's going on for you."

Good God. Amelia had not become an expert antiquarian and professor at the age of twenty-six by *having conversations.* "I'm fine," she said, which was as emphatic an end to the matter as any British person could offer.

Ottersock sighed. "Let me put it another way. I want to know what on earth you were thinking, young lady! Mishandling a thaumaturgic candlestick and causing a fire is one thing, but a girl should not be working alone in a museum after dark, let alone bantering with a male colleague!"

"Arguing," Amelia corrected him.

"Engaging in private intercourse," he corrected her right back, with all the authority of a faculty head and older white male.

Amelia was so alarmed by this definition, she nearly gasped aloud. She'd barely escaped losing her position at Oxford earlier this year due to Caleb Sterling. Although they had been friends since they met as eight-year-olds in boarding school, the moment Professor Throckmorton from Medieval History caught them hugging, that became impossible. Throckmorton, caring not that Caleb had merely been consoling her after she received news of her grandfather's death, spread such malicious gossip that she was officially told to either marry Caleb or quit her professorship. After all, just because women had been admitted to tertiary education after Queen Charlotte demanded it a hundred years earlier didn't mean that they were free to *act like men.* Heavens, if female academics started touching their male colleagues willy-nilly (so to speak), what would come next? Trousers on ladies?!

She'd survived the scandal, unmarried and employed, because

no one would call Caleb and her friends these days. Indeed, they were the very model of foes. And yet still she felt her job in peril.

"I'm afraid I have no time to discuss the matter," she told Ottersock. "I'm going to Hereford to follow up on a clue about treasure in the cathedral there." Actually, she'd planned it for tomorrow, but getting out of town fast seemed the only way to avoid this talk. "My train leaves in two hours."

Ottersock choked on his laudanum. "What? You can't just run off! I'm trying to discipline you! Sit down!"

Driven to desperate measures, Amelia looked at her wrist-watch, then raised big, imploring eyes to the faculty head. A fear that she might start crying blazed across Ottersock's face.

"Fine," he grumped. "Go! And for God's sake, don't blow anything up!"

She'd gone, only returning this afternoon in time for the symposium—and with *absolutely no awareness whatsoever* that Caleb also was staying at the Minervaeum. Indeed, when Professor Jemeson waylaid her in a corridor to inform her of it *("Now don't go burning down the club, little lady, ha ha . . . say, want to come to dinner with me?")*, Amelia had expressed complete surprise.

Unfortunately, Jemeson had not told her about the pre-symposium drinks being held in the library, and now here Caleb was, walking toward her through a crowd of people trained to tell stories. Amelia looked up to the ceiling's painted heaven, but its frolicking cherubs offered no inspiration. When she looked down again, Caleb was standing on the other side of the table, as if he'd magically folded space and time to reach her.

"Good evening, Mr. Sterling," she said in a prim voice.

"Miss Tarrant," he drawled. "Sitting alone in a corner, I see."

"Hoping to avoid unpleasant company," she replied pointedly.

He smirked. She stared. The atmosphere grew almost unbearably tense (perhaps because everyone in the library was holding their breath).

Then Caleb gave a dramatic sigh. Dropping into the chair opposite Amelia, he leaned forward, elbows on the table and chin set atop his linked fingers. His blue-eyed gaze seemed to twinkle behind wayward strands of hair. "Hey, Meely," he said.

Amelia glanced at the historians behind him, who hastily looked away as if they possessed no interest whatsoever in the conversation. "Please leave, Mr. Sterling," she replied. "I'm trying to work."

"You needn't call me Mr. Sterling when we're alone." He grinned with appallingly winsome charm. "*Professor* will do fine."

How anyone could make such a respectable title sound indecent, Amelia did not know. "We aren't alone," she pointed out. "There are fifty other people in the room."

"When I'm with you, it feels as if the rest of the world vanishes."

Amelia rolled her eyes.

"Speaking of vanishing," he continued, "you fled after the Ashmolean fire—"

"I went to Hereford," she corrected him.

"I've been worried."

"Nonsense. You've been sleeping half the day and reading—" She angled her head to see the title of his book, and her nose wrinkled. "Byron."

"Of course I've been reading Byron," he retorted, as if it were obvious. "My best friend disappeared into the ether!"

"Sh!" Amelia glanced again at the crowd, but they had given up hope of scandal and returned to their conversations. "I only went out of town for a few days. That's hardly a good reason to succumb to Romantic poetry."

"Was it because I got my eyebrows shaped and you were overwhelmed by their beauty?" he asked with apparent sincerity.

Amelia *tsk*ed. "No, I—" She paused, looking at his eyebrows, and he grinned. She speared him with a frown, although only briefly, in case she hurt him for real. "Scoundrel. No, Professor Ottersock started asking too many questions, and I needed an excuse to get away. You know that if he realized the truth about us not actually being enemies, he'd immediately fire me. He hasn't budged from his notion that a male and female professor being bosom friends would bring Oxford into disrepute."

"Well, if you're going to use a phrase like 'bosom friends,' I can't say I blame him," Caleb said, then smiled again as her frown deepened. "So when you sent me a note to meet here tonight, you weren't planning to tell me goodbye forever? And in public, where I couldn't make a scene?"

Amelia suppressed a laugh. "As if being in public ever deterred you from making a scene. No, I'm not planning to say goodbye. I wouldn't leave Oxford." She paused for the slightest of moments, then added, "My aunt Mary would get too lonely."

"Ah yes, poor Aunt Mary, with only her husband, your brother, your cousin, his wife, and your parents for company." He chuckled, and a dozen heads in the crowd whipped around to see what was happening and whether it signaled an imminent explosion.

"You are a pest!" Amelia declared at once in a strident voice.

Caleb straightened, shaking back his hair. "And you are poison!"

Murmuring, the crowd turned away again. Amelia and Caleb exchanged a look that mingled amusement, exasperation, and old remembrances—the kind of look only possible when you have known someone most of your life. Caleb leaned back in his chair, propping his feet up on the table. Amelia stiffened, imagining the germs that were no doubt leaping from his shoes to populate her books.

"What are you writing?" he asked.

"My speech for the symposium tomorrow."

"Is it about the amazing treasure you found in Hereford Cathedral?"

She raised an eyebrow. "How do you know I found anything?"

"Because I know you."

All of a sudden Amelia's interior twinkled, as if her cells had turned to stars. "It's just a trinket, nothing important," she said. (It was extraordinary.) "Not even worth discussing." (If she didn't win this year's Petrarch Award for Excellence in Historical Research, King Henry VIII was an exemplary husband.)

"Can I see it?" Caleb craned his head as if he might be able to read her notes from a distance, upside down.

Amelia laid a hand over the page. It contained a rough draft, and not even Caleb was allowed to see her grammatical errors. "You'll learn about it tomorrow."

Caleb's eyes widened with genuine astonishment. "You don't think I'm actually going to attend the symposium? Good God, there's nothing more tedious than listening to a gaggle of historians droning on."

"*You're* a historian."

"I'm an antiquarian. Haven't you heard, that's—"

"Entirely different," they chorused, and shared a brief, sardonic smile—then hastily erased it in case anyone was watching. "So . . ." Caleb said, rocking his feet back and forth. "Does your treasure do anything interesting? Would it turn Ottersock into a frog? Please say yes."

"*Caleb,*" she murmured chidingly.

"Sorry," he lied. "Come on, bella luna, show me."

Amelia drew breath to reply, then froze, noticing a nearby historian straining to overhear them. It was Dummersby from the British Museum, second only to Professor Throckmorton as academia's worst tattler. Immediately she glared at Caleb.

"*Do not even think about touching that teaspoon!*"

She flicked her gaze meaningfully toward Dummersby, and in a flash Caleb's feet were down and he was leaning forward, snatching her teaspoon from where it had been lying on a napkin beside her cup.

"Stop!" Amelia commanded, but he was already leaning back in the chair again.

"This?" he said, staring incredulously at the teaspoon. "This is your amazing treasure? Really? What does it do, turn tea into wine?"

Well, really! Even though they were pretending, Amelia felt a stab of offense. Getting to her feet, she rounded the table with a determination she'd learned from studying Queen Isabella, the She-Wolf of France. Caleb stood, his chair scraping against the floor, his grin twisting into a wary grimace.

"You are an unprincipled knave," Amelia told him.

"Mm hm," he agreed, nodding.

"Give. It. Back."

He held out the teaspoon. "Show me what it does. I dare you."

"Oh well, if you *dare* me," Amelia retorted sarcastically. She did not reach for the teaspoon—she'd known him far too long to fall for a trap like that—and he stepped forward, coming so close she could see the small, faded scar above his left eyebrow. The other historians had begun setting down their drinks, stuffing canapés into their pockets, and edging for the door, but Amelia didn't notice. Caleb's gaze was intense in its focus. He'd changed his brand of cologne while she'd been away, and the woodsy freshness infused her breath like a summer's morning. The warmth of his smile pressed against her lips, although they weren't touching.

"I *double* dare you," he said, his voice deep and shadowy.

Little flutters of sensation went through Amelia's stomach. *I must have bound my corset too tight,* she thought. After all, she wouldn't flutter for Caleb. Their relationship was entirely platonic, their touches innocent—for example, when she brushed a crumb from his sleeve, beneath which his arms had grown so muscular over the years; or when he reached for one of the lemon sweets she kept in her skirt pocket and accidentally stroked her thigh through layers of cotton and lace . . .

"Is it getting hot in here, or is it just me?" Beaulieu asked, fanning himself.

We're only friends, Amelia reiterated to herself. Friends who were fake hating to protect her reputation.

Flutter flutter, her stomach replied.

She glowered even more fiercely at Caleb, and he glowered right back. "Someone go fetch the building's fire warden, hurry!" a professor exhorted in a loud whisper.

Without taking his eyes off her, Caleb lifted the teaspoon and drew the tip of his tongue slowly up it.

Alarmed that her evidently shrinking corset might crush her, Amelia snatched the spoon from him. "For heaven's sake," she grumbled. "This is a very sensitive and dangerous item."

"It tastes like sugar," he said. "You stirred your tea with it." He cocked his head, smiling with fascination at her, and Amelia flushed, imagining him smiling like that before he kissed a woman.

"It's thaumaturgic silver," she said. "During the Anarchy, a vicar of Hereford hid it inside the cathedral's crypt, to be used as a final defense should the building be stormed. He left a vague mention of this in his journal, which I deciphered."

"Okay," Caleb said, still smiling.

The teaspoon began to feel warm in Amelia's hand as she clutched it even tighter. "It's *magical.*"

"Prove it."

Nearby, a lamp crackled.

"Please," he added, fluttering his eyelashes. And while Amelia was trying to decide whether he'd darkened them with cosmetics, he reached out to grab the teaspoon again. She automatically slapped his hand away. He slapped hers back.

At which point, both remembered they were standing in full view of their peers and proceeded to act accordingly.

In other words, a hand-slapping match broke out. Within seconds the teaspoon dropped to the floor, ignored.

"Ruffian!" Amelia exclaimed.

"Persnickitator," Caleb retorted.

"That's not a real word!"

"See what I mean?"

Tiny blue flames of magic began to flicker along the spoon's handle. In response, books tumbled from shelves, and the lamp's glass shade melted.

"You are outrageous!" Amelia declared. She almost skidded on the teaspoon, and Caleb caught her by one elbow to steady her. "You are obnoxious!" she added, pulling from his grip. *"You are overly opinionated!"*

"And you've clearly spent ages consulting a thesaurus to describe me. It's highly suggestive." He raised his eyebrows, but when Amelia lowered hers in a frown, he retreated. In doing so, he accidentally kicked the teaspoon. It went skittering across the floor, trailing sparks and making historians leap from its path.

"Being suggestive is the *purpose* of a thesaurus," Amelia said.

"You should try poetry instead."

The teaspoon clattered. Sausage rolls began levitating off the buffet table.

"You are a beetle-headed, flap-ear'd knave!" Amelia shouted, driven to the Shakespearean level of insults.

Thud thud thud. More books fell off their shelves or flew across the room, pages flapping, to slam against a wall. Historians ducked behind armchairs or cowered beneath desks. Beaulieu emitted a high-pitched scream and fainted into Dummersby's arms.

"Better that than a stinging wasp!" Caleb retorted.

Amelia blasted him with her fiercest stare, the one she usually reserved for students who claimed three grandmothers' funerals in one year. The usual pretense at enmity was escalating out of control, just as it had in the Ashmolean when a curator came upon them standing close together while they inspected the candlestick. She could not understand why, any more than she could stop it. Arguing with Caleb was beginning to have the same effect on her that the divine right of kings had on England's Parliament, and she couldn't seem to restore her calm head.

Suddenly the teaspoon leaped up, spinning as if it was stirring the air. Flares of blue light and fire burst from it. The historians began to shout and push one another as they made a dash for the exit. Finally noticing, Amelia turned to stare at the spoon with trepidation. Beside her, Caleb did the same.

"What's its power?" he asked from the side of his mouth.

"Intense combustion in response to environmental discord," Amelia said.

They glanced at each other with a silent *oh, damn* . . .

As THE EXPLOSION boomed through the Minervaeum, its staff sighed wearily and went to fetch the ever-present water buckets.

India Holton lives in New Zealand, where she has enjoyed the typical Kiwi lifestyle of wandering around forests, living barefoot on islands, and messing about in boats. Now she lives in a cottage near the sea, writing books about unconventional women and charming rogues, and drinking far too much tea.

Ready to find
your next great read?

Let us help.

Visit prh.com/nextread